She was doing this, she really was.

She was crossing that little line and getting into an elevator with Marcus.

"Okay?" he asked as the doors slid shut, blocking them off from the bright lobby. He slid his arm around her waist and pulled her in close. "Still okay?"

In her dreams, Marcus swept into the office and kissed her and told her how much he needed her and yes, they wound up in bed.

But in those dreams, Marcus was the one doing all the sweeping. She didn't do anything but let herself get carried away in the over-the-top romance of the whole situation.

This was stupid. This wasn't just a risk—this was practically career suicide. Yes, she wanted Marcus and yes, he wanted her, and thank God they were both unattached, consenting adults.

It didn't change the fact that she was initiating a physical relationship with her boss. It didn't change the fact that she'd kissed him back.

But there was no going back to the way things were.

"Better than okay," she said, pulling him down for a kiss.

Marcus's lips moved over hers as he spun and backed her against the wall of the elevator.

* * *

is part of Mills

HIS FOREVER FAMILY

BY
SARAH M. ANDERSON

MILLS & BOON

First Published in Great Britain 2016
By Mills & Boon, an imprint of HarperCollins*Publishers*
1 London Bridge Street, London, SE1 9GF

© 2016 Sarah M. Anderson

ISBN: 978-0-263-91847-2

51-0216

Our policy is to use papers that are natural, renewable and recyclable products and made from wood grown in sustainable forests.The logging and manufacturing processes conform to the legal environmental regulations of the country of origin.

Printed and bound in Spain
by CPI, Barcelona

Award-winning author **Sarah M. Anderson** may live east of the Mississippi River, but her heart lies out west on the Great Plains. With a lifelong love of horses and two history teachers for parents, it wasn't long before her characters found themselves out in South Dakota among the Lakota Sioux.

Sarah's book *A Man of Privilege* won the *RT Book Reviews* 2012 Reviewers' Choice Best Book Awards Series: Desire. Her book *Straddling the Line* was named Best Desire of 2013 by *CataRomance*, and *Mystic Cowboy* was a 2014 BBA Finalist in the Single Title category as well as a finalist for the Gayle Wilson Award of Excellence.

When not helping out at her son's school or walking her rescue dogs, Sarah spends her days having conversations with imaginary cowboys and American Indians, all of which is surprisingly well-tolerated by her wonderful husband. Readers can find out more about Sarah's love of cowboys and Indians at www.sarahmanderson.com.

To Sasha Devlin, my Spring Fling buddy.
We'll always have Chicago!
And when we don't,
we'll always have Twitter!

One

"Come on, Ms. Reese," Marcus Warren called over his shoulder. "It's not that hot."

He paused in the middle of the jogging path to wait for his executive assistant, Liberty Reese, to catch up with him. He looked around, checking for any vans with dark windows that didn't belong. It was an old habit, keeping an eye out for danger. But as usual, aside from some other runners, he and Ms. Reese had the shoreline to themselves. Thank God. The past was in the past, he repeated to himself until his anxiety faded.

Man, he loved Lake Michigan. The early-morning light made the rippling water a deep blue. The sky was clear and warmed by the sun, which seemed to hover just about a foot over the surface of the water. Later today, the heat would be oppressive, but right now, running along the lakefront with a cool breeze blowing in from the water?

This was as close to free as Marcus got to feel.

He checked his Fitbit. His heart rate was falling. "You're not going to let the heat beat you, are you, Ms. Reese?" he teased, stretching out his quads.

Ms. Reese puffed up next to him. "May I take a moment to point out—again—that you're not taking notes while you run?" she said, glaring at him.

But he wasn't fooled. He saw the way the corner of her lips curved up as she said it. She was trying not to smile.

He kept stretching so she could catch her breath. "But I'm talking. That counts for something, right?"

She rolled her eyes and finished off the water. That made him grin. He was Marcus Warren, heir to his father's Warren Investments financial empire *and* his mother's Marquis Hotel empire. He was the sole owner of Warren Capital, a venture capital firm he'd started with his trust-fund money. He owned half of the Chicago Blackhawks and a quarter of the Chicago Bulls, in addition to 75 percent of the pro soccer team, the Chicago Fire. He was one of the richest bachelors in the country and possibly the richest one in Chicago.

People simply did not roll their eyes at him.

Except for Ms. Reese.

She tucked the bottle back into her belt. Then, her fingers hovering over the Bluetooth earpiece she wore at all times, she asked, "So how do you want to proceed with the watchmakers?"

Rock City Watches was a boutique firm that had set up shop in downtown Detroit and wanted a fresh round of investing to expand its operations. Marcus looked at his watch, made just for him. The 24-karat gold casing was warm against his skin. "What do you think?"

Ms. Reese sighed heavily and began to plod up the jogging path again. She was not a particularly graceful runner—*plodding* was the only word for it—but she kept up with him and took notes while they ran. It was the most productive time of day. He did his best thinking while they ran.

Which was why they ran every single day, in rain or heat. Ice was about the only thing that kept them indoors, but he had a treadmill in a room off his office. Ms. Reese could sit at a small desk and record everything and provide her opinion.

He let her get a few feet ahead of him. No, she was not terribly graceful. But that didn't stop him from admiring the view. Ms. Reese had curves—more than enough curves to give a man pause.

He shook his head, pushing all thoughts of her backside from his mind. He was not the kind of billionaire who slept with his secretary. His father had done that enough for both of them. Marcus's relationship with Ms. Reese was strictly business. Well, business and running.

He caught up to her easily. "Well?"

"No one wears watches anymore," she panted. "Unless it's a smart watch."

"Excellent point. I'll invest twenty-five million in Rock City Watches."

Ms. Reese stumbled a bit in surprise. Marcus reached out and steadied her. He didn't allow his hand to linger on her warm skin. "You okay? We're almost to the fountain." Buckingham Fountain was the point where they turned around and headed back.

She gave him a hell of a side eye. "I'm fine. How did you get from *timepieces are a dead market* to *let's invest another twenty-five million*?"

"If no one wears watches anymore, then they become what they once were—a status symbol," he explained. "Only the wealthiest consumers can afford a watch that costs several grand. The timepiece market isn't dead, Ms. Reese. The mass-market timepiece market is. But the luxury timepiece market?" He held out his wrist. "It's a hell of a nice watch, don't you think?" This particular watch went for $4,500.

She nodded. "It'll be great PR, as well. Made in America and all that."

"But they need to accept the realities of the market."

She nodded. "Such as?"

"Marketing and wearables. Let's get back to the Rock City Watch people with requests to see their marketing mock-ups. I also want to set up a meeting to discuss a hybrid device—a luxury watch that can slot wearable tech into the band."

They reached the fountain and she stopped, her head down and her hands on her knees as she took in great gulps of air.

"What else?" he asked.

"You have to make a decision about attending the Hanson wedding," she said in between gasps.

Marcus groaned. "Do I have to?"

"You're the one who decided you should go to this wedding," she told him flatly. "You're the one who decided you should take a date. And you're the one who decided to kill two birds with one stone by scheduling the meeting with the producers of *Feeding Frenzy* the day after the wedding."

Marcus allowed himself to scowl at his assistant. Her lack of sympathy was not comforting. Attending the Hanson-Spears wedding in Los Angeles had not, in fact, been his idea. Who the hell wanted to watch his former fiancée get married to the man she'd cheated on him with? Not him.

But his mother had decreed that Marcus would attend the wedding with a date and put on a happy face so they could "put this unfortunate event behind them." Of course, if his mother had had her way, Marcus would have married Lillibeth Hanson anyway because what was a little affair in the grand scheme of things? Lillibeth came from old money. Marcus came from old money and made new money. Together, his parents had reasoned, they could apparently rule the world.

Marcus didn't see the point. He'd refused to reconcile with Lillibeth and he'd thought his parents had accepted that decision. But then the wedding invitation came.

And the hell of it was, his parents were not entirely wrong about the effects the scandal had had on Marcus's business. To some, his inability to see the truth about Lillibeth until it was too late might also indicate an inability to make good investment choices. So his parents had strongly suggested he attend the wedding to show that everyone was on good terms. And they *strongly* suggested he take a date because it would be an admission of defeat to show up at your ex's wedding alone.

All Marcus had to do was pick a woman.

He looked at Liberty. "What are my options, again?"

"Rosetta Naylor."

Marcus cringed at the celebutante's name. "Too shallow."

"Katerine Nabakov."

"Too Russian Mafia."

Liberty sighed heavily. "Emma Green?"

Marcus scowled harder. He had actually gone out with Emma several times. "Really?"

"She's a known quantity," Liberty explained. "No surprises."

"Wrong. People would think that us dating again is a sure sign of wedding bells." Specifically, his parents.

Marcus had done many things to keep the peace with his mother and father. Hell, he'd come damn close to getting married to Lillibeth Hanson, all because they thought that was best.

He wasn't going to risk that kind of trap again.

"The options are limited and time is running short, Mr. Warren," Liberty said in exasperation. She jammed her hands on her hips. "The wedding is in two weeks. If you insist on attending with a date, you need to actually ask someone to go with you."

"Fine. I'll just take you."

The effect of this statement was immediate. Liberty's eyes went wide and her mouth dropped open and, in a fraction of a second, her gaze dropped over his body. Something that looked a hell of a lot like want flashed over her face.

What? Did she actually *want* him?

Then it was gone. She straightened up and did her best to look imperial. "Mr. Warren, be serious."

"I am serious. I trust you." He took a step toward her. "Sometimes I think…you're the only person who's honest with me. You wouldn't try to sell all the details of a date to the gossip rags." Which had been a huge part of the scandal with Lillibeth. She had capitalized on her affair, painting Marcus as a lousy boyfriend both in and out of the bedroom.

Liberty bit at her lower lip. "Honestly? I don't think you should go at all. Why would you give her the chance to hurt you again?" Her voice had dropped and she didn't sound imperious at all. Instead, she sounded…as if she wanted to protect him.

It was a fair question. He didn't want to go. He didn't want to give Lillibeth the chance to cut him down again. But he'd promised his parents that he'd put a good face on it and make sure the Warren name still meant power and money.

"And for the record," she went on, "I think doing that *Feeding Frenzy* reality show is also a bad idea. The whole problem with Lillibeth was that your private life suddenly became public fodder. Going on television to bid on investment ideas? You're just inviting people to further make a commodity out of you."

"It's supposed to be a good way to build my brand."

Liberty rolled her eyes again, as if that was the stupidest thing she'd ever heard. "Seriously? You've built a successful venture capital firm without being a celebrity. You have plenty of people dying to pitch to you. Heck, I'm surprised we haven't been accosted by a 'jogger' lying in wait to pitch you his million-dollar idea yet."

He tensed at the idea of being accosted by anyone. But no—no suspicious vehicles with armed men were around. The past was in the past.

"But you know what?" Liberty took a step toward him, jabbing at him with her index finger. She could be a formidable woman in her own right. "You do this reality show, that's exactly what's going to happen. You won't be able to run along the lake without plowing through idiots in running shoes who want a piece of your time and your fortune. Don't feed the machine, Marcus. Don't do what 'they' think you should do. For the love of God, do what *you* want."

Marcus. Had she ever called him by his first name before? He didn't think so. The way her lips moved over his name—that was the sort of thing he'd remember. "Maybe I want to take you to the wedding."

It was hard to say if she blushed, as she was already red faced from the run and the heat. But something in her expression changed. "No," she said flatly. Before he could take the rejection personally, she added, "I—it—would be bad for you."

He could hear the pain in her voice. He took a step toward her and put a hand on her shoulder. She looked up, her eyes wide and—hopeful? His hand drifted from her shoulder to her cheek and damned if she didn't lean into his touch. "How could you be bad for me?"

The moment the words left his mouth, he realized he'd pushed this too far. Yes, Liberty Reese was an exceptional assistant and yes, she was beautiful—when she wasn't struggling through a summer run.

But what had started as an offhand comment about a d[...]
to a wedding now meant something else. Something mo[...]

She shut down on him. She stepped out of his touch a[...]
turned to face the lake. "It's getting warmer," she said in[...]
monotone voice. "We need to finish our run."

"Do you have any water left?"

She looked sheepish. "No."

He held out his hand. "Give me your bottle. There's[...]
water fountain a couple hundred yards away. I'll fill it u[...]

She unhooked her bottle and handed it over. "Thanks," s[...]
said, sounding perfectly normal, as if he hadn't just asked h[...]
out and touched her face. As if she hadn't turned him do[...]
flat. Somehow, it made him admire her even more. "I'll w[...]
here. Try not to get any brilliant ideas, okay?"

Marcus took off at top speed. He heard Liberty sho[...]
"Show-off!"

He laughed.

The water in the drinking fountain was too warm. He [...]
it run for a few seconds, hoping it'd cool off. As he waite[...]
he looked around. There was a trash can only a few f[...]
away, boxes and bags piled around it on the ground. M[...]
cus scowled at the garbage. Why couldn't people take ca[...]
of the park, dammit? The trash can was right there.

As he filled the water bottle and debated calling the may[...]
about the garbage pickup schedule, he heard a noise. It w[...]
a small noise, but it didn't belong. It wasn't a gull crying [...]
a squirrel scampering—it was closer to a...a cat mewing[...]

Marcus looked around, trying to find the source of t[...]
noise. A shoe box on the ground next to the trash can move[...]

Marcus's stomach fell in. Oh, no—who would throw[...]
kitten away? He hurried over to the box and pulled the l[...]
off and—

Sweet Jesus. Not a cat. Not a kitten.

A *baby*.

Two

Breathing hard, Liberty admired the view as Marcus sprinted away from her. When he reached the water fountain, she turned her attention back to the lake. It wouldn't do to be caught staring at her boss's ass. Even if it was a *fine* ass. And even if the owner had just made one of himself.

Instead, she took the time to appreciate the gift that was this morning. She hadn't set foot in a church in a good fifteen years. But every morning she stood here and looked out on Lake Michigan and gave thanks to God or the higher power or whoever the hell was listening.

She was alive. She was healthy. She had a good job that paid for food and a safe apartment. There was even some money left over for things like running shoes and haircuts.

"Liberty?" Marcus yelled from the water fountain. "Liberty!"

Even though Marcus couldn't see her, she glared at him. What the hell had gotten into him this morning? One of the reasons she worked for him—aside from the insane salary he paid her—was the fact that he treated her as an equal. It was a bit of delusion on her part to pretend that she was on par with the likes of Marcus Warren, but it was her delusion, dammit.

And that delusion worked only because it was just her and Marcus on these runs, both in running clothes. The delusion didn't work when he was wearing a four-thousand-dollar suit and she had on the finest suit she could find on 80 percent clearance at Macy's. And the delusion sure as hell wouldn't work if she accompanied him to a three-day destination wedding extravaganza that no doubt cost more than she'd ever earn in her lifetime.

Someone would see through her facade. It'd get ugly, fast.

"Liberty!" He was even louder this time.

Was he not used to women saying no to him? Oh, whom was she kidding? Women didn't say no to him. Why would they? He was gorgeous, single, richer than sin and eminently respectable. "What?"

"I need you!" he yelled over his shoulder. "Hurry!"

She realized he wasn't standing at the water fountain anymore. He was on his knees by a trash can in the gravel that surrounded the fountain. His shoulders were hunched over and he looked as if—oh, God, he wasn't having a heart attack, was he?

Liberty began to hurry. The three years of daily morning runs with Marcus had given her enough stamina that she broke into a flat-out run.

"Are you okay?" she demanded as she came up to him. "Marcus—what's wrong?"

He looked up at her, his eyes wide with fear and one hand over his mouth. Just then, something in front of him made a pitiful little noise.

She looked down. What she saw didn't make sense at

first. There was a box and inside was something small and dark and moving.

"Baby?" Marcus said in a strangled voice.

"Baby!" Liberty cried with a start. She didn't know much about babies, but this child couldn't be more than a week old. The baby was wrapped in a filthy rag, and dark smudges that might have been dirt but were more the color of dried blood covered its dark skin. Wisps of black hair were plastered to its tiny little head. Liberty stared in total shock, trying to make sense of it: an African American newborn in a shoe box by the trash can.

"It was—the box—it was closed," Marcus began to babble. "And I heard a noise and—baby. Baby!"

The baby opened its little mouth and let out another cry, louder this time. The sound broke Liberty out of her shock. Jesus Christ, someone had tried to throw this baby away! In a box in this heat? "Move," she commanded and Marcus dutifully scooted out of her way.

Her hands shaking, Liberty lifted the baby out of the box. The rag fell away from the impossibly tiny body—no diaper. A boy, and he was caked in filth.

"Oh, my God," she whispered as the baby's back arched and it let out a squeal. His little body was like a furnace in her hands.

"What do we do?" Marcus asked. He was clearly panicking.

And Liberty couldn't blame him. "Water," she realized. "He's too hot."

Marcus held out her water bottle, the one he'd been filling. She grabbed the rag and said, "Soak that in the fountain," and took her bottle.

The baby squirmed mightily in her arms and she had this moment that was almost an out-of-body thing, where instead of looking down at a little baby boy she'd just plucked from a shoe box, she was looking down at William, the baby brother she'd never gotten the chance to see, much less hold. Was this what he'd been like, after their mother gave birth in prison and the baby was taken away to a foster home? Had William died like this?

No. This baby, whoever he was, was not going to die. Not if she had anything to do with it.

"This is disgusting," Marcus said, but she didn't pay any attention to him.

She folded herself into a cross-legged position on the gravel, ignoring the way the rocks dug into her skin. "It's okay," she soothed as she tried to dribble some water into the baby's mouth. "You're a good boy, aren't you? Oh, you're such a sweetheart." The baby turned his head from side to side and wailed piteously. Panic gripped her. What if he wasn't going to make it? What if she couldn't save him? "You're loved," she told him, tears coming to her eyes. "And you're so strong. You can do this, okay?"

"Here," Marcus said, thrusting the rag at her. Except it wasn't the rag—it was his shirt.

She looked up and found herself staring right at Marcus Warren's bare chest. In any other circumstances she would have taken her time admiring the view because *damn*. He was muscled and cut—but still lean. He had a true runner's body.

The baby whimpered. Right. She had much more important things to deal with than her boss suddenly half-naked. She held the baby away from her body. "Drape it over him."

Marcus did as he was told, laying the sopping-wet cloth over the baby's body. The sudden temperature change made the poor thing howl. "It's okay," she murmured to him, trying to get a little water into his mouth. "You'll feel better soon."

"Should I go for help? What should we do?"

Help. That would be a good thing. "My phone is in my pack," she said. He didn't run with his phone—that was her job. "Call 911." She was amazed at how calm she sounded, as if finding a baby on the verge of heatstroke in the trash was just another Tuesday in her life.

Marcus crouched behind her and dug through the fanny pack that held her water, keys and phone. "Got it." She told him her password without a second thought and he dialed. "We're at Buckingham Fountain and we found a baby in the trash," Marcus said way too loudly into the phone.

"Shh, shh," Liberty soothed as Marcus talked to the 911 dispatcher. "Here, let's try this." She dipped her finger into the water and held it against the baby's mouth. He sucked at it eagerly and made a little protest when she pulled her finger away to dip it into the water again.

He latched on to her finger a second time—which had the side benefit of cutting off the crying. Liberty took a deep breath and tried to think. There'd been a baby at her second foster home. How had the foster mother calmed that baby down?

Oh, yes. She remembered now. She began to rock back and forth, the gravel cutting into her legs. "That's a good boy," she said, her ears straining for the sounds of sirens. "You're loved. You can do it."

Agonizingly long minutes passed. She couldn't get the baby to take much more water, but he sucked on the tip of her finger fiercely. As she rocked and soothed him, his body relaxed and he curled up against her side. Liberty held him even tighter.

"Is he okay?" Marcus demanded.

She looked up at him, trying not to stare at his body. Never in the three years she'd worked for Marcus had she seen him even half this panicked. "I think he fell asleep. The poor thing. He can't be more than a few days old."

"How could anyone just leave him?" Now, that was more like the Marcus she knew—frustrated when the world did not conform to his standards.

"You'd be surprised," she mumbled, dropping her gaze back to the baby, who was still ferociously tugging on her finger in his sleep. Aside from being hot and filthy, he looked healthy. Of course, she'd never seen William before he died in foster care, so she didn't know what a drug-addicted newborn looked like. This child's head was round and his eyes were still swollen; she'd seen pictures of newborns who looked like him. She just couldn't tell.

"You're just about perfect, you know?" she told the infant. Then she said to Marcus, "Here, wet your shirt again. I think he's cooling down."

Marcus did as he was told. "You're doing an amazing job," he said as she wrapped the wet cloth around the baby's body. The baby started at the temperature change, but didn't let go of her finger. Marcus went on, "I didn't know you knew so much about babies," and she didn't miss the awe in his voice.

There's a lot you don't know about me. But she didn't say it because it'd been less than—what, twenty minutes? If that. It'd been less than twenty minutes since Marcus Warren had said he trusted her because she was the one person who was honest with him.

She wasn't—honest with him, that was. But that didn't mean she wanted to lie outright to him. She hated lying at all but she did what she had to do to survive.

So, instead, she said, "Must be the mothering instinct." What else could it be? Here was a baby who needed her in a truly primal way and Liberty had responded.

The baby sighed in what she hoped was contentment and she felt her heart clinch. "Such a good boy," she said, leaning down to kiss his little forehead.

Sirens came screaming toward them. Then the paramedics were upon them and everything happened *fast*. The baby was plucked from her arms and carried into the ambulance, where he wailed even louder. It tore her up to hear him cry like that.

At the same time, a police officer arrived and took statements from her and Marcus. Liberty found herself half listening to the questions as she stood at the back of the open ambulance while the medics dug out a pacifier and wrapped the baby in a clean blanket.

"Is he going to be okay?" she asked when one of the paramedics hopped out of the back and started to close the door.

"Hard to say," the man said.

"Where are you taking him?"

"Northwestern is closest."

Marcus broke off talking with the cop to say, "Take him to Children's." At some point, he'd put his shirt back on. It looked far worse for wear.

The paramedic shrugged and closed the doors, cutting Liberty off from the baby. The ambulance drove off—lights flashing but no sirens blaring.

The cop finished taking their statements. Liberty asked, "Will you be able to find the mother?"

Much like the paramedic, the cop shrugged. She supposed she shouldn't have been surprised. After all, she'd barely survived childhood because, aside from Grandma Devlin, people couldn't be bothered to check on little Liberty Reese. "It's a crime to abandon a baby," he said. "If the mother had left the baby at a police station, that's one thing. But…" He shrugged again. "Don't know if we'll find her, though. Usually babies are dumped close to where they're born, and someone in the neighborhood knows something. But the middle of the park?" He turned, as if the conversation was over.

"What'll happen to the baby?" Marcus asked, but Liberty could have told him.

If they couldn't find the mother or the father, the baby would go into the foster system. He'd be put up for adoption, eventually, but that might take a while until his case was closed. And by then, he might not be the tiny little baby he was right now. He might be bigger. And he was African American. That made it that much harder to get adopted.

She looked in the direction the ambulance had gone.

The cop gave Marcus a sad smile. "DCFS will take care of it," he said.

Liberty cringed. She did not have warm and fuzzy memories of the Department of Child and Family Services. All she had were grainy memories of frazzled caseworkers who couldn't be bothered. Grown-up Liberty knew that was because the caseworkers were overwhelmed by the sheer number of kids in the system. But little-kid Liberty only remembered trying to ask questions about why her mom or even Grandma Devlin wasn't going to come get her and being told, "Don't worry about it," as if that would make up for her mother's sudden disappearances.

What would happen to the baby? She looked at her arms, wondering at how empty they felt. "Marcus," she said in a hoarse voice as the cop climbed into his cruiser. "We can't lose that baby."

"What?" He stared at her in shock.

She grabbed on to his arm as if she was drowning and he was the only thing that could keep her afloat. "The baby. He'll get locked into the system and by the time the police close his case, it might be too late."

Marcus stared down at her as if she'd started spouting Latin. "Too…late? For what?"

Liberty's mouth opened and the words *I was a foster kid—trust me on this* almost rolled off her tongue. But at the last second, she snapped her mouth shut. She'd created this person Marcus saw, this Liberty Reese—a white college graduate, an excellent manager of time and money who always did her research and knew the answers. Liberty Reese was invaluable to Marcus because she had *made* herself valuable.

That woman had had nothing in common with Liberty Reese—the grubby daughter of an African American drug addict who'd sold herself on Death Corner in Cabrini-Green to afford more drugs, who'd done multiple stints in prison, who hadn't been able to get clean when her daughter was shipped back to foster care for the third time, who couldn't tell Liberty who her father was or even if he was white, who'd given birth to a baby boy addicted to heroin and crack and God only knew what else.

That's not who Liberty was anymore. She would never be that lost little girl ever again.

She looked back in the direction the ambulance had gone. That little baby—he was lost, too. Just as her brother had been in the few weeks he'd been alive. Completely alone in the world, with no one to fight for him.

Liberty would *not* allow that to happen. Not again.

She opened her mouth to tell Marcus something—she wasn't quite sure what, but something—except nothing came out. Her throat closed up and tears burned in her eyes.

Oh, God—was she about to start crying? No—*not* allowed. Liberty Reese did not cry. She was always in control. She never let her emotions get the better of her. Not anymore.

Marcus looked down at her, concern written large on his face. He stepped closer to her and cupped her chin. "Liberty…"

"Please," she managed to get out. "The baby, Marcus." But that was all she could say because then she really did begin to cry. She dropped her gaze and swallowed hard, trying to will the stupid tears back.

The next thing she knew, Marcus had wrapped his arms around her and pulled her into his chest. "It's okay," he murmured, his hand rubbing up and down her back. "The baby's going to be fine."

"You don't know that," she got out, trying to keep herself from sinking against his chest because Marcus Warren holding her? Comforting her?

The feeling, the smell of his body—awareness of Marcus as a man—blindsided her. Want, powerful and unexpected, mixed in with the panic over the baby and left her so confused that she couldn't pull away like she needed to and couldn't wrap her arms around him like she wanted to. She was rooted to the spot, wanting more and knowing she couldn't have it.

Marcus leaned back and tilted her head up so that she had no choice but to look him in the eyes. It wasn't fair, she thought dimly as she stared into the deep blue eyes that were almost exactly the same color as Lake Michigan on a clear day. Why couldn't he be a slimeball? Why did he have to be so damned perfect, hot and rich and now this—this *tenderness*? Why did he have to make her want him when she didn't deserve him?

He swiped his thumb over her cheek, brushing away a tear she hadn't been able to hold back. "It's important to you?" he asked, his voice deep. "The baby?"

"Yes," was all she could say, because what else was there? Marcus Warren was holding her in his arms and comforting her and looking at her as if he'd do anything to make her happy and dammit all if this wasn't one of her fantasies playing out in real life.

"Then I'll make it fine," he said. His thumb stroked over her cheek again and his other hand flattened out on her lower back. One corner of his mouth curved up into a smile that she knew well—the smile said that Marcus Warren was going to get exactly what he wanted.

And although she knew she shouldn't—couldn't—she leaned into his palm and let herself enjoy the sensation of Marcus touching her. "You will? Why would you do that for me?"

Something shifted in his eyes and his head dropped toward hers. He was going to kiss her, she realized. Her boss was going to kiss her and she was not only going to let him, she was going to kiss him back. Years of wanting and ignoring that want seemed to fall away.

But he didn't. Instead, he said, "Because you're important to me."

She forgot how to breathe. Heck, she might have forgotten her own name there for a second, because she was important to him. Not just a valuable employee. She, Liberty Reese, was important.

The alarm on her phone chimed, startling them out of whatever madness they'd been lost in. Marcus dropped his hand from her face and took a step away before he handed her phone to her. In all that had happened, she'd forgotten he had it.

It was eight forty-five? They'd started their morning run at seven. "You have a phone call with Dombrowski about that proposed bioenergy plant in fifteen minutes," she told him. Despite the heat that was building, she felt almost chilled without Marcus's arms around her.

Marcus laughed. "We're a little off schedule today. We haven't even showered."

Liberty froze as the image of the two of them in the shower together barged into her mind. Normally, they ran back to Marcus's condo, where he got ready while she caught the train to the office. Marcus had installed a shower in the restroom, so she would shower and dress there. She'd get started on organizing the notes she'd made during the run and Marcus would show up by nine thirty, looking as if he'd walked off a red carpet.

There was no showering together. Heck, there wasn't even any showering in the same building. That's how it worked.

But then, before ten minutes ago, there hadn't been any tears or hugs, either. Their physical contact was limited to handshakes and an occasional pat on the back and that was it.

"Shall I call him and reschedule?"

"Please do. Then we'll head back and I'll make a few calls." That was a perfectly normal set of Marcus responses.

Liberty was confident they were going to pretend that the touching and the holding and even the wedding date invitation had never happened. And that was fine with her, really.

But Marcus leaned forward. Even though he didn't touch her again, she still felt the air thin between them. His gaze dropped to her lips and, fool that she was, she still wanted that kiss that hadn't happened. The kiss that *couldn't* happen. "I promise you, Liberty—we won't lose that baby."

Three

It took Marcus the better part of three hours to find the right bureaucrat to deal with. The CEO of Children's Hospital, while sympathetic to Marcus's plight, could not legally provide any information on the baby. He did, however, call Marcus back in twenty minutes with the number of a DCFS supervisor.

The supervisor was less than helpful, but Marcus got the name of the manager of DCFS Guardians, who was responsible for assigning workers to these cases. It took some time to get ahold of the manager, and when he did, Marcus discovered a caseworker hadn't even been sent out.

"We're doing the best we can, Mr. Warren," the tired-sounding woman said. "But we have a limited amount of social workers and a limited amount of funds available to us. The baby will probably be in the hospital for several days. We'll send someone out as soon as we're able."

"That's not good enough," Marcus snapped.

"Well, how do you propose we deal with it?" the woman shot back.

The same way he dealt with everything. He wasn't about to let something like red tape get in his way. Marcus did a cursory web search and discovered that the current head of DCFS had gone to school with his father.

Well, hell. He should have started there. He knew how to play this game. He'd been raised playing an extended game of Who's Who. Political favors and donations were the kind of grease that made the wheels in Chicago run.

It took another twenty minutes to get through to the director's office and an additional twenty before Marcus had the man's personal promise that a caseworker would be assigned within the hour. "Of course, we don't normally keep nonfamily members updated…" the director said.

"I'd consider it a personal favor," Marcus said and in that, at least, he was being truthful.

Because after watching Liberty fold herself around that infant and cuddle the baby until he calmed down? After seeing Liberty's anguish as the baby was driven away in the ambulance? After impulsively pulling her into his arms because she was going to cry and feeling her body pressed against his?

After seeing that look of total gratitude when Marcus had said he'd take care of things?

Yeah, this was personal.

"Give your father my best," the man said at the end of the call.

"Will do!" Marcus said with false enthusiasm. He'd rather his father not find out about this particular conversation or the reason behind it. If Laurence and Marisa Warren knew about this, they'd give Marcus that disappointed look that, despite the decades of plastic surgery, was still immediately recognizable. It was one thing to trade political favors—but to do so for this? For an abandoned baby? Because his assistant got a little teary?

"What do you hope to gain out of this?" That's what his mother would say in her simpering voice, because that's what life was to her. Everything, every single human interaction, had a tally associated with it. You either gained something or you lost.

Warrens were never losers.

And his father? The man famous for his affairs with his secretaries? "If you want her, just take her." That's what his father would say.

He didn't want to be that man. He didn't want to use Liberty because he had all the power in their relationship. He was *not* his father.

Still, his father cast a long shadow. Marcus had gone to the university his parents had picked. His girlfriends had been preapproved daughters of their friends. Hell, even his company, Warren Capital, had been his father's idea. What better way to curry power and favor than to literally fund the businesses of tomorrow?

It had taken him years to loosen the ties that bound him to his parents, but he'd managed to separate his life from theirs. Liberty was a part of that, too. His mother had some friend of a friend she'd wanted him to hire—someone she could use to keep tabs on Marcus. Instead, he'd defied her by hiring a young woman from a family no one had ever heard of based on the strength of her recommendations and her insistence that she jogged regularly.

Marcus had paid for that act of defiance, just as he'd paid for refusing to marry Lillibeth Hanson. He may have lost favor with his parents, but he'd gained much more.

He'd gained his independence.

Still, he couldn't have his parents finding out about this. It simply wouldn't do for them to interest themselves in his life again.

"Mr. Warren?" Liberty stuck her head through his office door. He didn't miss the way that he was "Mr. Warren" again, as if she hadn't called him Marcus by the side of the jogging trail this morning.

"Yes?"

"Mr. Chabot is on the line." Marcus must have looked at her blankly, for she went on, "The producer for *Feeding Frenzy*? He wants to confirm the meeting when you're in Los Angeles after the wedding."

Right. Marcus had spent his entire morning tracking down someone—anyone—who knew about the little baby. He did actually have work to do.

"What did you tell him?"

She notched an eyebrow at him. "I put him on hold." The panic-stricken woman from the run this morning was gone and in her place was his competent, levelheaded assistant. Ms. Reese was impeccably dressed in a gray skirt suit with a rose-colored blouse underneath. Her hair was neatly pulled back into a slick bun and her makeup was understated, as always.

He'd wanted to kiss her this morning. The impulse had come out of nowhere. He'd watched her hold that child and felt her palpable grief when the ambulance had driven off. He'd wanted to hold her, to let her know it'd be okay. And then she'd looked up at him with her deep brown eyes and…

"Thank you, Ms. Reese," he said because what he needed right now was not to think about that impulse or how he'd joked that he should take her to the wedding only to realize he hadn't been joking. Which was a problem. She was an assistant—not part of his social circle. If he showed up with her, people would talk. Marcus Warren, slumming with his secretary. Or, worse, they'd assume that Liberty was manipulating him just as Lillibeth had.

But he wanted to take her. She was safe and trustworthy. And she was the one telling him to do what he wanted.

She gave him a little nod and turned to go.

"Liberty," he said.

She paused for a beat before she turned back around. "Yes?"

"I've made some calls about the baby. I'll let you know when I hear anything."

Her face softened and he was struck by how lovely she was. Underneath that executive-assistant mask was a beautiful woman. He just hadn't realized how beautiful until this morning. "Thank you."

He had nothing to gain by tracking down that baby. The child wouldn't bring him more power or money. The baby boy wouldn't be able to return a favor when Marcus wanted.

But he'd made a promise to Liberty.

He was going to keep it.

The ad mock-up for Rock City Watch drifted out of focus as Liberty wondered about that little baby. It'd been four days since she'd held him to her chest. Was he still in the hospital? Was he okay?

She shouldn't be this worried, she decided as she tried to refocus on the ad. Worrying wasn't going to help anything. And besides, Marcus had promised he'd look into it and she had to have faith that he'd keep that promise to her.

Of course it'd also been four days since Marcus had wrapped his strong arms around her and told her he'd find the baby because the child was important to her and she was important to Marcus.

Since that time, there'd been no hugs, no long looks. There'd been no more mention of the wedding, although that would have to change soon. If he continued to insist on going, he needed to pick a date. A safe date, she mentally corrected herself. Someone who wouldn't look at him and see nothing but a hot body and a huge...

Bank account.

The phone rang. "Warren Capital Investments. How may I assist you?"

"Ms. Reese." The coquettish voice of Mrs. Marisa Warren floated from the other end of the line. Liberty gritted her teeth. So this was how today was going to go, huh? "How is my son today?"

"Fine, Mrs. Warren." But Liberty offered no other information.

When she'd first been hired, Marcus had made it blisteringly clear that she worked for him, not for Laurence or Marisa Warren. If he ever caught her passing information to his parents about his business, his prospects or his personal life, well, she could pack her things and go. End of discussion.

Luckily, Liberty had gotten very good at telling people what they wanted to hear without giving anything away.

"I was wondering," Marisa simpered, "if my son has settled on a date for the Hanson wedding? It's a few weeks away and he knows how important it is."

When she'd first started fielding these nosy calls, Liberty hadn't entirely understood why Marcus was so determined that nothing of his life leak out to his parents. After all, she'd grown up dreaming of having a mother and a father who cared about her. And Marisa Warren seemed to care about her son quite a lot.

But appearances were deceiving. "Mrs. Warren," she said in her most deferential tone because it also hadn't taken her long to realize that while Marcus might treat her with respect and dignity, to his parents she was on approximately the same level as a maid. "I couldn't speak to his plans for the wedding."

"Surely you've heard something…"

Liberty focused on keeping her voice level. "As you know, Mr. Warren doesn't share personal information with me."

She wasn't sure at what point this wedding had crossed from personal to business and back again. When Marcus's relationship with Lillibeth had blown up in the media, she'd read what she could—but he'd never once broached the topic during office hours. It was only when they were running that he'd even touch on the subject—and even that was more about damage control than "feelings" and "sharing."

He'd asked her to prepare a roster of acceptable women with whom to attend this wedding. And then he'd asked her—however jokingly—to be his date.

"Hmph," Mrs. Warren said. It was the least dignified sound she was probably capable of making and, in her honeyed voice, it still sounded pretty. "Have him call me when he's free." She never asked to speak to Marcus when she called his office number. That was the thing that Liberty had realized about that first call. Mrs. Warren wasn't calling to talk *to* Marcus. She was calling to talk to Liberty *about* Marcus.

Liberty knew where her loyalty lay, even if Mrs. Warren didn't. "Of course, Mrs. Warren."

She hung up and finished analyzing the Rock City Watch ads. If Marcus was going to push them as a high-end luxury good, then the ads needed to be slicker. There was too much text talking about Detroit's revival, and the photography needed to give off a more exclusive vibe, she decided.

What rich people wanted was exclusivity. That's what she'd learned in the three years she'd worked in this office on North LaSalle. Not only did they want the best, they wanted to be damned sure that it was better than what everyone else had. It wasn't enough to own a great watch or a fancy car or live in an expensive building. Rich people wanted to make sure that theirs was the only one. She figured that was why they spent so much money on artworks. By definition, those were one of a kind.

This world was all still foreign to her, but after three years she felt as if at least she was becoming fluent in the language.

She was just finishing her notes when Marcus called out, "Ms. Reese?"

"Coming." She grabbed her tablet and the ad materials and walked into his office. This place, for example, was a perfect example of how a rich person simply had to have the very best. Even though Warren Capital was a relatively small operation—Marcus employed fifteen people to handle the finances and contracts—the business was located on LaSalle Drive on the top floor of one of the most expensive office buildings in Chicago. Marcus's office sat in the corner behind walls of glass that gave him expansive views of downtown and Lake Michigan. Warren Capital was the only company on this floor—no one else could claim this view. It was the best—and it was his.

And through sheer dint of will, Liberty managed to carve out a place where she could fit in this world. Sure, it was as an assistant and yes, she had to buy new running shoes every six months. It didn't matter. She loved this office, this view. Everything clean and bright. There were no holes in the wall, no critters scurrying about. If something broke, maintenance had it fixed within hours, if not minutes. The lights were always on and the heat always worked. This office was as far away from the apartment in the Cabrini-Green projects as she could get.

"Your mother called," she said, taking her usual seat in front of Marcus's desk. His office furniture reflected a modern sensibility—black leather seating, glass-topped desks of ebony wood and chrome. Even the art along the wall was modern. Among others, he had an Edward Hopper and a Mark Rothko—names she'd had to look up online because she certainly hadn't heard of them before. Marcus had bought the Rothko for $35 million.

Yes, he had one hell of an impressive…bank account.

"I assume to pump you for information about my wedding plans?" he asked without looking up.

"Correct. She's concerned about your date. Or lack thereof."

Marcus sighed heavily. "I've had an update on the baby, if you're still interested."

"What?" Her heart began to pound as he glanced at her in surprise. She tried again. "I mean, of course I'm still interested. Why wouldn't I be?"

"You hadn't asked."

She blinked at him. "You promised you'd make some calls. I didn't want to bother you."

He gave her a look that was partly amused. But she also thought she saw some of the tenderness beyond why he'd made that promise to her in the first place.

"Liberty," he said in a gentle voice. A creeping flush started at the base of her neck and worked its way down her back. Was it wrong to like how he said her name? Was it wrong to want him to say it some more? "You are not a bother to me."

She swallowed, willing her cheeks not to blush. They were getting off track. "What did you hear? About the baby?"

"Ah, yes." He looked down at his computer. The moment he looked away, Liberty exhaled.

"The baby has been discharged from the hospital."

She gasped. "How is he? Is he okay? Did they find his mother yet?"

"Apparently he's surprisingly healthy, given the circumstances—but no, they haven't located his parents yet." He gave her an apologetic look. "They don't seem to be looking too hard, despite my encouragement. I don't think they'll find the mother."

Liberty didn't know what to think because on one hand,

that poor child—being abandoned and never knowing his parents?

But on the other hand, he'd already been abandoned once. What if they found his mother—then what? There were other ways to abandon a child than just leaving him in a park. That she knew personally.

Marcus said, "I've been assured that the foster mother is one of their best and that the baby's needs will be met."

She gaped at him for a moment before she realized her mouth was still open. She got it shut and tried to remember to look professional. This was probably as good as the news would get. One of their best foster mothers? Personal assurances that the baby would be well cared for? Those were all things she'd never gotten when she was in the system. "That's wonderful. Can I visit him?"

Marcus looked at her in surprise, as if she'd asked for a space pony. "I didn't get the address."

"Oh." She stared down at her tablet. "I just thought…" She cleared her throat and tried to get back on track. "Here's the analysis of the Rock City Watch ad. I don't think it's hitting the target market you were looking for yet. And you still need to find a date for the wedding."

She stood and handed the ad material over to Marcus. Then she turned and headed for the door.

It was better this way. She'd done her part. Marcus had upheld his end of things. The baby was going to be fine.

Besides, what was she going to do? Adopt a child? Please. She worked from 7:00 a.m. until 6:00 p.m., five days a week, and she came in on Saturday to prepare for the next week's meetings. She had to. There was so much about his world that she didn't know and she couldn't afford to be exposed as an outsider, so she did her homework day in and day out.

She was at the threshold when Marcus spoke. "Liberty."

She paused. He wasn't going to ask her to the wedding again, was he? "Yes?"

She turned to face him. The way he was looking at her—it wasn't right. It wasn't normal anyway. What she would give for that look to be right because there was something to it, something that was possessive and intense. It scared her, how much she wanted him to look at her like that.

So she went on the defensive. "You can't want me to go to this wedding with you."

His lips curved into a seductive smile. "First off, aren't you the one telling me to do what I want?"

He couldn't mean that he really *wanted* to take her—could he? "Yes, but—"

He held up his hand like a king. "Do you want to see him again? The little boy."

She gave him a long, hard look. Was this a game? If so, she wasn't playing. "Mr. Warren, you're not going to make this awkward, are you? You'll get me the foster mother's address *if* I agree to attend this ridiculous wedding as your—what, your personal human shield?"

A muscle in his jaw twitched and he looked quite dangerous. Very few people said no to Marcus Warren. But she was one of them. "Just answer the question—do you want to see the baby again?"

She gritted her teeth. "Yes," she said, bracing for his counteroffer.

"That will be all," Marcus said, turning his attention back to his computer.

The dismissal was so sudden and unexpected that she just stood there for a moment. Marcus didn't look back up at her. He didn't acknowledge her continued presence at all. He merely ignored her.

It was not a good feeling.

Four

This time, the DCFS supervisor didn't hesitate to give Marcus the name and address of the foster home. All he had to do was say who he was and the woman practically fell over herself to give him what he wanted.

Well. It was nice that someone was acting appropriately. Because his executive assistant sure as hell wasn't.

Marcus stared at the information he'd written down on a piece of company letterhead. Hazel Jones. He googled the address and saw that it was way up in West Rogers Park.

This was ridiculous. He should be game-planning how to survive this wedding, not diverting his time, energy and accumulated favors for an abandoned baby and his assistant. And yet, here he was, doing just that.

There was nothing to be gained here. He did not need Liberty as a personal human shield and the implication—that he couldn't attend this stupid wedding without one—was an insult to his pride. He was a Warren, dammit all.

He didn't hide from anyone or anything and woe unto the person who tried to stand between him and his goal.

Who, at this exact moment, was Liberty Reese.

He strode out of his office to find Liberty on the phone. She glanced up at him, and the fact that he saw a hint of worry in her eyes only made him madder. What had he ever done to make her afraid of him? Not a damned thing. His father would have had her pinned to her desk by the end of her first month here and if she'd so much as sneezed wrong afterward, he would have done everything in his power to bury her.

And what had Marcus done? He'd treated her with respect. He'd never once laid a hand on her, never implied that her job was in some way connected to her sexuality.

All he had done was ask her to go to a wedding with him. And now she was treating him as if he was some lecherous old man to be feared.

"Yes," she said into the phone. "That's correct. No—no," she said in a more severe voice. "That is not the timetable. That information needs to be on my desk by the twelfth." She notched an eyebrow at him and mouthed "Yes?"

He crossed his arms and mouthed back, "I'll wait."

There it was again, that hint of worry. Okay, so maybe he shouldn't have asked her to the damned wedding. Hell, if he had his way, he wouldn't even be going to the thing.

"No, the twelfth. What part of that isn't clear? *The. Twelfth,*" Liberty snapped at the caller. Marcus grinned. He'd hired her because she was outside his parents' sphere of influence and she ran. But she'd turned into an exceedingly good assistant who was not afraid to push when she needed to.

She rolled her eyes at the phone and then dug through a small stack of papers on her desk, pulled one out and handed it to him.

"Available for the Hanson-Spears wedding" was the label of a column. Below was a list of names and phone numbers.

Marcus gave her a dull look, which she ignored. "Yes. Excellent. We look forward to seeing what you put together." She hung up the phone and took a deep breath. "I have to say that, at this point, the baby-wearables people are not winning any points in terms of organization or professionalism. They may not be ready to move to the next level."

Ah, yes. The company that wanted funding for a line of baby clothes and blankets with smart technology built into the fabric so anxious parents could monitor sleeping and eating habits from the comfort of their phones. The idea was intriguing, but he didn't like to see his money squandered by poor planning. "So noted."

She turned a bright smile to him. It was not real. "Was there something I could help you with?"

He held out the name and address he'd copied down. "Here. It's in West Rogers Park, up on the north side."

Liberty made a small noise, like a gasp she was trying her best to hold in. "I…" She looked up at him and at least for right now, any hint of worry or fake smiles was gone and he found himself looking down at the same woman whom he'd held in his arms beside the jogging path.

She would do anything for that baby, he realized. *Anything.* Even attend a wedding.

He knew it. And given the way her cheeks colored a pretty pink and she dropped her gaze, she knew it, too.

It'd make his life a hell of a lot easier. A plus-one for this wedding in exchange for a little information, and he wouldn't have to worry about finding a media-ready, parent-approved date who wouldn't view the event as a stepping-stone to bigger and better things. He could go with Liberty and might even enjoy himself. At the very least, they could run on the beach along the Pacific Ocean in the mornings instead of Lake Michigan.

She wouldn't be able to say no.

And he wouldn't be any better than his father was.

"As promised," he said and turned to walk back to his office.

He heard her chair squeak as she got up to follow him. "That's it?"

"That's it," he said, sitting down. He felt strange and he wasn't sure why. It wasn't a bad feeling. He stared at the list she'd given him. He'd gone out with a half dozen of these women and he knew the other half. Any one of these women would make a great date to this wedding and appease his mother.

He crumpled the paper up and threw it in the trash.

"You're not going to…" She let the sentence trail off but he could hear the words anyway. *You're not going to force the issue?*

"Insist you do something you obviously don't want to that falls outside of your job parameters? No," he replied, trying to sound casual. He was seriously just going to let this go? If he didn't get a date and he didn't take Liberty, he'd just go alone. Sure, his parents might disown him for it. "Why would I?"

He glanced at her then and wasn't surprised to see her looking as if she'd stepped into a room full of snapping alligators. "That's…thank you."

Even stranger, that made him feel better, as if her appreciation was all that he needed. "You're welcome."

But she didn't leave. Instead, she took another step into the office. "Marcus…"

It wasn't as if she hadn't said his name before. She had. But there was something about the way she said it this time that held him captive.

"I know I shouldn't ask this—but…" She looked down at the paper again as if he'd given her a sheet of solid gold. "Can I leave early today? Just today," she hurried to add. "This won't be a regular thing. I just…"

And he remembered how she'd soothed the baby, how she hadn't just hummed a lullaby but had told that little child that he was loved and he was strong and he could make it. And Marcus remembered how watching her holding that baby had rocked him to his core.

"I'll come in on Saturday and finish up whatever I don't get done this week," she offered, mistaking his silence for disapproval.

He stared at her. Did she think he didn't know she came in on Saturdays anyway?

Liberty went on. "This won't affect my job performance at all."

And he was reminded that he held all the power here and that meant he could gain something from this interaction.

He looked at his watch. It was three forty-five—early by their standards. "Here," he said, holding out his hand for the paper. "Give it to me."

"Oh." The disappointment on her face was a painful thing to see. "Yes, of course." She trudged forward—there was no other word for it—and handed over the paper. Then, without looking him in the eyes, she turned and headed back to her desk.

"Get your things packed up," he said, picking up his phone. He had nothing to gain from this but he was going to do it anyway. Because he wanted to. "We'll go together."

Somehow, Liberty found herself sitting in the passenger seat of Marcus's Aston Martin, zipping up Lake Shore Drive. One minute, she'd been crestfallen that she couldn't immediately go see the baby. The next, Marcus had been hustling her into his car—his very nice car—and personally driving her to the foster home.

She'd never been in his car before. Oh, sure, she'd attended a few business functions with him, but those were either after-hours events when she'd take the El as she always did or business lunches with potential clients when he'd have her order a car big enough for the entire group.

The Aston Martin was his personal car. And he drove it like a bat out of hell. Of course he did, she thought as she surreptitiously tried to grab on to the door handle when Marcus took the curve without braking. He drove as he ran.

"We don't have to go this fast," she said, trying to sound calm. "I'm not in that big of a hurry."

"This isn't fast," he replied and then, the moment they hit the straightaway, he gunned it. Liberty was pushed back into the seat as Marcus accelerated, weaving in and out of traffic. Lake Shore Drive was still mostly clear—it wouldn't fill up for another half hour with commuters. Marcus took full command of the road.

If she wasn't so concerned with dying in a fiery heap by the side of the road, she'd be forced to admit that it was kind of sexy. How often did a billionaire act as her personal chauffeur? Never.

They zipped up the drive in record time and then cut over on Peterson. There, at least, Marcus slowed down.

She was nervous. What if this foster home was one of the best—and it still wasn't very good? She tried to think back to the three homes she'd been in. The first home was fuzzy. It was just after she'd started kindergarten. Less than two weeks into the school year, her mom wasn't there when she got off the bus one day. Liberty had done okay on her own for a few days, going to see Grandma Devlin for food, but before long, she'd been in a foster home.

She didn't remember much, just that it got cold in her

room and that the other girls were mean to her. But she hadn't been hungry and there hadn't been the same kind of screaming and fights as at home.

"Why do you need to see him so badly?" Marcus asked when they got stuck at a light.

Liberty tensed. Were they still in the tug-of-war they'd been in earlier? Or were they back to normal? Since they were out of the office, was this the kind of conversation they might have while they were running?

Marcus glanced at her. "I'm just asking, Liberty," he said, sounding tired. "And it has nothing to do with the wedding."

Oh, if only she could *just* answer honestly. But how would that be possible? Because the truth hurt. And what would Marcus think if he knew the truth about addict moms and foster homes and being an unwanted, unloved little girl? Would he still want to take her to this stupid wedding—or would he look at her and see an imposter who was not to be trusted?

Still, she understood what he wanted to know. It wasn't her deepest, darkest secrets. It was a simple question that was only one step removed from polite conversation. She had to hope he'd be satisfied with her answer. "I had a little brother," she said and she was horrified to hear her voice quaver.

She'd never said those words out loud. Who would she have said them to when she was a kid? Her foster parents? They had enough kids to worry about. Her teachers? That would have only made them pity her more, and she had enough of that. Her friends? *Ha*.

"I didn't realize," Marcus replied. "I'm sorry."

"It's no big deal," she lied because that lie came as naturally to her as breathing air. None of it had been a big deal because she'd survived. She'd thrived. She could afford to ignore her past now.

Or she had been able to. Right until she'd seen the little baby in the trash. Then everything had come back.

She swallowed and tried to get her voice to work right again. "He was born with a lot of birth defects and didn't make it long." Which was a version of the truth that was palatable for Marcus's refined taste.

An uncomfortable silence boxed her in. She could see Marcus thinking and she couldn't have that because if he kept asking questions and she kept having to come up with better versions of the truth, sooner or later she'd either let the truth slip or be forced to tell a real lie. So she barged into the silence and said, "I appreciate you coming with me for this, but it wasn't necessary. You should be focusing on the list I gave you."

"You mean the list I threw away?" There—they were back to their early-morning teasing and banter.

"I have other copies," she announced and was rewarded with Marcus rolling his eyes and grinning at her. "You need to be focused on the wedding and the meeting with the producers, not on taking me to see an abandoned baby."

"Maybe this is what I want to do."

"Be serious, Marcus."

They hit another stoplight. "I am serious. You think you're the only one worried about that baby?"

She stared at him. "You are?"

"I can't explain it," he said in a quiet voice. "But watching you hold him…"

Oh. That was bad. The way his voice trailed off there at the end? The way he sounded all wistful and concerned?

Very, very bad. Damned bad, even.

She was not good for him. She could never be anything more than a valuable employee who got up too early every morning to jog with him. "I can't do anything for your reputation except drag it down."

Marcus didn't even look at her. He kept his attention on

the road, but she saw him clench his jaw again, just as he had in his office earlier. "My reputation isn't everything."

She desperately wanted to believe that, but she knew that in his world, her mere existence would be a scandal. "I'm not good for you," she said in a whisper.

He pulled onto a side street and parked. "I'll be the judge of that."

That was exactly what she was afraid of.

Five

Marcus got out of the car and looked around. He'd only ever lived in the Gold Coast, with luxury high-rises and doormen and valets. He rarely left the downtown area and when he did, it was to see the White Sox play or catch a Bulls or Blackhawks game at the United Center—from his owner's box, of course.

He looked up and down the street at the two-story buildings that stood side by side with older bungalows. Most yards were mowed. Was this a good neighborhood?

"This is nice," Liberty said, sounding shocked.

"What did you expect—slums?"

There was something about the way she avoided looking at him as she laughed that bothered him. She stared down at the address on the letterhead. He saw her hands were shaking.

"This one," she said, indicating a trim little bungalow. It was white with a wall of windows framed in dark wood.

The paint around the windows was a little chipped and the white was grubby, but it didn't look bad. He hoped.

"Ready?" he asked.

She took a deep breath and gave him an apologetic look. "You don't think this is ridiculous, do you?"

He had that urge to once again pull her into his arms and tell her it was all going to be fine. But he didn't. Instead, he told her, "Coming to see the baby? No. I want to do this with you."

Her eyes got huge again, but she didn't say anything. They walked up to the front door of the house and knocked. And waited. Marcus knocked again.

"She knows we're coming, right?" Liberty said. The panic in her voice was obvious. "Should we have—"

The door opened. "Mr. Warren?" Marcus almost grinned at the appearance of the little old lady standing before him. Maybe she wasn't that old, but she was petite, with a crown of white hair cut into a bob and a huge pair of vintage-looking glasses on her nose.

"Mrs. Jones, hello. We spoke on the phone." He offered his hand but she just nodded and smiled. "This is Liberty Reese. We found the child together and we just wanted to see how he's doing."

"It's a pleasure to meet you, Mrs. Jones," Liberty said. She sounded stiff.

"How sweet of you to come. Please, call me Hazel. All my friends do. Come in, come in. Shut the door behind you, if you don't mind." She turned and began to climb up a short flight of stairs.

Marcus made sure to shut the front door behind him, which took a little shove. The entryway contained another set of doors that led both upstairs and downstairs, and he had to wonder if this was a single-family home or if someone else lived in the basement.

Hazel and Liberty finally went through the upstairs door and Marcus followed, shutting it behind him. Then he looked around.

Wow. Once, when he'd been really little, he'd had a nanny who loved *The Brady Bunch*. His parents didn't believe in television, so getting to watch any show was a big deal to him. The nanny—Miss Judy—let him catch a show if he got all his lessons done. She'd make a bowl of popcorn and they'd snuggle on the couch and for a half hour at a time, he'd gotten a glimpse at what normal might look like.

It'd been years since he'd thought of *The Brady Bunch*. But this was like walking into the Brady house. Everything looked as if it was original to the 1960s or '70s—the pine paneling, the vinyl covers over the sofa cushions, the preponderance of autumn gold and orange everywhere. Marcus leaned over to catch a glimpse through a doorway—yes, there were avocado-green appliances in the kitchen.

This was one of the best foster homes in the system?

"He's in the nursery," Hazel was saying. "He's still napping. Oh, they sleep so much the first week or so, but he's starting to wake up."

"Is he okay?" Liberty asked anxiously.

"I think he's perfect," Hazel said as she guided them through a small dining room and past two doorways that led to a bedroom and a television room. The third doorway was the nursery. "I understand your concerns, though. I've had children who were coming off drugs or the like and he doesn't seem to have those problems." She stopped and sighed. "His poor mother. One has to wonder."

"Yes," Liberty said. "One does."

Hazel gave Liberty a maternal smile as she patted her arm. "It's good you've come. This way."

They all crowded into the small room. A metal crib was by one wall and a larger, wooden crib up against another.

There was a dresser with a blue terry-cloth pad on it nex
to a worn rocking chair. Marcus had to wonder how lon
Hazel Jones had had these things—since her own childre
had been babies?

All over two of the walls were pictures of babies, he re
alized. Old pictures, with the edges curling and the colo
faded to a gold and brown that matched the furniture in th
rest of the house. There were hundreds of pictures of littl
babies all over the place.

Next to a window was an antique-looking swinging cha
that squeaked gently with every swing. And inside the swir
was the baby boy. He was clean and dressed and Marcu
swore he'd grown in the past five days, but there was n
mistaking that child. Marcus would know him anywher
How odd, he thought dimly.

Liberty made a noise that was half choking, half gasp
ing. "Oh—oh," she said, covering her mouth.

Hazel patted her on the arm again. "You're his guardia
angels, you and your boyfriend. He would have likely die
if it hadn't been for you."

"We're not—" Liberty started to say, but Hazel cut he
off.

"It'll be time for his bottle in a few. Would you like t
feed him?"

"Could I?" Liberty turned to Marcus, her brown eye
huge. "Do we have time?"

As if she had to get his permission. "Of course."

"I'll be right back." In contrast to her slow climb up th
stairs, Hazel moved quickly to the kitchen. "Don't go any
where!" she jokingly called out.

"Is this what you wanted?" Marcus asked Liberty as the
stared at the baby.

"Oh, God, yes. He's okay," she said as if she still couldn'
believe it. The baby exhaled heavily and turned his hea

away from the window. Liberty gasped and flung out a hand in his direction and Marcus took it. He gave her a squeeze of support and she squeezed back. "Look at him," she said in awe.

"Is this place okay for him, do you think?" Marcus looked around the room again at the worn, battered furniture. "They said it was one of their best homes..."

"No, it's really lovely." Marcus stared down at her, but she was still looking at the baby. "And it seems like she only has him right now. This is *amazing*."

There was something in the way she said it, the way she *meant* it, that struck him as odd. But before he could ask about it, Hazel said brightly, "Here we are."

He dropped Liberty's hand and stepped out of the way. Hazel handed him a bottle and he took it, even though he had no idea how to feed a baby.

"Does he have a name yet?" Liberty asked Hazel.

"Oh, no. He's still Baby Boy Doe." As if on cue, the baby began to lift his little hands and scrunch up his eyes. "I suppose he should have a name, shouldn't he?"

"William," Liberty said without hesitation. "He's William." She said it with such conviction that again, Marcus found himself staring at her.

"Oh, that's lovely. My husband was Bill. That's a good name." The baby began to fuss and Hazel deftly carried him over to the dresser and laid him out on the pad. She unzipped his blanket-thing—a blanket with arms? Was there a name for that? Hazel began to change his diaper with the kind of practiced motion that made it clear she could do this in the dark, in her sleep. Marcus wondered how many babies she'd changed just like that.

"We never had children," Hazel went on as she got out a clean diaper from the top drawer, all the while never taking her hand off the baby's belly. "But I loved babies so... I was offered an early retirement from my teaching position back in 1988 and I decided that I was going to be a grandmother one way or another."

"All babies?" Liberty asked.

"Oh, yes. I just love this age. They're such little angels. I can't keep up with them when they start crawling and walking, though." Hazel shook her head. "Babies are just my speed."

Marcus watched as Hazel changed the diaper. She made it seem easy but the mostly naked infant was squirming and then there was the cleaning part and...

Suddenly, he was terrified. It wasn't the same kind of terror he'd felt when he'd opened the box and found this child—that had been stark panic, with a life hanging in the balance. That danger was safely past, thank God. But when Hazel got the diaper on and asked Liberty if she wanted to help re-dress William, and Liberty still looked as if she might start sobbing with relief at any moment, the whole scene was so far outside his realm of experience that he might as well have landed on Mars.

Liberty got his tiny little feet back into the blanket contraption and zipped him up. "Here we go," Hazel said in a singsong voice as she picked William up. "Dear, why don't you sit in the rocker?"

Liberty sat and Hazel laid the baby in her arms. In that moment, everything about Liberty changed; it was as if he were looking at a different woman. This wasn't his take-charge assistant—this was Liberty, the real woman.

Hazel took the bottle from Marcus and showed Liberty how to hold it. The older woman got a little pillow that had been next to the rocking chair and used that to prop Liberty's arms up. "There we go. He's been eating quite a bit, poor dear." For the first time in a while, she seemed to notice Marcus. "Oh—would you like a chair?"

"I'm fine," he insisted. He couldn't take his eyes off Liberty and William. There was something about them—something he'd seen that first time in the park...

"You're amazing with him," he told Liberty and he meant it. Yeah, he'd found the child, but it was Liberty who'd cooled him down and got him to stop crying. It was because of Liberty that Marcus had used his clout to make sure the baby got into the best home.

It was Liberty who'd named him.

Then she looked up at him and smiled and everything that Marcus knew to be true about himself was suddenly... not true. Not anymore.

He was Marcus Warren. A trust-fund billionaire, gossip column fodder and a potential reality-television star. He had a business and a reputation to manage. He had to carry on the Warren family name.

And quite unexpectedly, none of it mattered. What mattered was seeing Liberty rock that tiny baby and smile at him with that silly joy on her face, as if she'd been waiting her whole life for this exact moment.

What mattered was knowing he'd made this moment happen. Because he wanted that silly joy on her face. He wanted to be the one who made her smile, who gave her everything her heart desired. Not because it would give him leverage, but because it made her happy.

His entire life had been about accumulation. Things, power, favors—more and more and more. Never enough.

What if...

William's mouth popped off the bottle and he squirmed. "Oh, is he okay?" Liberty asked Hazel.

The two of them fussed over the baby and Liberty got him burped. Then Hazel took William back and turned to Marcus. "Would you like to hold him?"

"Sure," he said, sitting in the rocking chair. Liberty

propped the pillow under his arm. He tried to position his arms the way she had.

She looked down at him skeptically. "Have you ever held a baby before?"

His face got hot. "No?"

Liberty sighed, but at least she was grinning as she moved his hands into approximately the right position as if it was no big deal to physically rearrange him. But it only made that nearly out-of-body experience he was having that much worse.

What if...

"Here we are," Hazel said, handing William to Marcus. The baby sighed and scrunched up his nose.

Marcus was dimly aware that Hazel and Liberty were still talking, but he didn't really hear them. Instead, he stared down at the child in his arms.

William was so small—how was this human going to grow up and be a regular-sized person? "Hi, William," Marcus whispered as the baby waved one of his hands jerkily through the air.

Without thinking about it, Marcus shifted and held one of his fingers up against William's hand. The baby grabbed on at the same time his little eyes opened up all the way, and in that moment Marcus was lost. How could anyone have walked away from this baby? This must have been what Liberty had felt when she'd held the baby in the park.

They couldn't lose this baby. He'd thought he'd done his part, getting William into one of the best foster homes— but now that Marcus had seen Liberty with him, now that he'd held William himself, how could he walk away from this child?

He looked around the room again. Hazel was a good foster mother for a baby, he decided. But the stuff she had to work with was ancient. Marcus eyed the baby swing William had been in when they got here. The thing looked like a death-trap of metal and plastic.

His phone buzzed in his pocket, which startled the baby. William began to fuss and Hazel swooped in and plucked him from Marcus's arms. "There, now," she soothed.

"Sorry," Marcus said as he dug out his phone. The missed call had been from his mother. This couldn't be good. It was already past five.

"We should go," Liberty said. "Hazel, thank you so much for letting us visit William. This was wonderful. I'm so glad he's got you."

With William tucked against her chest, Hazel waved the compliment away. "You're more than welcome to come back. Just give me a call!"

"Could we?" Liberty glanced at Marcus, her cheeks coloring brightly. "I mean, I'll do that."

"We can come back," he agreed. And he wasn't just saying that—he really did want to see the baby again. More than that, he wanted to see Liberty with the baby again.

Liberty gave him another one of her shy smiles, as if she'd been hoping he'd say that but hadn't dared to ask.

As they walked toward the front door, Hazel followed them. "You two should consider applying for adoption," she said. "A nice couple like you? And because you found him, you might have a better chance of getting him. If they don't find his birth mother, that is," she added, sounding sad. "Poor dear."

Liberty jolted. "I don't—"

"We'll discuss it," Marcus said. He put his hand on Liberty's back and guided her down the stairs. "Thanks so much."

He made sure to shut the door behind them.

Six

Liberty stood on the sidewalk in a state of shock. She knew she needed to pull herself together but she was weirdly numb right now.

"That place was a time warp," Marcus said, stepping around her to the car and opening the passenger door for her.

She blinked at him. Hazel was a warm, loving, capable woman who had only one child in her charge and, by all appearances, would dote on William as if he were her own. That was weird enough, but now? Marcus Warren was opening her door for her. In what world did *any* of this make sense?

"Liberty?" Then he was touching her again, his hand in the small of her back as he gently propelled her toward his waiting car as if he was her chauffeur instead of her billionaire boss. Warmth flowed up her back from where he touched her and she wanted nothing more than to lean into him. "Are you all right?"

No. No, she wasn't. Everything had changed and she

didn't know how she'd ever be the same again. But she had to try. "I can't—you don't have to come back."

Marcus snorted in amusement. "I never have to do something I don't want," he said. "You were right. We can't lose him."

"We?" That word sounded different in her ears now, foreign almost. There was no "we" where Marcus and she were concerned. Not outside the office or off the jogging path. Or beyond her carefully guarded fantasies. "But…"

"Come on," he said, almost pushing her into the car. "Let's get some dinner. We can talk then."

"Dinner?" She couldn't make sense of anything he was saying. *We. Dinner.* "No—wait," she said when he got into the driver's seat. "You don't have to take me to dinner. You should be taking a potential wedding date—not me."

"Maybe I am taking a potential date to dinner."

And they were right back to where they'd been earlier. Well, this time she was not going to mess around. The sooner he realized how radically inappropriate she'd be as a wedding date, the sooner they could get back to their regularly scheduled programming. "Marcus, I'm *not* going. I'm not good enough for you, for that crowd. I know it. Everyone else there will know it. You're the only one who doesn't seem to realize it."

"That's not—"

She cut him off because he had to see reason. She didn't know how much longer she could be this strong. "That's not all. Why would I want to go to this wedding? Why would I want to watch Lillibeth hurt you again? Because you know she's going to try. And everyone will be watching to see how bad it's going to be. You'll be back in the media again. And I don't want to be a part of that. I don't want to be another reason people try to tear you down. I care too much about you to let that happen."

The last part just slipped out. She hadn't meant to say that she cared about him at all, but she'd built up a head of steam. But it was the truth—a truth that she couldn't bury anymore.

"Liberty," he said. And then something horrible and wonderful happened—Marcus touched her. He cupped her face in the palm of his hand.

"I just don't want you to be hurt again," she breathed. And even though she knew she shouldn't, she reached up and held his palm against her skin.

"You won't hurt me. I know you too well for that."

There it was again, that blind trust he had in her. And she knew—*knew*—that if he learned the truth, the whole truth and nothing but the truth about her junkie mom and her unknown father, he would be hurt.

She wanted to lean into his touch, but she couldn't because she was already starting to slip up and if she let herself get swept away in his touch, in his longing looks, something even more damaging might come out of her mouth.

So she shook him off. "If you don't want to, don't. Don't go to the wedding. Don't do the reality show. You said it yourself—your reputation isn't everything. You don't need to do any of that stuff. Do what *you* want."

He stared at her for a moment, but she refused to make eye contact because she didn't know if she could handle it. One searing look from Marcus Warren might break her resolve. So she kept her gaze locked on the windshield.

He started the car and began to drive without answering.

"Please take me back to the office. I'll finish the work I didn't get done earlier."

"Don't worry about it," he said. He sounded distant.

She fought the urge to apologize, to backpedal—to take it all back. She wanted to go back to the way things had been a week ago, when he'd tease her during the run and she earned his respect by being invaluable to his business, when she didn't offer opinions on his personal life and she didn't run the risk of letting the facts of her life slip out at every turn.

But then, that'd mean not finding William—not knowing that he was alive and healthy and cared for. And she couldn't imagine that. She'd seen that baby for a total of an hour and a half and she couldn't imagine life without him.

You two should consider applying for adoption. Liberty would be lying to herself if Hazel's idea didn't sound like a dream come true. She'd long fantasized about Marcus. He was gorgeous, one of the richest men in the city, and she liked him. She hated running but she liked running with him. She liked his jokes and how he treated her and how he'd put that shower in the ladies' room so she could change without going all the way back to her apartment in Logan Square.

And she'd liked the way he looked holding that baby and smiling down at him as if he really did care. It hadn't mattered that he'd had on a suit that probably cost thousands or that William was one burp away from ruining that suit. Marcus had smiled and cooed and held his hand anyway. William was important to Marcus because William was important to her.

She'd spent her entire adolescence and adulthood trying so hard to overcome her abandonment. Her life was built around making sure no one could forget about her again. She worked harder than anyone else. She never stopped working. In college, she'd held down two jobs and carried a full class load and never done anything fun like party or date. Never. She'd passed as white because she could and because it meant she was that much further away from Jackie Reese's life, because passing meant that she had to work only twice as hard to get ahead, not four times as hard.

What if Marcus learned the truth about her? About her mother's criminal history and overdose death? About Liberty's time in foster homes? About how she wasn't really who she said she was?

Would he still look at her and smile as he'd smiled at William? Or would he look at her and see who she really was—a hooker's daughter who lied her way into a better life?

"We're here," he said, startling her out of her thoughts.

She looked up to see that, instead of pulling up to the office, they were in front of a restaurant. A valet in a red jacket opened her door. "Welcome to Alinea."

She turned to Marcus. "Wait, what?"

"Dinner," he said in his nonnegotiable voice.

"Marcus! We can't do this!"

Unexpectedly, he leaned over, his face very close to hers. "We can't? Why can't we?"

"I'm your assistant. You're my boss. I'm not…"

"Don't you dare say you're not good enough for me, Liberty, because it's not true."

Her heart began to pound. He really meant that. Worse, he believed it. He couldn't imagine that she was anything other than what she was. If he knew…

But when he said things like that, she wanted to tell him. She wanted to say yes, that she'd go with him—anywhere with him.

But her reality trumped any fantasy she had. Marcus simply couldn't know the truth. She clung to the only thing she could—their professional relationship. "But I work for you."

He lifted an eyebrow, which made him look like a fox. She felt like a hen, that much was for sure. "I could fix that."

She gasped. "Is that…are you *threatening* me?" She needed this job. She *was* this job. Getting another would mean risking exposure all over again. References would be checked. Questions would be asked. Judgments would be made.

He looked hurt by this. "No—of course not. It's just…" He sighed heavily. "Look, it's been a long day. I'm hungry. You're hungry. I want dinner. This isn't a date, okay? We'll talk business."

"You won't ask me about the wedding again?"

"I won't ask," he promised.

Marcus settled into the booth and watched as Liberty hesitated before sliding in opposite him. The maître d' said, "Mr. Warren, the wine list."

"Thank you, Winston."

When Winston had departed, Liberty whispered, "You come here often?"

Marcus shrugged. "Enough that they have a table waiting for me. I enjoy dining out."

"So," she said in a too-bright voice. "Business."

"Yes," he agreed, staring at the menu. "But first, dinner."

Liberty frowned at the menu. "What's good? I don't even…" Her voice trailed off. "What's haricots verts?"

"Green beans in French," Marcus said with a grin.

"Why don't they just say green beans?"

Marcus snorted. "Like commoners? Please."

Liberty gave him a nervous little smile and he remembered one of her excuses for why she wouldn't go to the wedding with him—because she wasn't good enough.

"What's a foam? A truffle-oil foam? Is that even food?"

"It's more of a taste—a flavor on the palate," he told her. "This isn't the first time you've eaten in a restaurant like this, is it? We've gone to lunches in similar places."

She didn't look him in the eyes. "We've never been here. I'd remember it." As she said it, a waiter walked past with a balloon. He deposited it at a nearby table and the diners popped the balloon and started eating it.

Liberty blanched. "I'd definitely remember *that*. Are they…"

"It's a house specialty." This was wrong, all wrong. At the time, he'd just wanted a nice meal with her, and Alinea was one of the nicest restaurants in the country, with prices to match. "What do you order when we dine out?" He felt bad that he didn't remember. True, when they ate together at a restaurant, he was entertaining clients, but that suddenly seemed like the sort of thing he should know about her.

She blushed. "I usually either order what you order or I order the special."

Why hadn't he ever noticed that before? "But what if you don't like what I order?"

"I'm not picky." She kept staring at the menu as if it were written in, well, a foreign language.

He plucked it from her hands. "What are you in the mood for? Steak? They have a lobster dish that's amazing."

She stared at him as if he, too, had started speaking in tongues. "There was steak on that menu?"

He grinned as the waiter came back. "I'll have the lobster plate and the lily bulbs. The lady will have the *wagyu* plate and the fourteen textures."

"Excellent choices," the waiter said. "May I recommend a 2000 Leflaive Bâtard white burgundy with that?"

"Is that the Montrachet Grand Cru?"

The waiter bowed in appreciation. "It is."

"That'll do."

"If I may be so bold," the waiter said, "we have the pâté sucrée tonight."

"That sounds fine," Marcus said, handing over the menus. He looked to Liberty. "Unless you wanted to try the balloons? They're quite fun. Apple flavored, right?" The waiter nodded again.

Liberty goggled at him. "No, what you ordered is fine."

In other words, she had no idea what he'd ordered. He made a mental note that the next time he took her out to dinner to pick some place more accessible—a nice steak house or something.

"Do I even want to know how much this is going to cost?"

Marcus waved this question away. "It's not important."

"What do you mean, it's not important? Of course it's important. I can't expect you to pay for my dinner."

That made him smile. "Did you think we were going Dutch here?"

"This isn't a business lunch, Marcus. You can't expect me to—"

Actually, he was rapidly losing his grip on what, exactly, he could expect from her. "Liberty, stop, for heaven's sake. That bottle of wine alone probably costs five or six hundred dollars."

All the blood drained out of her face. "And that's not important?"

He knew she was serious but… "What's a six-hundred-dollar bottle of wine to me?"

She still looked like a ghostly copy of herself. "I just—six hundred dollars? When I was growing up…" She stumbled over her words and went silent.

He went on. "Liberty, when you're a billionaire, at a certain point, money loses all meaning. If it were a six-million-dollar bottle of wine, well, it still wouldn't make a big impact in the long run."

He was not making things better, that much he could tell. She looked as if he'd stabbed her with the business end of a wine bottle. "You—you really mean that, don't you?"

"Money is like air. I don't think about it. I don't have to do anything to make more of it suddenly appear. It just *is*."

She stared at him, openmouthed. "I understand that most

people don't live like that—I'm not a complete idiot," he hurried to add, which did not necessarily improve things. "There's no way I'd expect you to foot part of the bill in a place like this."

He took her in—the pale face, the eyes and mouth wide with shock—and wondered about her life. She'd always been this smartly dressed, exceptionally prepared young woman. Sure, he knew the suits weren't Chanel or Armani, but she'd fit his image of a middle-class woman working her way up.

But was she?

"So," she said nervously. "Thank you for dinner. Whatever it's going to be."

"You're welcome." There was a pause, as if she didn't know what to say next. Frankly, he wasn't that sure, either. "So. We're not talking about the wine."

She gave him a baleful look. For some reason, it made him grin. "No. And we're not talking about the wedding."

"No." He considered. "Are we talking about William?" Because he had some questions for her. And they weren't necessarily fact-finding questions, per se. He had a flood of confused emotions that he hadn't anticipated and didn't know how to process. Tender emotions. It was…odd. He needed to make sense of what he was feeling and he wanted to know if Liberty was feeling the same way.

There it was again, that shy little smile. "I thought we were going to discuss business."

"Fine. Business." He thought back to something that had come up earlier. "Why do you work every Saturday?"

The question clearly caught her off guard. "What? I don't—I mean—you know about that?"

"Of course," he said. "There's very little that goes on in my company that I'm not aware of."

Her cheeks reddened as she stared at the top of the table. "I'm just trying to get a jump on the week." But there was something about the way she said it that didn't sit quite right. Then she looked up at him and gave him a sly smile. "I have this boss, you see—he appreciates an assistant who knows as much as she can about potential clients, market conditions and so on."

"Sounds like a real bastard," he agreed. "But every Saturday?"

She shrugged, as if that were no big deal.

There was something about this he didn't like, but he was having trouble putting his finger on it, which meant he liked it even less. "I don't pay you to work six days a week."

"You pay me a lot," she said and then added, "It's a very generous salary. I don't mind."

"But don't you have a life?" It came out before he realized what he was saying, but there was no taking it back.

Liberty's eyes narrowed as she drew herself up and squared her shoulders.

"I mean," he quickly backtracked, "even I don't spend that much time in the office and it's my business. It's not healthy. You've got to make time to have a social life and—I don't know, go grocery shopping or something."

He did some quick calculations. They ran five mornings in a row and she was basically putting in an extra workday. "You're working sixty-hour weeks, every week. I pay you for forty hours."

"You pay me to do a job. This is what it takes to do the job well," she countered, looking trapped. "And for the record, I have a life. I buy groceries. I shop. I watch television."

"Do you have a social life? Spend time with your family? Do you date?"

Her eyes flared. "Not that it's any of your business."

Maybe it wasn't. He didn't know why he'd asked about her dating, except that he wanted to know. "Here's what I don't understand," he went on. "When I first realized you were working weekends, I thought it was because you were trying to get ahead—which made sense. You'd put in the hours and prove yourself to be invaluable—which you are," he hurried to add because this seemed like a good place for a compliment. "People who work like you do have a plan. They have goals. They stay in a job for a year or two, learn everything they can, and then they move on. They take the next job that can challenge their skill set, the next job that can lay the groundwork for the job after that—they network, build up references, the whole nine yards. They climb a ladder. Yet it's been three years and you're still here with me, fending off my mother and scolding inventors who can't get their shit together. Why?"

"I like this job. It's a good job."

He scoffed at this. "It's not like there's one good job in the world and this is it. What about the time Jenner tried to poach you? He offered to make you his assistant—at, I believe, almost double the salary. And you didn't take it."

Erik Jenner was an old friend of his, going back to prep school. They played golf and talked sports and tried to outdo each other with bigger boats, better cars and everything else. It hadn't surprised him at all that Jenner had tried to poach Liberty for his real estate business. He was surrounding himself with the best talent money could buy.

What had surprised him was that Liberty had said no. Not that she'd told Marcus—Jenner himself had related this whole story with the air of one who had failed in his quest and didn't know why.

Marcus didn't, either.

"I didn't like Mr. Jenner," she countered. That got Marcus's attention. Then she quickly added, "I mean, I didn't like his business model. His real estate developments seemed unsustainable."

"You play it safe, Liberty. You're more than smart enough to go elsewhere and move up the ladder. But you won't take the risk. Are you really content to be my executive assistant for the rest of your life?"

She opened her mouth to answer, but just then their first courses arrived. The waiter explained their dishes for them and instructed Liberty on how to eat hers. She gamely sampled her dish while giving Marcus's lily bulbs the side eye.

"They're good," he told her, spearing one on his fork. "Try one."

He held out his fork to her and, after a moment's pause, she leaned forward. Her lips closed over the bulb and he suddenly realized exactly why he'd asked if she was dating anyone—it wasn't because he was concerned that she was burning herself out.

It was because watching her lips slide off the tines of his fork was close to a holy experience. Her eyes widened as she chewed and then the tip of her tongue slipped out and traced the seam of her lips.

"I don't know how you can accuse me of playing it safe," she said in a low voice, "when you're feeding me bulbs and God only knows what else." She dipped her spoon into her bowl and held it out for him to taste. "I take *lots* of risks."

Seven

Marcus leaned forward, with a glint in his eyes that she wasn't sure she'd ever seen before. "Do you?" he asked, and then took her spoon into his mouth.

Liberty's heart beat so fast that she wouldn't be surprised if Marcus could see it thumping in her chest. Him feeding her? Her feeding him? She stared at his mouth, at his lips. Was it wrong to wonder what it'd be like to feel his lips moving on her body as they moved on her spoon?

Would it be bad if she found out?

She shook her head. That must be the wine talking because right now? This was a hell of a risk. The kind that could put her job in jeopardy. Under any normal circumstances, it would be unacceptable.

But there was very little about today that felt normal. Including this dinner.

Especially this dinner.

Still, she didn't know how to answer him. So instead

she turned her attention back to her dish. She was forced to call it a dish because she simply had no other words to describe it. She wasn't sure that what she was eating qualified as food.

She took a sip of the most expensive wine she'd ever had. "This is good. Weird, but good."

"Next time, we'll go to a steak house," he told her in between bulbs.

"Next time?" Because this dinner walked a fine line between a business dinner and a date. Having more of the same would be decidedly date-like.

She couldn't date Marcus, no matter how wonderful it might be. She wasn't the kind of woman who belonged in a place like this, drinking wine that cost hundreds of dollars and eating things that barely met the basic standards of being edible while also probably costing several hundred dollars. There hadn't been any prices on the menu, which, in her experience, was a bad sign.

She was the kind of woman who considered a five-dollar bottle of wine and a carryout pizza to be a rare treat. If she got really wild, she'd go to the small Thai restaurant a block away and get *pad see ew*.

"The question remains," Marcus said, finishing his bulbs. "You haven't left me. Why?"

"Because." She was aware that wasn't much of an answer. But it was the only answer she had.

Because Marcus was right. She'd worked her ass off to get this position, to get to a point in her life where she wasn't living on the line that divided poverty and extreme poverty. The fact that she'd made it this far? Gotten off public assistance, paid off all her college debt and was finally able to say that she was comfortable? *Valuable?*

Why on God's green earth would she want to risk that?

"*Because* is not an answer," Marcus said. The waiter reappeared, cleared their dishes and refilled their wineglasses. Liberty sipped—slowly.

You haven't left me. That was what he'd asked and she'd truly never thought of it in that light. She'd stayed with a job. She hadn't stayed with the man.

Had she?

She thought back to Erik Jenner, how he'd arrived in the office unexpectedly one day. He'd propped himself up on the corner of her desk and smiled down at her. It wasn't the kind of smile that Marcus gave her—no, this was different. Jenner was attractive and rich—on paper, he wasn't that different from Marcus. But the way he'd looked at her made her uncomfortable.

He'd offered her a lot of money and a lot of responsibility if she'd jump ship. And she'd be lying if she said the money wasn't tempting.

But she hadn't wanted to risk it—any of it. Having a boss who made her uncomfortable. Starting over in a place where people would ask questions about her: where she'd gone to school, who her family was. As tempting as the money had been, it hadn't made up for the stability—the safety—that Marcus offered her.

"I don't want you to work on Saturdays anymore," Marcus announced over the lip of his wineglass.

"It would affect my job performance," she informed him.

"Fine. Then I'm giving you a raise. I pay you now for a forty-hour week. I'll up that by twenty percent."

She choked on her wine. "You'll *what*?"

Oh, that lazy smile—that could be her undoing, if she let it. She wouldn't let it. "Really, Liberty, you need to work on your negotiation skills. A good negotiator would have come back with thirty percent."

"I wasn't even asking for a raise!"

"True. A good negotiator would have used Jenner's job

offer to ask for one. He offered you thirty percent more than I'm paying you with stock options. The benefits package was considerable and you didn't even tell me about it." He wagged a finger at her as if he were scolding her. "I've seen you be a hard-ass with clients for me. Can't you do that for yourself?"

"I don't—" She exhaled.

"Ask me for something," he demanded, leaning forward and pinning her with his gaze. "Right now. Tell me what you want."

Liberty began to panic because she'd had enough wine that she couldn't be 100 percent sure that she wouldn't say something horrible, such as she wanted him. Because she did. This felt like a dream: Marcus Warren sitting across from her in a dimly lit restaurant, offering her what her heart desired. All she had to do was say the word.

She bit down on the inside of her cheek—hard. The pain snapped her out of her reverie. "I want my food," she said in a light tone. "I think your bulb thingies were better than my—my whatever it was."

He stared at her. "Are you afraid of me? Is that it?"

"Don't be ridiculous," she retorted.

"Then why won't you tell me what you want? Come on, Liberty! Do you realize that today, asking if you could leave early to go see William—that was the first time you've *ever* asked to leave work early? That's not normal. People have appointments, stuff comes up. People get sick. But not you."

"Did it ever occur to you that I already have everything I want? I like my job. I like working for you. Nothing has to change."

He gave her a look then that seared her. Heat flushed her, starting low in her back and racing upward like a forest fire. He leaned forward and although she knew she needed to lean back, to break his gaze—to do anything to put a little distance between them—she felt the pull of his body on hers. He was like gravity. That's what this was—an unseen force that guided her every movement.

"What if it's already changed?" He reached out and put his hand on top of hers. His touch was warm against her skin—intimate, even. The air around them felt charged with electricity, and the shock of it all made it hard to sit still. "What if we can't go back?"

The waiter arrived with their dishes and Liberty pulled her hand away and put it in her lap. Marcus had forgotten what he'd ordered, but he didn't care. Liberty stared at her food with open distrust—he couldn't blame her. Her *wagyu* steak looked like charcoal briquettes, complete with embers. The waiter went through the premeal instructions again but Marcus wasn't listening.

What if everything had already changed?

There was no what-if here. Everything *had* changed. Nothing had been the same between them since the moment he'd found that little baby boy and watched Liberty clutch him to her chest. In that moment, he'd seen her differently. She'd been more than his employee then—much more.

Liberty gamely poked at her steak dish. "This is food, right?"

"Eat slowly. The experience is almost as important as the food," he told her, looking at his own plate. Ah, yes—he remembered now. The lobster.

"Eating quickly could be deadly," she quipped as she blew out a smoking ember on her beef.

Why wouldn't she tell him one thing she wanted? Why wouldn't she demand a raise, more perks—anything of him?

I care too much about you. That's what she'd said in the car and that was another moment they couldn't back away from.

He watched her pick at her food. "This is good," she said, diligently forging ahead as if, in fact, nothing had changed.

"I'm glad," he said casually. What if these things were connected? The fact that she cared for him and the fact that she never asked anything of him? Except when it came to William.

Because she cared for that little baby, too.

"What are we going to do about William?" he asked, trying to keep his tone light.

Not that it worked. She paused, her fork halfway to her mouth. He had the urge to lean over and kiss her, but he was pretty sure he'd get a steak knife to the palm if he did that. "We?"

"Yes, we. We're in this together. When do you want to go see him again?"

She took her time answering and he worked on his lobster. Not that he tasted much of it. He was too busy watching her. "I was unaware there was a *we* where William was concerned."

"Of course there's a *we*. We found him. We rescued him. We're checking on him." *You should consider applying for adoption*, Hazel had said, right before she'd called them a nice couple. Was that how they looked to the rest of the world? Is that how the people in the busy restaurant saw them?

He hadn't been in a couple since Lillibeth, and even then he'd felt more like an accessory than a man in a relationship.

"You really are worried about him? About what will happen to him?"

He couldn't help himself. He reached out and took her hand in his again. "I would be a monster if I wasn't, Liberty."

More to the point, he'd be like his parents. They didn't worry about Marcus. They worried about whether they were maximizing the value they could get from him.

A flicker of doubt flashed over her face, but at least this

time she didn't pull her hand away. It stayed there, under his—light and warm. "We should wait a week," she finally said and he didn't miss that *we*. "Otherwise Hazel might start to get ideas. How about next Thursday? That's before you leave for the wedding."

"I suppose I don't have to ask about my schedule."

"You're fine," she said, a half grin curving her lips. Then, her gaze flicked over his body so fast that if he hadn't been watching, he would have missed it. "But the wedding is coming up fast…"

He bristled. "We're not talking about the wedding, Liberty. Not unless something changes."

"Like you deciding not to go?"

"Like you deciding to go with me."

She looked down to where they were holding hands. "I don't think that would be a very good idea," she murmured softly as she pulled her hand away.

He wanted to take her hand back, to hold on to it. He didn't. Instead he said, "I'm not even asking you as my date, you know."

She raised an eyebrow at him. "Oh, of course not. It's a legitimate business expense, no doubt."

"Having you with me when I meet with the producers the next day would be," he defended. "At the very least, you should be there for that. I'll need you to take notes."

That got her. She screwed her mouth off to one side and glowered at him. There was no other word for it. "Fine. But the wedding… Your mother would have my head on a platter, and God only knows what she'd do to you."

He sighed because he knew that was the truth. His parents might very well disown him if he went against the plan in such a public way.

But would that be so bad? For one thing, his parents' ire would be strictly private. They wouldn't dare risk the scandal of publicly disowning him. And if he was disowned, then they might very well keep their noses out of his business—for a while, at least.

"It'd be worth it to me," he told her. "Not to see your head on a platter but just to piss them off."

"I don't want to be the rope in your tug-of-war, Marcus."

"If you came with me, I would do everything in my power to make sure you weren't."

She took in a deep breath. "Why do you want me to go so badly? Why does it have to be me?"

"Because I trust you."

She looked stunned. "Why would you do that?" she asked in a quiet voice.

"Because you've earned it. Look," he said in frustration. "Trust is the one thing in this world that I literally cannot buy. I can't put a price on it. No one can. You can buy loyalty, but the risk with that is that someone else can offer a higher price for the same loyalty."

"Is this just because I didn't take Jenner's job?"

"No." This was going nowhere fast. Why couldn't he make her understand? "It's because you work weekends without letting me know. It's because you run with me every day. It's because you are the only person to tell me to do what I want instead of what you think I should do. It's because you…"

Because you care about me.

Because I care about you.

But he didn't say it. He couldn't, not with the way she was looking at him. "I don't think you should go to the wedding," she said softly. "But then, I don't think you want to go. So it's the same thing."

"It's not." He needed to run—to move. To do something other than to sit here and make an ass of himself trying to explain it to her. "And you? What do you want? You can't want to work every weekend."

She shrugged and dropped her gaze. He could feel her retreating, as if what she wanted wasn't important. But it was.

"Let me ask you this—if this wasn't Lillibeth's wedding, would you go with me?"

She didn't hesitate. "No. I don't fit in your world, Marcus. It's foolish to assume I could."

"But would you want to?"

Her mouth opened and then closed, and he knew the answer was *yes*.

"That's beside the point," she finally said but it was too late.

"What is the point?"

"We work together. We come from two different worlds. This…" She looked around at the people eating taffy balloons and drinking expensive wine. "I don't belong here, Marcus. What I want is what I have—a good job working for a good boss who trusts me."

"You don't want anything else? Something more?" That couldn't be all. Hell, as rich as he was, he still wanted.

He wanted someone he could trust with his deepest secrets, his darkest moments. He wanted a woman in his bed he could trust unequivocally, without worrying about how the story might show up on the gossip sites the next day.

He wanted someone a hell of a lot like Liberty.

Color flamed at her cheeks, but she didn't even blink as she said, "No. There's nothing else I want."

Wouldn't you know, she was the one thing money couldn't buy. "Come on," he said, tossing his napkin onto the table. "I'll take you home."

Eight

Marcus barely glanced at the bill before he paid it, which was enough to remind Liberty of the huge gulf that separated them.

Hell, an ocean the size of the Pacific separated them.

So what if the idea of a three-day weekend with him was exactly what she wanted? So what if he looked at her as if she was the woman of his dreams? So the hell what if she was physically shaking from the effort it took not to lace her fingers with his when he touched her hand?

It didn't matter what she wanted. What mattered was that she was safe and happy and had managed to make something out of her life.

Something foolish like fantasizing about Marcus, how he'd shower her with affection and gifts and make her feel like a princess—that was the quickest way to lose everything she'd fought for. And she wasn't that foolish. She didn't need to be rescued by Prince Charming. She'd already rescued herself.

She needed to get away from him, away from his pleading looks and his demands that she tell him her heart's desire.

"I'll just catch a cab," she said when they emerged onto Halstead. She was having trouble shifting her mental gears from a meal that probably cost a thousand dollars—not including tip—to her one-bedroom apartment wedged into a carriage house behind a two-flat.

Good Lord. That meal had probably been more than her rent.

She clung to that fact when Marcus came up behind her and put his hand in the small of her back, propelling her toward the valet. "I'll drive you home," he insisted.

"You don't have to do that," she said, the desperation growing. Because if he drove her home—all that time in the car together? This situation was rapidly moving beyond awkward and fast approaching dangerous.

"But I want to. It would be ungentlemanly of me to not see you home."

"Why?" Why did he insist on playing with fire?

She knew the answer, of course. It was because the flames would not burn him, not as they would her. He might get a little singed around the edges, but that would be the worst of it.

Men like Marcus Warren didn't face the same set of consequences women like Liberty Reese did. That was just a simple fact of life. He could whisper sweet nothings in her ear and kiss her and then, when the morning regret came crashing down on his head, he could simply fire her.

Well, she didn't think he'd do that, not to her. But she might suddenly have another job offer from one of his friends—Jenner, even—and this time, he'd insist she take it. For her own good, no doubt.

This was why she didn't have romantic entanglements. The risk always outweighed what little reward she might glean from a brief physical coupling.

She could not expose herself, not like that. Intimacy would lead to questions and questions and more damn questions.

She didn't want anything to change. Not at work, not between her and Marcus. She wanted him to stay firmly in his office and her fantasies to stay firmly in her head.

The valet pulled up in the Aston Martin and hopped out. He tried to get Liberty's door, but Marcus waved him off. "I've got her."

Against her better judgment, she sank down into the Aston Martin's seats and tucked her feet up so Marcus could shut the door. She watched him as he walked around the front of the vehicle. What had she done to deserve this? It wasn't just that he was gorgeous, a blond god with blue eyes and a runner's body. It wasn't even that he was so rich that money was little more than air to him.

It was that he looked at her as no one else ever had. Marcus *saw* her. She'd spent her entire adult life—and most of her adolescence—trying to be invisible. Burying herself in her homework so she could get ahead, get out of the projects, get to college—get this job. The only way anyone had ever paid any attention to her was because she was a good student and now, a good assistant. By herself, Liberty was worthless. Well, maybe not worthless. Grandma Devlin had done the best she could, and she wasn't even Liberty's grandmother. She was just a kindly old neighbor who'd lost her own children to the streets and who saw a little girl who needed help.

But Grandma Devlin was the exception that proved the rule. No one else could be bothered with Liberty Reese. She had been invisible to the world—to her own mother. She was valuable only because she made herself valuable.

Maybe too valuable. Did Marcus want her, Liberty Reese? Or did he want what he thought she represented—someone trustworthy and honest, someone who knew her place?

Because he didn't know her, not the real her.

He couldn't. Not now, especially after he'd sat there and told her all the reasons he trusted her.

She would do anything to not destroy his version of Liberty Reese. Anything.

"The address?" Marcus said in a casual tone once he was behind the wheel.

She gave him her address. "It's off of Fullerton." When he looked at her, she said, "Logan Square."

"Ah," he replied, as if he'd ever been there before. She highly doubted he had.

As he drove, she began to panic. What would he say when he saw the run-down two-flat building? When he realized she didn't even live in the building, but in the carriage house out back? Would he start in on how she should ask— no, demand—more of him? And, by extension, of herself?

He simply didn't realize how much she'd already demanded—of herself, of her world. The fact that she'd made it this far was not to be taken lightly.

"This is pretty far from the Loop," Marcus observed as they negotiated Friday-night traffic on the Kennedy.

"It's not that far, really."

"But what time do you have to leave to get to my place for the morning run?" The way he asked it made it clear that this was the first time he'd ever thought of it. "You're at my door at seven every single day."

She fought the urge to squirm in her seat. Point of fact, she was at his door at 6:50 a.m. every day. Then she stashed her backpack of work clothes in a closet where the doorman had reserved a space just for her and waited for Marcus to come down. "The Blue Line is only two blocks from my apartment," she hedged. "It's a straight shot to the Loop and then I catch a bus to your place. It's not bad. At that time in the morning, there's hardly ever any traffic jams."

"Liberty," he said in a stern voice. "I asked you a question. What time do you leave your place?"

She was trapped. "I catch the six oh nine—the train runs every five minutes," she added, as if that somehow made it better.

It didn't. "So you get up—what, at five thirty? Every morning?"

"Basically."

"And you work until six or so every night?"

"Yes," she said, getting irritated. "Do I need to account for my time in between six at night and five in the morning?"

They finally edged off the Kennedy and onto Fullerton. "No, no," he said, sounding lost in thought. "That's not it. It's just…"

"It's just that the rest of us don't have lakefront condos, personal chefs, cars and drivers, and an unlimited budget?"

"I'm not clueless, you know. I realize that very few people live like I do."

"Sure you do—as an abstraction. Have you ever been here? Or to Rogers Park? Ever ventured out of the trendy, safe areas of Chicago?"

His silence answered the question for him.

"This is what I mean, Marcus. This is why I can't go with you to that wedding, why it's ridiculous to think I should even want to. You see me in a specific set of circumstances, but that's not the whole of me. This," she said, gesturing out the window, "this is a nice neighborhood. I have a nice place. I've worked hard for it. But that's not what you're going to see."

He turned onto her street and pulled up to the curb in front of her landlord's two-flat. Then to her horror, he shut the car off and turned to face her. "What am I going to see, Liberty? What am I looking at, right now?"

Me. You're looking at me. That's what she wanted to say. This was a nice place compared with the slum she'd grown up in. This was her getting above her station in life. She'd come up so far that sometimes she looked around and got scared of the heights she now occupied.

Because what he was looking at was a nobody who dared to act as if she were a somebody.

"Money isn't air," she whispered. "Every dollar I make is spoken for. Every grocery trip I make, every lunch I pack, every pair of running shoes I buy is a risk because what if that's it? What if there's no more?"

"Then why didn't you take Jenner's job offer? Why didn't you take a bigger paycheck?"

"Because money isn't the only thing I need from this job."

Damn that truth.

The space between them was already tight. This was not a big car. But there was no mistaking it—that space was shrinking. She didn't know if she was leaning toward him or he was leaning toward her. All she knew was that his gravity was pulling her in and she couldn't fight it any more than she could decide she could fly.

"What else do you need?" he asked in a serious voice. She felt his breath whisper over her skin and she shivered.

"Marcus…" But whatever else she was going to say was cut off as he cupped her cheek in his palm and lifted her face toward his.

"Do you need something else? Something more? Because I do."

In her last grasp at the safety of the way things were, she said, "This will change everything."

His nose touched the tip of hers and she felt his fingers on her skin—pulling her toward him. "What if everything has already changed and we can't go back?"

"I'm not good for you," she warned him even as her

hands moved, touching his face, feeling the slight prick of his stubble against her palm. A sign that he wasn't some perfect god of a man but someone real and warm and hers. Hers, but not for the taking. "I'm *not*."

"Then be bad for me," he murmured against her lips.

All at once, he was kissing her and God help her, Liberty was kissing him back. Her first real kiss. She so desperately wanted to catalog each moment to remember it for all time—she was kissing Marcus Warren!

But any hope of memorizing the moment disappeared under the pressure of his skin against hers. Touching Marcus, tasting him—she couldn't think, couldn't rationalize. This was really happening, she thought over and over. Heat burned through her limbs, making her fall into him.

This was weakness, temptation—things she'd always been above because survival was more important than a kiss. But she'd come to a place where she wasn't on the ragged edge anymore—thanks to him.

His lips moved over hers gently at first and she instinctively opened her mouth for him. She wanted this—him. She was horribly afraid she might *need him*.

When his tongue swept into her mouth, she jolted in her seat. The shock of the intimacy was enough to pull her out of the moment, and the weight of what she was doing hit her like a hammer to the chest. "I can't do this," she sputtered, pulling away from him. She fumbled for the seat belt but she was so disorientated that it took several tries before she clicked the right button.

"Wait—what?" He latched onto her forearm, halting her before she could get the door open. "Can't—or won't?"

She jerked her arm out of his grasp and somehow let herself out of the car. Then she was walking up the sidewalk, her head down and her steps quick. She didn't have his money and, when he touched her like that, she didn't have much air, either.

She heard his car door open behind her but she didn't slow down and she didn't look back.

"Liberty?"

She didn't answer. What could she say? *I want you? I've fantasized about you for years? I would do anything you ask of me—just don't ask me about my past?*

He trusted her. He thought she was honest with him.

If anyone saw them together and did a little digging, she could ruin him.

And she cared too much about him to see him hurt like that.

So she walked away from him.

It was all she could do.

Nine

"**M**r. Warren," the security guard said, standing to attention when Marcus walked into the building.

"Hello…" He leaned forward to read the guard's name tag. "Lester."

He knew the guards who were in the lobby every weekday, but he couldn't remember the last time he'd dropped by the office on a weekend. When he worked on the weekend, it was reading reports Liberty had prepared for him from the comfort of his sofa, usually with a game on in the background. "Were you the one I talked to earlier today?"

"Yes, sir," the older man said, still standing smartly at attention. Maybe he was a former military man?

"Ah, good. Is Ms. Reese still here?"

"Yes, sir," Lester repeated. "Ms. Liberty got here at eight thirty, like she does every Saturday."

Marcus got the feeling that Liberty wouldn't have had to look at Lester's name tag. "And she stays until…"

"Three, three thirty," Lester said warmly. "A hard worker, that one."

"Yes," Marcus agreed. He was beginning to realize exactly how hard Liberty worked.

Every Saturday for close to three years, she had worked an extra seven hours.

He definitely didn't pay her enough.

"Thanks, Lester," Marcus said, heading for the elevators.

The ride up to his floor had never felt so long. Hell, the whole morning had been long. He'd wanted to get here first thing, but even he saw the folly of that. If he burst into the office right after Liberty got there, she'd most likely panic and bolt on him.

Just as she'd done last night.

Jesus, this was a mess. And the hell of it was, he wasn't sure he'd do anything different. Well, maybe he wouldn't take her to that restaurant. But everything else?

He'd wanted to go with her to see the baby.

He'd wanted to take her to dinner.

He'd wanted to kiss her.

And what a kiss it'd been. Raw need had coursed through his body at the touch of her lips against his, her skin in his hands. He'd wanted to strip her out of her sensible skirt suit and lay her out on a bed and lavish her with attention until she was crying out his name.

He still wanted that. But he didn't think he was going to get it.

The elevator doors opened and he strode out into Warren Capital's offices. Somehow everything felt different on the weekend. The heat of summer seemed to seep in through the windows and pop music played in the background. He saw an open snack container on a desk.

Liberty was not at her desk.

Marcus stared at the empty chair, not grasping what he saw. She was here. Lester had said so. He peeked into his office—maybe she was in there? No. The place was empty. Where could she have gone?

Then behind him he heard the door to the bathroom open. Before he could turn around, Liberty exclaimed, "Marcus! What are you doing here?"

"I came to see you," he said. And then he *saw* her.

Instead of the woman in the running shorts and a shapeless unisex T-shirt or the woman in the business suits, Liberty stood before him in a short khaki skirt, flip-flops and a sleeveless shirt covered in a brightly colored pattern. The only part of her that was the same as ever was her hair, but even that was different. Instead of her polished buns or sleek ponytails, her hair was messily knotted at the nape of her neck.

She looked young and sweet and everything about her made him want to pull her into his arms and kiss her all over again.

"I didn't expect—I mean, you never come in—oh," she finally said and stopped talking. Her gaze swept up and down his body and he could guess that she was having the same reaction he was. She'd probably never seen him in a T-shirt, cargo shorts and deck shoes. She crossed her arms over her chest and rubbed her bare skin as if she were suddenly cold.

"I needed to come in today," he said, clenching his hands at his sides so he wouldn't rub her arms for her. "I needed to talk to you."

"Is this about work? I'm getting caught up."

"You work every Saturday," he reminded her, wondering why she phrased it like that. "This isn't about work. We have a problem."

"Oh?" she asked drily, which made him grin. "Only one?"

"One big problem, which spawns several smaller issues." She looked at him wryly. "And that is?"

"You care for me." She opened her mouth to say something, but he didn't give her the chance to deny it. "And I care for you."

"Oh." The word rushed out of her in a burst of air, but that was all she said. She didn't try to talk her way out of it or make excuses.

He couldn't tell if that was a good *oh* or a bad one. "Yes. And you seem to think that it's a problem."

This time, when she exhaled, it was clearly in frustration. "Because it is, Marcus. You saw where I live. You saw how I couldn't even navigate dinner at a restaurant where they know you by name. The only way our worlds ever cross is in this office or on the jogging path. It doesn't matter how I feel about you, and believe it or not, it doesn't matter how you feel about me. It simply won't work."

That answer made him mad. It didn't matter how he felt? How she felt? That sounded like something his mother would say—something she had said when the Lillibeth situation had blown up. It hadn't mattered that he'd been hurting. What had mattered was putting on a good face for the public.

"The kiss last night—are you telling me it didn't matter?"

She touched the tips of her fingers to her lips. "It doesn't change anything."

"The hell it doesn't, Liberty. Did you want to kiss me last night?" Because the thought niggled at him: Had he kissed her against her will?

He wasn't going to prey on his assistant, not as his father preyed on his secretaries.

"That's not important," she said in a shaky voice. "What I want isn't important."

"Don't give me that crap. What you want is just as important as what I want." She opened her mouth to argue with him but he wasn't having it. "Answer the damned question, Liberty. Did you want the kiss?" She looked at him as if he were making for her fingernails with a pair of pliers, but he couldn't walk away from this—from her. He had to know. "Do you want me?"

The silence hung in the air for a beat too long as they stared at each other. "Of course," she whispered, all the blood draining out of her face. "Of *course* I do. But—"

There were no *but*s here. He closed the distance between them in two long strides, pulled her into his arms and kissed her with everything he had. After a squeak of surprise, he was thrilled when Liberty sighed into his mouth, her body molding itself to his.

When the kiss ended, he looked her in the eye and brushed an errant strand of hair away from her face. "Don't tell me *that* doesn't matter, Liberty. It does. Because *you* matter to me."

She closed her eyes and breathed deeply. "It won't end well. I'm not good for you."

She'd said that last night and it'd bothered him then. It bothered him even more now. "But what if I can be good for you? No one cares about me like you do, Liberty. No one worries about what's good for me or what's bad for me. I could disappear off the face of the earth tomorrow and you know what people would mourn? They'd mourn the senseless loss of my money, my looks, my power. My parents wouldn't miss me. They'd only miss being able to use me for their own purposes. You are the one person in this world who would miss me."

It hurt to admit that out loud but not as much as it hurt to know it was 100 percent the truth.

Her eyes widened. "You don't mean that. People love you."

"Do they? Or do they just love what they think I can do for them?" He paced away from her, desperate to move, to think. "You don't know what it was like growing up in my house. Do you have any idea how crushing it is to realize that your parents don't love you? That they wouldn't fight for you, not even if you really needed them to?"

He'd learned that so early. He'd been what, six? Six years old when the men with the guns had tried to take him and his nanny. Miss Judy had screamed and chased the bad guys off and saved him. And what had his parents done? Nothing—except to get rid of his nanny.

Even now, the crushing loneliness of that time filled him with despair. He began to pace.

"I do," she said in a gentle voice, crossing to him. But she didn't try to slow him down. "More than you can know." He paused and looked at her. "But—"

"Don't you dare say it doesn't matter, Liberty. You want to know what doesn't matter? All of this. This office, this company, this life. You're so worried about my reputation and I couldn't give a rat's ass about it." He pulled up short and stared at her. He didn't know where the words were coming from. All he knew was that they'd been building up since last night—since before that, if he were honest. Ever since he'd found that little baby boy—and seen Liberty care for him.

Ever since he'd found someone he wanted to fight for.

And now that the words were coming out, there was no stopping them. "It's not me. It's not who I am. It's what they wanted me to be."

"Who did you want to be?" she asked softly.

He laughed bitterly. "Do you realize you're the first person to ask?"

"You talk like it's too late, like you don't have the power to do what you want. But that's not true, Marcus. It's never too late."

"I thought you didn't want anything to change."

She gave him a long look then, full of heartache and sorrow. "Do you think I'd be happy knowing that I was one of the wardens who kept you locked in a cage of someone else's making? Do you really think that I'd sacrifice you just so I wouldn't have to do something risky?"

"Everyone else would. Lillibeth would have."

"I'm not everyone else and I am *not* Lillibeth." This time, she was the one who crossed to him, grabbed his face in her hands and hauled him down to her lips.

It wasn't an expert kind of kiss, but that didn't matter to him. He wrapped his arms around her and clung to her as she kissed him again and again. His blood sang through his body. Nothing separated them except a few thin layers of clothes. When she nipped at his lower lip, he went hard for her.

He slammed on the brakes before they went too far. "Liberty," he groaned, holding her tight, her chest heaving against his. He felt as if he'd run a marathon in record time.

"I know who you are," she whispered against the sensitive skin of his neck.

"Do you?" Was that even possible when he wasn't entirely sure he knew?

"You're a good man, Marcus Warren." Right now, with her in his arms—her body pressed against his—he did not feel like a good man. "You treat your employees well," she went on, kissing her way up his neck. "You care about a baby that no one else does."

Her teeth skimmed over his skin right below his ear and he couldn't have fought back the groan if he'd tried. His hand slid down her back and he cupped her bottom, pushing her against him so she could feel exactly what she did to him.

He couldn't remember being this turned on.

Oh, sure, he was no innocent. He liked sex. He had his pick of beautiful women, models and actresses and heiresses, all making eyes at him from the time he'd hit puberty. Sex was easy, fun.

Or it had been, once. When had he last been this excited? When was the last time he'd wanted not just sex, but the woman?

Because this was Liberty. This wasn't just sex. This was something else entirely.

"You make me feel important," she murmured in his ear and he was powerless to stop her as she wrapped her lips around his lobe and sucked.

"You are important," he got out through gritted teeth. But when she shifted, rubbing against his erection as her hands began to drift down his backside, he forced himself to breathe again. "Is this what you want? Because if you keep kissing me like that…"

She angled his face so she could look him in the eye. "What I want," she said in all seriousness, "is to get out of this office."

Out of this office, out of these clothes—yeah, he was on board with that. "My place? Would you come home with me?"

"It'll change everything," she said, but this time she wasn't trying to warn him off. Instead, for the first time, she sounded as if she accepted that it *had* to change, that staying the same would mean a slow death for both of them.

He held her tight and buried his nose in her hair. "I want it to. I need it to."

"Then let's get out of here."

Liberty had been to Marcus's condo building, of course. Every weekday morning she waited for him in the lobby. But she'd never crossed the inlaid tile line in the lobby that divided the doorman's territory from the rest of the building, and she'd certainly never been up to Marcus's floor.

Thankfully, Joey, the usual doorman she dealt with, wasn't working at noon on a Saturday. "Todd," Marcus said to the man in the fancy coat.

"Mr. Warren," Todd replied, giving Liberty a little smile.

Jesus, she was doing this, she really was. She was crossing that little line in the tile and getting into an elevator with Marcus.

"Okay?" he asked as the doors slid shut, blocking them off from the bright lobby. He slid his arm around her waist and pulled her in close. "Still okay?"

Yes. And no, but yes. In her dreams, Marcus swept into the office and kissed her and told her how much he needed her and yes, they wound up in bed.

But now? At this exact moment?

This was stupid. This wasn't just a risk—this was practically career suicide. Yes, she wanted Marcus and yes, he wanted her and thank God they were both unattached, consenting adults.

It didn't change the fact that she was initiating a physical relationship with her boss. It didn't change the fact that she'd kissed him back.

But he was right. There was no going back to the way things were. She cared for him and he cared for her and that was a hell of a thing.

"Better than okay," she said, pulling him down for a kiss.

Marcus's lips moved over hers with an urgent pressure as he spun and backed her against the wall of the elevator. "I want you so much," he whispered in her ear as his hands slipped down her bottom. "I want to do everything you like."

Well. There was that. She didn't, technically, know what she liked. Her childhood and adolescence had been about self-preservation and besides, when a girl spent every weekend in the library, who had time for dating?

So she did what she always did—she hedged the truth. Just a little. "I want to see what you've got," she murmured. Then she boldly slipped her hand down between their bodies and over the bulge in his shorts. "Oh, my." Was that all *him*?

"Liberty," he hissed, his hips flexing against her palm. That really was all him, hot and hard and barely contained by his shorts.

The elevator came to a stop. She tensed—what if someone were waiting to get on and saw them?

But Marcus grinned down at her. "Relax, babe. I own this entire floor." He gave her another quick kiss and then pushed away, leading her out into a small room with a door. "I didn't like that the elevator opened up directly into my place," he explained as he unlocked the door. "Too much of a chance that my parents could bribe their way into the building."

He threw the bolt and exhaled in what looked like relief before he pulled her back into his arms.

"We're safe here," he told her.

Then he was kissing her again and for the first time, she let herself get fully lost in his touch. It wasn't the same fall-off-the-edge-of-the-earth sensation that she'd had in his car last night.

"Let me give you the tour," Marcus said, backing her up. She kicked off her dollar-store flip-flops and let him guide her. "This is the entryway." As he spoke, he grabbed at the hem of her shirt and started to pull.

"It's lovely," she replied, not looking at the entryway one bit. Instead, she was studying him. This—this was how they really were. Teasing and talking, just as they did on their morning runs. Except now, they were touching.

"Oh, Liberty," he said in awe as he dropped her shirt on the floor. His hands touched the sides of her waist for a brief second before he started stroking upward, over her ribs. Then he was cupping her breasts, his thumbs brushing over her plain white bra. "Look at you, babe."

Liberty shivered—actually shivered—at his touch. She wasn't clueless, just inexperienced. She'd seen men touch women and women touch men, but she hadn't quite grasped how overwhelming those touches could be.

"Good?" Marcus asked, leaning down to press a kiss to the top of her left breast, right above the bra cup.

"Keep moving," she ordered. She didn't want her first time to be in a hallway.

An image assembled itself for her, of Marcus backing her against the wall right there, lifting her up and wrapping her legs around his waist while he thrust into her.

Okay, right. Not her first time. But maybe her second time. And her third time.

"Hmm," Marcus hummed, his tone light. But he kept pushing her backward, one hand snaking down to her lower back and slipping beneath the waistband of her skirt to brush at the skin hidden there. "And here we have the sitting room. Sometimes, I sit there."

She burst out laughing. "We should maybe try it sometimes. The sitting."

"Want to try other things first," he murmured as her bra strap gave under his expert fingers. The straps slid down her arms and he tossed the bra aside. "These, for example."

He leaned down and took her right nipple in his mouth. Then he sucked.

The sensation was almost too much for her. Looking down and seeing Marcus Warren doing that to her?

But, no, she reminded herself. He was just Marcus.

She threaded her fingers through his golden hair and held him to her. Her head fell back and a low moan pulled itself from her throat. "Oh. The sitting room," she managed to say. "Got it."

"I love this room," he agreed, switching to the other breast.

"It's a great room. Great views." But her eyes had fluttered shut so she could focus on the feeling of Marcus's tongue sliding over her bare skin, of his fingers gripping into her flesh.

A flash of panic popped up out of nowhere as Marcus turned her to the left and continued to back her up. Was this really happening? Or was this a dream? The most realistic, most erotic dream she'd ever had? Maybe she'd fallen asleep at work. She hadn't slept well last night, not after bolting out of Marcus's car. She could be hallucinating this entire thing.

"Dining room," he murmured.

Liberty was only vaguely aware that they were moving through a room that contained tables and chairs. Instead, she was more focused on how Marcus's hands snaked down her hips and how he was pulling her skirt up. "Wait," she said and the moment the word left her mouth, he froze.

"Wait?" In that moment when he stopped, she fell a whole lot more in love with him. It wasn't an act. He wasn't telling her how special, how important she was just to get her in bed. He really did want her and he really did want to do right by her.

"Don't pull it up," she told him. She didn't want a boring khaki skirt bunched up around her middle. Nothing sexy about that. In her fantasies, he stripped her bare. "Just take it off."

"Woman," he growled, relief flooding his face. Whereas he'd been slow and gentle with her shirt and her bra, he jerked at the button at the top of her skirt with an almost savage force.

He didn't even get the zipper the whole way down before he was pushing at the skirt, sliding it over her hips. The fabric hit the ground with a dull *whump* and Liberty took a mental second to thank the laundry gods that she'd put on a cute pair of undies today, white with little pink flowers printed on them and an edge of lace all the way around.

"Office," he said, jerking his head at a doorway.

"Mmm," she hummed, pulling him up and working at the buttons on his shirt. Which was not easy, as she was walking backward and he was sliding his fingertips under the leg bands of her panties and kissing her neck. She managed to get the top two undone before she gave up and jerked the shirt over his head.

"Look at *you*," she whispered, running her hands over Marcus's bare chest. "Do you have any idea how long I've dreamed about this?" She rubbed her thumbs over his flat nipples.

He shuddered into her touch. "I didn't want to be that boss," he said, pivoting her to the left this time. "I didn't want to hurt you."

This was going to hurt, in the end. Not the sex so much—although it might—but falling into bed with Marcus would, in the long run, be bad for both of them.

But not falling into bed with him right now? That wasn't even an option. "Then don't hurt me," she told him, trying to unbutton his shorts.

"Bedroom," he grunted, picking her up. "Bed." The next thing she knew, Marcus was laying her out on a massive bed with crisp white sheets.

Liberty fell back, surrendering herself to the plush softness of his bed and the hard muscles of his body. She touched him everywhere, but it wasn't enough—he still had his shorts on. "I like your bedroom. Nice place."

"Better with you in it." Liberty got the button on his shorts undone but when she went for his zipper, her hands brushing his massive bulge, he sucked in a breath and grabbed her hands. "Slow down, babe. Let me just…"

He pinned her hands to the bed and kneed between her legs. "Let me learn you," he murmured, leaning down and sucking on her nipple.

"Oh, Marcus," she moaned as he kissed and sucked at her. In all the times she'd thought about this, she'd never taken into consideration the wet warmth of his mouth. All that light and heat that flowed around her focused on where his mouth touched her, and her nipple went hard under his attention.

"You like that, don't you?"

"Yes," she hissed as his mouth closed over her other nipple, pulling and tugging until she was writhing on the mattress. *"Yes."*

"You taste so good," he said as his mouth moved lower. He let go of her hands and slid his palms down her sides, hooking into the waistband of her panties. "I want to taste all of you."

He pulled and her panties came off. She was nude before him. She'd have thought that she might feel nervous or self-conscious about this—being naked, having Marcus look at her with that lust in his eyes. But she wasn't.

A strange pressure was building up inside her, like lightning getting ready to strike. She shimmied against the bed when Marcus put his hand over her heart and let his fingertips drift over her midsection. "I'm going to touch you here," he said as his hand moved lower.

"You better," she replied, impressed at how confident she managed to make that sound. He was in no hurry, though, and the anticipation was killing her. She fisted her hands in the sheets.

"Impatient? That's not like you, Ms. Reese," he said with a confident grin.

"I just want to do—" She gasped as his fingers stroked over her sex. "I just want to do a good job, Mr. Warren," she managed to say through clenched teeth as he started to rub her.

"Oh, I have no doubts that you'll do an excellent job, Ms. Reese. You always take care of everything I need, don't you?" His other hand came up between her legs and touched her opening, but he didn't stop rubbing.

"I want to be good for you," she whispered, unable to look away from where he was touching her.

"You are," he said, his voice ragged with need. "So let me be good for you."

One of his fingers slid into her.

"Oh." She sucked in air as he moved inside her and rubbed outside her. "Oh, Marcus."

"That's it, babe," he said, his own breathing coming in hard, fast bursts. "Open up for me."

Then he leaned down and his mouth replaced the finger rubbing against her and he was licking her and stroking into her, and everything about her tightened down until a wave of electricity spiked through her and her mouth fell open in a silent scream of pleasure.

It was unlike anything she'd ever felt. She'd touched herself, but those little pops of release had nothing on the way Marcus had effortlessly brought her to orgasm.

Marcus knew it, too. He looked up from between her legs and stared at her. She was powerless to do anything but stare back as her muscles pulsed around his fingers. "Ms. Reese," he said, but that was as far as he got because Liberty had grabbed hold of his face and hauled him up to her mouth.

This was what she'd guarded herself from for so long— this feeling of his weight pressing her back against the mattress, the feel of his mouth on hers, the sound of her name on his lips.

She was his now. She'd always been his.

But now?

Now he knew it, too.

Ten

The taste of Liberty still on his tongue, Marcus forced himself to push back. *Mine*, he wanted to say as he looked over her body, splayed before him with delicious wantonness. *Mine*.

Condoms. He needed condoms before he lost what little control he had. He managed to get them out of the bedside table as she was pushing his shorts off him, pulling his briefs down and going, "Oh, *Marcus*," when he sprang free.

"Babe," he managed to say, but then she wrapped her hands around him and stroked up, then down, and he lost all thought except the sensation of Liberty's hands on his shaft. He couldn't *not* move. He thrust into her hands and braced himself against the side of the bed and thrust harder.

"Do you like this?" she asked, and he didn't miss the almost innocent note to that question.

"God, yes," he groaned. It would have been easy to just go on and lose it right there in her hands, but he wasn't going to be selfish about this.

He managed to pry her hands away from his throbbing erection and roll the condom on. She watched the whole process with wide eyes. "What position works for you?" he asked, finally climbing into the bed. Before she could even answer, he pulled her into his arms and kissed the hell out of her.

Her hands were all over his body, her fingers digging into his backside—urging him on. She rolled onto her back and pulled him with her. "Like this," she said.

"Anything you want, babe." Her lower lip tucked up under her teeth as he positioned himself at her entrance, and for a second she looked so nervous that he paused. "Okay? Yes?"

"Yes," she said decisively, flexing her hips to rise up and meet him.

Marcus tried to go slowly, tried to hold himself back as he joined his body to hers. It should have been easy—for years, he'd always been able to restrain himself when it came to sex. He'd convinced himself it was because he was a considerate lover, always putting his partner's needs first.

But the truth of the matter was, it'd been safer that way, safer to make sure he didn't get hurt. Even with Lillibeth, the woman he'd resigned himself to marry, he'd never given himself over to uncontrolled passion like this. Maybe because there hadn't been all that much passion in the first place.

He trusted Liberty with his life. And he couldn't hold himself apart from her. Not any longer.

She sucked in a hot breath when he sank home into her tight body, so he kissed her and let the feeling of her warmth surround him.

Then he began to move. Liberty made little gasping noises as she clung to him, her hands digging into his shoulders, her lips on his neck, his mouth. Every so often she would move in a different way and he'd have to pause and realign, but after a while, they learned each other's pacing better and she began to rise up to meet his thrusts.

And he was lost in her. The only thing that kept him from going over the edge was his runner's stamina. He pushed himself past the point of pleasure and pain as his muscles burned and his lungs cried out for more air.

She made a noise high in the back of her throat and then her shoulders came off the bed. She clung to him before she fell back, panting and moaning his name. He couldn't hold back any longer, not when she looked up at him, her eyes glazed with desire and satisfaction.

He groaned through his climax and collapsed, his heart racing. "Liberty," he whispered into her hair. He had things he wanted to say, things he needed to tell her. But he didn't have the words—that's how lost he was.

She leaned back, her gaze searching his face. Then, when he continued to fail to come up with a single sweet nothing to whisper, she kissed him hard.

For the first time in a long time, he felt right. Definitely since Lillibeth's betrayal but even before then. He was safe here.

Liberty lay on her back, staring up at the ceiling. "So... wow."

"Yeah, wow." He grinned. "Just think—we'll have three days to do that when we go to the wedding."

The moment the words left his mouth, he realized that hadn't been the right thing to say. He felt her body tense up, felt her withdraw from him. She cleared her throat. "Um, I need to get cleaned up, I think."

"Through that door," he said, pointing to the master bath. She scooted off the bed without looking at him.

He stared at her retreating form until the bathroom door shut with a decisive click. Bringing her to his place and making love to her *had* changed everything. There was something between them, something that ran deeper and truer than anything he'd ever felt before.

It wasn't a feeling that he wanted on a part-time basis. He couldn't go back to running with Ms. Reese in the morning and working with her in the afternoon and pretend that what they'd had here didn't exist during business hours.

If they were going to be together, they were going to be *together*. Marcus Warren didn't settle.

He hurried to the bathroom down the hall, took care of the condom and cleaned up quickly, and then headed back to the bedroom. He didn't have anywhere he needed to be and there was no way in hell that he was going to let Liberty head back to the office, no matter how much she thought she needed to get ahead.

He was pulling the covers down when the bathroom door opened. Liberty, in all her nude glory, leaned against the door frame, one arm seductively wrapped around her waist. Marcus was glad to see the satisfied little smile on her face, glad to know he'd given that to her.

"Hi," she said in a quiet voice.

He patted the bed next to him. "Come here."

He watched her as she crossed to him. Her body was beautiful in a real way that he wasn't sure he'd ever appreciated before. Lillibeth had had her nose fixed and her boobs enlarged and she worked out slavishly to keep her weight a ridiculous 115 pounds. Lying in bed with her had sometimes been like lying in bed with a bag of bones, all pointy and hard.

Liberty had curves. Her hips were a sight to behold and, as she slid into bed next to him, he was already having a hard time keeping his hands off them. Her nipples were far darker than he'd been expecting, but he liked them, and her breasts, although small, were more than enough to fill his hand.

He pulled her against him and touched her breast. "I can feel your heartbeat," he murmured as he pulled the covers up over them.

She put her hand on his chest. Amazing how even that simple touch warmed him. "Yours, too." She leaned forward and kissed his chest. "So, what happens next?"

"A couple of options. We could stay in bed for the next several days."

She leaned back to give him a sharp look. "You know that's not going to work."

"You're not going back to the office today and that's final," he told her. "I'll fire you if you do."

"Again with the threats," she murmured, but she didn't sound menaced. If anything, she sounded sleepy. Warm and content. And although Marcus didn't nap, per se, he felt his eyelids drifting shut as they snuggled deeper into the covers. "Fine. Twist my arm. I guess I'll just have to stay here with you."

"That's option two—the best option," he agreed, curling his body around hers. He realized he was stroking her perfect little breast, his fingers drawing over her skin toward her stiff nipple.

"What's the third option?" she asked warily.

"I understand why you're nervous about the wedding, so I can call my personal shopper and we can get some things for you. That way you won't have to worry about finding something to wear. Eventually," he added, kissing her bare shoulder.

Her hand covered his as he still stroked her breast. "Marcus... Why do you want me to go so badly?"

"Because." She didn't respond to this unhelpful comment. She just waited.

Now it was his turn to roll onto his back and stare at his ceiling. "Do you know what I wanted to be when I grew up?"

"No." She nestled into him, her hand on his chest, right over his heart. "I take it billionaire investor wasn't it?"

"No. I was actually scouted. I had scholarship offers for soccer, track and baseball from a bunch of different schools with really good programs. Not that I needed the scholarships."

"But coaches wanted you."

"They did. I had an offer from a few teams in Europe to come play soccer. Germany, I remember. There were two teams in Germany that wanted me. There was a bidding war, even."

"Really?" She leaned up on her elbow and looked down at him. "How come I don't know this? I mean, before I took the job, I googled you pretty hard."

"Nothing ever came of it. My parents didn't approve. It simply wasn't done," he said, in a reasonably good impression of his mother's simper.

Liberty winced. "Beneath a Warren?"

That made him smile. She got him in such a fundamental way. He threaded his fingers into her hair. It was coarser than he'd thought, but that just made him like it more—an extra layer of sensation. "Exactly. A few words from my father and the scholarship offers were rescinded. I have no idea how he made the Europeans go away, but he did."

"Wait—what do you mean, he made them go away?"

"I was going to go. I was eighteen and all the college offers disappeared and I had had it. I was going to go to Germany, as far away from my parents as possible, and play soccer for a few years. College could wait, right?"

She was staring at him now, the concern on her face obvious. "So, what—you decided to play professional soccer and because your father didn't approve, he made the team rescind the offer?"

"Basically. I never did know for sure, but I suspect he actually bought the team I chose—for a short while anyway."

"How could they do that to you?" She was genuinely shocked.

He smiled bitterly. "For my own good, they said. To protect me."

"What on earth would they need to protect you from so badly they had to buy a soccer team in Germany?"

"Well…" He opened his mouth to tell her about the men and the guns and losing his nanny, Miss Judy. But the words didn't come. So he didn't answer the question. Instead, he said, "It wasn't to protect me. It was to protect the family name. I went to Columbia instead and Northwestern for business school. It was literally the only option they left open for me. Everything else has been their idea."

She thought about this for a while. "Is that why you hired me? Because it wasn't your parents' idea?"

"Well, that and you said in your interview that you jogged two miles every day."

The corner of her mouth quirked up a bit. "I did, didn't I? I'm a lot faster now."

He grinned at her as he ran his hands up and down her back. "I like running with you. It's the best time of my day. You and me and the jogging path along the lake."

Her smile was wistful, almost. "It's my favorite part of the day, too."

He leaned up to kiss her because that honest touch of his lips to hers said what he couldn't seem to find the words to say.

"I want you to come with me, babe," he told her when the kiss ended. He brushed her hair back from her face and cupped her cheek. "When I'm with you, it's like I can still see that man I thought I'd be once, and I don't want to fall into line and do what I'm told, only do what's good for the family image. I want to fight for you."

She leaned into his touch. "I won't fit in your world," she warned him. "I'm not good for you." But again, it didn't sound as if she was arguing with him. It sounded as though she was accepting this fact just as she accepted that the sky was blue.

"You keep saying that." He leaned up on his elbows to stare at her. "So you're not a trust-fund baby. You keep your private life private and you've got my respect."

She didn't reply, except to look at him with her big, dark eyes.

A whisper of doubt crept into the edge of his mind. She did keep her private life private—so private, in fact, that after three years, he'd seen where she lived only last night.

In his mind, Liberty was this beacon of honesty and respectability, always on time and under budget, outperforming herself every quarter. But what if…

What if there were something she kept hidden, something that could hurt him?

He looked at her. She was lying on his stomach, her chin resting on her hands as she looked right back at him. "Do you really want to know?"

"Only if you want to tell me. The past is in the past, babe. As long as you didn't kidnap or murder anyone…" He paused.

She laughed out loud. "Good Lord, no. I have led a remarkably crime-free life. Never even been arrested."

He exhaled a breath he hadn't realized he'd been holding. She was safe and he trusted her. She was just going to have to get used to it. "You may not be good for Marcus Warren, billionaire," he conceded. "But," he went on, "you are very good for me. Come with me. Let me fight for you."

She broke eye contact first, tilting her head to the side

and resting it on his chest. "No one has ever fought for me," she said in a voice so quiet he had to lean up to catch all the words.

"No one? What about your parents?"

She shrugged. It was a seemingly casual gesture, but he could see the tension in her shoulders. He stroked her bare skin.

"As you said, it's in the past. I don't like to talk about it. But if you want me to tell you, I will."

"You don't have to. It won't change how I feel about you. I want you to be happy."

She traced a small circle on his chest with the tip of her finger. "Is that the reason you're looking out for William? Because of me?"

"Yes. But it's not the only reason. It's…" He sighed. "It's because you care about him, but it's also because when I see you with him—I didn't anticipate how it would make me feel."

She propped herself up and stared at him. "Yeah?"

What if… That's what he'd thought looking at her with that tiny baby, the love on her face obvious. "Watching you hold him, feed him—it's like I was looking at this other life, the path I didn't get to take. Maybe in another life…"

In another life, he might have already married for love, not for power or reputation. He might have a baby, or a bunch of kids, and they'd do normal things such as spend every Saturday running around soccer fields and cooking dinners together, and then he'd help put the kids to bed and pull Liberty into bed and…

"But he's African American," Liberty said, her tone careful. "Does that bother you?"

Marcus shook away the image of him and Liberty and one big, happy family. "It might bother my parents. I couldn't care less."

She continued looking at him, her eyes full of what he hoped like hell was love. Normally, when women made eyes at him, it was because of his money, his looks—or some combination of the two.

But the way Liberty looked at him was different. God, how he wanted it to be different.

"We'll go see him before we leave, okay?" he said. It was so odd. She didn't want anything from him for herself—she was adamant about that. But she wanted someone to fight for the baby. "Thursday. But I'll have my assistant check my schedule."

That got a huge grin out of her. "I think it can be arranged."

"And you'll come with me to the wedding? As my date?" He held his breath because if she said no, he would have to let it drop.

She sighed, a world-weary noise that almost made him rescind the offer. He'd backed her into a corner and it was maybe too selfish of him to ask this of her. "It's important to you?"

"You're important to me."

The corners of her eyes crinkled and he thought she might be smiling at him. Unexpectedly, she rolled off him and sat up on the edge of the bed. He wanted to pull her back down into his arms, but instead, he leaned forward and pressed a kiss between her shoulder blades, high on her back. "Then I guess we have to go shopping. I don't have a thing to wear."

Eleven

"This," Liberty said, staring down at the orange designer bikini covered in huge flowers, "is *ridiculous*."

Cathy, the Barneys New York saleslady in charge of transforming Liberty into a member of the upper crust, met her eye in the mirror of the private dressing room. "The rehearsal dinner has a theme," she reminded her. "Beach Blanket Bingo. Everyone is supposed to dress like something from an Annette Funicello movie."

"Well?" Marcus called out from the other side of the curtain.

"Do I at least get a cover-up?" Something to hide her hips would be nice. Like pants.

Cathy selected a drapey cover-up with an orange-tinted peacock-feather pattern. Liberty slipped it over her head, careful to avoid looking at the price tag. She didn't want to know. Ignorance was bliss.

What didn't help in any of this was the way the space between her legs throbbed gently with every movement, a constant physical reminder of how much things had changed.

After years of fantasizing about Marcus, she'd finally had him—her first. She hadn't had her virginity taken by force or coercion, which had always been a threat when she'd been younger and growing up with very few people to watch over her. She'd given herself to Marcus freely, and he'd done the same.

So why did she feel so damn weird about the whole thing?

Finally dressed, Liberty pushed the curtain aside and strode out into the sitting room. Marcus was reclining on a leather love seat, drinking champagne and generally looking as if he was having fun. Of course he was. He wasn't the one being trussed up like a Christmas goose.

"Like I said, ridiculous. Is this normal? For the entire guest list to be invited to a—a what? A bonfire the night before the wedding?"

Not that she would know what a normal wedding looked like—she didn't. She'd ordered gifts delivered to other people's weddings on Marcus's behalf, but she'd never been to a wedding, normal or extravagant.

Nor had she ever been to a store like Barneys. She'd thought they might be going to one of the stores on the Magnificent Mile, and that alone had been mildly overwhelming—but at least she'd been in Bloomingdale's a few times, stalking the sale rack for those few good pieces that could carry the rest of her clearance wardrobe through.

Barneys, on the other hand, was so far out of her comfort zone that the only thing she could do to keep from hyperventilating was to focus on exactly how ridiculous this entire thing was.

"Who demands that their guests show up in bikinis?" she asked, stalking to the dais in the center of the room so she could model for Marcus.

"You're lucky Lillibeth's not getting married in Vienna like the wedding I went to a few years ago. The dress code for that was lederhosen and dirndls for the women."

Liberty dropped her head into her hands. "I don't even want to know what a dirndl is, do I?"

"Probably not," he agreed. Then he added, "I'd like to see the bikini, please."

She scowled at him in the mirror. "I don't have a bikini body. I won't take the cover-up off at this party."

"You have a body. You're wearing a bikini. Ergo, you have a bikini body," he said. "Besides, if you don't go swimming in the ocean with me, you'll have to stay on the beach making small talk with all the other women who claim they don't have bikini bodies, hmm? I believe there will be surfboards and paddle boards available, as well."

"You don't fight fair." Liberty scowled harder, but she pulled the cover-up over her head. "And what will you be wearing?"

"Board shorts and a Hawaiian shirt. I won't swim in the shirt," he added. To Cathy, he said, "What shoes would you pair with that?"

Cathy disappeared back into the changing room, where racks and racks of clothing had been waiting for their arrival after Marcus had called ahead.

Liberty fought the urge to chew on her thumbnail. She was wearing a swimsuit that probably cost as much as two weeks' rent. Maybe three. "Aren't there sharks in the ocean? Things that sting and bite?"

Marcus snorted, his gaze traveling over her nearly naked body. Liberty didn't know whether to cover up or pose. "Of course. But trust me, the ocean will be much safer than the land."

Cathy reappeared with a pair of gladiator-style sandals in one hand, flip-flops in the other. Liberty dutifully put a foot in each style of shoe and stood while Marcus decided on the flip-flops. And of course the look had to be paired with huge gold earrings and a collar-style necklace and some gold bangles, according to Cathy.

Liberty winced as she was draped in finery. And she kept right on wincing as she spent the next hour and a half trying on dresses suitable for a beach wedding. If all the clothing had been pretty, that might have been one thing. But some of it wasn't pretty. Some of it—like a maxi dress that looked as though it'd been sewn out of old curtain sheers, as if she'd attempted high fashion on her own—was just hideous.

Finally, Cathy picked up a bright coral dress that was sleeveless with an asymmetrical hem. The neck was a high twist halter that tied in the back in a huge, drapey bow.

The dress was *pretty*. More important, Liberty didn't feel like an imposter in it.

Marcus knew it, too. When she walked out into the sitting room, he sat up and whistled. "Wow," he said in what sounded like awe.

"That color is fabulous with her skin tone," Cathy agreed warmly. "And since she'll be walking on the beach..." She scurried back for the gladiator sandals.

Liberty examined herself in the mirror. The dress made her seem tall and elegant—willowy, even. The color was good with her skin—she was glowing.

It didn't look like her. It looked like some alternate-reality Liberty, one who'd had a normal childhood, and a loving set of parents, and hadn't had to claw and fight for every single thing.

For the first time in a very long time, Liberty realized how much she resembled her mother. Not the woman who couldn't stay clean and out of jail, but there'd been one time...

"Mama, why do you look so pretty?" That was what

Liberty had asked. She must have been around nine. Mama had gotten clean during her first stint in prison and she'd been trying.

"I've got a date with Prince Charming, baby girl, and he's going to save me from…this," Jackie had said as their neighbor from two floors down had zipped Jackie into the borrowed pencil skirt and Grandma Devlin had unrolled the hot rollers from her hair. Mama had had "good enough hair," as she'd called it. She'd claimed her mother was half-white and that was why Liberty's hair was so good. No mention was made of Liberty's father, who was probably white, as well. But that was only Liberty's guess. They didn't speak of her father. Ever.

"Real proud of you, sweetie," Grandma Devlin had said as she teased a curl into a voluminous wave.

It was the only time Liberty had ever glimpsed the woman her mother could have been, if only she'd tried to save herself instead of expecting someone else to do it for her. Her date hadn't saved her. Maybe nothing could have.

And now here stood Liberty, wearing a four-thousand-dollar dress that was made of the softest silk and feeling as if she was trying to be something she wasn't. Was this how her mother had felt that night? In three days—or, more specifically, after three days at this destination wedding—would Liberty still be swept off her feet by a prince who promised to fight for her?

Or would she be right back where she started, waiting for life to smack her down for daring to get above her station?

Marcus stood, breaking her reverie. God, she didn't want life to smack her down again. She didn't need this Prince Charming to rescue her—she could save herself. But was it wrong to want more out of life than to just survive? Was it wrong to want something more than just an afternoon or a long weekend with Marcus?

He was looking her over and she struck a pose, mimicking the way she'd seen models stand.

"Do you like it?" he asked.

She smiled at him in the mirror. He was plunking down God-only-knew how much money on a wardrobe for her. He could just decree it was fine or not. But he still asked her opinion. "I do, actually. It doesn't feel like a costume, you know?"

"Cathy, I'll need a new tie," he said when she came back into the room.

"You went with a linen suit, correct?" Cathy said, which made Liberty look at her sideways.

"Yes," Marcus said, clearly unsurprised that the saleslady would recall his clothing options.

"I think we have something that will complement her outfit beautifully," Cathy said as she hurried from the room.

The moment the door was closed, Marcus stepped up onto the dais with Liberty. "You look gorgeous," he told her, leaning forward to press a kiss against her bare shoulder. He caught her eye in the mirror and slid his arm around her waist. "You do fit in my world, you see? You fit with me."

"It's just the dress," she said, feeling a little weird because she was wearing a gown and he was still in cargo shorts. "It's a great dress."

"It's not the dress. It's you. Babe, I know this makes you nervous, but what's the worst that will happen?" She gave him a suspicious look in the mirror, which made him grin. "You'll be your normal confident, capable self, and we'll have some fun together and *maybe* a few bored, vicious people make snide comments. So what? There's nothing inherently scandalous about you."

She swallowed. There'd been a moment this afternoon,

lying in his arms, listening to him tell her his deepest secrets, that she'd wanted to tell him hers.

And he'd said the past was the past. So it wouldn't matter that Jackie Reese had been African American or an addict or a hooker in her free time. It wouldn't matter that Liberty was a foster kid. None of it would change his opinion of her, right?

Maybe she was foolish, but she desperately wanted to believe that. He hadn't asked for details, so she hadn't told him. It wasn't dishonest because she would tell him if he asked.

"I know how these things go," Marcus went on, his fingers drifting over her bare arms. "I've weathered worse, remember? It'll only be a few short days and then people will move on to the next scandal."

She could still stop this. She could come down with the plague or something—anything to make sure that her past couldn't be used against him.

But she'd backed herself into a hell of a corner and she had no choice but to brazen it out in a pretty dress. Still, she gave him one final out. "Are you sure about this?" she asked even as she leaned into him. "It's not too late. We could just spend the three days in bed here."

He turned her into his arms and looked her in the eye. "We still have time before the trip, if you want to come home with me."

"You mean, spend the night?" She'd be lying if she said the idea didn't appeal to her. A night curled around Marcus? Waking up by his side in his gorgeous home, the lake spread out beneath them?

It was like something out of a fairy tale.

He cupped her face. "Yes. It's fine if you don't but…" Then he lowered his lips and kissed her. Her blood began to pound and the space between her legs throbbed even harder. It wasn't a bad thing, that throbbing. If only he'd touch her there again, take some of the pressure off her body as he'd done earlier… "I want you to stay."

How could she refuse? "I'll need to go back to my apartment at some point before work on Monday," she said in a quiet voice. "I'll need my running shoes. I have this boss, you see…"

His eyes lit up with hope—and excitement. "We can stop by after this, then grab some dinner."

"Not at that fancy restaurant?"

"No," he quickly agreed. "Let's get some takeout and watch the sun set. Just you and me. Let me show you how good I can be for you."

"Here we are," Cathy announced loudly as the door cracked open. Liberty jumped and tried to step clear of Marcus, but he didn't let her go and Cathy didn't come rushing in. "This tie will match her dress perfectly, but I brought a few others, just in case. I've got pocket squares and sock options, as well."

Marcus barely looked at the ties before giving his approval to the first one. Then, stepping off the dais, he said, "I think that we're ready to move forward."

Twelve

This time, when Marcus and Liberty got out of the car in front of the little bungalow in Rogers Park, they held hands as they walked to the door.

It was a brilliantly hot Thursday afternoon, one of those days that's so warm the sky is no longer blue but a nearly colorless gray. It was the kind of day when Liberty stayed at work as long as she could. She was lucky she had a window air conditioner in her apartment, but air-conditioning wasn't cheap. She ran it only when she was home.

Of course, she hadn't exactly been at home much in the past six days. And she hadn't been working late in the office, either. Instead, she'd spent nearly every moment with Marcus.

The whole week had a dreamlike quality to it. Dining out at nice—but not too weird—restaurants with Marcus. Going to see a White Sox game Tuesday evening. Even the morning runs were different. She ran faster because instead of having to catch the train to work to shower, she raced Marcus back upstairs to his home and they showered—together.

But the thing about dreams was that they always ended sooner or later. And since they were flying out on Marcus's private jet early tomorrow morning for that wedding—the wedding she had a completely new wardrobe for—she was afraid that the ending would definitely be sooner.

And it would be no one's fault but her own.

The door popped open before Marcus could ring the bell. "Mr. Warren!" Hazel Jones stood in the open doorway, beaming a megawatt smile at them. "Ms. Reese! Oh, it's just…" Her voice trailed off as honest-to-goodness tears formed in her eyes.

"What's wrong? Is William okay?" Liberty demanded, releasing Marcus's hand and rushing toward the older woman.

She was surprised when Hazel pulled her into a hug. "It's just the most wonderful thing ever!" she said in a quavering voice. "William's fine, just fine. Do come in."

"I trust everything was delivered satisfactorily?" Marcus asked as Hazel began her slow climb up the flight of stairs. Liberty paused and looked back at him.

"What did you do?" she asked in a whisper as he pushed the door shut.

Marcus winked at her. "You'll see."

"I know you called," Hazel was saying, "but I had no idea you meant to replace it all. And when the men showed up! Oh, my heavens!"

"Replace *what*?" Liberty whispered at him. But his only response was to place his hand on her lower back and propel her forward.

"William's just waking up," Hazel said as she disappeared into the nursery. "Oh, those men did such a quick job—I hardly had to worry about a thing!"

"What…" Liberty walked into the nursery and her words died on her lips.

The walls were the same, with all the curled and faded photos of tiny babies tacked up. But the rest of the room?

Gone were the rickety metal swing and the metal crib. Gone was the dresser that doubled as a changing table and the second crib. The ancient rocker that had barely rocked wasn't there anymore, either.

Everything was brand-new. There were two sturdy wooden cribs finished in a high-sheen gloss. Instead of threadbare cotton sheets, there was new bedding and, Liberty was willing to bet, new mattresses. The swing was up-to-the-minute and the rocker was so clean that it practically glowed. The changing table was an actual table now, with stacks of diapers underneath. The dresser next to the table matched the cribs and the rocker.

"This is simply the most thoughtful thing anyone has ever done for me," Hazel said, clasping her hands in front of her as if she were giving thanks to God.

"It was nothing," Marcus said warmly, moving toward the crib where William was beginning to fuss. "You're doing so much good in this world, helping these babies out. I just wanted to make your life a little easier."

Then, as Liberty stared at him, he leaned over and picked William up—correctly, even, supporting his head and everything. "Hey there, buddy," he said in a soft voice. "Did you grow? I think you grew!" He tucked William into his arms and began to sway gently from side to side. "How do you like your new swing?"

Something clenched in Liberty's stomach, some need she couldn't even name. As she watched, completely dumbstruck, William blinked and focused on Marcus. His little mouth opened and he made a sighing sound. It was a noise of contentment.

A hundred images flooded her mind—images she knew she couldn't have, but she wanted anyway. A baby—not just any baby, but their baby. And Marcus would be right there with her. He wouldn't disappear and abandon them. They'd get up in the morning and load the child into the jogging stroller and they'd all run together and then, when he got older, they'd spend Saturdays at the parks, playing soccer and baseball. Afternoons on the beach, trips to the museums.

What she wanted more than anything else in the world was a family—with Marcus, with William, with babies of their own. A family where no one had to hide from drug dealers or pimps or even overbearing parents. A family where they had lots of good food and a nice place to live and they never had to worry about tomorrow. A family where everyone was happy and laughing and smiling.

She'd always wanted that, ever since she'd realized that other people had it.

But now? Watching Marcus coo at William?

She wanted that with them. The wanting was so strong that she couldn't even seem to breathe.

"Those men—they even washed the bottles!" Hazel was saying. "I never! They put everything together, took all the old things away and even organized the drawers!"

Marcus turned to her. "Was everything acceptable? Is there anything I missed? I don't really know what a baby needs, so I had to take the salesman at his word."

"My heavens!" Hazel wiped a tear of joy from her eye. "It's so much more than I could give the little angels." She turned to Liberty. "Did you help pick out the clothing? So thoughtful, to send clothing for little boys and little girls."

Liberty realized that her mouth was hanging open to her chin. She shook her head, trying to make sense of all of this.

Marcus, who had just spent maybe ten thousand dollars on a weekend wardrobe for her, had at some point spent an-other God-only-knew how much on a complete nursery, including bottles and clothes. And all for an abandoned baby boy he had no earthly reason to care for.

"No," Liberty finally said, her voice weak. "He did this all."

"Why," Hazel said, turning her attention mercifully back to Marcus, "you're just a guardian angel, aren't you?" William made a high whining noise in the back of his throat. "Oh," Hazel said, "he's hungry. I'll go get his bottle and you can feed him."

"Okay," Liberty said. Somehow, despite the fairy-tale qualities of the past six days, this took the cake. When Hazel was out of earshot, she turned to Marcus. "*When* did you do this? *How* did you do this?"

The man had the nerve to look pleased with himself as he sat in the chair and began to rock William. "I wanted it to be a surprise. Before I came to find you at the office last Saturday, I made some calls."

"*Why* did you do this, Marcus?"

He gave her a long look. "You have to ask?"

"Here we are," Hazel said, bustling back in. "Oh, just look at the two of you," she added, beaming down at William and Marcus. "Don't they make a handsome pair?"

"They do," Liberty agreed automatically.

The panic hit her like a Mack truck barreling down the highway at seventy miles an hour, and suddenly she couldn't breath. This was all well and good, this little delusion she and Marcus were enjoying. All of her private fantasies were not only seeing the light of day, but Marcus was proving to be better than she ever could have dreamed. She knew sex was fun—why else did people do it so much? But being in bed with Marcus, where she could pretend their world was just big enough for the two of them—that was one thing.

But this? Him sending professional baby people over to revamp Hazel's house? Him taking her for a wardrobe makeover so she could fit into his world—no, not even that. So she could fit into a very specific social setting, complete with cheating ex-girlfriend and overbearing, borderline abusive parents?

No. Not only was this not going to work, was this going to fail—it was going to fail epically. Marcus may think that a few vicious people might whisper behind their hands at this wedding and then people would move on, but Liberty knew the truth. People didn't move on from something like this.

She'd come so far. She'd literally, figuratively and metaphysically pulled herself up by her own bootstraps through the sheer force of her will and a promise she'd made to Grandma Devlin all those years ago—she would save herself. Because no one else would do it for her. Not her mother, not her nonexistent father—not even Grandma Devlin could save Liberty from her own mother or from foster care.

But Liberty had gone too far. She'd fallen in love with a billionaire—someone so far above her station that she shouldn't have even been able to see him, much less talk with him, work with him—run with him. She'd gotten too close to the sun and when the truth burned bright, she would fall back to earth and her carefully constructed life would fall with her.

For so long, that had always been the worst thing that could happen to her—someone would learn the truth and she'd be out of a job, back on the streets, struggling to start over once again. But now she knew the real truth.

Marcus looked up at her as if he could sense her racing thoughts. "Liberty?"

"I'm sorry," she said, her voice shaky. Because she was. When she fell, she wouldn't just lose her job. She'd lose Marcus. She'd hurt him because he was naive enough to think that he could trust her.

"I asked if you two had discussed applying for adoption." If a little old lady could do puppy-dog eyes, Hazel was doing them right now. "William would be lucky to have two loving parents like you." She sighed happily. "Such a handsome family you'd be."

Marcus looked at Liberty as if he were expecting her to come up with some sort of reasonable response to this statement, but she had nothing. So he finally said, "We're still thinking about it."

Oh, God—he *was* thinking about it. She could tell from the way he gazed down on William's little face as he happily drank his milk.

And just as she'd stood in front of that mirror and seen a different version of her mother—a path not taken—she knew that right now, Marcus was looking at a different version of himself, one where he found a way to make her fit into his life and a way to make this baby fit into his life and just like that—*poof!*—they were this instant family that was supposed to live happily ever after.

He thought he could make it happen, just as he'd made this nursery happen. He was rich and powerful and he could bend reality to his will because his illusion was that he was in control of his own life.

He would hate her when she took that away from him.

He looked up at her and there was no missing it—the way his face relaxed into that peaceful smile. The way his eyes lit up when he caught her gaze. Even—oh, God—even the way he leaned down and pressed a tender kiss to the top of William's fuzzy little head.

She was shaking with want, with need, with the wish to make this fantasy reality. *I don't want to wake up*, she decided. *If this is a dream…*

She was in love with her boss, one of the richest, most powerful men in Chicago.

No, that wasn't true. It had been, once, but not anymore.

She was in love with Marcus, with a man who cared for a baby boy he didn't have to, who'd once almost run away to Germany just to be free. She was hopelessly in love with a man who used his power, his influence, to pull her up next to him, instead of lording it over her.

If only there wasn't a wedding or a reality television show. If only they could go on ignoring the rest of the world.

But they couldn't. She had to end this charade before it destroyed both of them. She couldn't go to the wedding with him and that was that.

"I think Liberty needs to cuddle a baby," Marcus said, half to her and half to William.

So she took the infant in her arms and sat in the finest rocker money could buy and tried to stop looking as if she'd been flattened by a semi.

She gazed down at the baby boy in her arms. William. Her William, her second chance to redeem her mother's greatest mistake. She hadn't been able to save her little brother, hadn't had the power or the money or the skills to keep that baby alive. He'd never been anything but a ghost of regret that haunted her. But here this baby was, just as alone and lost as William had been.

Except for Marcus, his guardian angel.

What would happen to William when she and Marcus ended? Would Marcus still invest this kind of money and time in the baby? She didn't want to think that he'd punish her by punishing William. The child was innocent.

But she couldn't risk that. She couldn't risk losing another William, not when she had the power to save him this time.

She looked up at Marcus, who was making good-natured small talk with Hazel about cribs and diapers and babies.

She hadn't wanted anything to change. She hadn't wanted to risk the comfortable life she'd made for herself. And if they hadn't found this tiny baby in a shoe box by the trash, maybe they would have gone on as they had, Marcus gently teasing her during their morning runs and Liberty working every Saturday and their worlds crossing only in safely defined ways.

But everything had changed.

And there was no going back.

Thirteen

Liberty paused at the top of the stairs, her hand on the railing that led down to the beach. She just stood there for a moment, her eyes fixed on some point way out in the ocean.

"Beautiful," she murmured, turning a strange smile in Marcus's direction.

"Yes," he agreed, slipping his arm around her waist and pulling her into a light hug. They needed to get going. They'd delayed arriving for the Beach Blanket Bingo party as long as they could. They were quickly becoming unfashionably late and that would create its own set of problems.

But he didn't want to ruin this moment. Liberty was framed by the bright blue sky and the deep blue ocean. The salty breeze whispered softly through the sands on the private beach on Catalina Island, blowing the strands of her hair around her neck. He wanted to bury his face against her and let those hairs play over his skin.

No, he didn't blame her for not hurrying down to the beach.

He looked down to where the party was in full swing. Even though it was only three in the afternoon and the sun wouldn't set for hours, the tiki torches burned bright and the bonfire was already going. Easily a hundred people were lounging in the sand, getting drinks from one of the two bars that had been set up on opposite sides of the beach, or sitting around the bonfire. From this safe distance, it looked like fun. But he knew better.

He gritted his teeth and said, "Are you ready?"

She turned a quick smile to him, but he didn't miss the glimmer of fear in her eyes. "There's no going back, is there?"

"We'll go down, make the bare minimum of polite greetings, and then we'll hit the water, okay?" He pointed to where a cabana had been set up close to the water. "See all the boards? I'll get you a paddle board and we'll be out on the waves in fifteen minutes—twenty, tops. And most people aren't out in the water. It'll be just us."

She took a deep breath. "I'm going to hold you to that," she said, tugging her cover-up down over her bottom before she started down the steps.

"You look great," he told her again. He'd been telling her that ever since they'd gotten on the plane early this morning because she'd been extremely nervous. She'd tried to hide it, but he'd seen right through her confident smiles and stiff shoulders.

She'd spent the plane ride with her hands glued to the armrest. She hadn't said much of anything when they'd landed in Los Angeles to refuel and she'd said even less when they'd taken off to fly to Catalina Island, where Lillibeth's wedding was being held on the private lands owned by the Wrigley family. Liberty had turned an unnatural shade of green when they'd landed on the tiny airstrip carved into the top of the highest point on Catalina four hours ago. He'd never seen a single person drink so much ginger ale at one time in his life.

"You're just saying that because I'm mildly terrified," she said in an almost normal joking tone.

"I'm not. You're gorgeous independent of your fear level."

They made it to the bottom of the stairs, where she waited for him. "Fifteen minutes," she murmured, linking her hand with his.

"You'll fit in," he promised.

But as they strolled down the beach, approaching the bonfire—complete with pig roasting on a spit—Liberty's apprehension began to affect him.

It only got worse when Lillibeth caught sight of them and waved. In the space of time it took for her to make her way over to them, he realized he should have listened to Liberty. He shouldn't have come. To hell with putting on a happy face and showing the world that Lillibeth hadn't actually trampled on his heart and, by extension, trampled on the Warren name.

He'd thought he'd been making an acceptable compromise with his parents by agreeing to come to this wedding, but now? With the woman who cheated on him and publicly humiliated him strolling toward him wearing nothing but a tiny little white string bikini and a whole lot of gold jewelry?

Bad idea. This wasn't saving face. This was rubbing his face in his failures.

"Marcus, darling!" she cooed, as if he were a toy poodle. "Where have you been? You're looking marvelous."

"Lillibeth," was all he got out before she was planting kisses on his cheeks. He shot a helpless look at Liberty, who rolled her eyes. "This is quite...something."

She slid her arm around his waist and leaned her head against his shoulder as if Liberty wasn't standing a foot away. "Isn't it? I wanted something private and intimate." The tips of her fingers brushed against the buttons on the front of his garish pink-and-blue Hawaiian shirt. "Somewhere we could all just relax and…see what happened."

Warning bells went off in Marcus's head—was she flirting with him? Was that even possible? The bride flirting with the man she sold out to the press the night before her own wedding?

But then again, this was Lillibeth. She had not proven herself to be the most trustworthy of significant others. Of course she could be flirting with him. He wondered if her groom knew—or cared.

In a panic, he looked at Liberty. She was outright glaring at Lillibeth. Well. At least they were all on the same page.

Lillibeth looked up at him, her limpid blue eyes composed into some variation of regret. "I'm so glad you came. I feel terrible about how it ended between us, you know. I hope that we can—" she lifted one of her smooth shoulders in a shrug and then, unbelievably, lifted on her toes and leaned toward him "—make amends."

"I don't think that's possible." Marcus removed Lillibeth's arms from around his waist and moved to Liberty's side. She looked as if she was going to erupt at any moment. He took her hand in his and squeezed it. "Lillibeth, this is my guest, Liberty Reese."

Lillibeth blinked in confusion, as if she couldn't believe he'd say no to her. "Wait—Reese?" When Lillibeth's eyes focused, they zeroed in on Liberty like a heat-seeking missile. "Ms. Reese? You brought your *secretary* to my wedding?"

"It's nice to see you again," Liberty said in the kind of voice that made it clear it was anything but nice. "And actually, I'm an executive assistant."

"Really, Marcus," Lillibeth said, her nostrils flaring in a most horselike manner, as if she'd stepped in something unpleasant.

Marcus felt Liberty tense but before a catfight could break out, the situation got a whole lot worse.

"Marcus!" a high-pitched voice called out over the beach. Marisa Warren, draped in a sheer caftan that was blindingly lime green, sauntered up to them, a cigarette in one hand and a drink in the other. "There you are, you naughty boy!"

"Mother," he said, turning his head so she could kiss him on the cheek. This was fine. This was going according to plan. They'd get this over with, and then he and Liberty could hit the water. "Where's Father?"

Marisa waved the hand with the cigarette dangerously close to his shirt. "Oh, he's around, I'm sure."

Translation: he was probably screwing around. Jesus, was this entire wedding party going to devolve into an orgy? What happens on a private island beach stays on a private island beach? He felt nauseous.

Marisa's gaze passed over Liberty, categorizing and dismissing her in the blink of an eye. "Dear," she said, dropping her voice to a more conspiratorial whisper that did nothing to prevent Liberty from hearing every word she said, "I was so hoping to see you with Emma Green. She's such a darling young woman..."

"Oh, I love Emma," Lillibeth added, smiling at Marisa. "She'd be great for Marcus, don't you think?" The two women shared a friendly smile.

Liberty's grip tightened on his hand to the point of pain. "No," Marcus said in a fierce whisper. "I'm here with Liberty."

"Your secretary?" Lillibeth said, trying to pull off an innocent tone and failing completely.

But it worked on Marisa—too well. Her gaze cut back to Liberty with renewed interest. "Your *what*?"

Marcus pried his fingers out of Liberty's grip and slipped his arm around her waist. "Mother, you know Liberty."

"What are you doing, Marcus?" Marisa hissed in a whisper, as if everyone else were listening in. Gone was the soft, delicate voice she used in public. Instead, her tone could cut glass. He knew the warning when he heard it, but he refused to buckle. "We agreed," she said, dropping her cigarette and digging her fingers into his upper arm, "that you were going to bring a suitable date to this event."

"Liberty is perfectly suitable." Lillibeth made a highly unladylike snorting noise. "She is my guest," he said, shaking his mother off. "I am a grown man, Mother. I can see whomever I want."

For a moment, her mask of social acceptability snapped back into place. "But, darling, what do you think can be gained from this?" she said, looking at Liberty as if she weren't a woman, but a thing. A bargaining chip.

He stared at his mother. "I thought I might try being happy. Isn't that enough?"

Marisa's face twisted into a mask of rage. "You are an embarrassment to the Warren name," she threatened as if he were still eighteen and a flight risk.

But he wasn't eighteen, not anymore. He was not afraid of her, of any of them. "You're doing a fine job of that yourself," he replied, pointedly looking at her glass.

Marisa's eyes blazed with righteous anger. "I am trying to protect you, *dear*."

And he was six again, holding his nanny's hand, and crying as he stood in front of his parents and told them about how the men in masks in the big black car had pulled up next to them on their way home from the park and pulled out guns and threatened to take them away the next time. How his nanny had yelled and scared the bad guys off. Marcus had asked if they were going to call the police because the police were the good guys who'd catch the bad guys.

That's when his parents had exchanged a look and said, "Dear, we can't risk the Warren name. We'll protect you."

And two days later, Miss Judy—the woman he'd spent most of his six years with—had been gone and Marcus had been very much alone.

All to protect the Warren name.

He was only dimly aware that he'd taken a step toward his mother, dimly aware that he'd dropped his arm from Liberty's waist. Marisa took a step back, her eyes widening in alarm.

"Protect me?" He barked out a harsh laugh. "Is that what you tell yourself so you can sleep at night? You don't care about me. You never have."

"That's not true!" Marisa gasped.

"Isn't it? You got rid of my nanny for protecting me. And Father—he made all those scholarship offers disappear. He made the offer from the German soccer teams disappear. How was *that* protecting me?"

"German soccer teams?" Lillibeth asked in genuine confusion.

Marisa shot Lillibeth a hard look. Lillibeth crossed her arms and took a step back, her head down. She may well cower before Marisa Warren, but Marcus wouldn't cower. Not anymore. "We are in public," Marisa said in a harsh whisper, her gaze darting around.

"That's all that matters, isn't it? What the public thinks. God, what an idiot I've been. To think, after all this time, I'd been telling myself that things would get better if I just did what you wanted. If I went to school where you wanted me to, if I started the company you wanted me to—if I slept with the women you wanted me to."

His mother gasped. "Marcus!"

"It never mattered, did it? No matter how hard I tried to be the perfect Warren, it was never enough. Well, I'm done pretending we're a happy family because we never have been and we never will be. You wanted me to marry her?"

he went on, jerking his chin back in Lillibeth's direction. "Why? So we could spend the rest of our lives making each other as miserable as you and Father make each other? *No.*"

"That's not why," Marisa said and this time, he heard a note of desperation in her voice. "Be reasonable, Marcus."

"Be reasonable?" He laughed again. Heads turned in their direction, but he didn't care. "You mean, do as you're told, Marcus—right?"

"That's not what I said. Please, Marcus," she begged, her eyes huge. "People will talk."

"Like Lillibeth talked to the press? She hurt me and yet you insisted I take her back, insisted I make amends—the only reason I'm here is because it was the lesser of the evils. Let them talk. They can't do any more damage than she's done, than you've done."

"Hey!" Lillibeth protested from somewhere behind where he now stood.

"Be quiet," Liberty snapped. "You sold your story. You sold him out."

"Funny coming from you," Lillibeth fired back. "Who the hell are you? Just a secretary trying to sleep your way to the top. You're nothing."

"That's executive assistant and I'm a hell of a lot more to him than you'll ever be."

Marcus felt a welling of pride for Liberty. She would not be cowed, either. But more than that, she was defending him. God, he loved that woman.

"Marcus, everything we've done was to protect you," his mother offered weakly. "You don't understand. We just wanted to keep you safe."

"No, you just wanted to control me. I'm nothing but a pawn to you. I'm not here for her," he said, jerking his thumb at Lillibeth. "I'm not here for you. I'm not here for Father and I'm sure as hell not here for the Warren family name.

I'm here with Liberty. Stay out of my life." He turned to Liberty. "You were right. Let's go."

"Marcus, you *will* stay," his mother demanded. "You came all this way—it would be a scandal."

He stopped and made eye contact with Liberty. "What do you want to do?" she asked in a soft voice.

Honestly? He didn't want to admit that his mother had a point. It wasn't a great point—but storming out of here less than ten minutes after he'd arrived would make people talk.

"Fine."

He took Liberty's hand and turned back to Lillibeth. "Congratulations on your nuptials," he said as he pulled Liberty after him. Without looking back, they walked down to the water's edge.

Liberty barely had time to kick off her shoes and tug her cover-up over her head before Marcus was hauling her into the water. They walked straight out into the waves, hand in hand, and they didn't stop until the water was at her chest and she was beginning to panic.

"I can't swim," she reminded him when a wave jumped up and smacked her in the chin.

"Here," he replied, turning and scooping her into his arms as if she weighed nothing.

She let him and the water carry her as she looped her arms around his neck. She rested her head against his shoulder as he turned and began to walk parallel to the beach.

They were silent until Marcus stopped. They had moved far past the actual beach—maybe a hundred yards from the last cabana. They were, as promised, completely alone on the edge of the ocean. The other guests who were in the water were so far away she couldn't hear them splashing in the water.

Confident they wouldn't be seen or heard, Liberty leaned

back to look up at Marcus. His face was drawn tight, but she couldn't tell if it was sorrow or anger. The two emotions blended together too completely to see where one left off and the other started.

What had he said about a nanny? Whatever it had been, it had hit a true nerve with his mother. Liberty wouldn't have thought she could ever feel anything for Marisa Warren, but in that moment, the older woman had looked her age, haggard and worried. She'd looked like a mother who truly did care for her son.

One thing was clear. Liberty wasn't the only one with secrets.

"The past is in the past," he said in a tight voice, his eyes focused on a point so far in the distance, she wasn't sure human eyes could actually see it. "That went well."

"Swimmingly," she agreed.

Marcus looked down at her, a small grin on his face. "You can't swim."

"And yet, here we are. I believe I was promised a paddle board or something," she added.

"Later." His grin faded. "You stood up for me."

"I just backed you up. Your flank was exposed." But then she thought of how Lillibeth had looked when she'd called Liberty a nothing—vicious and victorious. And that woman hadn't been wrong. Liberty was a nobody. No name, no family. And in this crowd—where a mother would throw her son under the bus for the sake of the family name—being a nobody who came from nobodies was a cardinal sin. Liberty would never be forgiven, no matter how industrious or smart or loyal she was.

It was bad enough that he was sticking his neck out for her with his mother, in front of all these people. She just couldn't bear the thought of him realizing how much of a nobody she really was.

God help her, she never should have let it get to this point, where Marcus Warren was cradling her in his arms in the Pacific Ocean.

But she hadn't been able to help herself. He cared for her and she was terribly afraid she might love him, and if that meant she might have to beat the hell out of a debutante bride, then so be it. And he didn't ask, so she didn't tell him.

"Thank you for standing with me. For being here with me. This is why I wanted you here, Liberty. Because I knew, deep down, that this was how it was going to go." He sighed heavily and looked out onto the ocean. "Because this is how it always goes and I need things to change—"

"Hello?" The voice boomed off from their left, interrupting Marcus.

Dammit! She wanted to hear what Marcus was about to say. Scowling, Liberty twisted in his arms to see Erik Jenner paddling toward them on a surfboard.

Jenner waved and Liberty couldn't help but note that he looked relieved to see them. "Are you two hiding over here?"

Yes, Liberty thought, frowning at him. Why did it have to be Jenner—someone who knew that she was Marcus's assistant?

She was in no mood to have to tell one of the most powerful real estate moguls in Chicago to shove off. But she would, dammit. Friend of Marcus's or no.

"Jenner," Marcus said, his voice dropping in register. And just like that, he was back to being Marcus Warren, Billionaire. "How are the waves?"

"Lousy. This whole beach is pretty subpar," Jenner said. His casual tone didn't match the way his eyes were darting between Marcus and Liberty.

She was still in his arms. And he was in no hurry to set her down.

"I thought she was going to get married in Hawaii," Jen-

ner went on after a moment's pause. "Better beaches there."
When Marcus didn't reply, Jenner leaned forward and ad-
dressed Liberty. "I'm Erik Jenner. We've met, right?"

"We have. Liberty Reese." Liberty reached over the surfboard to shake his hand.

Jenner's eyes went wide as he said, "Ah," in a long ex-
halation. "I didn't recognize you out of your suit." He shot
Marcus a knowing look. "That certainly explains *that*."

Marcus's eyes narrowed in challenge. "Comments?"

"None," Jenner said quickly. "Who the hell am I to judge?
But your mother—"

"No," Marcus interrupted. "Don't tell me. I'm sure she's
having heart palpitations or something melodramatic.
Hence we're all the way over here."

"Fair enough." Jenner looked from Liberty to Marcus
again. "So."

"So," Marcus echoed.

Liberty floated in Marcus's arms. She didn't know what,
if anything, she was supposed to say right now. Lillibeth
and all her vitriol she could handle. But Jenner was a friend
of Marcus's. Guy friendships were not Liberty's specialty.

Marcus was the one who broke the silence. "Listen,
Jenner—do you still need an assistant?"

"I might," he said hesitantly. "Why?"

Liberty looked up at Marcus in surprise. "Why?"

Marcus looked down at her, his eyes full of tenderness.
"Things have changed."

"Marcus," she said in a low voice, "what are you doing?"

"Trying to make sure your boss isn't taking advantage
of you," he whispered back.

"I thought you told me you couldn't survive without her,"
Jenner said, his tone cautious.

Marcus grinned at Liberty. "I can't."

She saw then what he was doing and she loved him for it.

Anyone else might have tried to keep her closer—keep her in his office and his bed. Or anyone with as much money as Marcus had could have easily told her she could quit her job and stay at home and he'd pay for everything. And it would be tempting. To be his? To not have to worry about money, about security?

But that would mean that Liberty would be a kept woman—as long as he wanted to keep her. That would mean giving up everything she'd fought for to hope and pray a man would marry her and take her away from her life.

That would mean she would be no better than her mother, who refused to save herself on the off chance a prince might do it for her.

That's not who Liberty was. And, God bless him, even though Marcus didn't know about her mother and her princes and everything Liberty had done—every lie she'd told—to get where she was today, he knew that she would always need her job, always need the security it promised.

He didn't need to know about her past. He understood her anyway.

"I have a job open. It's not as an executive assistant, though. That position was filled. I need an office manager. More responsibility, more involvement in the business."

"I know someone," Marcus said, still grinning at her. "Great people skills, amazing at organization. A quick learner." Her cheeks flushed, but she couldn't help it. "She's got amazing recommendations, too. She's worked for the best."

Jenner snorted. "Man, you are *gone*."

In the distance, a gong sounded. An honest-to-God gong. Talk about pretentious wedding accessories. They all looked up the shoreline.

"Luau," Jenner said. "I guess that means we have to go back and eat a pig."

Hearing the note of resignation in his voice, Liberty

looked at him. Out here, in his swim trunks, sitting astride a surfboard, he didn't look like the real estate mogul who'd tried to woo her away from Marcus. He looked like a regular guy—attractive, yes, but there was something about him that gave her the impression he didn't want to be here any more than she or Marcus did.

"I guess we do," Marcus agreed. "Hey, can we borrow your board? I promised Liberty."

"I can't swim," she explained when Jenner looked at her. "I hope that's not a job requirement."

Both men laughed at that and some of the melancholy tension dissipated. "Sure." Jenner slid off the side. "But after we suffer through this, I'm coming back out. You guys are welcome to join me."

"You're not going to give me and Liberty any crap, are you?" Marcus asked, helping Liberty up onto the board.

Jenner let go and held up his hands in surrender, which made the board shift underneath Liberty. "I'm not your mother, man." Jenner looked back up the beach and added, "Someone in this crowd should get what they actually want."

"We all should." He looked at Liberty. "Ready?"

Ready? For what? To go back and face a mostly hostile crowd who thought of her as nothing more than a secretary who was trying to snag her boss right out from under their noses?

No, that wasn't right. Was she ready to go back and stand by Marcus's side, protecting his flank while he defended her right to exist? Was she ready to do what it took to protect him—to protect them? Even if that meant taking a position with Jenner's company?

"Yes," she said, trying to paddle without falling over the side of the board. "I am."

Fourteen

When they returned to shore, Lillibeth stayed well clear of them, which suited Marcus just fine. He and Liberty ate enough of the roast pig to be polite and then got boards of their own and headed back out into the ocean. There weren't really any decent waves here but, given how Liberty squealed as she rode out the smaller waves, Marcus knew this was all she could handle. He stayed within easy reach of her at all times, but she fell off her board only twice.

When dusk draped itself over them, he and Liberty sat on their boards, holding hands as the golden sun dropped below the surface of the waters. "And I thought sunrise over Lake Michigan was something," she said, her voice reverential.

"It's beautiful out here," he agreed, stroking his thumb over her knuckles. "I'm glad we came. It was worth it to share that with you."

She turned a smile back to him, but it faded with the last red streaks of light as she turned to look at the beach behind them. "I suppose we have to go in."

"We can stay out," he said because he really didn't want to go back in. Out here, floating in the ocean with Liberty by his side, he didn't have to deal with Lillibeth or his mother's guilt or anyone's side-eye glances.

But he knew that, sooner or later, they'd have to face the reality waiting for him back on the beach.

"Marcus," she said in that teasing tone, "may I remind you for the fortieth time today that I don't know how to swim? So being in the ocean after dark seems like a particularly bad idea?"

"Fortieth? Is that all?" He tried to grin, but he knew she was right.

"I've made it through a whole day of not drowning," she quipped. "I'd hate to ruin my streak at this point. Besides, it's getting colder."

Without realizing it, his gaze dropped to her chest. He could just make out the stiff peaks of her nipples straining against the wet fabric of her bikini top. Yeah, they could get out of the water—and skip the bonfire entirely. "Come on," he replied. "But we don't need to hang out. They're all just going to get drunk anyway. More drunk," he corrected himself.

"I'd rather be in the hut with you," she said, catching his eye and giving him a sly smile.

He laughed. He wouldn't necessarily call it a hut. It was a cabin—a rustic cabin. Three walls, a bed, a small bathroom and expansive views of the ocean—and that was it. There wasn't even a shower—that was up at the big house, where most of the wedding party and the less intrepid guests were staying, including his parents. The estate had a few of these small cabins scattered around, complete with thatched roofs and open views of the ocean.

And a sense of privacy. Their cabin was down a rocky path, maybe three hundred yards from the rest of the estate.

They made it to the shore without a problem and dropped off their boards. It didn't take long to see that he'd been right—the bartenders were still pouring and the DJ had started playing thumping club music.

He looked around. Trust-fund babies, hedge-fund managers, debutantes and minor celebrities, all partying together under the haze of the bonfire's smoke in an alcoholic daze. This was his crowd. These were his friends.

But were they? Had he ever been happy with them? Or had it just been a never-ending game of one-upmanship and drinking?

He and Liberty gathered up their things and began the long walk back to their hut. Tiki torches marked the path, so at least they weren't stumbling around in the dark.

Then a voice called out behind them. "Marcus?"

His mother.

He almost kept going. But Liberty was the one who stopped and turned back. And since she was holding his hand, he had little choice but to do the same.

His mother was still in her lime-green caftan. The shadows the torches were throwing over her face made her look older than he'd ever seen her before. It was almost like looking at a ghost of a woman he'd known in a previous life. "Yes?"

She didn't reply until she caught up to him. "Marcus, I have something I need to tell you."

"I'm sure you do. That doesn't mean I need to hear it. Come on, Liberty." He started to turn but his mother latched onto his arm.

"Don't you turn your back on me, young man. I am still your mother. And…and I owe you an apology."

That tripped him up, so much so that Marcus physically stumbled. "You what?"

Marisa stepped into him, touching his face with the palm of her hand. It was almost a tender gesture. But Marisa Warren didn't have a tender bone in her body. "You don't understand what your father and I have done to protect you."

He stiffened. He didn't want to do this, didn't want to deal with the guilt and the burden of being the one to carry on the Warren name—at all costs.

She went on. "That's our fault. Perhaps we did our jobs a little too well."

"Yes, of course. You were obviously Parents of the Year." He tried to turn again but she wasn't letting him go.

"I didn't realize you remembered that nanny," she said, halting him in his tracks for a second time. "I'd hoped you'd forgotten about her."

He stared down at her in shock. "Forgotten about Miss Judy? I was almost kidnapped and she's the one who saved me—not you, not Father. And what did you two do? You didn't call the cops. You didn't find out who was behind it. You got rid of her. And you left me all alone."

Beside him, Liberty gasped in shock.

"But, dear," his mother said in a pleading tone, "that's not what happened." She sighed heavily, as if the truth weighed on her. Marcus didn't buy her act for a minute. This was nothing but manipulation, pure and simple. "She was the one who organized the fake kidnapping."

Marcus recoiled in disbelief. Miss Judy? The one who'd given him baths and taken him to the park and read him stories at night? The woman who'd make a big bowl of popcorn so they could watch *The Brady Bunch* together? The one who'd loved him? "I don't—*what*?"

"Why do you think we fired her? She staged the whole thing."

"How…" He was so surprised that he couldn't even form the words. All he could see was the woman with the graying streaks in her hair and the warm smile on her face. "She wouldn't have. She cared about me!"

Marisa shook her head. "She might have. But desperation makes people do funny things. We had a private eye investigate what happened. Why would kidnappers be scared off by a woman screaming? It didn't make sense."

He reached out behind him for Liberty. When her hand slid into his and he felt her step closer to his side, the panic that was building in his body eased back enough that he could try to think again. "Why should I believe you? Because you've lied to me before. You've told me what you thought I needed to hear to get me to do what you wanted. Why is this different?"

His mother gave him a long look. "You should believe me because it's the truth. What do I stand to gain by telling you this? You're going to be very mad at me, I know. I just… I never realized that you hated us for that. I thought we'd made it clear that we were doing what was best for you."

"Yes, you made it quite clear that I was not to worry about it. That doesn't mean I was able to stop the nightmares."

A look of guilt stole over his mother's face. "She was in trouble. She needed money. The day after the attack, we got a ransom note—we were to pay a million dollars or next time, we wouldn't be so lucky. It was a scam—she'd get the money and look like the hero. I'm just sorry that she saw fit to use you as a means to an end."

Confusion rolled through him—that and anger. His whole life spent checking over his shoulder for vans—all for nothing. "Why are you just now telling me this? Why didn't you have her arrested? Why did you let me live my whole life thinking there were people out to get me?"

His mother took a step back. "You were a child," she said in a pleading tone. "What was I supposed to tell you? That the nanny you loved had put you directly in harm's way? That she'd arranged for her brother-in-law and his friends to don masks and use real guns to scare your father into giving them a million dollars?"

"Yes," he said through gritted teeth. "You should have been honest with me."

Marisa scoffed. "You wouldn't have understood then. We didn't want to subject you to the police, to a trial—and, yes, the publicity. You were six, Marcus. You would have forever been the boy whose nanny tried to kidnap him. People wouldn't have treated you like a Warren. They would have treated you like this thing to be pitied. No," she said decisively. "We did the right thing."

"You only cared about the Warren name." That's what he'd spent the past thirty years thinking—they loved the name and the power that went with it. Not him. Never him.

His mother looked incredulous. "Of course we did. Your father was involved in high-level negotiations with the Saudis for oil then and our first thought was that the negotiations had gone sour. We couldn't risk showing weakness."

"You let those people go because you wanted to save face for a *business deal*?" That he could believe. That was exactly what his father would do.

Unexpectedly, her expression turned dark. "We *ruined* those people for what they did to you. Their hands were not clean and we dug every single misdeed of theirs up. They went to jail for other reasons, but you can be damned sure they knew we had put them there. No one messes with a Warren."

Part of him wanted to believe her, wanted to believe that his parents had actually cared enough about his well-being to mete out punishment as they saw fit. And there was a time in his life when he might have bought everything she said, hook, line and sinker.

But he wasn't that naive little rich boy anymore. And this woman no longer held that power over his life. So he drew himself up to his full height and glared down at her. "And I'm just supposed to believe you? All those scholarships that Father made disappear? Was my life in mortal danger then, too?"

His mother waved those questions away as if they were mosquitoes. "Wanting to run off and play soccer? Do you know how embarrassed your father was?"

"Yes, I can clearly see how I've been nothing but a massive failure my entire life. Well, get used to disappointment, because I'm done. I always did everything you wanted—the schools, the girls, the company. Now I'm going to do what I want and I dare you to try to stop me."

"Oh, Marcus, please—you're being melodramatic." Anything sympathetic about his mother disappeared in the flickering light of the torches. "Do you not see what we did for you? You're one of the most powerful men in Chicago. You could run for office. You *can* do whatever you want. That's what we gave you. The world is yours."

Marcus heard a strangled-sounding noise and realized it had come from his own throat. "Run for office?"

"Now," his mother went on, as if she'd won and he'd lost and everything would go on as it had. "It's unfortunate that you decided to go public with your little affair, but at the very least, we're on a private island. This can be suppressed. No one needs to know you were dallying with your assistant." She straightened the collar on his shirt. "Nothing needs to change. You're still a Warren and that means something."

This was it. This was the rest of his life right here. His mother might claim that she had no ulterior motive telling her little story about his nanny, but he saw through that lie. She was trying to pull him in, trying to make him trust her.

"…Emma would be a perfect choice," his mother was

saying, as if Liberty were nothing more than set dressing. "From such a good family."

"No."

"No?" His mother paused. "Well, there are other options if Emma doesn't work for you."

"I'm with Liberty," he said.

"Yes, well, just keep it quiet," Marisa said impatiently. "That's what—"

"No," he insisted, louder this time. "No, Mother. You don't get to pick. You don't get to dictate my life anymore. I didn't want Lillibeth. I don't want Emma. For God's sake, I didn't want to come to this wedding and have to put on a good face all because it fits some twisted version of what the Warren name stands for." His mother opened her mouth, but Marcus cut her off. "I'm with Liberty. I'm not going to cheat on her and I'm not going to use her and I'm sure as hell not going to cast her aside because you think I can do better. I want her and I'm damned lucky that she wants me."

His mother glared at him. "You're being difficult, Marcus. Do you really think she—"

"She's the only person in my adult life who has cared about me. Not about what I could do for her, not about what I can buy her—but about me, Marcus. I want someone who's honest with me, who would never lie and cheat. I want the one thing money can't buy. I want her love. And if that means I'm not protecting the Warren name, then so be it."

His mother's eyes narrowed to slits; she looked like a snake on the verge of striking. No, she wasn't going to let him go that easily. "This is exactly why we didn't tell you about your stupid nanny. You always were a fool. You—"

"I," he interrupted, jerking his arm free from her grasp, "am going to do exactly what I want."

Lesser men had cowered before that look of intense

hatred. But Marcus would not give. "Are you, now?" It wasn't a question, but a threat.

No, she wasn't going to let him go at all, if she could help it. "I am. And if you try to interfere? I will do everything in my power to drag the Warren name through the mud. You think we lost face when Lillibeth sold me out? You have no idea how much damage I can inflict."

That got his mother's attention. Her eyes widened and she physically recoiled in horror. "You wouldn't *dare*."

"Try me and we'll find out."

They stood in a furious silence for a moment, trying to outglare each other. "I am very disappointed," his mother said softly, the simper back in her voice. "Very disappointed."

"So am I. God knows that when I have children, I won't treat them like pawns in some game that's rigged from the start." He turned, still holding Liberty's hand. "Goodbye, Mother. Don't look for me at the wedding tomorrow. I won't be there."

"Marcus?" Marisa called after him. "Marcus, this is not acceptable!"

But he didn't stop, he didn't try to figure out what twisted definition of love his parents had been using for the past thirty-some-odd years. Maybe they did love him and this was the only way they knew how to show it.

No, that was a cop-out because he'd grown up in that world, and even he knew that wasn't love. That was control. And he was done being their puppet.

Everything had changed.

And now he was free.

He began to run.

Fifteen

She had to tell him the truth. And she would, just as soon as he stopped sprinting along the dimly lit path—and pulling her with him. Liberty stumbled to keep up in her flip-flops. Somehow, she managed to keep her balance. But that was only physically.

Emotionally, she wasn't sure she'd ever find her balance again. How was she supposed to make sense of what she'd just heard? No, what his mother thought of her wasn't a huge shock. Nor was it shocking that what Marisa Warren had a problem with wasn't that Marcus was sleeping with Liberty, but that he'd gone public.

But… He'd almost been kidnapped as a kid? By his nanny? And his own parents—people who should have loved and protected him at all costs—had…well, she couldn't make sense of it. They'd put the perpetrators behind bars—but completely ignored Marcus while they did it? They'd kept him locked away from the world, as if it'd been *his* fault?

Her own mother had been a horrible person. Liberty knew that. Jackie Reese had been a sheep without a flock, lost in a hell of her own making. She'd ignored Liberty for drugs and men for years and years.

But no matter how bad it'd been—and Lord knew it had been pretty damn bad—Liberty had always had hope. She'd had Grandma Devlin teaching her to read. As shitty as the foster homes had been, the foster parents had fed her three squares a day and made her go to school. There had always been the promise that if Liberty put her head down and worked her ass off, she could save herself.

But Marcus—with all his money and all his power—had never had that hope. All she wanted to do was pull him into her arms and tell him it was going to be all right.

If only that were the worst of it.

But it wasn't because he really was going to fight for her. He really was going to risk everything—his name, his fortune—for her. He'd promised her that and he was going to keep his promise.

She'd tried to tell him that she wasn't good for him, that she'd hurt him. But he hadn't listened.

Well, that had to change, starting right now. She'd tell him about her childhood, about her times in foster care, about all those lies she lived with. He'd understand. After all, he understood how much she needed to make sure William was okay. It hadn't mattered to Marcus that William was a lost baby boy. Marcus would see that Liberty had done what she needed to in order to survive.

They crested the small hill in front of their cabin hut. He didn't even break stride as he ran up the single step that led inside. He only stopped when they reached the raised platform that held the bed.

Hands linked, they stood there for a short second, both of them panting from the run. His head was down and she knew he was hurting. And she knew telling him that she wasn't exactly the woman he thought she was would hurt him even more.

But she couldn't be yet another woman who lied to Marcus Warren. She was better than that. She had to be, if she wanted to be good enough for him. "Marcus," she began, trying to find the words. *I'm black—but I've been passing as white my entire adult life. My mother was an addict and a hooker. And I'm in love with you.*

"Don't talk," he said gruffly, turning and yanking her into his arms. Before she could react, his mouth crushed down onto hers.

It was not a tender kiss, not when his teeth clipped her lower lip. But she didn't pull away, didn't do anything but tilt her head to give him better access. She could taste the desperation on his lips—the confusion, the despair.

"Marcus," she said, pulling back enough that she could form the words. "I need to—"

"Don't want to talk." He jerked at the clasp of her bikini top and savagely pulled it off. The cold air hit her chest, still damp with ocean water, and she shivered when her nipples went tight. Then his mouth was against her bare skin, sucking her nipple into his mouth. "Let me take care of you."

"Marcus…" This wasn't about him taking care of her— she needed to take care of him. She needed to protect him. But his mouth was on her body and he was yanking down her bikini bottoms and sliding his hands up between her legs and…and she couldn't fight the rising surge of desire.

Still, she knew this wasn't about her. It wasn't. This was about him and dammit all, she needed to do something to tell him that she'd be here for him, however he needed her. "It's going to be okay," she said because that's what he needed to hear. Because that was what she'd always wanted to know when she was being thrown around by her mother's fate. She reached for his board shorts and began to pull them down. "Everything's going to be okay."

"Stop talking." He pushed her back down onto the bed and grabbed a condom. Before she'd even gotten his shorts all the way off, he spread her legs and plunged into her with a savageness that she'd never experienced before. She gasped as he filled her completely in one sure stroke, her body shuddering to take him in.

He paused, hovering over her, his head down. He was breathing hard, although she didn't know if that was from the sprint back to their hut or from the conversation with his mother or what.

"It's okay," she murmured. She ran her fingers through his hair, trying to lift his face so she could see him. They'd been lovers for only a week now and she was still getting used to the feeling of Marcus's body joined to hers. "It's okay, baby." She wasn't sure if she was telling him or herself.

She expected him to move—but she didn't expect him to grab her hands and hold them over her head. Then his mouth closed over hers again and he furiously kissed her as he began to thrust.

For the first time, she was completely at his mercy. He'd spent the past week making sure that she was comfortable, that she was okay with what was happening. Any sweetness was gone, however, as he drove into her harder and harder.

If it'd been anyone else, she might have been scared. But this was Marcus and she was his. She'd always been his.

But more than that, he was hers. This raw coupling, this furious need? This was how much he needed her. So instead of trying to reassure him, instead of struggling to get her hands loose so she could touch him, she gave herself over to him completely. This was what he needed and she could give it to him.

He shifted and held both of her wrists with one hand and then grabbed at her bare breast. He pinched her nipple with just enough pressure to make her gasp and, when she did, he covered her mouth with his.

He shifted again, slipping his free hand under her left leg and holding her thigh up so that he could thrust deeper. Electricity filled the air between them, making her skin prickle as her climax began to build. "Yes," she hissed at him. "Oh, yes, Marcus."

"Babe," he groaned, his teeth scraping over the sensitive skin at the base of her neck. Then he pushed back and reached down between her legs, his fingers finding the place where she needed him most.

He pressed and thrust into her, and Liberty couldn't control herself any more than she could control the storms. Her climax broke over her like a clap of thunder. Marcus thrust a few more times before he froze. Then, groaning, he fell forward onto her.

She pulled her arms free of his grasp and hugged him to her. She didn't say anything, though. She didn't need to. She just needed to be here for him.

They lay tangled together, breathing hard, for several minutes before Marcus leaned up on his elbows, a sheepish grin on his face. "Okay?"

"Okay," she agreed. "More than okay." Except she needed to tell him. And she hadn't yet.

Before she could get her mouth to form the words, Marcus said, "Before I had you, I didn't know I could fight back, babe. But I'm going to fight for you—for us. You and me and even William."

The mention of the baby shocked her out of her little speech about mothers and prison and foster care. "William?"

Marcus rolled over and pulled her up into his arms. "I think maybe we should try to apply for custody. Together."

She sat bolt upright. "We should *what*?"

His smile this time was more confident—the smile of a man who knew what he wanted and was used to getting it. This was, after all, Marcus Warren—and very few people said no to him. "I know I'm screwed up and I know my parents probably aren't done with me yet. But it doesn't matter what they think, what anyone thinks, I'm not going to hide you and I'm not going to let you go. I'm going to fight for you, Liberty." He touched her face, his fingertips trailing over her cheek. "I can give you anything you want. And you want William."

"But—I work. I *need* to work. And what about Jenner?"

"I know it bothers you to carry on an affair with your boss. I'm not that fond of the circumstances myself. My father is notorious for sleeping with his assistants, and I want to be better than that. I want us to be on a level playing field."

"But—the baby?"

He shrugged. "We can hire a nanny or you can take some time off. A year."

She stared at him openmouthed. "But…"

"There are no *but*s here, Liberty. I want you. I think I've known that for a long time. I want to wake up in the morning with you in my arms and I want you in my bed every night. You are the one person I trust and I can't imagine life without you anymore. Come live with me." He sat up and touched his head to hers. "Come be my family. You and me and William."

"Marcus…" *I'm black. My mother was a convict.* "You should know—"

He shook his head. "No, I don't want to know. Really, Liberty—it doesn't matter. I can't change your past any more than I can change mine. It doesn't matter any more than my mother's version of what my nanny did matters. It's over and done and I'm not looking over my shoulder anymore. I know what I need to know—that I love you and I want you," he whispered, his thumb stroking over her cheek.

She couldn't. She shouldn't.

Then he said, "Let me be your family, Liberty—that's what I want. Be my family. Be mine."

And how was she supposed to say no to that? If the life she'd been born into truly didn't matter to him, then it didn't matter to her. Jackie Reese was dead and gone, and so was her grubby little baby girl. The woman she was now—that was who mattered. She mattered because Marcus loved her.

"That's what I want, too," she told him.

He began to laugh, a happy noise that couldn't be stopped. And she laughed with him.

Because she wanted to.

Sixteen

"Why are we doing this again?" Liberty stopped in front of the nondescript building that held the offices for the producers of *Feeding Frenzy*.

It'd been two days since they'd left Catalina Island early Saturday morning—hours before the Hanson-Spears wedding had been scheduled to take place. Since then, they'd been ensconced in a suite at the Beverly Hills Hotel, feasting on room service and each other.

Marcus had no idea if Lillibeth had actually gotten married or what his mother had told people about their absence. And what was more, he didn't care. "We have a meeting. It would be rude to bail."

Liberty made a noise of frustration. "I didn't think meeting with reality-show producers was a good idea before we got involved," she said. "And now? I think it's a *really* bad idea."

"I'm not going to do the show," he said, holding her hand as they headed inside. The fact that she was arguing with him made him smile. He couldn't have this kind of honest conversation with anyone else. Just her.

"Then why meet with them at all? You don't have to do this."

"Look." He stopped and turned to face her. "My parents are insane."

"No argument here," she replied, wrinkling her nose.

"But," Marcus went on, "they're right—to a degree," he hastily added when Liberty rolled her eyes. "I do have a business image to maintain. So this isn't about building my brand name. This meeting is more about keeping investment options open. I'll listen to their pitch, politely say it's not for me and who knows? Maybe in a year or three, someone remembers this meeting and they reach out to me with an investment opportunity." He squeezed her hand, hoping she'd see that this was a good compromise. After all, it would be foolhardy to close the door on potential investments. That was his whole business. "I could make movies."

"You could do that anyway. You're Marcus Warren," she reminded him, trying to look stern. But he saw the way the corner of her mouth curved up into a tiny smile. "You can do whatever you want."

"Speaking of that," he murmured, pulling her in closer. "What do you want to do after this? We can see the sights or…" He pressed a kiss right underneath her ear and was rewarded when she shivered.

They'd get this meeting out of the way and then they'd take another day or two to do whatever Liberty wanted. And after that, they'd head back to Chicago and he'd start working on assembling the necessary paperwork to get custody of William.

Liberty would move in, of course. And if she didn't like his place, they'd get a new place, one that was theirs and not just his. And he'd have to get a ring. "Or we could fly to Vegas and get married."

Liberty jolted against him. "Marcus..." she said in a quiet voice. "Let's—let's get through this first."

He looked at her—was that reluctance in her voice? But she gave him a huge smile, as if maybe getting married was exactly what she was thinking, too. "Think about it—but no Beach Blanket Bingo. That's final."

She laughed and he laughed with her. This was right. This was his life on his terms.

They were shown into a conference room. Liberty sat beside Marcus, her tablet out. He smiled to himself as she slipped back into her role as executive assistant as if nothing had happened. The only thing that seemed different about her was the business suit he'd bought for her. Everything else was the same.

The show staff filed into the room. In general, they were all slightly rumpled looking. Rick Chabot, the producer of *Feeding Frenzy*, introduced himself and his coproducers, assistant producers and executive assistants—seriously, how many people were in this entourage?

Finally, all the hands were shaken and they all sat down, Marcus and Liberty at one end of the table, Chabot and his crew at the other. "Now," Chabot said in a different tone from the one he had just used to introduce half of Hollywood. Marcus shot Liberty a look, but all she did was shrug. Chabot was studying his own tablet. "Let's get down to business. You and Ms. Reese are a couple, is that correct?"

"Yes," Marcus said in what he hoped was a casual voice. He'd just spent five minutes introducing her as his assistant. Where the hell had this guy gotten that information?

"That's going to be a problem for *Feeding Frenzy*," Chabot went on, without bothering to look up. One of his group tapped his arm and tilted a screen in his direction.

Chabot nodded and continued. "Gotta be honest with you, Warren—part of your appeal is your availability. You're hot, you're rich—you've got to be single for this show. Someone with her background isn't going to send the right signals to our target viewers, especially not women."

"Excuse me? What background?" He looked at Liberty and was surprised to see that she'd turned a ghastly shade of green.

Chabot studied his tablet before turning a critical eye on Liberty. "Is this correct? Your mother was a convicted drug mule and hooker? She died of an overdose?"

A different person leaned over and pointed at the screen. "Is that a picture of Liberty with her mother? But is she...?" The producer turned the tablet around so that Marcus could see the photo of a young girl, clearly Liberty, standing in front of an apartment building with a gaunt-looking, light-skinned African American woman.

There was a moment of total silence. Marcus knew he needed to say something—it was completely unnecessary to blindside Liberty like this. And it was patently untrue.

Except...

Except Liberty wasn't denying it. She wasn't doing anything—maybe not even breathing. If everything Chabot had just said had been a lie, Liberty would have laughed it off. She wouldn't just be sitting there, looking as if she'd been shot.

Because it wasn't a lie, Marcus realized.

"Where are you getting your information?" Liberty managed to ask in a strangled voice.

"We received an email," Chabot said. "We vet all our candidates thoroughly so we followed up." For the first time, he looked up at Liberty. "It's not personal, you understand."

"No, of course not," she mumbled.

"Now—you have a child you gave up for adoption, is that correct?"

That got an immediate response out of her. "What? No."

Chabot scrolled. "A boy named William? Is that not correct?"

Marcus gaped at her. She couldn't possibly—could she have?

"I do not have a child," Liberty said firmly. "Your source is mistaken."

"We're selling a specific image here—wealthy, powerful," Chabot went on as though Marcus gave a flying rat's ass for what he was saying. "Now, if you two were already married, that might be one thing, but if we're going to take this to the next level…"

He said other things about image and selling, but Marcus didn't hear him. All he could do was stare at Liberty. She did not meet his gaze.

Her mother was African American? An addict? And a hooker? Why hadn't she told him? She couldn't possibly think that it mattered to him, could she? Or had there been another reason she'd kept that part of her hidden?

No, not even hidden. She'd lied to him. And for what? She had to realize that her race was a nonissue to him. But what would she have gained by making him think she was something she wasn't?

I'm not good for you. That's what she'd said, over and over. All those times she'd tried to convince him not to take her to the wedding? Not to do this stupid reality show?

Was this what she'd tried to tell him? Was *this* what he'd said didn't matter?

"…market share," Chabot was saying. "And you can be listed as a producer, of course."

He'd rather gouge out his eye with a rusty spoon. "Well," Marcus said, standing up before he quite knew what he was doing. Because this mattered. This history—he couldn't wrap his head around it. He'd thought…well, he'd thought wrong.

All he knew was that there was no way in hell he was doing anything that would take him to "the next level." He shuddered at the mere thought. What did that even mean? His face on lunch boxes? Did people even have lunch boxes anymore? He didn't know and he didn't want to find out. "We'll be in touch," he lied. Then he turned on his heel and walked right out of that crowded room.

He didn't know if Liberty followed him and he didn't wait around to find out. He didn't want to hear her excuses. He'd heard it all before—from his mother, from Lillibeth. From everyone who wanted a piece of the Warren name, the Warren fortune—but not him. Never him.

They all told him what they thought he needed to hear. To "protect" him. No doubt Liberty would say the same thing. She'd been trying to protect him from the truth—but why? So it could be used against him? Or had there been something more to it? Something sinister?

Idiot. That's what he was. A fool of the first-class order. Because people always wanted something from him. His money, his power, his body—but not him. Never just him. He'd thought Liberty was different. But was she? She'd pushed back against coming to the wedding with him, against this meeting—and she'd made it sound like it was because she was worried about him.

But he saw the truth. She'd been protecting herself and her secrets. How many more did she have? Was this just the tip of the iceberg?

There was always a cost. Everything was a transaction. And if you didn't gain something you lost.

God, he was tired of being the loser. And this time, it was no one's fault but his own.

He realized he was already outside. He didn't remember walking out of the conference room or down the hall.

"Marcus," Liberty said in a soft voice behind him that, yes, had a tinge of fear to it. He could hear her footfalls now as she hurried to catch up.

He kept going. He had a car around here somewhere, a car with a driver. The guy couldn't have gone far.

"Marcus, wait—please."

He didn't want to. He didn't want to give her another second of his time. But he didn't know where his car was and he had no idea where he was going. The confusion metastasized into rage. This was his fault—because he'd dared to be a real man with her.

He didn't feel as real anymore. "Why?" He turned on her. "Why, Liberty?"

She stood before him, her eyes painfully wide. She looked awful and the foolish part of his brain that hadn't gotten the message that she was not to be trusted, she was not safe—she was just like all the rest—wanted to pull her into his arms and tell her it was going to be all right.

It wasn't, though. So he did no such thing.

"I…" She swallowed, clutching her tablet to her chest. Her bag gaped open on her shoulder. She looked as if she'd run after him. Maybe she had. He didn't care. "I called for the car. He's coming right away."

"That's what you have to say? That's it?"

"I didn't—we should—" Her back stiffened. "Can we at least wait for the car? If I'm going to be humiliated for the second time in less than an hour, at least I'd like it to be in private."

"Oh, yes—sure. We wouldn't want any more public humiliations, would we?"

For a moment, he thought she was going to bend. Her

chin dropped and her shoulders hunched and she looked small and vulnerable.

Fine. Good. She could just look that way. It was a trick, a play on his feelings. Well, he'd show her. He'd stop having feelings. That was his mistake; he saw that now. He'd allowed himself to care about someone. Her. He should have learned his lesson after Lillibeth a little better.

But then Liberty rallied. She straightened up and glared at him. "Can we wait for the car, please? Or is it going to make you feel better to put me in my place with an audience?" She glanced around them with an exaggerated motion.

Yes, people were milling around. No one was paying them a lot of attention, though. "You know what? It's not. It's not going to make me feel any better. But how tender of you to pretend you care."

"I do care," she responded, the fire lighting in her eyes. "Don't you dare imply I don't."

The rage in his chest built, swirling back on itself like a hailstorm picking up speed. God dammit, he could do some damage right now. He could leave a wake of destruction in his path and watch the world burn.

"You're a fine one to be talking about daring. When were you going to tell me? Or were you going to wait until we'd adopted that baby? Until we had children of our own?"

"William is not my child." She paused, as if she was collecting herself. Or was she just trying to get her story straight? "He couldn't be. You were my first."

"You were a *virgin*?" he roared.

She flinched as if he'd slapped her. Heads around them turned. If people hadn't noticed them before, they sure as hell did now. "Marcus—the car—"

But the storm of rage kept on swirling and he couldn't fight it. "And you didn't feel like you should have mentioned that at some point?"

"I tried," she snapped. "I tried to tell you about all of it. You're the one who said the past was the past, and my past didn't matter any more than yours did. You're the one who cut me off. So, yes, I did feel like I should have mentioned it at many points. And I didn't because you didn't want me to."

"Because I thought you'd gotten your heart broken or you had to, I don't know, work your way through college—something common like that! I never imagined you were passing as white and hiding this! Because that seems important to me. I was going to marry you, for God's sake! I wanted to have a family with you! I trusted you with everything, Liberty. Everything. Things I've never told anyone else because I love you. And you didn't. You obviously didn't trust me at all."

"Marcus," she pleaded as tears started to drip down her cheeks. "I wanted to tell you but—"

"No. If you'd wanted to, you would have." Her tears were not going to move him. Not even a bit. "And you know what? It doesn't even matter. I don't care."

"You…don't?" Her chest hitched up as her eyes swam.

"An honest conversation, Liberty. That's all I wanted. That's what I thought I was having. I mean—is it all a lie? Did you even run?"

She flinched. "No. I never ran before I met you."

Everything he thought he knew about her was based on a lie. The past three years, their morning run together—that time had saved him. Because he had Lake Michigan and Liberty and the freedom to run, he'd been able to get past Lillibeth's betrayal. He'd been able to deal with the pressure his parents put on him.

He didn't think he'd be able to run his way out of this storm. "Nothing but lies. And why? Was it just so you could trick me into marrying you? So you could have a piece of the Warren name?"

That got a reaction out of her. "Don't be ridiculous, Marcus. I hate your name and I hate what your family has done to you because of it." The force of her anger pushed him back a step.

"Then why? And I want a real answer, Liberty. No more lies."

"Why? Have you ever tried being a black woman in this world? We aren't all born with a collection of silver spoons to choose from, Marcus."

He wasn't going to be relieved that she was fighting back, that he'd always loved how she argued with him when most everyone else would tell him what they thought he wanted to hear. The Liberty he'd loved had been a lie.

"Yes, my mother was black and yes, my father was probably white. I don't know. All I know is that passing meant I only had to work twice as hard to get out of the gutter instead of four times as hard. So yes, I passed. Yes, I let everyone think I was a middle-class white girl. I'm not about to apologize for what I had to do to survive."

"I don't want you to apologize for surviving, dammit."

"Then what do you want from me?"

"I wanted the *real* you, Liberty."

Her eyes flicked behind him. "The car is here. I'll be happy to tell you what it was like growing up with a hooker junkie for a mother and being bounced around from foster home to foster home—in the damned car, Marcus."

"No, I'm done. I'm *done*, Liberty. Do you realize that I risked everything for you? I stood up to my mother for you, I bailed on commitments for you—I would have done anything for you." His voice caught in his throat but he ignored that. "I would have fought for you, Liberty."

She looked at him with so much pity in her eyes that it made him physically nauseous. All his rage seemed to blow itself out and suddenly he was tired.

He'd wanted things to change and change they had. Why hadn't he considered the option that they might change for the worse?

Because it got worse when she stepped in closer to him and laid her palm against his cheek and, fool that he was, he let her. He should push her away and put her in her place and make sure she knew that no one screwed over a Warren. No one. "I didn't want you to fight for me," she said, her voice soft and gentle. "I wanted you to fight for yourself."

Her words hit him like a gut punch. What the hell was she talking about? Of course he fought for himself! He was Marcus Warren, dammit all!

But before he could tell her that, she turned and, head held high, walked off. He thought she was heading for the front gate, but he wasn't sure. "What are you doing?" he called after her.

"Take the car. I'll make my own way home."

"That's it?" For some reason, he didn't want to watch her walk away. It wasn't that he wanted her to stay—he didn't. He just…he wanted the last word. He wanted to do the walking, dammit.

She stopped and looked back at him and he was horrified to see she was crying again. "That's all there can be. We both know it. Maybe we always did."

"Sir?" Marcus started. The driver was standing next to him, looking deeply concerned. "Sir, would you like me to get the young lady?"

That's all there can be.

"Can you get me another car here within ten minutes?"

"Yes, sir."

Marcus nodded toward Liberty's retreating form. "Take her wherever she wants to go."

That's all there was.

And she was right, damn her. They both knew it.

Seventeen

If Liberty knew where her mother was buried, she'd go to the graveside. She had so many questions and for maybe the only time in her life, she felt as if her mother might have had some answers.

Or at least, one answer. Was this what Jackie Reese had felt like when her prince in polyester failed to rescue her?

Not that Liberty had wanted Marcus to rescue her. But for a few days—less than two weeks—he'd been her knight in shining armor, ready to take on all comers to defend her from the cruelties of the world.

Liberty didn't know where her mother was interred. For that matter, she didn't know where Grandma Devlin had been buried, either. Liberty had no connection to her childhood. She didn't see people from the projects. She didn't have any old friends who kept her up-to-date on the neighborhood gossip. Hell, there wasn't even a neighborhood anymore. Most of the Cabrini-Green projects had been leveled to make way for trendy new housing, the likes of which all her old neighbors would've never been able to afford. Maybe that was the point.

Her old life was so far removed from the person she'd willed herself to be that it didn't seem as if she could be both versions of Liberty Reese. And being Jackie Reese's daughter was not the better option.

So she'd stopped being Jackie's daughter. That hadn't been a chapter—it'd been a completely different book, one that was finished and done and had no other bearing on her life now. As Marcus had almost come to believe, the past was past.

Except it wasn't. Liberty would never be free of Jackie.

She hadn't lied to Marcus. Okay, well—she had maybe bent the truth. But that wasn't the real problem.

No, Liberty had lied to herself. She'd convinced herself that Jackie Reese's daughter didn't exist and, as such, wasn't important. That's what little Liberty had always felt like back then. Unimportant.

But the woman she'd become? That Liberty was *important*. She was valuable because she made herself valuable. She worked harder and longer than anyone else. She had saved herself. To hell with princes.

She had no prince. In fact, she had no one.

Well, almost no one. Two days after she'd walked away from Marcus Warren, she knocked on Hazel's door and waited. She should have called before she came, but she'd been afraid that Hazel might not have let her come over. The older woman still might not let her in, but Liberty was desperate. She knew that this William was not the same as the little brother who had died all those years ago, unwanted and unloved. But this baby, here and now, felt like her only living connection to a past she'd tried to bury.

"Yes? Oh, Ms. Reese!" Hazel's large eyes looked up at

her through her thick glasses. "I wasn't expecting you or Mr. Warren today." She peered around Liberty, looking for Marcus.

"Actually, he's not here," Liberty said. There. She'd managed to keep her voice surprisingly level. She could do this.

"Oh." Hazel gave her an odd look, but Liberty ignored it.

"May I see William?"

"Of course, dear. Come in. Mind the door."

Liberty entered and followed Hazel up the steps. Tomorrow, she was going to go into Marcus's office after hours, when she knew he wouldn't be there, and clean out her desk. Then she was going to start applying for jobs. She wasn't even going to bother contacting Erik Jenner. That was too close to Marcus.

She was unemployed and starting over from scratch for the second time in her life. Which had led her to one unavoidable conclusion—this would be her last visit with William. She couldn't afford to let herself get any more attached to the child than she already was because she could not afford the child and if she did get a job, she didn't know where she'd wind up. It'd be for the best if she weren't in Chicago anymore. Too many versions of her past here.

"...Ms. Reese?"

Liberty shook herself out of her thoughts. Hazel was standing just inside the nursery, a look of concern on her face. "I'm sorry?"

"I asked if everything was all right." She peered at Liberty with owlish eyes. "With you and Mr. Warren."

Oh. That. "I don't..." But her words trailed off as she saw William rocking in the brand-new swinging chair that Marcus had bought just for him, and her chest felt as if it was going to collapse back into itself. The whole room was a giant reminder of how very much Marcus had cared—for William, for her.

This was going to hurt more than she'd thought it would.

She understood that he felt betrayed. She couldn't blame him for that. But what stung even more was that he'd promised to fight for her—and he hadn't. It hadn't mattered how valuable she'd made herself and it hadn't mattered how much she truly cared for him. All that had mattered was that she hadn't fully disclosed the most painful parts of her life.

"I don't think that Mr. Warren and I will be able to apply to adopt William," she said, plucking the infant out of the swing. William made a small mewling noise as Liberty tucked him against her chest. His tiny body was so warm, so fragile.

"Dear, I'm so sorry to hear that. You two… I had hoped…" Hazel's voice trailed off.

Yeah, they'd all hoped. Liberty sat down and stared at William's face, trying to commit every last detail to memory. She'd come so close to being able to hold on to this child—to being able to hold on to Liberty Reese. But she'd flown too close to the sun and what went up had to come back down. "I came to say goodbye." She said it more to the baby than to Hazel.

William blinked up at her, his tiny little mouth stretching out. She desperately wanted to think that he knew her now, that the sound of her voice or the smell of her skin was familiar to him. That, somehow, he'd remember there once had been a woman who loved him so much that she'd risked her safe, comfortable life for him.

And Marcus said she never risked anything.

"Will you take our picture together?" she asked, shifting to retrieve her phone. The company phone, with all the company communication on it. She'd have to bite the bullet and get her own phone after this. She couldn't keep Marcus's property. And the dresses—those would have to go back, too. Part of her wanted to return them herself or sell them—that money could carry her for months while she hit the job market.

But that would be another level of dishonesty. Marcus would assume that she'd been with him only for the money. As much as she was worried about her financial future, she couldn't bring herself to lower his opinion of her any more.

Hazel cleared her throat and took the phone. With some fussing, she managed to take a few pictures. "You belong together," she said, handing the phone back.

"I know." It was only after she'd said it that Liberty realized she didn't know whom Hazel was referring to— Liberty and William? Or Liberty and Marcus?

"Dear," Hazel began delicately. "It might be best—for the baby—if you kept visiting for as long as you're able."

"Really?" Oh, how Liberty wanted to believe that. But was Hazel telling her what she thought she needed to hear?

"Oh, yes. He knows you, you know. And he's still settling in after that rough start…" Hazel looked at her hopefully. "I know it can't be a permanent thing. When you're a foster mother, everything is in a constant state of change. Babies come and go, and all I can do is try to give them the best start I can. He's already lost his mother. They haven't found her, you know. I don't think it'd be good for the little angel to lose you so soon, too."

Liberty's throat started to close up. "I'm—" She had to pause and take a breath. "I'm going to be looking for a new job. I might have to move soon."

"I understand. But even for a few more weeks…" She looked at William and smiled. "They know when they're loved. Trust me, it makes such a difference later on."

Wasn't that the thing that had saved her? Grandma Devlin had loved her. She'd never been able to take Liberty in, but knowing the older woman was right down the hall with a cookie and a story and a hug—that she'd be there when Liberty left the foster homes—that was what had kept Liberty going throughout a hellacious childhood.

"All right," Liberty agreed, trying her hardest not to sob and doing a lousy job of it. "If you say so."

Hazel made satisfied noises and bustled off to get William a bottle. When Liberty and the baby were alone, she leaned down and whispered, "I love you, William. I always will."

He sighed against her cheek.

And Liberty let herself cry.

Marcus waited at the office the next day and the day after that, but Liberty did not show up. He took that to mean that she didn't intend to come back to work. Fine. Great. He needed a new assistant and that was inconvenient, but whatever. He'd work around it.

This did not explain why he left explicit instructions with the security guards to call him the moment she came back. She'd left all of her things, after all. She'd be back. And when she did finally show up…

Well, he'd know about it.

He didn't want to speak to her again. But when his phone rang at nine fifteen at night and Lester the security guard was on the other end, telling him that Liberty had entered the building, Marcus still hurried down to his car and took off for the office.

As he drove, he wondered what the hell he was doing. He didn't need to confront her. He'd pretty much said what he needed to say. He was just…making sure she didn't walk off with office supplies or change all the passwords out of spite. That was all.

She wasn't there. "You just missed her," Lester said, sounding sympathetic.

Marcus noticed that the older man wasn't meeting his gaze. "Is that a fact?"

"Yes, sir," Lester said. He had nothing else to add.

Marcus went up to the office anyway—just to be sure. Liberty's shower supplies were missing from the bathroom. Her area was as neat as a pin, as always—but the drawers were empty. He checked.

She was just…gone. It was almost as if she'd never even existed.

Then he saw it—her company phone sat on the corner of his desk and underneath it was a small white envelope with *Marcus* written in Liberty's neat hand across the front.

He didn't want to read it.

But that's exactly what he did.

Marcus,

I will never forgive myself for the pain I have caused you. This was never my plan. I didn't want things to change because I thought I had everything I needed. I was wrong about that, too.

I think it's best for me to move on. I won't take the job with Jenner, so you won't have to worry about explaining anything.

Please don't hold any of this against William. None of this was his doing. I just wanted something better for him than what I had.

I hope you figure out what you want and you fight for that. Not for me, not for your parents—for you, Marcus. If there's one thing life has taught me, it's that you have to save yourself. No one else is going to do it for you.

Thank you for everything. The last three years have been a gift I don't deserve.

Love,

Liberty

He picked up her phone. He didn't know why he remembered her password and he didn't know why he entered it.

The phone didn't open up on the home screen. Instead, it opened up on the last app that had been used, and Marcus wasn't ready for what he saw.

There was Liberty, looking as if she hadn't slept in days. She had William in her arms.

The sight of the two of them—it tore right through him. Because he'd spent the past two weeks allowing himself to think of a different life from the one he had. He'd pictured running in the morning with Liberty as they pushed the jogging stroller. And later, Saturdays at soccer parks and movies on the couch and silly songs and dancing around. Taking Liberty to bed at night and waking up with her in his arms in the morning.

He had everything he wanted, he told himself as he stared at that photo. He didn't need her. He didn't need kids. He absolutely did not need a big, happy family.

And what the hell was she talking about? He was Marcus Warren and that meant something. That's what his mother had said and she was right. She was…

Marcus froze, his heart suddenly pounding so hard he was afraid it would rip right out of his chest. *His mother.*

She and his father—they'd hired a private investigator who'd dug up enough dirt on his old nanny to put her and most of her family in jail.

She was very disappointed in him.

And suddenly, Liberty's past had appeared out of nowhere.

He grabbed his phone out of his pocket and, before he could think better of it, dialed his mother. "Marcus, darling," she cooed. "How are you? Are you all right? I've been so worried about you."

He didn't even have to ask the question—she'd already answered it. No one else knew that Liberty was gone.

But she knew. Of course she did. She—she and his father—had been behind the breakup.

There were, however, a few questions remaining. "How long have you known?"

There was an unnervingly long pause before Marisa Warren cleared her throat and said, "Known about what, darling?"

"About Liberty. About her past."

"Really, Marcus—you've got to be smarter about these things. Once you're settled down with the right kind of woman—"

"Answer the damned question, Mother. How long have you known about her?"

"Why, since you hired her, dear. You didn't really think I was going to let a nobody with no name and no family just ingratiate herself into your life without finding out something about her, did you?"

Why was he surprised? He shouldn't be. And he wasn't going to give his mother the satisfaction of thinking she'd one-upped him. "So let me get this straight—you dug up all the dirt you could find, or thought you could find—on my assistant and then sat on it for three years?"

His mother didn't reply.

Keeping his voice level was the hardest thing he'd ever done. But he wouldn't give her the satisfaction, dammit. "You've been waiting this whole time for the chance to use Liberty's past against her, haven't you? Not even against her. Against me. You sat on this information for three damned years because you knew you could use it to keep me in line, didn't you? *Didn't you?*"

So much for keeping his voice level. He didn't care. No one was around to hear him. He was completely alone because he'd fallen right into the trap without even realizing it had been set for him.

He'd done exactly what his mother wanted him to do. He'd pushed Liberty away.

"You're being ridiculous, Marcus. Think of what she could have cost you. And that baby? What were you think—"

He hung up. And when she called him right back, he turned his phone off.

Everything had a price and you either gained or you lost. That was the game he'd been raised to play. You gained favors and cashed them in when you needed them. Failure to do so meant you lost the game—you lost face, you lost business, you lost your name. Winners or losers, that's who made up the world, and Warrens were always winners. Always.

Except the game was a lie. He wasn't a player. He was a pawn. He was never supposed to win anything. He was nothing more than a favor to be accrued or cashed in. Everyone wanted something from him.

Except for Liberty. She hadn't asked him for anything. Not even a recommendation. And she would do anything for that baby. Including risking her job—and her heart.

If there's one thing life has taught me, it's that you have to save yourself. No one else is going to do it for you. That line from Liberty's note jumped out at him.

He hadn't thought he needed saving. He hadn't realized he had to fight for himself. He wasn't some helpless newborn. He had the ways and means to accomplish what he wanted.

But had he? Or had he just gone along with his parents to get by? He saw now what Liberty meant—what she'd always meant when she'd told him not to go to the wedding because he didn't want to, not to meet with the producers because he didn't want to.

All this time, she'd been telling him to fight for what he wanted.

He picked up her phone again and looked at the picture of Liberty and William. He loved her—he loved them both. What he'd wanted was a family. Liberty and William and more babies—one big happy family. His forever family.

He knew what he wanted.

Now he just had to fight for it.

No one was going to stand in his way this time.

Eighteen

"Ms. Reese? This is Trish Longmire of the One Child, One World charity."

"Hello," Liberty said, stopping in the middle of the sidewalk and fiddling with her new phone so that she could hear better. She had about two blocks to go before she got to Hazel's house. This was her third visit this week to feed and cuddle William.

She tried to think—had she applied at this organization? She'd sent out a lot of résumés, but she didn't recognize the name. The sun beat down on her head and she began to sweat. "How can I help you?"

"One Child provides basic school supplies to children living at or below the poverty line and grants to upgrade classroom technology at schools in need, primarily schools on reservations."

"A noble cause," Liberty said. Education had saved her from crushing poverty, after all. "But I have to ask—what does this have to do with me?"

"The Longmire Foundation has given us a considerable endowment and a mandate to get computers into classrooms."

The Longmire Foundation? That name she recognized—Nate Longmire was the Boy Billionaire of Silicon Valley who'd made headlines when he'd married a young woman no one had ever heard of from...

Oh, God. "I'm sorry—did you say Trish *Longmire*?"

Trish laughed. "Yes. We're expanding our efforts. I'd like to offer you the job of our urban outreach coordinator. You were highly recommended."

"But—who? I haven't applied for the job!" she said, her voice squeaking. Was this happening?

"Marcus Warren," Trish said, although Liberty should have guessed—who else could it be? "We need someone who's comfortable in both underprivileged classrooms, and organizing and attending fundraising events. I understand that you can personally attest to the value of a good education in changing your circumstances, but you've spent the last three years singlehandedly managing Warren Capital," Trish went on. "That makes you uniquely qualified."

"I—am?" Liberty cleared her throat. She needed to be making a better impression here. But she'd spent years—*years*—hiding her childhood. And this woman was telling her it was an asset? "I am, of course. Qualified, that is. I, um..." she babbled. "I'm sorry. This is quite unexpected."

"I understand. I'd like to fly you out to San Francisco next week so we can work out the details, if you're interested in the position."

"Of course. That would be—San Francisco. Yes!"

She and Trish exchanged emails, and then the call ended. Liberty sagged against the parking meter, staring at the screen of her new phone. What had just happened? Had Marcus really called up the wife of another billionaire and recommended Liberty? For a job? For which she was "uniquely qualified"?

She hadn't seen him since the blowup in the parking lot a week and a half ago. She hadn't heard from him, either— not so much as a peep. True, she hadn't exactly left her new number or anything but...

It was over. She'd kept the truth from him and he'd broken his promise to fight for her and that was that. That's all there could be.

Wasn't it?

On shaky legs, she managed to walk the rest of the way to Hazel's house. The shocks just kept right on coming, though, because Marcus's sleek Aston Martin was parked out front.

Oh, God. Marcus was here. Liberty was physically a hot mess—she'd sweat through the back of her tank top and her hair was frizzing. And Marcus was here. With William.

Oh, *God*.

But before she could bolt, the door swung open and there was Hazel, all big smiles. "Ah, Ms. Reese—Mr. Warren is waiting for you."

"He is? How did he know when I'd be here?"

"Oh," Hazel said, shooing her inside and waiting until Liberty hip checked the door shut, "he called shortly after your last visit." She scurried up the stairs with more energy than Liberty had ever seen out of her. "William is so glad to see him again—you can just tell."

Liberty stared at Hazel's back. Maybe none of this was real. Maybe she'd fallen getting off the bus and hit her head and was currently hallucinating. That would be almost as plausible as a job offer out of the blue and Marcus cuddling a happy William.

Stuck somewhere between panic and disbelief, she followed Hazel upstairs and into the nursery. What was Marcus doing here? What was he doing, period?

Oh. He was playing with a baby, that's what. Marcus Warren, one of the most powerful men in all of Chicago—if not the nation—was sitting on the floor of Hazel's nursery, making circles with William's legs and going "whee!" And William? He was kicking his little legs in what looked like sheer joy every time Marcus paused.

"She's here!" Hazel crowed in victory.

Marcus paused mid-*whee* and looked up at Liberty. "Hey, William," he said, carefully turning the infant around. "Look who's here."

William's legs kept right on kicking and his plump arms lifted in her direction. Hazel was right. William did know her.

"Marcus?" she managed to get out. "What did you do?"

That grin—that was the look he always got on his face when he didn't take no for an answer. And he was looking at her. When she didn't pick William up, he tucked the little boy against his chest and surged to his feet. "Hazel," he said, leaning around Liberty, "could you give us a moment?"

"Of course!" Hazel clapped—actually clapped—before she hurried to the kitchen. Liberty heard humming.

"Marcus," she said again, trying to sound stern. "What are you doing?"

The smile dimmed a bit. "Visiting William. Asking Hazel about what I need to do to apply for custody."

Liberty's mouth dropped open, but she quickly got it closed again. "Custody? Why would you do that?"

"Because I want to," he said simply.

"And—the charity? I just got a job offer—in San Francisco? What was that about?"

He shrugged, as if personally getting her a job was no big deal. "You need the work. I know you. I know you won't be happy if you don't have something to manage."

"But…why? Why did you do that for me? My past—you're done. We're done."

"About that." He shifted William in his arms and pressed a gentle kiss to the top of William's fuzzy little head. "I've been thinking about what happened and I owe you an apology."

She didn't even bother trying to get her mouth closed this time. "But—"

"No *but*s. Hear me out. Did you stop and wonder about how those producers knew so much about you? Do you remember Chabot saying they'd gotten an email?"

"I…guess? But so much happened—I didn't think…" But now that he mentioned it, that had seemed odd. "Who?"

"Well. It turns out that my mother had you investigated back when I first hired you and she'd been…saving these details, shall we say, until she could use them to her best advantage."

Liberty gasped, her hand against her chest. The violation was a physical thing, one that made breathing hard. Marisa Warren had known the whole time. "She *what*?"

There had been hundreds of opportunities for Marisa to use that information, too. She could have demanded that Liberty do what she wanted or she'd expose Liberty and all her little lies. But she hadn't. She'd waited for three years.

Marcus nodded grimly. "It was a lousy thing to do to you. You didn't deserve to be ambushed like that. She wouldn't deign to apologize, so I'll do it for her. I'm so sorry, Liberty."

"You're apologizing for her?"

William made a little noise and Marcus adjusted his hold on the baby. "And for myself. I should have listened to you—you were right. The whole weekend was a disaster and I…" He sighed. "I acted like a Warren. And that's not who I am. I want to be better for you. If you'll give me a second chance, I'll be better."

Liberty looked at the tiny baby, her second chance to make things right. "There's something else I should tell you, though, Marcus. The last time my mother went to prison—she went three times—and I was in my third foster home, she had a baby. He was born addicted to God only knows what. He didn't live past three weeks. I don't think he ever had a name. I never saw him. But I named him William because it was a good, strong name. Just like I named this baby."

"Is that all? Because if we're going to make this work, Liberty, I need you to be completely honest with me."

Were they going to make this work? Was that what he was doing here? For the first time, she began to hope this wasn't a dream. If this were really happening... "I don't like to run. But I do it anyway because I get to do it with you. Not at first—at first it was just because I needed a job. I needed to make myself valuable and if that's what it took, then that's what I did. I needed to be someone important, Marcus. And then, when I actually became that person, I couldn't untangle myself from all the little lies I'd told. I wanted to tell you, I did. But I was so afraid that if I did, you wouldn't look at me and see the woman I'd made myself into—all you'd see was Jackie Reese's daughter, and I didn't want to be that person ever again. I never did it to hurt you. I never tried to trick you. I tried to tell you. I just..."

He nodded, as if he truly did understand. "You just did it to survive."

"Yes," she agreed weakly. "I hope you can forgive me."

"Oh, babe," he said. Somehow, he'd gotten closer to her. With William cradled in one arm, he reached out and cupped her face. "Only if you can forgive me. That producer caught me off guard, but that doesn't excuse my actions. I made a promise to you—that I would fight for you, that I would protect you—and when the shit hit the fan, I didn't."

"You didn't," she said. She couldn't get her voice any higher than a whisper, though. Marcus Warren, the billionaire, was apologizing—to her. "You said it didn't matter, but it did."

No, that wasn't right. Because this was just Marcus. He was a little messed up, but he was a good and honorable man trying to make things right.

"It doesn't matter. Does knowing my nanny might have tried to kidnap me matter to you? Or the fact that I almost ran away to Germany—does that matter?"

"Of course not. That's not who you are now."

"Just like your mother's past isn't your present—or our future. I know I haven't earned your trust, but I'd like another chance." He slid his hand down her neck and pulled her in closer. "This time, I won't fail you."

Please don't let this be a dream. Or, if it was, Liberty didn't ever want to wake up. "But I'm a nobody. Why would you do that for me?"

"Because," he said, his lips curling up into a smile. He leaned down and, without squishing the baby, touched his forehead to hers. "The smartest, kindest woman I know told me to figure out what I wanted and go do it. Not because anyone else thought I should, but simply because that's what I want. So that's what I'm doing."

"But…me?" The baby sneezed and they both looked down at him. Liberty touched the top of his head with her hand. "And William?"

"I want you—both of you. I want to be a big happy family." He tilted her head back and stared down into her eyes.

"But you just got me a job in San Francisco."

That made him grin. "No, I recommended you for a job as an urban coordinator. They're branching out. As Nate explained to me, not all Native Americans live on reservations. And we happen to live in Chicago, which is urban. But even if you can't be based here, we could go together. We can start someplace new. I'll be happy anywhere—as long as I have you." He lowered his face to hers. He was going to kiss her, she realized—and she wouldn't have it any other way.

"I'm not good for you." She whispered the words against his lips. "I'll always be the daughter of a convicted criminal. People will always talk."

"Then be bad for me. None of that matters. What's important is you and me and what we know is true. Marry me, Liberty. Be my forever family. Let me prove that I'll never stop fighting for you—for us." He glanced down at William, who was watching this whole thing with big eyes. "For all of us. Right, buddy?"

William cooed.

"Oh, Marcus." Then there weren't any more words because she was kissing him and he was kissing her and they were trying not to squish the baby in between them.

"Is that a yes?" he asked.

"Yes." She lifted William from his arms and then leaned into Marcus as he pulled her against his chest. "*Yes*. I'm yours. I always have been."

"And you always will be."

* * * * *

He came to a dead stop and swallowed hard.

Every bit of what she was wearing was borrowed. Yet somehow his new assistant managed to look like a fashion model for an outdoor company. Suddenly, he realized that Dylan was correct. Libby Parkhurst had a kick-ass body.

Libby's eyes snapped open, her expression guarded. "Good morning," she said.

He hated the guilt that choked him. "Libby, I—"

She held up a hand, stopping his instinctive words. "I don't want to talk about it."

They stared at each other for several long seconds. He forced himself to zero in on basics.

He slid one backpack off his shoulder. "I need to make sure the straps are adjusted correctly for you." Without asking, he stepped behind her and helped settle the pack into position. With a few quick tugs, he was satisfied. Finally, he moved in front of her and fiddled with the strap at her chest.

Libby made some kind of squawk or gasp. It was only then he realized his fingers were practically caressing her breasts. He stepped back quickly. "I'm sure you can manage the waistband," he muttered.

"Uh-huh." She kept her head down while she fiddled with the plastic locking mechanism. After a moment, she stared off into the woods. "I'm good."

* * *

How to Sleep with the Boss
is part of The Kavanaghs of Silver Glen series:
In the mountains of North Carolina, one family
discovers that wealth means nothing without love.

HOW TO SLEEP
WITH THE BOSS

BY
JANICE MAYNARD

First Published in Great Britain 2016
By Mills & Boon, an imprint of HarperCollins*Publishers*
1 London Bridge Street, London, SE1 9GF

© 2016 Janice Maynard

ISBN: 978-0-263-91847-2

51-0216

Our policy is to use papers that are natural, renewable and recyclable products and made from wood grown in sustainable forests.The logging and manufacturing processes conform to the legal environmental regulations of the country of origin.

Printed and bound in Spain
by CPI, Barcelona

USA TODAY bestselling author **Janice Maynard** knew she loved books and writing by the time she was eight years old. But it took multiple rejections and many years of trying before she sold her first three novels. After teaching kindergarten and second grade for a number of years, Janice turned in her lesson plan book and began writing full-time. Since then she has sold over thirty-five books and novellas. Janice lives in east Tennessee with her husband, Charles. They love hiking, traveling and spending time with family.

Hearing from readers is one of the best perks of the job!

You can connect with Janice at twitter.com/janice maynard, facebook.com/janicemaynardreaderpage, www.wattpad.com /user/janicemaynard, and instagram.com/janice maynard.

For Caroline and Anna: beautiful daughters,
dear friends, exceptional women…

One

"I want you to push me to my limits. So I can prove to you that I can handle it."

Patrick stared across his paper-cluttered desk at the woman seated opposite him. Libby Parkhurst was not someone you would pick out of a crowd. Mousy brown hair, ordinary features and clothes at least one size too big for her slender frame added up to an unfortunate adjective. *Forgettable.*

Except for those eyes. Green. Moss, maybe. Not emerald. Emerald was too brilliant, too sharp. Libby's green eyes were the quiet, soothing shade of a summer forest.

Patrick cleared his throat, absolutely sure his companion hadn't intended her remark to sound provocative. Why would she? Patrick was nothing more to her than a family friend and a prospective employer. After all, Libby's mother had been his mother's best friend for decades.

"I appreciate your willingness to step outside your comfort zone, Libby," he said. "But I think we both know this job is not for you. You don't understand what it involves."

Patrick's second in command, Charlise, was about to commence six months of maternity leave. Patrick needed a replacement ASAP. Because he had dawdled in filling the spot, his mother, Maeve Kavanagh, had rushed in to supply an interviewee.

Libby sat up straighter, her hands clenched in her lap, her expression earnest and maybe a tad desperate. "I do," she said firmly. "Maeve described the position in detail. All I'm asking is that you run me through the paces before I have to welcome the first group."

Patrick's business, Silver Reflections, provided a quiet, soothing setting for professionals experiencing burnout, but also offered team-building activities for high-level management executives. Ropes courses, hiking, overnight survival treks. The experience was sometimes grueling and always demanding.

The fill-in assistant would be involved in every aspect of running Silver Reflections. While Patrick applauded Libby's determination, he had serious doubts about her ability to handle the physical aspects of the job.

"Libby…" He sighed, caught between his instincts about filling the position and his obligation to play nice.

His unwanted guest leaned forward, gripping the edge of his desk with both hands, her knuckles white. "I need this job, Patrick. You know I do."

Libby had him there. He'd witnessed in painful detail what the past year had been like for her—as had most of the country, thanks to the tabloids. First, Libby's father had been sent to prison for tax fraud to the tune of several million. Then eight weeks ago, after months of being hounded by the press and forced to adopt a lifestyle far below her usual standards, Libby's emotionally fragile mother had committed suicide.

Quite simply, in the blink of an eye, Libby Parkhurst

had gone from being a sheltered heiress to a woman with virtually no resources. Her debutante education had qualified her to host her father's dinner parties when her mother was unable or unwilling to do so. But twenty-three-year-old Libby had no practical experience, no résumé and no money.

"You won't like it." He was running out of socially acceptable ways to say he didn't want her for the job.

Libby's chin lifted. She sat back in her chair, her spine straight. The disappointment in her gaze told him she anticipated his rejection. "I know your mother made you interview me," she said.

"I'm far past the age where my mother calls the shots in my life." It was only partly a lie. Maeve Kavanagh wielded maternal guilt like a sharp-edged sword.

"I don't have anything left to lose," Libby said quietly. "No home. No family. No trust fund. It's all gone. For the first time in my life, I'm going to have to stand on my own two feet. I'm willing and able to do that. But I need someone to give me a chance."

Damn it. Her dignified bravery tugged at heartstrings he hadn't tuned in ages. Why was Libby Parkhurst his problem? What was his mother thinking?

Outside his window, the late-January trees were barren and gray. Winter still had a firm hold on this corner of western North Carolina. It would be at least eight weeks before the first high-adventure group arrived. In the meantime, Libby would surely be able to handle the hotel aspects of the job. Taking reservations. Checking in guests. Making sure that all reasonable requests were accommodated.

But even if he split Charlise's job and gave Libby the less onerous part, he'd still be stuck looking for someone who could handle the outdoor stuff. Where was he going to find a candidate with the right qualifications willing to work temporarily and part-time?

If this had been an emotional standoff, Libby would have won. She never blinked as she looked at him with all the entreaty of a puppy begging to be fed. He decided to try a different tack. "Our clients are high-end," he said. "I need someone who can dress the part."

Though her cheeks flushed, Libby stood her ground. "I've planned and overseen social events in a penthouse apartment overlooking Central Park. I think I can handle the fashion requirements."

He eyed her frumpy clothing and lifted a brow...not saying a word.

For the first time, Libby lowered her gaze. "I suppose I hadn't realized how much I've come to rely on the disguise," she muttered. "I've dodged reporters for so long, my bag-lady routine has become second nature."

Now he was the one who fidgeted. His unspoken criticism had wounded her. He felt the taste of shame. And an urgent need to make her smile. "A trial period only," he said, conceding defeat. "I make no promises."

Libby's jaw dropped. "You'll hire me?"

The joy in her damp green eyes was his undoing. "Temporarily," he emphasized. "Charlise will be leaving in two weeks. In the meantime, she can show you how we run things here at the retreat center. When the weather gets a bit warmer, you and I will do a dry run with some of the outdoor activities. By the end of February, we'll see how things are going."

He had known "of" Libby for most of his life, though their paths seldom crossed. Patrick was thirty...Libby seven years younger. The last time he remembered seeing her was when Maeve had taken Patrick and his brothers to New York to see a hockey game. They had stopped by the Parkhurst home to say hello.

Libby had been a shy redheaded girl with braces and a ponytail. Patrick had been too cool at the time to do more than nod in her direction.

And now here they were.

Libby smiled at him, her radiance taking him by surprise. "You won't be sorry, I swear."

How had he thought she was plain? To conceal his surprise, he bent his head and scratched a series of numbers on a slip of paper. Sliding it across the desk, he made his tone flat...professional. "Here's the salary. You can start Monday."

When she saw the amount, Libby's chin wobbled.

He frowned. "It's not a lot, but I think it's fair."

She bit her lip. "Of course it's fair. I was just thinking about how much money my family used to spend."

"Is it hard?" he asked quietly. "Having to scrimp after a lifetime of luxury?"

"Yes." She tucked the paper in her pocket. "But not in the way you think. The difficult part has been finding out how little I knew about the real world. My parents sheltered me...spoiled me. I barely knew how to cook or how much a gallon of milk cost. I guess you could say I was basically useless."

Feeling his neck get hot, he reached for her hand, squeezing her fingers before releasing her. Something about Libby brought out his protective instincts. "No one is useless, Libby. You've had a hell of a year. I'm very sorry about your mother."

She grimaced, her expression stark. "Thank you. I suppose I should tell you it wasn't entirely a surprise. I'd been taking her back and forth to therapy sessions for weeks. She tried the suicide thing twice after my father's trial. I don't know if it was being without him that tormented her or the fact that she was no longer welcome in her social set, but either way, her pain was stronger than her need to be with me."

"Suicide never makes sense. I'm sure your mother loved you."

"Thank you for the vote of support."

Patrick was impressed. Libby had every right to feel sorry for herself. Many women in her situation would latch onto the first available meal ticket…anything to maintain appearances and hang on to the lifestyle of a wealthy, pampered young socialite.

Libby, though, was doing her best to be independent.

"My mother thinks the world of you, Libby. I think she always wanted a daughter."

"I don't know what I would have done without her."

Silence fell suddenly. Both of them knew that the only reason Patrick had agreed to interview Libby was because Maeve Kavanagh had insisted. Still, Patrick wasn't going to go back on his word. Not now.

It wouldn't take long for Libby to realize that she wasn't cut out for the rigorous physical challenges that awaited her at Silver Reflections. Where Charlise had been an athlete and outdoorswoman for most of her life, Libby was a pale, fragile flower, guaranteed to wilt under pressure.

Over the next two weeks, Patrick had cause to doubt his initial assessment. Libby dived into learning her new responsibilities with gusto. She and Charlise bonded almost immediately, despite the fact that they had little in common, or so it seemed.

Charlise raved about Libby's natural gifts for hospitality. And the fact that Libby was smart and focused and had little trouble learning the computer system and a host of other things Charlise considered vital to running Silver Reflections.

On the second Friday morning Libby was on his payroll,

Patrick cornered Charlise in her office and shut the door. "Well," he said, leaning against the wall. "Is she going to be able to handle it?"

Charlise reclined in her swivel chair, her amply rounded belly a match for her almost palpable aura of contentment. "The girl's a natural. We've already had four clients who have rebooked for future dates based on their interactions with Libby. I can honestly say that I'm going to be able to walk away from here without a single qualm."

"And the outdoor component?"

Charlise's glow dimmed. "Well, maybe a tiny qualm."

"It's one thing to run this place like a hotel. But you and I both know we work like dogs when we take a group out in the woods."

"True. But Libby has enthusiasm. That goes a long way."

"Up until a year ago I imagine she was enjoying pedicures at pricey Park Avenue salons. Hobnobbing with Fortune 500 executives who worked with her dad. It's a good bet she never had anyone steal her lunch money."

Charlise gave him a loaded look. "You're a Kavanagh, Patrick. Born with a silver spoon and everything that goes with it. Silver Reflections is your baby, but you could walk away from it tomorrow and never have to work another day in your life."

"Fair enough." He scratched his chin. "There's one other problem. I told Libby that she would have to dress the part if she planned to work here. But she's still wearing her deliberately frumpy skirts and sweaters. Is that some kind of declaration of independence? Did I make a faux pas in bringing up her clothing?"

"Oh, you poor, deluded man."

"Why does no one around here treat me with respect?"

Charlise ignored his question. "Your mother offered to buy Libby a suitable wardrobe, but your newest employee is independent to say the least. She's waiting to go shopping until this afternoon when she gets her first paycheck."

"Oh, hell."

"Exactly."

"Wait a minute," he said. "Why can't she wear the clothes she had when her dad went to prison? I'll bet she owned an entire couture wardrobe."

"She did," Charlise said, her expression sober. "And she sold all those designer items to pay for her mom's treatments. Apparently the sum total of what she owns can now fit into two suitcases."

Patrick seldom felt guilty about his life choices. He did his best to live by a code of honor Maeve had instilled in all her boys. Do the right thing. Be kind. Never let ambition trump human relationships.

He had hired Libby. Now it was time to let her know she had his support.

Libby was in heaven. After months of wallowing in uncertainty and despair, now having a concrete reason to get up every morning brought her something she hadn't found in a long time…confidence and peace.

For whatever reason, Patrick Kavanagh had made himself scarce during Libby's first two weeks. He'd left the training and orientation entirely up to Charlise. Which meant Libby didn't constantly have to be looking over her shoulder. With Charlise, Libby felt relaxed and comfortable.

They had hit it off immediately. So much so that Libby experienced a pang of regret to know Charlise wouldn't be coming back after today. Just before five, Libby went to Charlise's office holding a small package wrapped in blue paper printed with tiny airplanes. Charlise and her accountant husband were looking forward to welcoming a fat and healthy baby boy.

Libby knocked at the open door. "I wanted to give you this before you go."

Charlise looked up from her chore of packing personal items. Her eyes were shiny with tears. "You didn't have to do that."

"I wanted to. You've been so patient with me, and I appreciate it. Are you okay? Is anything wrong?"

Charlise reached for a tissue and blew her nose. "No. I don't know why I'm so emotional. I'm very excited about the baby, and I want to stay at home with him, but I love Silver Reflections. It's hard to imagine not coming here every day."

"I'll do my best to keep things running smoothly while you're gone."

"No doubts on that score. You're a smart cookie, Libby. I feel completely confident about leaving things in your hands."

"I hope you'll bring the baby to see us when the weather is nice."

"You can count on it." She opened the gift slowly, taking care not to rip the paper. "Oh, Libby, this is beautiful. But it must have been way too expensive."

Libby grimaced. She had been very honest with Charlise about her current financial situation. "It's an antique of sorts. A family friend gave it to my parents when I was born, engraved with the initial *L*. When I heard you say were going to name the baby Lander, after your father, I knew I wanted you to have it."

"But you've kept it all this time. Despite everything that's happened. It must have special meaning."

When Libby looked at the silver baby cup and bowl and spoon, her heart squeezed. "It does. It did. I think I held on to the set as a reminder of happier times. But the truth is, I don't need it anymore. I'm looking toward the future. It will make me feel good to know your little boy is using it."

Charlise hugged Libby tightly. "I'll treasure it."

Libby glanced at her watch. "I need to let you get out of here, but may I ask you one more thing before you go?"

"Of course."

"How did you get this job working with Patrick?"

"My husband and Patrick's brother Aidan are good friends. When Patrick put out the word that he was starting Silver Reflections, Aidan hooked us up."

"And the high-adventure stuff?"

Charlise shrugged. "I've always been a tomboy. Climbing trees. Racing go-karts. Broke both arms and legs before I made it to college. At different times, thank goodness."

"Good grief." Libby thought about her own cocoon-like adolescence. "Do you really think I can handle the team building and physical challenges in the outdoors?"

The other woman paused, her hand hovering over a potted begonia. "Let me put it this way…" She picked up the plant and put it in a box. "I think you'll be fine as long as you believe in yourself."

"What does that mean?"

"I've heard you talk about Patrick. He intimidates you."

"Well, I—" Libby stopped short, unable to come up with a believable lie. "Yes."

"Don't let him. He may come across as tough and intense at times, but underneath it all, he's a pussycat."

A broad-shouldered masculine frame filled the doorway. "I think I've just been insulted."

Two

Libby was mortified to be caught discussing her new boss. Charlise only laughed.

Patrick went to the pregnant woman and kissed her cheek, placing his hand lightly on her belly. "Tell that husband of yours to call me the minute you go to the hospital. And let me know if either of you needs anything… anything at all."

Charlise got all misty-eyed again. "Thanks, boss."

"It won't be the same without you," he said.

"Stop that or you'll make me cry again. Libby knows everything I know. She's exactly who you need… I swear."

Patrick smiled. "I believe you." He turned to Libby. "How about dinner tonight? I've tried to stay out of the way while Charlise showed you the ropes, but I think it would be good for the two of us to get to know each other better. What do you say?"

Libby felt herself flush from her toes to the top of her head. Not that this was a date. It wasn't. Not even close.

But Patrick Kavanagh was an imposing specimen. Despite his comfortably elegant appearance at the hotel, she had the distinct sense that beneath the dark suits and crisp ties lurked someone who was very much a man's man.

The kind of guy who made a woman's toes curl with just one look from his intense blue-gray eyes. He was tall and lean and had a headful of unruly black hair. The glossy, dark strands needed a comb. Or maybe the attention of a lover's fingers.

Her heart thumped hard, even as her stomach tumbled in a free fall. "That would be nice," she said. *Great.* Now she sounded like a child going to a tea party at her grandma's house.

Charlise picked up her purse and a small box. Patrick hefted the larger carton and followed her out of the room, leaving Libby to trail behind. Outside, the air was crisp and cold. She shivered and pulled her sweater more tightly across her chest.

Patrick stowed Charlise's things and hugged her. The affection between the two was palpable. Libby wondered what Charlise's husband was like. Obviously, he must be quite a guy if he let his wife work day after day with the darkly handsome Patrick Kavanagh.

Charlise eased behind the wheel, closed the car door and motioned for Libby to come closer. Patrick's phone had rung, and he was deep in conversation with whoever was on the other end.

Libby rested a hand in the open window and leaned down. "You're going to freeze," she said.

The pregnant woman lowered her voice. "Don't let him ride roughshod over you. You're almost too nice sometimes. Stand up to him if the occasion warrants it."

"Why would I do that? He's the boss."

Charlise grinned and started the engine. "Because he's too damned arrogant for his own good. All the Kavanagh men are. They're outrageously sexy, too, but we women have to draw a line in the sand. Trust me, Libby. Alpha males are like dangerous animals. They can smell fear. You need to project confidence even when you don't feel it."

"Now you're scaring me," Libby said, only half joking.

"I've known Patrick a long time. He admires grit and determination. You'll win his respect. I have no doubt. And don't worry about the survival training. What's the worst that could happen?"

Libby watched the car drive away, burdened with an inescapable feeling that her only friend in the world was leaving her behind in the scary forest. When she turned around, the lights from the main lodge of Silver Reflections cast a warm glow against the gathering darkness.

Since Patrick was still tied up on the phone, she went back to Charlise's office—now Libby's—and printed out the staff directory. She planned to study it this weekend. Facts and figures about everyone from the housekeeping staff to the guy who kept the internet up and running. Even at an executive retreat center famed for creating an atmosphere of solitude and introspection, no one at the level of these guests was going to be happy without a connection to the outside world.

Patrick found her twenty minutes later. "You ready to go? I guess it makes sense to take two cars."

Silver Reflections was tucked away in the mountains ten miles outside of town. In the complete opposite direction stood the magnificent Silver Beeches Lodge. Perched on a mountaintop overlooking Silver Glen, it was owned and operated by Maeve Kavanagh and her eldest son, Liam. Libby hesitated before answering, having second thoughts. "I'm sure you must have better things to do with your weekend. I'm not really dressed for dinner out."

Patrick's eyes darkened with a hint of displeasure. "If it

will make you feel better, I'll include these hours in your paycheck. And dinner doesn't have to be fancy. We can go to the Silver Dollar."

Patrick's brother, Dylan, owned a popular watering hole in town. The saloon was definitely low-key. Certainly Libby's clothing would not make her stand out there. "All right," she said, realizing for the first time that Patrick's invitation was more like an order. "I'll meet you there."

During the twenty-minute drive, she had time to calm her nerves. She already had the job. Patrick wasn't going to fire her yet. All she had to do was stick it out until they did some of the outdoor stuff, and she could prove to him that she was adaptable and confident in the face of challenges.

That pep talk carried her all the way into the parking lot of the Silver Dollar. The requisite pickup trucks were definitely in evidence, but they were interspersed with Lexus and Mercedes and the occasional fancy sports car.

Libby had visited this corner of North Carolina a time or two over the years with her mother. Silver Glen was a high-end tourist town with a nod to alpine flavor and an unspoken guarantee that the paparazzi were not allowed. It wasn't unusual to see movie stars and famous musicians wandering the streets in jeans and baseball caps.

Most of them eventually showed up at the Silver Dollar, where the beer was cold, the Angus burgers prime and the crowd comfortably raucous. Libby hovered on the porch, waiting for Patrick to arrive. The noise and color and atmosphere were worlds away from her native habitat in Manhattan, but she loved it here.

At Maeve's urging, Libby had given up the New York apartment she could scarcely afford and had come to North Carolina for a new start. Truth be told, her native habitat was feeling more and more distant every day.

Patrick strolled into view, jingling his car keys. "Let's

grab a table," he said. "I called Dylan and told him we were on our way."

In no time, they were seated. Libby ordered a Coke… Patrick, an imported ale. Dylan stopped by to say hello. The smiling, very handsome bar owner was the second oldest in the seven-boy Kavanagh lineup. Patrick was the second youngest.

Patrick waved a hand at Libby. "Do you remember Libby Parkhurst? She's going to fill in for part of Charlise's maternity leave."

Dylan shook Libby's hand. "I do remember you." He sobered. "I was sorry to hear about your mother. We have an apartment upstairs here at the Silver Dollar. I'd be happy to give it to you rent-free until you've had a chance to get back on your feet."

Libby narrowed her gaze. "Did your mother guilt you into making me an offer?"

Dylan's neck turned red. "Why would you say that? Can't a man do something nice without getting an inquisition?"

Libby stared from one brother to the other. Apparently, down-on-her-luck Libby had become the family *project*. "If you're positive it won't be an imposition," she said slowly. "I'm taking up a very nice guest room at Maeve's fancy hotel, so I'm sure she'd rather have me here."

Dylan shook his head. "Maeve is delighted to have you *anywhere*. Trust me. But she thought you'd like some privacy."

Patrick studied Libby's face as she pondered the implications of living above the bar. It was hardly what she was used to…but then again, he had no idea what her life had been like after the tax guys had swooped in and claimed their due.

Dylan wandered away to deal with a bar-related problem, and on impulse, Patrick asked the question on his mind. "Will you tell me about this past year? Where you've been? How things unfolded? Sometimes it helps to talk to a neutral third party."

Libby sipped her Coke, her gaze on the crowd. Friday nights were always popular at the Silver Dollar. He studied her profile. She had a stubborn chin, but everything else about her was soft and feminine. He would bet money that after one night in the woods, Libby was going to admit she was in over her head.

When she looked at him, those beautiful eyes gave him a jolt—awareness laced with the tiniest bit of sexual interest. He shut down that idea quickly. Maeve would have his head on a platter if he messed with her protégé. And besides, Libby wasn't his type. Not at all.

Libby's lips curved in a rueful half smile. "It was frightening and traumatic and definitely educational. Fortunately, my mother had a few stocks and bonds that were in her name only. We managed to find an apartment we could afford, but it was pretty dismal. I wanted to go out and look for work, but she insisted she needed me close. I think losing the buffer of wealth and privilege made her feel painfully vulnerable."

"What about your father?"

"We had some minimal contact with him. But Mama and I both felt betrayed, so we didn't go out of our way to visit. I suppose that makes me sound hard and selfish."

Patrick shook his head. "Not at all. A man's duty is to care for his family. Your father deceived you, broke your trust and failed to provide for you. It's understandable that you have issues."

She stared at him. "You speak from experience, don't you? My mother told me about what happened years ago."

Patrick hadn't expected her to be so quick on the uptake. Now he was rather sorry he'd raised the subject. His own father, Reggie Kavanagh, had been determined to find the lost silver mine that had made the first Kavanaghs in North Carolina extremely wealthy. Reggie had spent months, years…looking, always looking.

His obsession cost him his family.

"I was just a little kid," Patrick said. "My brother Liam has the worst memories. But yeah…I understand. My mother had every right to be bitter and angry, but somehow she pulled herself together and kept tabs on seven boys."

Libby paled, her eyes haunted. "I wish I could say the same. But not all of us are as strong as Maeve."

He cursed inwardly. He hadn't meant to sound critical of Libby's mother. "My mother wasn't left destitute."

"True. But she's made of tough stock. Mama was never really a strong person, even in the best of times."

"I'm sorry, Libby."

Her lips twisted, her eyes bleak. "We can't choose our families."

In an instant he saw that this job idea was laden with emotional peril for Libby Parkhurst. When it became glaringly obvious that she couldn't handle the physically demanding nature of Charlise's role as his assistant, Libby would be crushed. Surely it would be better to find that out sooner than later. Then she could move on and look for employment more suited to her skill set. Libby was smart and organized and intuitive.

There was a place for her out there somewhere. Just not at Silver Reflections.

He drummed his fingers on the table. "I looked at the weather forecast. We're due to have a warm spell in a couple of days."

"I saw that, too. Maeve says you almost always get an early taste of spring here in the mountains, even if it doesn't last long."

"She's right. And in light of that, why don't you and

I go ahead and take an overnight trip, so I can show you what's involved."

Libby went from wistful to deer in the headlights. "You mean now?"

"Yes. We could head out Monday morning and be back Tuesday afternoon." Part of him felt guilty for pushing her, but they had to get past this hurdle so she could see the truth.

He saw her throat move as she swallowed. "I don't have any outdoor gear."

"Mom can cover you there. And my sisters-in-law can loan you some stuff, too. No sense in buying anything now."

"Because you think I'll fail."

She stared him down, but he wasn't going to sugarcoat it. "I think there is a good chance you'll discover that working for me isn't what you really want."

"You've made up your mind already, haven't you?" He was surprised to see that she had a temper.

"No." Was he being entirely honest? "I promised you a trial run. I've merely moved up the timetable, thanks to the weather."

Libby's gaze skewered him. "Do I need a list from you, or will your mother know everything I need?"

"I'll email you the list, but Mom has a pretty good idea."

Libby stood up abruptly. "I don't think I'm that hungry, after all. Thank you for the Coke, *Mr. Kavanagh*. If you'll excuse me, it sounds like I have a lot to do this weekend."

And with that, she turned her back on him and walked out of the room.

Dylan commandeered the chair Libby had vacated, his broad smirk designed to be irritating. "I haven't seen you crash and burn in a long time, baby brother. What did you say to make her so mad?"

"It wasn't a date," Patrick said, his voice curt. "Mind your own damned business."

"She could do better than you, no doubt. Great body, I'm guessing, even though her clothes are a tad on the eccentric side. Excellent bone structure. Upper-crust accent. And those eyes... Hell, if I weren't a married man, I'd try my luck."

Patrick reined in his temper, well aware that Dylan was yanking his chain. "That's not funny."

"Seriously. What did you say to run her off?"

"It's complicated."

"I've got all night."

Patrick stared at him. "If you must know, Mom shoved her down my throat as a replacement for Charlise. Libby can handle the retreat center details, but there is no way in hell she's going to be able to do all the outdoor, back-country stuff. When I hired her, she asked me to give her a chance to prove herself. I merely pointed out that the weather's going to be warm the first of the week, so we might as well go for it."

"And that made her mad?"

"Well, she might possibly have assumed that I expect her to fail."

"Smart lady."

"How am I the bad guy here? I run a multilayered business. I can't afford to babysit Mom's misfits."

Dylan's expression went from amused to horrified in the space of an instant.

Libby's soft, well-modulated voice broke the deadly silence. "I left my sweater. Sorry to interrupt."

And then she was gone. Again.

Patrick swallowed hard. "Did she hear what I said?"

Dylan winced. "Yeah. Sorry. I didn't have time to warn you. I didn't see her coming."

"Well, that's just peachy."

The waitress appeared, notepad in hand, to take Patrick's order. "What'll you have?" she asked.

Dylan shook his head in regret. "Bring us a couple of burgers, all the way. My baby brother needs some cheering up. It's gonna be a long night."

Three

Not since the wretched aftermath of her father's arrest had Libby felt so small and so humiliated. She'd thought Patrick liked her...that he was pleased with her work to date. But in truth, Libby had been foisted on him, and he resented her intrusion.

Her chest hurt, almost as if someone had actually sucker punched her. When she made it back to her room on the third floor of Maeve's luxurious hotel, Libby threw herself on the bed and cried. Then she cussed awhile and cried some more. Part of her never wanted to see Patrick Kavanagh again. The other part wanted to make him ashamed for having doubted her. She wanted to be the best damn outdoorswoman he had ever seen.

But since that was highly unlikely to be the actual scenario come Monday, perhaps the best course was to explain to Maeve that the job hadn't worked out.

There would be questions, of course, lots of them. And although there might be other jobs in Silver Glen, perhaps as a shop assistant making minimum wage, it would be difficult to find a place to live on that kind of paycheck. She owed Maeve a huge debt of gratitude. Not for anything in the world did she want to seem ungrateful.

Which left Libby neatly boxed into an untenable situation.

Saturday morning she awoke with puffy eyes and a headache. It was only after her third cup of coffee that she even began to feel normal. Breakfast was out of the question. She felt too raw, too bruised. There was no reason to think Patrick would be anywhere near the Silver Beeches Lodge, but she wasn't taking any chances.

After showering and dressing in jeans and a baggy sweater, Libby sent a text to Maeve, asking her to drop by when she had a minute. In the meantime, Libby studied her paycheck. She had planned to buy the first pieces of her professional wardrobe this weekend. But if she was going to be fired Tuesday night, it made no sense to pay for clothes she might not need.

One step at a time.

When Maeve knocked on the door around eleven, Libby took a deep breath and let her in.

Maeve hugged her immediately. "I want to hear all about the job," she said, beaming. "I saw Charlise in town Wednesday, and she said you were amazing."

Libby managed a weak chuckle. "Charlise is being kind."

The two of them sat down in armchairs beside the gas log fireplace. Although now Libby could barely afford the soap in the bathroom, the upscale accommodations were familiar in their amenities. Growing up, she had traveled widely with her parents.

Maeve smoothed a nonexistent wrinkle from her neatly pressed black slacks. Wearing a matching blazer and a fuchsia silk blouse, she looked far younger than her age, certainly too young to have seven adult sons. "So tell me," she said. "How do you like working for Patrick?"

"Well…" Libby hesitated. She'd never been a good liar, so she had to tiptoe through this minefield. "I've spent most of my time with Charlise. But everyone on the staff speaks very highly of your son."

"But what do *you* think? He's a good-looking boy, isn't he?"

At last Libby's smile felt genuine. "Yes, ma'am. Patrick is a hottie."

"I know I'm prejudiced, but I think all my sons turned out extremely well."

"I know you're proud, and rightfully so."

"Five of them already married off to wonderful women. I think I'm doing pretty well."

Uh-oh. "Maeve, surely you're not thinking about playing matchmaker. That would be extremely uncomfortable for me."

Maeve's face fell. "What do you mean?"

"I'm starting my life from scratch," Libby said. "I have to know I can be an independent person. Although I was too naive to realize it at the time, my parents sheltered me and coddled me. I want to learn how to negotiate the world on my own. Romance is way down the list. And besides, even I know it's not a good idea to mix business with pleasure."

If a mature, extremely sophisticated woman could sulk, that's what Maeve did. "I thought you'd appreciate my help."

"I *do*," Libby said, leaning forward and speaking earnestly. "You looked out for me at the lowest point in my life. You helped me through Mama's death and took me in. I'll never be able to thank you enough. But at some point, you have to let me make my own choices, my own mistakes. Otherwise, I'll never be sure I can survive on my own."

"I suppose you're right. Is that why you wanted to see me this morning? To tell me to butt out?"

Libby grinned, relieved that Maeve had not taken offense. "No. Actually, I need your help in rounding up some hiking gear. Patrick wants to take advantage of the warm weather coming up to teach me what I'll need to know for the team-building, outdoor-adventure expeditions."

"So soon? Those usually don't begin until early April."

"I think he wants to be sure I can handle the physical part of the job." Libby spoke calmly, but inwardly she cringed, Patrick's words still ringing in her ears. *I can't afford to babysit Mom's misfits.*

Maeve stared at her intently. Almost as if she could tell something else was going on. "Write down all your sizes," she said. "I'll gather everything you need and meet you here tomorrow around one."

"I really appreciate it."

Maeve stood. "I have a lunch appointment, so I need to run. You'll get through this, Libby. I know how strong you are."

"Mentally or physically?"

"They go hand in hand. You may surprise yourself this week, my dear. And you may surprise Patrick, as well."

Patrick's mood hovered somewhere between injured grizzly and teething toddler. He was ashamed of himself for letting his aggravation make him say something stupid. But damn it, he'd been talking to his brother…letting off steam. He didn't go around kicking puppies and plucking the heads off flowers.

He was a nice guy.

Unfortunately for him, he could think of at least one person who didn't think so.

During the weekend, he gathered the equipment he would need to put Libby through her paces. Normally, he and Charlise shared the load: supervising the employees who organized the meals, interacting with the executives, teaching skills, coaching the group through difficult activities.

But Charlise was not only accustomed to being outdoors, she also had a great deal of experience in living off the land.

Libby didn't. It was as simple as that.

Patrick tried to juggle things in his mind, ways for him to take over some of Charlise's duties so that Libby could handle a lighter load. But that would only postpone the inevitable. This first experience had to play out as closely as possible to the real thing, so Libby would understand fully what was involved and what she could expect.

By Monday morning, his mood hadn't improved. He'd gone through his checklist on autopilot, but of course, he'd had to cover Charlise's prep, as well. He arrived at Silver Reflections several minutes before eight so he would have some time to mentally gear up for the day's events.

Libby's car was already parked in the small wooded lot adjacent to the building. It was an old-model Mercedes with a badly dented fender. Suddenly Patrick remembered where he had seen the car before. Liam's wife had driven it a couple of years ago until a teenage kid backed into her at the gas station.

Liam had decided it wasn't worth fixing and bought Zoe a brand-new mommy van. The damaged car had been in Liam's garage the last time Patrick saw it. Apparently, Maeve wasn't opposed to getting the whole family in the act when it came to her "rescue Libby" plan.

Patrick headed inside, greeted the receptionist with an absent wave and holed up in his office. Taking a deep breath, he leaned a hip against his desk, pulled his phone out and sent a text.

We'll leave at nine if that works for you…

Libby's response was immediate: I'll be ready.

Meet me out front.

He wondered if Libby was nervous. Surely so. But he knew her well enough already to be damned sure she wouldn't let the nerves show.

At 8:55 he hefted all their gear and headed outside, only to get his first shock of the day. Libby leaned against a tree, head back, eyes closed. On the ground at her feet lay a waterproof jacket. From head to toe, she was outfitted appropriately. Sturdy boots, lightweight quick-dry pants, a white shirt made of the same fabric and an aluminum hiking pole. He came do a dead stop and swallowed hard.

Every bit of what she was wearing was borrowed. Yet inexplicably she managed to look like a model for some weird amalgam of *Vogue* and L.L.Bean. The clothing fit her better than anything she had worn so far in his employ. Suddenly, he realized that Dylan was correct. Libby Parkhurst had a kick-ass body.

When he shifted from one foot to the other, he dislodged a piece of gravel. Libby's eyes snapped open, her expression guarded. "Good morning," she said.

He hated the guilt that choked him. "Libby, I—"

She held up a hand. "I don't want to talk about it."

They stared at each other for several long seconds. He couldn't get a read on her emotions. So he shoved aside the memory of her face in Dylan's bar and forced himself to zero in on basics.

"Three things," he said tersely. "The moment you feel

anything on your foot begin to rub, we stop and deal with it. A major key to hiking in the mountains is taking care of your feet. Blisters can be incapacitating. Understood?"

"Yes, sir."

Her smart-ass tone was designed to annoy him, but he didn't take the bait. "Secondly, if I'm walking too fast for you, you have to say so. There's no need to play the martyr."

"Understood."

"Lastly, you have to drink water. All day. All the time. Women don't like the idea of peeing in the woods, so they tend to get dehydrated. That's also dangerous."

The look on Libby's face was priceless. "Got it," she mumbled.

"Am I being too blunt?" he asked.

She gnawed her lip. "No. I suppose I hadn't thought through all the ramifications."

"That's what this trip is about."

He slid one of two backpacks off his shoulder. "I need to make sure the straps are adjusted correctly for you." Without asking, he stepped behind her and helped settled the pack into position. With a few quick tugs, he was satisfied. Finally, he moved in front of her and fiddled with the strap at her chest.

Libby made some kind of squawk or gasp. It was only then that he realized his fingers were practically caressing her breasts. He stepped back quickly. "I'm sure you can manage the waistband," he muttered.

"Uh-huh." She kept her head down while she dealt with the plastic locking mechanism. After a moment, she stared off into the woods. "I'm good."

"Then follow me."

Libby had taken yoga classes from the time she was fourteen, although during the past year, she'd had to keep up the discipline on her own. She was limber and more than moderately fit. But Patrick's punishing pace had her gasping for breath by the third mile.

His legs were longer than hers. He knew the rhythm of walking over rough terrain. And she was pretty sure he had loaded her pack with concrete blocks. But if Charlise could do this, so could she.

Fortunately, the boots Maeve had found for Libby were extremely comfortable and already broken in. Given Patrick's warning, Libby paid close attention to her feet. So far, no sign of problems.

It helped that the view from behind was entertaining. Patrick's tight butt and long legs ate up the miles. She had long since given up estimating how far they had come or what time it was. Since her phone was turned off to save the battery, she was dependent upon Patrick's knowledge of the forest to get them where they needed to go.

At one point when her legs ached and her lungs burned, she shouted out a request. "Water, please." That was more acceptable to her pride than admitting she couldn't keep up.

Patrick had a fancy water-thingy that rested inside his pack and allowed him to suck from a thin hose that protruded. Not the kind of item a person borrows. So he had tucked plastic pouches of water for Libby in the side pockets of her pack. She opened one and took a long, satisfying gulp. It took everything she had not to ask how much farther it was to their destination.

The two of them were completely alone…miles away from the nearest human. The wind soughed through the trees. Birds tweeted. The peace and solitude were beautifully soothing. But a chasm existed between Patrick and her. At the moment, she had no desire to breach it.

As forecasted, the warming trend had arrived with a

vengeance. Temperatures must already be in the upper sixties, because Libby's skin was damp with perspiration.

Patrick hadn't said a word during their stop. He merely stood in silence, his attention focused on the scenery. The trail had ascended a small ridgeline, and through a break in the trees, they could see the town of Silver Glen in the distance.

"I'm good," she said, stashing the water container. "Lead on."

Her body hurt and her lungs hurt, but eventually, she fell into a rhythm that was almost natural. *One foot in front of the other. Zen-like state of being. Embrace the now.*

It almost worked.

When they stopped for lunch, she could have sworn it was at least seven in the evening. But the sun was still high in the sky. Patrick had a more sophisticated standard for trail food than she had anticipated. Perhaps a certain level of cuisine was de rigueur for his Fortune 500 clients. Instead of the peanut butter and jelly she had expected, they enjoyed baked-ham sandwiches on homemade bread.

When the meal was done and Patrick shoved their minimal trash into his pack, she finally asked a question. "What do you do if you have someone who can't handle the hiking?"

He zipped his pack and shouldered it. "Companies apply to come to Silver Reflections. We have a long waiting list. Most of the elite businesses institute some kind of wellness programs beforehand. They'll include weight loss, stress management, regular exercise…that kind of thing. So by the time they come to North Carolina, most of the participants are mentally and physically prepared for the adventure rather than dreading it."

"I see." But she didn't really. Patrick was already walking, so she stumbled after him. "But what about people that aren't prepared? Do they make them come anyway?"

Patrick didn't turn around, but his voice carried. "A lot of top corporations are beginning to realize the importance of physical well-being for their employees as a means to increase the bottom line. If an executive has a physical limitation, then of course he or she isn't forced to come. But if an otherwise physically capable person chooses not to attend to his or her health and fitness, then it might be a sign that a top-shelf promotion isn't in the cards."

With that, the conversation ended. Patrick was walking as quickly as ever, making it look easy. Maybe Libby had slipped into the numb stage, or maybe she was actually getting used to this, but her aches and pains had receded. Perhaps this was the "runner's high" people talked about. Endorphins at work, masking the physical discomfort.

At long last, Patrick stopped and took off his pack to stretch. Libby followed suit, looking around curiously. It was obvious they had reached their destination. Patrick stood on the edge of a large clearing. The area was mostly flat. About thirty feet away, a narrow creek slid and tumbled over rocks, the sound of the water as soothing as the prospect of wetting tired feet in the chilly brook.

Patrick shot her a look, clearly assessing her physical state. "This is base camp."

"There's not much to it," she blurted out.

"Were you expecting a five-star hotel?"

His sarcasm on top of everything else made her angry, but she didn't want him to get the best of her. So she kept her mouth shut. If he wanted her to talk, he was going to have to initiate the conversation.

Somehow, it seemed almost obscene to be at odds with another human in the midst of such surroundings. Though it would be several more weeks until the new green of spring began to make its way through the sun-kissed glades, even now the forest was beautiful.

She dropped her pack and managed not to whimper.

Though it galled her to admit it, maybe Patrick was right. Maybe this job was not for her. It was one thing to come out here alone with him. But in the midst of an "official" expedition, Libby would be expected to pull her weight. Her new boss wouldn't be free to coach her if she got in over her head.

He knelt and began pulling things from his pack. "The first thing Charlise usually does is put up our tents. I'll be teaching the group how to do theirs."

"Okay." How hard could it be? The one-man tents were small.

"First you'll want the ground cover. It's the thing that's silver on one side and red on the other. Silver side up to preserve body heat."

Libby was a fast learner. And she was determined to acquit herself well. "Got it."

Patrick pointed. "Leader tents go over there." He stood, hands on hips, while she struggled to spread the ground tarps and smooth them out.

Next came the actual tents. Claustrophobically small and vulnerably thin, they were actually not that difficult to set up. Lightweight poles snapped together in pieces and threaded through a nylon sleeve from one corner of the tent to the opposite side. Repeat once, and it was done. The only thing left was to secure the four corners to the ground with plastic stakes.

All in all, not a bad effort for her first time. Even Patrick seemed reluctantly impressed. He handed her a rolled-up bundle that was about eighteen inches wide. "Look for a valve on one corner. It's not difficult to blow up. And it won't look like much when you're done. But having this pad underneath your upper body and hips makes for a much more comfortable night."

He was right. Even when she inflated the thin *mat-*

tress, it didn't seem like much of a cushion. But she wasn't about to say so.

To give Patrick his due, he didn't go out of his way to make her feel nervous or clumsy. Still, having someone watch while she learned new skills was stressful.

At last, both tents were up, pads and sleeping bags inside. The full realization that she and Patrick were going to spend the night together hit her hard. No television. No computers. Nothing at all for a distraction. He was gorgeous and unavailable. She was lonely and susceptible.

Nevertheless, the job was what she needed. Not the man. She couldn't let him see that she was seriously attracted to him. Cool and casual was the plan.

She stood and arched her back. "What next?"

Four

Patrick hadn't expected much from a young, pampered, New York socialite. But perhaps he was going to have to eat his words. During the morning, he had set an intentionally punishing pace as they made their way through the woods. Libby stayed on his heels and never once complained.

Was it the past year that had made her resilient, or was she naturally spunky and stubborn? That would remain to be seen.

He glanced at his watch. Even with this current spring-like spell, it was still February, which meant far less daylight than in two months when he traditionally scheduled his first team-building treks. Kneeling, he pulled a small camp stove from his pack. "I'll show you how to use this," he said. "The chef at the retreat center has a couple of part-time assistants who prepare our camping meals the day before."

"I assumed the execs would have to cook for themselves. Isn't that part of the outdoor experience?"

"In theory, yes. But so far, we've only done short trips... two days, one night. So our time frame is limited. Since we want them to do a lot of other activities, we preprepare the food and all they have to do is warm it up. We don't spend too much time on meals."

Once Libby had mastered the stove, she glanced up at him. "Surely you don't expect the entire group to use something this small."

"No. I have a group of local guys who come along to carry the food, extra stoves and extra water."

He stared at her, disconcerted by feelings that caught him unawares. He was *enjoying* himself. Libby was a very soothing person to be around. When she stood up, he walked away, ostensibly picking up some fallen limbs that had littered the campsite.

Grappling with an unexpected attraction, he cursed inwardly. With Charlise, he never felt like he was interacting with a woman. He treated her the same way he did his brothers. Charlise was almost part of his family. While he was delighted that she and her husband were so happy about the upcoming birth, he would be lying if he didn't admit he was feeling a little bit sorry for himself. Silver Reflections had been going so well. He had honed these outdoor events down to the finest detail. Then Charlise had to go and get pregnant. And his mother had saddled him with Libby. A remarkably appealing woman who'd already managed to get under his skin.

What was he going to do about it? Nothing. It would be a really bad idea to get involved personally with his mother's beloved Libby. Not only that, but with Charlise out of commission, he had no choice but to work twice as hard. And ignore his libido.

Surely he could be excused for being a little grumpy.

Libby called out to him. "What now?"

He turned around and caught her rolling her shoulders. She'd be sore tomorrow. Backpacking used a set of muscles most people didn't employ on a daily basis.

"I'll show you how we string our packs up in the trees," he said.

"Excuse me?"

He sighed, the look of befuddlement on her face the sign of an outdoor newbie. "Once we set up camp, we won't be hauling our backpacks everywhere. We'll use this as home base and range around the area."

"Why can't we leave the packs in our tents?"

"Bears," he said simply.

Up until that point, Libby had done an admirable job keeping her cool, but now she paled. "What do you mean, *bears*?"

"Black bears have an incredible sense of smell. And they're omnivorous. Anytime we're away from camp— and at night when we're sleeping—we'll hang our packs from a high tree limb to discourage unwanted visitors. Don't keep any food in your tent at all, not even a pack of crackers or scented lip balm or toothpaste."

"I washed my hair with apple shampoo this morning." Her expression was priceless.

"Not to worry. I should have told you. But the scent won't be strong enough by the end of the day to make a difference."

"Easy for you to say," she grumbled as she glanced over her shoulder, perhaps expecting a bear to lumber into sight any moment.

Patrick unearthed a packet of nylon rope. "There will be plenty of tall men around to do this part, but it never hurts to gain a new life skill. Watch me, and then you can try."

"If you say so."

He found a rock that was maybe four inches around

and tied it to the end of the rope. "Stand back," he said. Fortunately for his male pride, his first shot sailed over the branch. He reached for the rock again and removed it. "Now all you have to do is attach one end to your pack, send it up, and tie it off." When Libby seemed skeptical, he laughed, his good humor restored for the moment. "Never mind. I won't make you practice this right now. We have better things to do."

"Like what?"

He grabbed a couple of water pouches and a zippered nylon case, then hefted both packs toward the treetops, securing them. "I'm going to show you where I teach the groups how to rappel."

Libby's expression was dubious. "Does Charlise do the rappelling thing?"

It was the first time she had seemed at all reluctant to approach something new. "No. Not usually. So if you don't want to try it, you can watch me. But I do want you to get a feel for the whole range of activities we offer. C'mon… it's not far."

As they passed the two tents, neatly in place for the up-coming night, he felt his pulse thud. He'd never thought of camping out as sexual or even sensual. When he spent time with a woman, it was in fine restaurants or at the theater. Perhaps later on soft sheets in her bedroom. But certainly not when both parties were sweaty—and without a luxurious bathroom at hand.

He stumbled. Damn it. Libby was messing with his head.

The large rock outcropping was barely half a mile away. He strode automatically, only slowing down when he realized that Libby was lagging behind. When she caught up, he moved on without speaking.

Though she had been cooperative and pleasant all day, his inadvertent insult from Friday hung between them like a cloud. He would have to address it sooner or later, whether she liked it or not.

When they arrived at their destination, he unzipped the bag and pulled out a mass of tightly woven mesh straps. "Sometimes, if we have women along, I might ask you to help them get into their gear. If a female seems extremely modest or uneasy, it can be difficult for me or one of the guys to help with the harness…you know…too much touching."

Libby nodded. "I understand."

She stared at him intently as he prepared the equipment. Something about her steady regard made the back of his neck tingle. "I'm going to go around the side of that ridge and come out on top," he said. "That cliff is only about thirty feet high, but it looks really far off the ground when you're standing up there, particularly if you've never done anything like this before."

"I can imagine."

He tossed her a thin ground cloth to sit on. "Feel free to relax while I get up there. And you don't have to worry about ticks or other bugs. It's still too early for a lot of creepy crawlies."

Libby *hadn't* been worrying about creepy crawlies, but she was now. Ick. Her legs itched already from the power of suggestion.

If her companion had been any man other than Patrick Kavanagh, she might have assumed he was showing off. He could have explained how the rappelling worked without a demonstration. Maybe he just liked doing it. It was a sure bet he didn't have any interest in impressing her.

Without Libby to slow him down, he appeared at the top of the small cliff in no time at all. She shaded her eyes and watched as he secured himself to a nearby tree. He checked all of his connections and waved. Then, looking like an extremely handsome and nimble spiderish super-hero, he stepped backward off the rock shelf and danced his way to the bottom.

His skill was striking.

Something about a man so physically powerful and at ease with his body was very appealing. For a moment, she thought about other, more primal things he might do exceedingly well...but no. She wouldn't go there.

Once before when she was young and immature, she'd fallen under the spell of a magnetic, powerful man—with disastrous results. History would not be repeating itself. She was older now, old enough to be tempted. But sex and romance were off the table. Keeping this job had to be her focus.

The demonstration took some time. Once Patrick reached the bottom, he had to go back to the top and untie his ropes.

Finally, he reappeared, striding toward her. She handed him his water. He dropped down beside her, barely breathing heavily, and took long gulps. Already, the sun was sliding lower in the sky, and a chill began to linger in the shadows.

Libby pulled her knees to her chest and linked her arms around her legs. "That was pretty cool. Have you always been fond of the outdoors?"

Patrick wiped the back of his arm across his forehead. "Would you be surprised to know that I worked in advertising for several years in Chicago?"

She gaped at him. "Seriously?"

His smile was self-mocking. "Yes. I loved the competitive atmosphere—stealing big accounts, coming up with the next great ad campaign. Brainstorming with smart, focused, energetic colleagues. It was a great environment for a young man."

She snorted. "You're still young."

"Well, you know what I mean."

"Then what changed?"

He shrugged. "I missed the mountains. I missed Silver Glen. I didn't know how deeply this place was imprinted on my DNA until I left. So one day, I turned in my notice, and I came home."

"And started Silver Reflections."

"It took a couple of years, but yeah…it's been a pretty exciting time."

"So who's the real Patrick Kavanagh? The man I just watched scramble down a cliff? Or the sophisticated guy who roams the halls of his übersuccessful, private, luxurious executive getaway?"

His quick grin startled her. "Wow, Libby…was that a compliment?" Without waiting for an answer to his teasing question, he continued. "Both, I guess. Without the time in Chicago, I doubt I would have understood the needs of the type A men and women who eat, sleep and breathe work. I was one of them…at least for a few years. But I realized my life was missing balance. For me, the balance is here. So if I can offer rest and recovery to other people, then I'm satisfied."

"And your personal life?" Oops. That popped out uncensored. "Never mind. I don't want to know."

He chuckled but kept silent.

They were sitting so close, she could smell his warm skin and the hint of whatever soap he had used that morning. Not aftershave. That would be the equivalent of inviting bears to munch on his toes. Even mentally joking about it gave her a shiver of unease.

Not long from now, it was going to get dark. Very dark. Her nemesis, Patrick Kavanagh, was the only person metaphorically standing between her and the wildness of nature.

To keep her mind off the upcoming night, she asked another question. "Do you have any regrets?"

"Yes," he said quietly. "I'm sorry I said something so stupid and unkind, and I'm sorry you heard it."

She flushed, though in the fading light, maybe he couldn't see. "I told you I don't want to talk about it. You're entitled to your opinion."

He touched her knee. Briefly. As if to establish some kind of connection. "I admire the hell out of you, Libby. I didn't mean what I said on Friday night. My mother is one of the best people I know. Her instincts are always spot-on. Her compassion and genuine love for people have influenced my brothers and me more than we'll ever know."

"You called me a misfit."

Patrick cursed beneath his breath. "Don't remind me, damn it. I'm sorry. It was a crappy thing to do."

"I think the reason it hurt me was because it's the truth."

Patrick leaped to his feet and dragged her with him, his hands on her shoulders. "Don't be ridiculous."

He looked down at her, his jaw tight. He was big and strong and absolutely confident in everything he did. With the five-inch difference in their heights, it would be easy to rest her head on his shoulder. She was tired of being strong all the time. She was tired of not knowing who she was anymore. And she really wanted the luxury of having a man like Patrick in her life. But survival trumped romance right now.

"You've been a trouper today," he said quietly.

"But I'm not Charlise."

One beat of silence passed. Then two.

"No. You're not. But that doesn't mean you aren't capable in your own way."

He wasn't dodging the truth. Where she came from they called that *damning with faint praise*.

"I can learn," she said firmly. Was she trying to convince Patrick or herself?

His small grin curled her toes in her boots. "I know that. And I'm sorry I hurt your feelings. I'm not usually such an animal. Please forgive me."

She wasn't sure who was more surprised when he bent his head and kissed her. When either or both of them should have pulled away, some spark of longing kept them together. At least it felt like longing on her part. She didn't know *what* Patrick was thinking.

His lips pressed hers firmly, his tongue teasing ever so gently, asking permission to slide inside her mouth and destroy her with the taste of him. Her arms went around his neck. Clinging. Her body leaned into his. Yearning. It had been well over a year since she had been kissed. Echoes of past mistakes set off alarms, but she ignored them.

The moment of rash insanity set her senses on fire, helping her forget that she'd walked through her own kind of purgatory. It felt so good to be held. So safe. So warm. She trembled in his embrace.

"Patrick…" She whispered his name, not wanting to stop, but knowing they were surely going to regret whatever madness had overtaken them.

He jerked as if he had been shot. Staggered backward. "Libby. Hell…"

The exclamation encompassed mortification. Shock. Regret.

It was the last one that stung, despite knowing that keeping distance between them was for the best.

She managed a smile, though it cost her. "We'd better get back to camp. I'm starving, and it's going to be dark soon."

His apology should have erased the friction, yet they faced each other almost as adversaries.

He nodded, his expression brusque. "You're right."

This time, following him through the forest came naturally. No matter the strained atmosphere between them, in this environment, she trusted him implicitly to take them wherever they needed to go.

Dinner was homemade vegetable soup warmed on the camp stove. The chef had made the entrée and added fresh Italian rolls to go with it. While Libby tended to the relatively foolproof job of preparing the meal, Patrick started a campfire and rolled a log near the flames so they would have a comfy place to sit.

With the cup from a thermos, Patrick ladled soup into paper bowls that would later be burned in the fire. He'd explained that the aluminum spoons they used were light in a pack and good for the environment.

Libby ate hungrily. It was amazing how many calories one consumed by walking in the mountains. Neither she nor Patrick spoke. What was there to say? He didn't really want her here. Not to replace Charlise. And beyond that, they were nothing to each other. Virtual strangers. Except she normally didn't go around kissing strangers. She jumped when an owl hooted nearby. Though she was wearing a long-sleeved shirt and the day had been warm, she scrambled to find her jacket. Huddling into the welcome warmth, she stared into the fire and tried not to think about the night to come.

If she had any hope of convincing Patrick that she was capable of filling Charlise's shoes, she had to act as if spending a night in the dark, scary woods was no big deal.

She stared into the mesmerizing red and gold flames, listening to the pop and crackle of the burning wood. The scent of wood smoke was pleasant…a connection, perhaps, to her ancestors who had lived closer to the land.

She and Patrick had eaten their meal in complete silence. Libby was okay with that. All she wanted to do now was get through this overnight endurance test without embarrassing herself.

She cleared her throat. "So, it's already dark. And it's awfully early to go to bed. What do people do in the woods when they camp out during the winter?"

Patrick's face was all planes and angles in the glow of the fire. He was a chameleon—dashing and elegant as a Kavanagh millionaire, but now, a ruggedly masculine man with unlimited physical power and capability. Looking at him gave her a funny feeling in the pit of her stomach.

The sensation was no secret. She was seriously in lust with her reluctant boss, despite his arrogance and his refusal to take her seriously. He could be funny and charming. He had been remarkably patient, even when saddled with his mother's charity case.

But the truth was, he didn't want her on his team. And when it came to the attraction that simmered between them? Well, that was never going to amount to anything, no matter how many hours they spent alone in the woods. She pressed her knees together, her heart beating a ragged tempo as she waited for an answer to what was one part rhetorical question and the other part a need to break the intimate quiet.

If she had a tad more experience, or if she honestly believed that Patrick felt a fraction of the sexual tension that was making her jumpy, she might make a move on him. But despite his kiss—which was really more of a hands-on apology—she didn't delude herself that he had any real interest in her.

Women like Charlise were more his type. Athletic superwomen. Not timid females afraid of the shadows.

Besides, she had to stay focused on starting her life over. She was on her own. She had to be strong.

She had almost forgotten her question when he finally answered.

Five

"Speaking for myself, I suppose it depends on who I'm with."

Patrick wasn't immune to the intimacy of the moment. He still reeled from the impact of the kiss. But all else aside, his mother would kill him if he played around with Libby. Libby was emotionally fragile and just coming out of a very rough period in her life. He couldn't take advantage of her vulnerability, even if she was already worming her way into his heart.

A part of him wanted to tell her how much fun sleeping-bag sex could be. But that would be crossing the line, and Libby Parkhurst was off-limits. He'd be exaggerating anyway. Most of the women he'd been serious about would run for the hills if he suggested anything of the sort.

It occurred to him suddenly that his love of outdoor adventure had largely been segregated from his romantic life. He hiked with his brothers. He took clients out in the woods with Charlise. But he'd never really wanted to bring a woman along in a personal, *intimate* sense.

Yet with Libby, he was tempted. Unfortunately, temptation was as far as it went. He had to keep her at a distance or this whole scenario might blow up in his face. Particularly when he had to fire her.

He picked up a tiny twig and tossed it into the fire. "You can always listen to music. Did you bring an iPod? It was on the list."

Libby nodded, her profile disarmingly feminine in the firelight. "I did. But if I have earbuds in, I won't be able to hear the wild animals when they come to rip me limb from limb."

Patrick chuckled. Despite Libby's lack of qualifications for the job as his assistant, he enjoyed her wry take on life. He also respected the fact that she acknowledged her fears without being crippled by them. As if he needed more reasons to be intrigued by her. But that didn't make her an outdoorswoman.

"I won't let anything happen to you, I swear." It was true. Libby might not be the one to cover the maternity leave, but he felt an overwhelming urge to protect her.

Eventually, Libby needed a moment of privacy in the woods. He had known it was coming. But he was pretty sure she wasn't comfortable about the dark.

When she stood up, she hedged. "I, uh…"

"You need to go to the bathroom before we call it a night."

"Yes."

He'd seen her blush before. Right now her face was probably poppy red. But he couldn't tell in the gloom. He handed her a flashlight. "Do you want me to go with you, or shall I stay here and face the fire?"

Long silence.

"Face the fire. But if I'm not back in ten minutes, send out the rescue squad."

Again, that easy humor. He sat and concentrated on the flames, feeling the heat on his face. His libido thrummed on high alert. It had never occurred to him that spending a night in the woods with Libby Parkhurst would test his self-control.

He had forgotten to glance at his watch when she left. How long had she been gone? Now she had *him* hearing all sorts of menacing sounds in the forest. "Libby," he called out. "You okay?"

He held his breath until she answered.

"I'm fine." Her voice echoed from a distance, so he stayed put.

At last she reappeared. "What time do we need to be up in the morning?" she asked.

"I'll get breakfast going…most importantly, a pot of coffee. You can pop out of your tent whenever you're ready."

"What about our packs?"

"I'll take care of it. When you get in your tent, make sure to take your boots off and put them by the exit. That way you won't get your sleeping bag muddy. The bedding I brought is warmer than the type we use in April. I hope you'll be comfortable."

"I'll be fine. Good night, Patrick."

He wished he could say the same. He was wired and horny. That was a dangerous combination.

With moves he had practiced a million times, he scattered the coals and made sure the fire was not in danger of spreading while they slept. Then he took both packs and hung them from a nearby treetop.

After crawling into his own tent and taking off his boots, he zipped the nylon flap and got settled for the night. His sleeping bag was high-tech and very comfortable. The temperature outside was perfect for snuggling into his down cocoon and sleeping.

Which didn't explain why he lay on his back and stared into the dark. The noises of the night were familiar to him. Hooting owls. Sighing wind. The *click-clack* of bare winter branches rubbing together.

Libby's tent was no more than four or five feet away from his. If he concentrated, he thought he might be able to hear her breathing.

He was almost asleep, when a female whisper roused him.

"Patrick. Are you awake?"

"I am now." He pretended to be gruff.

"What am I supposed to do if a bear tries to eat my tent?"

He grinned, even though she couldn't see. "Libby. People camp out in this part of the country all the time. We're not far from the Smoky Mountains. It's perfectly safe, I swear."

"I was kidding. Mostly. And I'm not being a wimp. I just want to be prepared for anything. But people *do* get attacked by bears. I went online and did a search."

"Are you sure you weren't reading stories about grizzlies? We don't have those in North Carolina."

"No. It was black bears. A woman died. They found her camera and she had been taking pictures."

"I remember the story you're talking about. But that was a long time ago and the woman, unfortunately, got too close to the bear."

"But what if the bear gets too close to me?"

He laughed. "Would you like to come sleep in my tent?" As soon as the words left his mouth, he regretted them. He hadn't consciously meant to flirt with her, but the feelings were there.

Long silence. "You mean with you?"

"Well, it doesn't make much sense just to swap places. If it will help you be more comfortable, I'm sure we can manage to squeeze you in here if we try."

Another, longer silence. "No, thank you. I'm fine. Really."

"Your choice." He paused. "Tell me, Libby. Did your family never vacation outdoors? National parks? Boating adventures? Anything like that?"

He heard the sound of rustling nylon as she squirmed to get comfortable.

"No. But I have a working knowledge of all the major museums in Europe, and I can order a meal at a Michelin-starred restaurant in three languages. I've summered in the Swiss Alps and wintered in Saint Lucia. Still, I've never cooked a hot dog over a campfire."

"Poor little rich girl."

"Not funny, Patrick. I happen to know the Kavanaghs are loaded. So you can't make fun of me."

"*Can't* or shouldn't?"

She laughed, the warm sound sneaking down inside him and making him feel something both arousing and uncomfortable.

"I'm going to sleep now," she said.

"See you in the morning."

Aeons later, Libby groaned. Morning light meant the dawn of a new day, but she was too warm and comfortable to care. For the past hour, she had actually been sleeping peacefully. Now, however, she had to go to the bathroom. And unlike any normal morning, she couldn't crawl back into bed afterward, because she would be completely awake.

She felt as if she had barely slept all night. Every noise was magnified in her imagination. She would doze off finally, and then minutes later some ominous sound would wake her up. It was an endless cycle.

To make matters worse, Patrick had fallen asleep almost instantly after their "bear" conversation. She knew this, because he'd snored. Not an obnoxious, chain-saw sound, but a quiet masculine rumble.

How did he do it? How did he sleep like a baby in the middle of the woods? Her hips were sore from lying on the ground, even with the pad, and she didn't know how *anyone* could manage restful slumber without some white noise.

Hiking enthusiasts talked about the peace and quiet of nature. Clearly they had never actually spent a night in the outdoors. The forest was *not* a silent place.

Though the temperatures were supposed to hit the sixties again this afternoon as the February warm spell lingered, this morning, there was a definite nip in the air. She shivered as she sat up and fumbled her way into her jacket. She could already smell the coffee Patrick had promised.

She rummaged in her pocket for the small cosmetic case she'd brought with her. A comb and a mirror and some unscented lip balm. That was it. Fortunately, the mirror was tiny, because she didn't really want to see her reflection. She had a feeling that her appearance fell somewhere between "dragged through a bush backward" and "one step away from zombie."

Putting on boots was her first challenge. Then, after struggling to tame her hair and redo her ponytail, she shook her head in defeat. She didn't need to impress Patrick with her looks. Why did it matter?

When she unzipped her tent and climbed out, she didn't glance in Patrick's direction. Instead, she headed off into the relative privacy of the forest. After taking care of her most urgent need, she returned to the campsite. Patrick looked rested, but his hair was rumpled and his jaw was shadowed with dark stubble.

Still, he looked gorgeous and sexy. Life wasn't fair at all.

He looked up from his contemplation of the fire when she sat down. "Mornin'," he said. The word was gruff.

She nodded, unable to come up with a scintillating response. The mood between them was undeniably awkward.

He poured her a cup of coffee. "Careful, it's hot."

"Thanks." Adding sugar and a packet of artificial creamer, she inhaled the steam, hoping the diffused caffeine would jump-start her sluggish brain. So far, the five-word conversation between her and her boss was taxing her will to live.

Two cups later, she began to feel slightly human. Even so, the fact that she had been wearing the same clothes for twenty-four hours made her long for a hot shower.

"What next?" she asked. The sooner Patrick taught her the drill, the sooner they could go home.

"We break down camp. With a group event, we'll have the camp stoves set up right over there. The guys that packed in the food and supplies will be your assistants. The meal is simple, homemade oatmeal with cinnamon and brown sugar for those who want it. Precooked bacon that we crisp up in a skillet. Whole oranges. And of course, coffee."

"Will I have to cook the oatmeal?"

"No. Only warm it. It's mostly a matter of being organized and making sure everyone gets served quickly. They're always eager to get started on the rest of the day, so we try not to drag out the meal process."

"I can handle that."

"You ready to head out?"

Gulp. Of course. She noticed he didn't say "head home." Clearly there was more to be learned.

She paid close attention as Patrick showed her how to

break down the tents and put out the fire. Once they re-loaded their packs, the site was pristine. It went without saying that a company like Silver Reflections would re-spect the sanctity of the natural world.

Patrick wasn't very talkative this morning. Perhaps he was regretting their momentary lapse. Or maybe he had other issues on his mind. Losing Charlise's expertise for six months had to be frustrating for him. Maybe everyone would have been a lot happier if Patrick had simply stood up to Maeve and told her he would find his own, far more qualified, temporary employee.

Still, even given the circumstances far beyond her com-fort zone, Libby realized she really wanted this job. Be-neath the physical challenges she was experiencing lurked exhilaration that she was facing her fears and conquering them…or at least trying to…

This morning's hike was shorter, no more than three or four miles. And Patrick's pace was more of a stroll than a death march. With the sun shining and the birds singing, it was almost easy to dismiss her sleepless night.

When they stopped for a snack, Patrick didn't take the time to unpack any kind of seating tarp. Instead, they leaned against trees. Recent rains had left the ground damp, particularly beneath the top layer of rotting leaves. He fished salted peanuts and beef jerky from his pocket. "This will give you energy," he said.

"Do I look that bad?"

His lips quirked. "Maybe a little frayed around the edges. Nothing to worry about. But it will be several hours before we get home, so you have to keep up your strength."

She bit off a piece of jerky, grimacing at the taste. "That sounds ominous. What's next? Building a canoe from a tree? Making blow darts from poison berries? Killing and skinning a wild animal with my bare hands?"

Patrick chuckled. "You've been watching too many movies."

"Then what?"

"We're going underground."

Her stomach fell somewhere in the vicinity of her boots. "Um, no. I don't think so. I got locked in a closet for several hours when I was a little kid and I've been claustrophobic ever since. I don't do caves."

It seemed as if he were baiting her, but she couldn't be sure.

"No caves in these mountains," he said. "It's the wrong kind of geology. You might find some large rock overhangs that provide shelter...but not the places where spelunkers investigate tunnels deep into the earth."

"Then what?"

"A mine." He didn't smile. In fact, his face was carefully expressionless.

Was this the part where she was supposed to throw up her hands and say "I quit"? "What kind of mine?" she asked, thinking about every Appalachian horror story she had heard about shafts collapsing and miners being buried alive.

"Years ago, it was one of hundreds of silver mines in the area, but it's long since been tapped out."

"Then why go in?"

"The claustrophobia you mentioned is a very real fear for many people. When we bring groups out, I go down into the mine with three at a time. Usually, the participants have been prepped in advance about what to discuss. Something simple, but work-related. We sit in the dark as they try to carry on a conversation without panicking."

"And if someone *does* freak out?"

"Their colleagues talk them through it...part of the team-building aspect. You'd be surprised. Sometimes it's the tough macho guys who can't handle it. It's an eye-opener all the way around."

"Well, thanks for telling me about it," she said, her voice high-pitched and squeaky. "I'll do absolutely everything you want me to do *above*ground, no questions asked. But I think I'll take a pass on the mine thing. I hope that's not a deal breaker."

Patrick took her hands, staring into her eyes like a hypnotist. "You can trust me, Libby, I swear."

She exhaled, an audibly jerky sigh. "This might be a good time to mention that my childhood was spent learning how to be scared of everything. My mom wouldn't take me into Central Park because of muggers. No Macy's Thanksgiving Parade because of lurking kidnappers in the crowd. If a spider ever had the temerity to invade our apartment, things went to DEFCON 1 in a hurry. She didn't want me to have a boyfriend, so she told me I could get pregnant from kissing."

"You and I are in trouble, then."

She ignored his attempt at levity. "I was afraid of drowning in the bathtub and being exposed to radioactivity from the microwave. My Halloween candy had to be checked for razor blades, even though it was all a gift from our neighbors across the hall, people we had known for years. I could go on, but you get the idea."

"You know that your mother had serious issues."

"Yes." It was hard to admit it out loud.

"People don't commit suicide for no reason. Your father's fall from grace may have devastated her, but surely it was more than that."

"I know." She swallowed hard, chagrined to feel hot tears threaten her composure. "I also learned to be afraid that I might be like her."

"Bullshit."

Patrick's forceful curse shocked her.

He squeezed her hands, and released her only to pull her against his chest for a brief hug. Then he stepped back and brushed a damp strand of hair from her forehead. The compassion in his gray-blue eyes stripped her raw.

"Libby," he said quietly, "you may not be the right person for this job, but you're strong and independent and amazingly resilient. Not once have you whined about what the last year has been like for you. During terrible, tragic circumstances, you cared for your mother when she couldn't care for herself. You did everything a loving daughter could do. And even though it may seem like it wasn't enough, that's not true."

"I tried to get help for her."

"By selling all your clothes and jewelry to pay for treatment."

"How did you know that?"

He shrugged. "Charlise told me."

Of course. "It wasn't like I had a use for all that stuff," she said.

"Doesn't matter. You gave everything you had. You walked a hard road. You're nothing like her, I promise. Nothing at all. And you don't have to go down into a mine to prove it."

Six

Patrick felt out of his depth. He was neither a grief counselor nor a psychiatrist. All he could do was make sure Libby knew how much he respected and admired her. And better yet, he could resist the urge to muddy the waters with sex.

She stared at him, her expression impossible to decipher. "I've changed my mind," she said quietly. "I want to do it. Not to impress you or to convince you to let me keep the job, but to prove something to myself."

"There are other ways," he said quietly, now suddenly positive that he had made a mistake in bringing her.

"But we're here. And the time is right. Let's go."

She took off down the clearly marked trail, forcing him to follow along behind. Their destination was a little over two miles away. With Libby setting the pace, they made it to the mine's entrance in forty-five minutes. She stopped dead when he called out to her.

The mine was unmarked for obvious reasons. No reason to tempt kids and reckless adults into doing something stupid.

He caught Libby's arm. "We've had engineers reinforce the first quarter mile. Enough to withstand even a mild earthquake. We do get those around here. I wouldn't take clients in there if it was dangerous."

"I know." She bit her lip. "How do we do this?"

"We'll carry our packs in our arms. I'll go first, using a headlamp. You stay on my heels. When we get to a certain spot, I'll spread something on the ground and we'll sit. At any moment if you change your mind, all you have to do is say so."

"How long do you normally stay underground?"

"An hour."

When she paled, he backpedaled quickly. "But we can always walk in and simply turn around and walk out." He hesitated. Was his role to encourage her or to talk her out of this? "Are you sure, Libby?"

She nodded, her pupils dilated. "I'm sure. But since I'm pretty nervous, you won't mind if I disappear into the woods for a minute?"

He looked at her blankly.

"To relieve myself."

"Ah." While she was gone, he followed suit and then waited for her return.

Though the day was bright and sunny, Libby's skin was clammy when she reappeared. He touched her shoulder. "You might want to roll down your sleeves and put on your jacket. It will be cool in the mine." They had shed layers as they walked and the air grew warmer.

Libby did as he suggested and then stared at him. "What now?"

"Let's do this." He pushed aside the undergrowth that had taken over the mine's entrance since last year. Facing him was a wooden door set into the dirt. He wrestled it loose and pushed it aside. "Door stays open," he said. "No getting locked inside, I swear."

"Is that supposed to make me feel better?"

He shot her a glance over his shoulder. She was smiling, but in her eyes he saw apprehension. Even so, her jaw was set, her resolve visible.

"Follow me," he said.

Libby put one foot in front of the other, blindly trusting Patrick Kavanagh to lead her into the bowels of the earth. Months ago when she and her mother were grief stricken and displaced, trying to start a new life, Libby had been anxious and stressed and worried.

But not like this. Her skin crawled with unease. People were meant to exist in the light. Her heartbeat deafened her. "Patrick!" She called out to him, her stomach churning.

He stopped immediately, dropping his pack and turning to face her. The beam of his headlamp blinded her. They weren't far into the mine. Daylight still filtered in behind them.

"Steady," he said. Knowing his eyes were on her only amplified her embarrassment.

She held up a hand. "Don't touch me. I'm fine."

Patrick nodded slowly. "Okay."

Suddenly, she wanted to throw herself into his arms. He was strong and self-assured and utterly calm. She was a mess. No wonder he thought she couldn't handle Charlise's job.

Slowly, they advanced into the mine. A quarter of a mile sounded like nothing at all. But in reality, it felt like a marathon.

Her panic mounted. No matter how slowly she breathed and how much she told herself she could do this, her chest tightened and her stomach curled. "Wait," she said. Frustration ate at her resolve. Mind over matter wasn't working.

She dropped her pack and wrapped her arms around her waist. "Give me a couple of minutes. I can make it."

Patrick dumped his pack as well and removed his headlamp so that the light pointed at their feet. "It speaks volumes that you even tried this, Libby."

Wiping her nose with her sleeve, she shook her head. "I hate being so stupid." Now would be a good time for him to hold her and distract her with his incredibly hot and sexy body. But apparently, that wasn't going to happen anytime soon. Or ever.

"You're not stupid. Lots of people have fears…heights, spiders, clowns."

His droll comment made her laugh. "Clowns? Seriously?"

"Coulrophobia. It's a real thing."

"You're making that up."

She heard him chuckle.

"I wouldn't lie to you."

"What are you afraid of, Patrick?"

Before he could answer, a muted rumble sounded in the distance.

"Hang on, Libby," he said.

Before she could ask what or why, a roaring crash reverberated in the tunnel. Debris rained down on them, first in a gentle fall, and then in a heavy shower that choked them and pelted their heads.

She heard Patrick curse. And then she stumbled.

Patrick fumbled in total darkness for Libby's arm. They had both gone down in the chaos. His brain looked for answers even as he searched frantically for his companion. He latched onto her shoulders and shook her. "Say something, damn it. Are you hurt?"

Dragging her into his lap he ran his hands over her head and limbs, checking for injuries. When he found none, he sighed in relief. He chafed her hands and rubbed her face until she stirred.

"Patrick?" she muttered.

"I'm here." Just then, her entire body went rigid and she cried out.

"We're okay," he said firmly. "There's no need to panic."

She was silent, telling him louder than words she thought he was crazy. After a moment she tried to sit up. "What happened?"

He kept an arm around her, feeling the shudders that racked her body. Though he would walk through hot coals before admitting it, the infinite, crushing darkness was pretty damn terrifying. "I'm not exactly sure, but I can make a guess. The mine hasn't caved in. I told you we've had it checked and reinforced."

"Then what?" Her head was tucked against his shoulder, her hands curled against his chest, her fingernails digging into his shirt, as if she wanted to climb inside his skin.

"I think it was a quick tremor…a small earthquake."

"In North Carolina?"

"I told you. It happens. And we've had so damn much rain in the last three weeks, it's possible there was a landslide that blocked the entrance."

Nothing he could say was going to make the facts any more palatable. Libby's skin, at least the exposed part, was icy cold, far colder than warranted by the temperature in the mine. He worried she might be going into shock. So they had to take action…anything to break the cycle of panic and disbelief.

"I need to walk back to the entrance and see what it looks like."

Her grip on his shirtfront tightened. "Not without me."

He smiled in the dark. "Okay. But first we have to find the headlamp."

He let go of his precious cargo with one hand and sifted through the debris.

Libby was pressed so close to his chest he could feel the runaway beat of her heart. "Is it there?"

He found the elastic strap and lifted it out of the pile of dust and twigs and small stones. But when he flicked the switch, nothing happened. Feeling carefully around the outer portion of the LED lamp, he realized that the whole lens had shattered.

"It's here," he muttered. "But it's broken."

"What about our phones?"

How exactly was he supposed to answer that? Did he need to tell her they could be stranded for days and needed to preserve the batteries? On the other hand, if they were going to be rescued, it made sense to get as close to the entrance of the mine as possible. Unless, of course, there was another landslide. Highly unlikely, but possible.

"I have a couple of backup flashlights," he said. "All I have to do is locate my pack and get them. Will you be okay for a minute if I let go of you?"

"Of course."

The right words, wrong tone. She was perilously close to the breaking point.

Cursing himself for bringing her down into this hell-hole, he set her aside and reached out his hands like a blind man. The first pack he found was Libby's. Since he had loaded it himself, he knew the exact contents. But he had put the flashlights in his pack, because they were heavy.

Moments later, he found his own equipment. When he located the item he wanted and flicked the switch, the small beam of light was as welcome as fresh water in the desert.

Libby stared at him owlishly. "Thank God," she said simply.

"You have stuff in your hair," he said. "Not insects," he

added quickly. Leaning forward, he combed his fingers through the ends of her ponytail and picked tiny debris from the rest of her head. "There," he said. "All better."

His conversation was nonsensical. He freely admitted that. But what in the hell were you supposed to say to the beautiful woman you were buried alive with—the very one you were hoping to keep at arms' length because she was vulnerable and trusting and not the woman you needed in your life either personally or professionally?

"It's not my real color," Libby said.

"Excuse me?" He was befuddled, maybe a little bit in shock himself.

"The color," she said. "I'm a redhead. Maybe you remember from when I was a kid. But after the mess with my father, I started dying my hair so I would blend into the crowd. Now I'm afraid to change it back."

"Tomorrow," he said firmly. "Tomorrow you should make an appointment with a stylist and go back to being you."

At last, she smiled. A weak smile, but a smile. "You are so full of it."

"I'm serious. Men love redheads."

"You know what I mean. I'm not an idiot. The chances of us getting out of here anytime soon are pretty slim. No one is expecting us back until dinnertime. That's several hours from now. And by the time they start to wonder where we are, it will be dark."

"So we'll wait," he said. "We have a decent amount of food and water. If we're careful, it will last."

"How long?" The question was stark.

"Long enough."

He got to his feet, ignoring the lash of pain in his left calf. "Come on, woman. Let's see what happened. We'll take our gear with us."

They hadn't really come all that far. It didn't take long

to retrace their steps. Unfortunately, his guess was spot-on. With or without a tremor as the inciting incident, a goodly portion of the hillside had come sliding down on top of the mine opening. Wet, sludgy earth filled the entrance. Trying to burrow out would only make the whole pile shift and slither, much like digging a hole at the beach.

But Libby looked at him with such naked hope he had to do something. "Stand back," he said. "Maybe it's not as bad as it looks."

"May I hold a flashlight, too?"

It wasn't a good idea. Batteries were like gold in their situation. Still, she needed the reassurance of sight. Later on they could sit in darkness.

He reached into his pocket for the spare flashlight and handed it to her. "I'm serious," he said. "Don't get too close."

For a moment, he was stymied. Using his bare hands to dig seemed ineffective at best, but even mentally cataloging the contents of his backpack, he couldn't think of a damn thing that might serve as a shovel.

In the end, he tucked the flashlight under his armpit and awkwardly began to gouge his fingers into the wet mess. Dry dirt wouldn't have been so bad, but the mud was a frustrating opponent.

After ten minutes of concerted effort, he had made no headway at all. Not only that, he was starting to feel dizzy. He stumbled backward, his filthy arms outstretched. "This isn't going to work. I'm sorry, Libby."

"You're hurt," she said, alarm in her voice. "You're bleeding below the knee."

He blinked, trying to focus his thoughts. Maybe adrenaline had masked his injury, because now his leg hurt like hell. "I don't want to touch the flashlight with all this gunk on my hands. Can you look at my leg?"

Libby squatted and touched his shin. "Whatever it was cut all the way through the cloth."

"Probably a piece of glass. We've found all kinds of broken bottles and crockery down here over the years."

He flinched when she carefully rolled up the leg of his pants.

"Oh, God, Patrick," she gasped. "You need stitches. Sit down so I can look at it."

"Wait. Find the tarp in my pack. We're going to have to make a place to get comfortable." *Comfortable* wasn't even on the map of where they were located. But they would take what they could get.

Libby moved quickly, locating the large tarp and spreading it with one side tucked up against the wall of the mine so they could lean against something. When she was done, he pointed to an outside zip pocket of his pack. "There's a small, thin towel in there. Can you wet it, just barely, so I can get the worst of this off?"

Libby did as he asked, but instead of giving him the towel, she took his hands in hers and began wiping his fingers clean. It was a difficult chore, especially given the lack of water.

He still held the flashlight under his arm. Though he couldn't see Libby's face, there was enough illumination for him to watch as she removed the muck. It was an intimate act...and an unselfish one...because the process dirtied her skin, as well.

But finally he was more or less back to normal.

"Sit down now," she urged.

He was happy to comply.

With his back against the wall of the mine, he took a deep breath. He felt like hell, and his leg had begun to throb viciously. There's a first aid kit," he said gruffly. "Big outer pocket. Antiseptic wipes."

Libby put a hand on his thigh, perhaps to get his attention. "You've lost a lot of blood, Patrick. A lot. The cut is four inches long and gaping."

"Clean it the best you can. We'll use butterfly bandages." The words were an effort. "I'll hold the flashlight."

It occurred to him that he could reach his own leg…do his own medical care. But he couldn't seem to work up the energy to try.

Libby's touch was deft but gentle. Wisely, she didn't waste time getting rid of all the blood. He watched her concentrate on the cut, making sure the edges were clean, dabbing at tiny bits of dirt that might cause infection later. When she was satisfied, she sat back on her heels. "I'll let it dry a minute," she said, "before I use the butterfly thingies."

"Can you get me a couple of painkillers?" he asked, hurting too much to act macho at this particular moment.

"Of course."

He took them with a sip of water and sighed. "Is the skin dry?"

Libby traced around the wound with a fingertip. "Yes." She tore open a small packet and gently affixed the Band-Aid, pulling the open edges of the cut together. It took two more before she was satisfied. "The bleeding has stopped."

"Good." He closed his eyes. "Sit between my legs," he said. "It will keep us both warm."

He needed the human contact, but more than that, he needed a connection to Libby specifically. She might be completely wrong for him on far too many levels, but right now, they had each other and no one else. He wanted to feel her and know she was okay.

Seven

Libby felt like she was in a dream. But when she settled between Patrick's thighs, her legs outstretched, her back against his chest, the situation got a whole lot more real.

Strong arms wrapped around her waist. Big masculine hands clasped beneath her breasts. Patrick's breath warmed the side of her neck. "Are you going to be okay?" she asked. The tenor of his breathing alarmed her. That and his silence.

"It's just a cut. Don't worry about it."

She might be inexperienced when it came to medical care, but she wasn't stupid. Patrick needed a proper hospital, an IV of fluids and red meat. Instead, he was stuck down here with her.

"What time is it?" she asked, feeling her anxiety rise again now that the immediate crisis was past.

"We have to turn off the flashlights," he said quietly, the words ruffling her hair.

She didn't know which part worried her the most—the

fact that he deliberately ignored her question, or the regression to pitch-black darkness. Without vision, the world seemed ominous.

"Do you sing?" she asked.

He groaned. "You don't want to hear that, I promise."

"I'm sorry, Patrick, but if you don't talk to me, I might go bonkers."

"Okay, okay." The words held amusement.

"Tell me about your family. My mother used to keep in touch with Maeve all the time, but I don't really know much about the Kavanagh clan. What are your brothers up to these days?"

"Liam is the oldest. He married a woman named Zoe who is sort of a free spirit. We love her, and she's a perfect match for my stick-in-the-mud brother."

"Go on."

"You saw Dylan at the pub. His wife is Mia. Dylan adopted her little girl."

"Next is Aidan?"

"That's right. He and Emma divide their time between New York and Silver Glen. Then comes Gavin. He runs a cybersecurity firm here in Silver Glen. His wife is Cassidy, and they have twin baby girls."

"What about Conor? Wasn't he the big skier in the family?"

"Still is. He ended up marrying a girl he knew way back in high school. Her name is Ellie."

"Which leaves you and James…is that his name?"

"Yep. My baby brother…who happens to be four inches taller than I am and thirty pounds heavier. We call him the gentle giant."

"You love him. I hear it in your voice."

"Well, when you're the last two in a string of seven, you end up bonding. It was either that or be terrorized by our siblings on a regular basis. With James on my side, I had a tactical advantage."

"Your mother takes credit for marrying off the first five. I suppose you and James are next in her sights."

"Not gonna happen."

The blunt, flat-toned response shocked her. "Oh?"

"Let me rephrase that. I can't speak for my brother, but I'm not interested in tying the knot. Earlier, you asked me what I was afraid of and I never got a chance to answer you. The truth is, it's marriage. I tried it once and it didn't pan out. So I plan on being happily single."

She turned toward him, which was dumb, because she couldn't see his face. "You're divorced?"

"Worse than that."

"She died?" Libby gaped in the darkness, horrified, feeling as if she had stepped in the middle of a painful past Patrick didn't want to share. But now that the door was open, she couldn't ignore the peek inside this complicated man.

Patrick sighed, his chest rising and falling. He pulled her back against him. "No. The marriage was annulled."

It was a good thing Patrick was willing to talk about his past, because the only thing keeping Libby from climbing the walls was concentrating on the sound of his voice. All around her, the dark encroached. Would they have to sleep here and wake up here and slowly starve to death?

Panic fluttered in her chest. "What happened?" she asked.

Patrick wasn't a fan of rehashing his youthful mistakes, but he and Libby had to do something to maintain a sense of normalcy. The medicine had dulled the pain in his leg, though he still felt alarmingly weak.

He rested his chin on her head, inhaling the faint scent of her skin. Her upper-class upbringing meant she'd been taught the rules of polite behavior at an early age. He was sure Libby would never ask that kind of personal question under different circumstances.

But here in the mine, such considerations were less important than the need to feel connected.

He played with the fingers of her right hand, fingers that were bare. Where were the diamonds, the pearls, the precious gems this young, wealthy woman had worn? All sold for her mother's treatment. Libby's mom had betrayed that sacrifice by killing herself.

The picture of Libby he'd had in the beginning was fading rapidly, the colors blurred by the reality of who she was. She'd been a Madison Avenue heiress…no doubt about that. But Libby Parkhurst was so much more than the sum of what she had lost.

His feelings toward her were confusing. He wanted to protect her, both physically and emotionally. And though it was disconcerting as hell, he was beginning to *want* her. In the way a man wants a woman.

Even here in this dank, dark mine shaft—and even though he had a throbbing wound in his leg—his body reacted to the feel of her in his arms. Their relationship had been thrown into fast-forward. He was bombarded with emotions—tenderness, affection and definitely admiration. For a woman who had barely been able to contemplate walking into the mine shaft and back out again, it was nothing short of remarkable that she was still able to function, considering what had happened.

He realized she was still waiting for an answer about his marriage. "My girlfriend got pregnant," he said. "One of those terrible clichés that turns out to be true. I'd been careful to protect both of us, but…"

"Accidents happen."

"Yes. My brothers and I had been brought up with a very strict code of honor. Her parents wanted us to get married, so I agreed. In hindsight, I doubt my mother was thrilled, but what could she do?"

"And the annulment?"

"When the little boy was born, he was dark-skinned… African-American. Even for a girl who was terrified to tell her parents she was involved in a mixed-race relationship and even though she was embarrassed to admit she'd been cheating on her boyfriend, it was clear that the gig was up. We didn't need to have a paternity test done. The truth stared us in the face."

"Oh, Patrick. You must have been devastated."

He winced, even now reacting to a painful, fleeting memory of what that day had done to him. "We'd been living together as husband and wife. We had both graduated from high school…rented a small house. Even though I'd been upset and angry and not at all ready to become a father, after nine months, I'd finally come around to the idea. I was so excited about that little boy."

"And then you lost him."

"Yes. I walked out of the hospital and never looked back. I went home. Slept in the bed where I'd grown up. But nothing was the same. You can't rewrite history and undo your mistakes. All you can do is move forward and not make those same mistakes again."

He wanted to know what Libby was thinking, but he kept on talking. It was cathartic to rehash what had been a chaotic, deeply painful time in his life. It was a subject never broached by the Kavanagh clan. They had swept it under the rug and moved on.

"I didn't abandon the baby," he said, remembering the infant's tiny face. "I want you to know that. His father stepped up. As soon as the annulment was final, he married the mother of his child and they made a family."

"You must have been so hurt."

It was true. He'd been crushed. But he had never let on how much it affected him.

"Adolescence is tough for everybody," he muttered.

Libby turned on her side, nestling her cheek against his chest and drawing up her knees until they threatened his manhood. "You're a good man, Patrick Kavanagh."

He stroked her hair. "I'm sorry about this," he said.

Libby sighed audibly. "It will be something to tell our children one day." She stopped dead, realizing what she had said.

"Don't worry about it, Libby. I'm a very popular uncle, and I like it that way."

"Have you told Maeve how you feel?"

"I think she guesses. She hasn't quite put the marital screws on me like she has the others."

"I'm warning you, it's only a matter of time. You'd better watch your step around her. She's wonderful, but sneaky."

After that, they dozed. Patrick dreamed restlessly, always fighting an ominous foe. Each time he awoke, his arms tightened around Libby. She was his charge, his responsibility. He would do everything in his power to make sure she got out of this mess in one piece.

At last, they couldn't ignore the rumbles of hungry stomachs. "What do you want?" he asked. "Beef jerky or peanuts?"

"I'll take the nuts, I guess."

He handed her the water. "Three sips, no more. We have to be smart about rationing."

"Can we please turn on one of the phones and find out what time it is? Do you think there's any hope of getting a signal down here? We're near the surface."

"I'll look. And no. I don't think there's a chance at all of having a signal."

"You really suck at this cheering up thing."

He checked the time, oddly comforted by the familiar glow of the phone screen. "Seven fifteen."

"So it's dark outside."

"Yes." He turned off the electronic device and stowed it. "It doesn't really matter, though, does it? Not to us?"

"I suppose not." She sighed. "Tell me something else. Do you have big plans for the weekend?"

"I'm flying up to New York Friday morning to do an orientation for one of the teams coming in April. Peabody Rushford is a world-renowned accounting firm with A-list clients. We'll sit around a big conference table, and I'll go over the checklist with all of them. They'll ask questions…"

"May I go with you?"

He paused, taken aback. Maybe Libby was simply trying to convince herself she wouldn't still be trapped underground come Friday. "I'm not sure there's any reason for you to be there," he said. "I don't want to hurt your feelings, but this job is not the one for you. I think you know that."

"Maybe so. But I was thinking of a more personal agenda."

His mind raced, already inventing sexual scenarios where he and Libby ended up naked on soft sheets. "What kind of agenda?"

"I haven't been back to my building since the day my mother and I had to leave. I thought I could go see it. I can't get inside the apartment, of course. Someone else lives there now. But I think even standing on the street would give me some closure."

"Then of course you can come with me," he said. "I wish I could fly us up there in my new toy. I bought a used Cessna recently, but it's still being overhauled. So we'll have to take the jet."

"*Now* who sounds like the poor little rich kid?" she teased.

"You've got me. But to be fair, the Kavanaghs share the jet with several others owners."

"Well, that makes it okay, of course."

"If I were you, I don't think I would alienate the only human being standing between me and solitary confinement."

"Not funny, Patrick."

"Sorry."

They sat in silence. The teasing had kept the darkness at bay for a few moments, but the truth returned. They were trapped…with no hope of rescue until morning at least, and maybe not even then.

Libby stood up, accidentally elbowing him in the ribs. "I have to stretch," she said.

"Don't go far."

"Hilarious, Kavanagh."

He might as well stand up, too. But when he moved, he cursed as pain shot up his leg, hot and vicious.

Libby crouched beside him. "Give me the flashlight."

"Why? We need to save the battery."

"I'm going to look at your leg. Don't argue with me."

She was cute when she was indignant. He surrendered the flashlight wordlessly.

In a brightly lit room, he would have been able to examine his own leg. With nothing but the thin beam of the flashlight, though, he had to rely on Libby for an up-close diagnosis. "How does it look?"

"Bad."

"Bad as in 'needs an antibiotic,' or bad as in 'heading for amputation'?"

She turned the flashlight toward his face, blinding him. "That isn't funny. If we stay in here much longer, you could be in serious trouble."

He covered his eyes. "I choose to laugh instead of cry."

"I'll bet you've never cried in your life. Alpha males don't do that."

"I cried when my father disappeared."

Eight

"Oh, Patrick." Libby's heart turned over. She would bet every dollar of her first paycheck that he hadn't meant to say something so revealing. She sat back down, feeling warm and almost secure when he enfolded her in his arms again. "I know we touched on this during my interview, and I'm sorry to open up old wounds... Did he really just go away?"

"I was a little kid, so some of my memories are fuzzy... but I've heard the story a hundred times. My father was obsessed with finding the silver mine that launched the Kavanagh fortunes generations ago. He would go out for days at a time...and then one weekend, he simply never came back."

"I'm sorry."

"It was a long time ago."

Libby had a blinding revelation, which was really pretty funny considering she was sitting in total darkness. She and Patrick had both been betrayed by their fathers. But luckily for Patrick, *his* mother was a rock.

"Did anyone have a valid theory about what happened?"

"In the beginning, there were lots of possibilities. The police posed the idea that he might have simply abandoned us, started a new life. But his passport was in the safe at home and none of his clothes or prized possessions were missing. He couldn't have left the country, and since none of the family vehicles had been taken, the final conclusion was that he had been killed somewhere in the mountains."

"You mean by wild animals?"

"It's possible. Or he could have fallen."

"But his body was never found."

"Exactly. Which meant that everyone's best educated guess was that my dad went down inside a mine—looking for remnants of a silver vein—and the mine collapsed."

"Oh."

Patrick's arms tightened around her. "This probably isn't the best conversation for us to be having at the moment."

"It does have a certain macabre theme."

"Remember, Libby…this mine we're in *didn't* collapse. It's just that the entrance has been blocked."

"A fine distinction that I'm sorry to say is not very comforting."

"You have *me*. That's something."

Actually, that was a lot. Patrick's reassuring presence was keeping most of her panic at bay…at least for stretches at a time. But their enforced intimacy had created another problem.

In the two weeks she had worked for him, she'd done her best to ignore the fact that he was a handsome, funny, intellectually stimulating man on whom she had a perfectly understandable crush. She'd kept her distance and been a model employee.

But now, with his strong arms holding her tight and his rumbly voice giving her goose bumps when his warm breath tickled her neck and cheek, she was suddenly, madly infatuated. That's all it was. An adrenaline-born rush of arousal. Part of the fight-or-flight response.

The same thing would have happened if she and Patrick had been cave people fleeing from a saber-toothed tiger. Of course later, once they were safe, they might have had wild monkey sex on a fur pelt by the roaring fire.

Her mouth went dry, and the pit of her stomach felt funny. "Patrick?" Clearly her brain cells were being starved of oxygen. Or maybe she was truly losing it, because the next words that came out of her mouth were totally inappropriate. "Will you kiss me?"

She felt his whole body stiffen. "Never mind," she said quickly. "That was just the claustrophobia talking."

"We're not going to die. I promise." His voice sounded funny…as if he had swallowed something down his windpipe.

"And by extrapolation I'm supposed to understand that imminent death is the only situation in which you could see yourself kissing me? Because I'm *one of your mother's misfits*, and a general pain in the ass?"

"You're not playing fair, Libby."

She turned in his embrace, her hands finding his face in the dark. His jaw was stubbly. She rubbed her thumbs over his strong chin. "Kiss me, Patrick," she whispered. "I know I'm taking advantage of you in your weakened state, but please. I've wondered for days what kind of woman you want. I know it's not me. Under the circumstances, though, you could bend the rules…right?"

"Libby, darlin'…"

The way he said her name was pure magic. "I'm listening."

He made a noise that sounded like choked laughter. "You were never spanked as a child, were you?"

She shrugged. "My nannies loved me. So, no. Is that an offer?"

"What about the spiders and the mud and the dungeon ambience?"

"Are you stalling?"

"I don't want you to be embarrassed when we get out of here."

"Embarrassed that I asked for a kiss, or embarrassed that I kissed my boss? I don't think that last one is a problem. You've pretty well admitted that my days are numbered when it comes to working for Silver Reflections."

His hands tangled in her hair, his lips brushing her forehead. "For the record, I haven't completely made up my mind about your status at Silver Reflections. Plus, kissing will make us want other things."

"Too late," she said, breathless…longing. "I already want those other things, but I'm willing to settle for a kiss."

"God, you're a brat."

Somehow, the way he said it turned the words into a husky compliment. "Shall I leave you alone, Patrick?"

His fingers tightened on her skull. "No. That's not what I want at all."

Before she could respond, he angled her head and found her mouth with his. The first kiss was barely perceptible… no more than a faint brush of lips to lips. Even so, she melted into him, stung by a wild burst of hunger that couldn't be satisfied by anything less than full body contact.

The kiss deepened. Patrick muttered something, but she was too lost to translate it. They had done this once before. That "sort of an apology" kiss they had shared in the woods. But she hadn't taken him seriously at the time. She'd thought he was just being nice. Charming. Offering sophisticated reparation for a thoughtless, hurtful mistake.

This was different. This was desperation. Need. Raw, unscripted masculine hunger.

Her fingers fumbled with his shirt buttons, tearing at them until she could rest her cheek against hot male skin. She nipped a flat nipple with her teeth. "I'm getting used to the dark," she whispered.

He groaned. "I'm not." He did his own version of seek-and-find, palming her breasts and squeezing them gently. "I want to see you...all of you."

There were no words to describe the feel of his hands on her bare flesh. It didn't matter that his fingers were probably still mud streaked...or that she shivered with her shirt unbuttoned. She was drowning in pleasure.

Need became a demanding beast, telling her there was a way...insisting that the less-than-perfect circumstances weren't as important as the yearning to take Patrick Kavanagh and make him hers. Her brain made a bid for common sense, reminding her that getting involved sexually with Patrick Kavanagh was a really bad idea.

But other parts of her body spoke more loudly. "How big is this tarp?" she asked, her fingers trembling as she unbuckled his belt.

Patrick found himself in uncharted territory. At any given moment he could find his way through a dense forest on a moonless night with no more than a compass and his knowledge of the mountains. Right now, however, he was a blind man struggling in quicksand.

This was insanity. Complete and utter disregard for the seriousness of their situation. He had to call a halt...

"Touch me," he begged.

When Libby's fingers closed around his erection, he sucked in a sharp breath.

"You fascinate me, Patrick," she said softly, her firm

touch on his body perfect in every way…as if they had been lovers forever and knew exactly what the other liked.

"I'm no different from any other guy," he croaked, feeling his temperature rise as sweat broke out on his brow. "We see, we want, we take."

"And what if *I* take *you*?"

His heart stopped. He tried to remember all the reasons why he was supposed to be a gentleman. The family connection. Libby's recent losses. His mother's disapproval.

Nothing worked. He wanted Libby. Badly. Enough to ignore his better judgment.

After that, it was only a matter of logistics. It could work. Not ideal, but doable. He fumbled with his pants, trying to lower them, but Libby was plastered against his chest, and he couldn't bear to shove her away, even for a moment.

"Wait," she cried. "Stop."

"Damn it, woman, this was *your* idea." He would stop if he had to, but why in the hell was she blowing hot and cold?

She put her hand over his mouth. "Listen," she said, urgency in her tone. "I heard something."

Patrick heard something, too. But it was the sound of his libido crying out in frustrated disbelief. "What are you talking about?"

"Shut up and listen."

Now she was making him mad.

And then he heard it. A scraping sound. And something else. Something human. *Holy hell.* "Button your blouse."

He struggled with his own clothing, and then cursed when he needed her help to stand up. The pain meds had worn off, and his leg was one big ache. Funny how lust was a stunningly effective narcotic. Fumbling for the flashlight, he took Libby's hand and they moved forward.

"We can't get too close," she whispered.

He squeezed her hand. "Cover your ears. I'm going to yell. *"We're down here!"* His plea echoed in their prison.

But from the other side of the mud and rock, a garbled response told him someone had heard the three simple words.

Libby's fingernails dug into his palm. "Who do you think it is?"

"Does it matter? As long as it's not the Grim Reaper, I'm a fan."

They clung to each other, barely breathing.

Suddenly, an unwelcome sensation intruded. "Libby," he said hoarsely. "My ankle is wet."

She reached inside his jacket. "Is that a flashlight in your pocket, or are you glad to see me?" Dropping to her knees, she shone the light on his leg. "Oh, hell, Patrick. The butterfly strips came loose. You're bleeding like a stuck pig. We have to sit you down. Let me find the tarp."

"No," he muttered, feeling woozy. "A little dirt won't hurt me." Leaning on Libby with a death grip, he bent his knees and stumbled onto his butt, cursing when his leg cried out in agony.

She hovered at his side, crouching and combing her fingers through his hair. "Are you okay?"

"Never better."

Without fanfare, a hole opened up in the mud. The unmistakable sounds of shoveling reverberated off the tunnel walls.

A voice, oddly disembodied, floated through the twelve-inch opening. "Patrick! You okay, man?"

Patrick swallowed. "I'm fine."

He licked his lips, shaking all over. "That's James, my brother. How did he know we were here?"

Libby put her arms around him, holding him close. "To quote a man I know, does it matter? Hang on, Patrick. It won't be much longer."

At last, the opening was large enough so they could

lean through and allow themselves to be tugged out like bears from honey pots. Patrick staggered but made it to his feet. He blinked, seeing four of his brothers staring at him. He must look worse than he thought. "Thanks for coming, guys."

And then his world went black.

Libby had her arm around Patrick's waist, but she was no match for his deadweight when he lost consciousness. They both went down hard, despite the fact that James reached for his brother.

"What's wrong with him?" James asked, alarm and consternation in his voice. Then he eased Patrick onto his back and saw the injury for himself.

Libby disentangled herself but stayed seated. "He's lost a lot of blood. The cut will need stitches."

After hasty introductions, Liam Kavanagh rescued the two backpacks from the mine. James and Dylan hoisted their injured sibling onto a portable litter and started back. Gavin gave her a weary smile. "I'm gonna piggyback you," he said. "It will be faster that way."

In the end, the trip through the forest took over two hours. The Kavanagh men had to be exhausted. It was four in the morning by the time they walked out of the woods and into the main lodge of Silver Reflections. Maeve was waiting for them, her face creased with worry.

The only brothers missing were Aidan, who, she learned, was out of town, and Conor who had gone to summon an ambulance. He'd kept his mother company during the rescue operation.

Maeve grabbed Libby into a huge hug. "Oh, my God. We've been out of our minds with worry." She bit her lip, eyeing Patrick's pale face as his brothers set the litter on a padded bench seat. "The ambulance is waiting."

Liam had radioed ahead to let Maeve know they were on the way.

In the hustle and bustle that followed, Libby found herself curled into a deep, comfy armchair by a fire someone had been kind enough to build in the middle of the night. When all the men disappeared, Maeve touched her arm. "Come on, sweetheart. I'll take you back to the hotel before I follow them to the emergency room. Are you sure you don't need medical attention?"

"No, ma'am. I'm fine."

Libby dozed in the car, waking up only as Maeve pulled up in front of Silver Beeches.

Maeve gazed at her, exhaustion on her face. "Do you need help getting upstairs?"

Libby knew her older friend was anxious to check on her son. "I'm fine, Maeve. Go see to Patrick. I'm going to bed as soon as I can get there."

Looking at her reflection in the bathroom mirror a short time later was a lesson in humility. Libby had seen corpses who had more color…and more fashion sense for that matter. Her clothes were filthy and torn, her hair was a tangled mess and, as an added indignity, her stomach rumbled loudly, making it known that sleep was going to have to wait.

The shower felt so good, she almost cried. After shampooing her hair three times and slathering it with conditioner, she used a washcloth to scrub away the grime from the rest of her body. She wove on her feet, fatigue weighting her limbs.

When she was clean and dry, she ordered room service. Six in the morning wasn't too early for bacon and eggs. She had every intention of cleaning her plate, but she managed only half of the bounty before she shoved the tray aside and fell facedown onto the soft, welcoming bed.

Nine

Patrick wolfed down half of a sausage biscuit and watched as the female doc stitched up his leg. Thanks to several shots of numbing medicine, he was feeling no pain.

James leaned against the wall, as if guarding the room from unwanted intruders. Since they were the last people in the ER, Patrick was pretty sure any danger had been left behind at the mine. He and James had finally convinced all the others to go home and get some rest.

Patrick looked at his brother over the doctor's head. "Thanks, bro. You want to explain to me how you knew where I was?"

James's grin was tired but cocky. "I came up to Reflections yesterday to grab one of your gourmet lunches and see if you wanted to hike with me. The people at the front desk said you were in the forest teaching a new recruit the ropes. I set out around the mountain to catch up with you."

"You know where the campsite is...but have you ever even *been* to the mine?"

"No…but I've heard you talk about it. So I used my Boy Scout tracker skills and followed your trail. I eventually stumbled across the landslide. The mud was thick and slimy and fresh. It was then I realized you might be in trouble."

"Me and Libby…"

"Yeah. Since when do you camp out with pretty ladies?"

"It wasn't like that."

"I saw how she looked at you."

"We'd been through a tough time. It was a bonding experience." Patrick managed to keep his expression impassive, but his body was another story. "How did you dig us out?"

James grimaced. "That was the bad part. After I discovered I had *nothing* that was going to do the job, I ran back several miles to the knoll where we can usually get a phone signal and called Conor. He alerted everyone else. We all met up and brought the proper supplies."

"I owe you one, baby brother."

"Don't worry. I'll collect sooner or later. Like maybe an introduction to your newest employee?"

"I don't think so," Patrick snapped.

James raised an eyebrow. "Feeling a little territorial, are we?"

"She's not your type."

"Mom told me her story. She sounds like an amazing woman."

"She is. But she's had a tough time, and she doesn't need strange guys sniffing around."

"I'm not a strange guy… I'm your brother."

The doctor looked up from her work and smiled. "Do I need to referee this squabble?"

Patrick looked down at the long, red, angry wound on his leg. He hadn't needed a transfusion, but it was a close call. "No, Doc," he said, shooting his brother a glare.

Fortunately, Patrick's medical care wrapped up pretty quickly. In the car, James lifted an inquiring eyebrow. "Am I taking you home?"

Patrick gazed out the window, feeling exhausted and surly. "I want to go up to the hotel and make sure Libby is okay."

"She'll be asleep by now."

"Mom would give me a key."

James drummed his fingers on the steering wheel. "I know the two of you just spent the night together in a creepy, dark tunnel, but that doesn't give you the right to act like a stalker. Think, man. You can't open her door and peek in on her. That's way over the line."

Patrick slumped into his seat. His selfish need to see her would have to wait. "I guess you're right. Take me home."

After a shower, a light meal and five hours of sleep, Patrick found himself awake and antsy. The cut was on his left leg, so he wasn't limited as far as driving. When he couldn't stand being inside his house for another minute, he drove to Silver Reflections. His employees seemed perplexed to see him after his ordeal, so he holed up in his office.

Liam had left the two backpacks inside Patrick's door. Patrick dumped them out and started putting things away. One of the staff would take care of cleaning the tarps and other items. The rest Patrick stowed in specially labeled drawers along one wall of his suite.

When all of that was done, he couldn't wait any longer. He sent a text to Libby.

Hope you're feeling okay. You don't have to go Friday if you're not up to it. And stay home tomorrow...you deserve a rest...

He didn't dare say what he was really thinking…that he needed time to figure out what to do about her.

He hit Send and spun around in his leather chair. Maybe he'd been more affected by the experience in the mine than he realized, because his concentration was shot. When someone knocked at his door, he frowned, tempted to pretend he wasn't there.

But, after all, he was the boss. "Come in. It's open."

Libby was the last person he expected to see. She smiled. "I just got your text. Thanks for the consideration, but I couldn't sleep all day. I've been in my office talking to a guest who's disgruntled because he came here to relax and it's too peaceful to sleep. Apparently he lives in a brownstone walk-up across the street from a fire station."

"Ah. Maybe he needs more help than we can give."

"Maybe."

"I'm serious, Libby. Take tomorrow off. And do you still want to go to New York?"

"If you'll have me."

He would be damned glad to have her six ways to Sunday, but that wasn't what she meant. "You're welcome to come with me. As long as you know this isn't a nod from me about the job. I'll book you a hotel room this evening."

"Are you sure you want to do that? I've been learning how to manage on a budget. One room is definitely cheaper than two."

The challenging look in her eyes sent an unmistakable message. He stood up slowly and backed her against the door. "Are you sure it wasn't the adrenaline rush of certain death that sent you into my arms?" He kissed the side of her neck to test his hypothesis. His hips nudged hers. She was soft where he was hard.

Libby sighed as their bodies aligned with satisfying perfection. Her green eyes sparkled with excitement. "Perhaps it has escaped your notice, but you're a very sexy man."

"It was the bloody leg, right? Women can't resist a wounded hero."

"To be exact, I believe James was the hero."

She was taunting him deliberately. He knew that. And still, it pissed him off. "My brother is a great guy, but I doubt the two of you would get along."

"And why is that? I found him quite charming."

"If any Kavanagh is going to end up in your bed, it's going to be me." The declaration ended only a few decibels below a shout.

"Ooh…so intense. I have goose bumps. Still," she said, drawing the single syllable out to make a point. "I'm not sure it's a good idea to sleep with the boss."

"Then we won't sleep," he said. He kissed her wildly, feeling the press of her generous breasts against his chest. How had he ever thought she was meek and mousy?

Libby leaned into him, moaning when he deepened the kiss. "Your mother feels bad about our ordeal. She's treating me to a spa day and a shopping trip tomorrow. But I'll tell her no if you want me here. I'm not going to parlay this whole 'stuck in a mine' thing into special privileges."

"I *want* you to stay away," he said, entirely truthful. "I can't concentrate when you're around."

"How nice of you to say so."

He cupped her cheeks in his hands. "Be sure about this, sweet thing. If I do anything to hurt you, my mother will string me up by my ba—"

Libby clapped a hand over his mouth. "Watch your language, Mr. Kavanagh." She rubbed her thumb over his bottom lip. The simple caress sent fire streaking to his groin. "Are you *planning* on hurting me?"

He shifted from one foot to the other. "Of course not."

"Then relax and go with the flow. If nothing else in the last year, I've learned that's the only way to live…"

* * *

Libby took Patrick at his word about staying home the next day. She'd suffered no lasting physical effects from their unfortunate incarceration, but she *had* been tormented by dark dreams Wednesday night. She *needed* employment. But she *wanted* Patrick. Climbing into bed with him was not going to be in her best interests. The conflicting desires went around and around in her head. She woke up feeling groggy and vaguely depressed.

Maeve, however, refused to let any notion of gloom overshadow their day. When she met Libby in the lobby, she clapped her hands, practically dancing around like a child. "I'm so glad you're finally going to put your hair back to rights. I know your mother disliked that boring brown."

Libby raised her eyebrows. "Has anyone ever accused you of being overly tactful?"

Maeve chuckled, heading out to the large flagstone driveway where her silver Mercedes was parked. "I consider you family, my dear. And as your honorary aunt or stepmother or whatever you want to call me, I'm only doing my duty when I tell you that you have taken a beautiful young woman and turned her into a drudge."

Libby couldn't take offense. Maeve was absolutely too gleeful about restoring Libby's original looks. For a moment, Libby felt a surge of panic. She'd hidden behind her ill-fitting clothes and her nondescript hair color for the better part of a year. What if someone in New York recognized her?

As Maeve navigated the curvy road down the mountain, Libby took several deep breaths. She had started a new life. Did it matter if people knew who she was? *Libby* hadn't committed tax fraud.

Besides, most of the friends in her immediate social circle had melted away when the Parkhurst fortunes began

to shatter. It was doubtful anyone would even want to acknowledge her. And as far as reporters were concerned,
Libby Parkhurst was old news.

When Maeve found a parking spot in Silver Glen, the
day of pampering began. First it was private massages,
then manicures and pedicures at an upscale spa. Of course,
most everything in Silver Glen was upscale. The beautiful alpine-themed town catered to the rich and famous.

An hour and a half later, once her Tahitian Sunset pol-
ish had dried, Libby admired her fingers and toes. This
kind of self-indulgence had been one of the first things to
go when she and her mother had been put out on the street.

It was amazing that something so simple could make a
woman feel like she was ready to take on the world.

Next was the hair salon. Libby pulled a photo out of
her wallet, one from her college graduation, and showed
the stylist her original color. The woman was horrified.
"Why would you ruin such an amazing head of hair? Never
mind," she said quickly. "I don't even want to know. But
before you leave here, young lady, I'm going to remind you
what the good Lord intended you to look like."

Libby allowed the woman to whack three inches, since
it had been ages since her last cut. Not only had Libby
dyed her hair as part of her plan to go incognito, she had
straightened it, as well. Little by little, the real Libby returned.

The stylist kept her promise. When it was done, Libby
gazed in the mirror with tears in her eyes. Her natural hair
was a curly, vibrant red that complemented her pale skin,
unlike the dull brown that had washed her out and made
her seem tired.

Now, the bouncy chin-length do put color in her cheeks.
Parted on one side and tucked behind her ear on the other,
the fun, youthful style framed her face and took years off
her age.

Maeve beamed. "Beautiful. Absolutely beautiful."

Next stop was a charming boutique with an array of trendily clad mannequins in the window. Libby put her foot down. "I have money, Maeve. My first paycheck went in the bank this morning."

Patrick's mother frowned. "You nearly died in the service of a Kavanagh business. If I want to buy you a few things as a thank-you for not suing us, that is my prerogative."

Libby gaped. "You know I would never sue you. That's ridiculous."

But Maeve had already crossed the store and engaged the services of a young woman about Libby's own age. The clerk assessed Libby with a smile. "What kinds of things are we looking for today?"

Maeve shushed Libby when she tried to speak. The older woman steamrollered the conversation. "A little of everything. Casual chic. Business attire…not a suit, I think, but a little black dress. And a very dressy something for dinner…perhaps in ivory or even green if that's not too obvious with her fabulous hair."

The couture makeover became a whirlwind. Libby tried on so many garments, she lost count. When the frenzy was done, Maeve plunked down a credit card. "She'll wear the jeans and stilettos home…plus the peasant blouse. We'll take all the rest in garment bags."

Libby gave up trying to protest. In the months ahead, when she was able, she would do her best to repay Maeve. In the meantime, it was exciting to know that she would be able to accompany Patrick to New York looking her best.

Maeve declared herself exhausted when they returned to the Silver Beeches Lodge. "I'm going to see if Liam needs me," she said. "And if not, I'm headed home to put my feet up."

Libby hugged her impulsively. "Thank you, dear Maeve. I love you."

This time it was Maeve who had tears in her eyes. She took Libby's hands, her expression earnest. "Your mother was a precious woman…fragile, but precious. I still remember how proud she was when you were born. You were the light of her life. When you remember her, Libby, try not to think of the woman she became at the end, but instead, the woman she was at her best…the friend I knew so well."

Libby managed a smile. "It's no wonder your sons adore you."

Maeve waved a dismissive hand. "They think I'm a meddling pain in the ass. But then again, they know I'm always right."

Libby said her goodbyes and wandered upstairs to her room. She was determined to move to the apartment over the Silver Dollar saloon very soon. How many paychecks would it take before she could afford a rent payment? She chafed at the idea of living on Kavanagh charity, even if it was extremely luxurious and comfortable charity.

She and Maeve had lunched out before their appointments, so tonight, the only thing Libby ordered from room service was a chef salad. Often she ate downstairs in the dining room, but it had been a long, though pleasant, day. Sometimes it was nice to be alone and contemplate the future.

After her modest dinner, she packed the suitcase Maeve had loaned her. At one time, Libby had owned a wide array of expensive toiletries. Now she was accustomed to nothing more than discount-store moisturizer, an inexpensive tube of mascara and a couple of lipsticks for dressing up.

Her lace-and-silk nightgown and robe were remnants of the past. As were the several sets of bras and undies she possessed. It was one thing to sell haute couture at a resale shop. No one wanted underwear.

As she crawled into bed, she checked her phone. Patrick had messaged her earlier to let her know he would be sending a taxi to pick her up at seven o'clock tomorrow morning. They would rendezvous at the brand-new airstrip on the other end of the valley.

Patrick's brief text—and her equally brief response— was the only communication Libby had shared with him since she'd walked out of his office Wednesday afternoon. She missed him. And she had gone back and forth a dozen times about whether or not she was doing the right thing.

Their flirtatious conversation had left the status quo up in the air. What was going to happen when they got to New York?

She could tell herself it was all about finding closure… a bid for saying goodbye to her old life. And maybe trying one more time to convince Patrick she could do the job at Silver Reflections.

But she had a weak spot when it came to her fascinating boss. The possibility of sharing his bed made her shiver with anticipation. Right now, that agenda was winning.

Ten

Patrick had decided to bring in one of the standby pilots the Kavanaghs sometimes used instead of flying himself. For one thing, the deep cut in his leg was still sore as hell. And for another, he liked the idea of sitting in the back of the jet with Libby. She was no stranger to luxury travel… so it wasn't that he wanted to see her reaction when he dazzled her with sophistication and pampering.

It was far simpler than that. He wanted to spend time with her.

He arrived at the airstrip thirty minutes early. The past two nights, he hadn't slept worth a damn. He kept reliving the moment the landslide happened. The instant Libby faced one of her worst fears. Because of him. Residual guilt tied his gut in a knot.

Not that she had suffered any lasting harm. Nevertheless, the experience in the mine was unpleasant to say the least. He never should have let her go down there.

He was already on the jet when the taxi pulled up. Peeking through the small window of the plane, he saw Libby get out. The day was drizzly and cold. She was wearing a black wool coat and carried a red-and-black umbrella, her face hidden. All he could see was long legs and sexy shoes.

The pilot was already in the cockpit preparing for take-off. Patrick went to the open cabin door and stood, ready to lend a hand if Libby needed help on the wet stairs. She hovered on the tarmac as the cabdriver handed a suitcase and matching carry-on to Patrick. Then she came up the steps.

Patrick moved back. "Hand me your umbrella." He'd been wrong about the coat. It wasn't wool at all, but instead, a fashionable all-weather trench-style, presumably heavily lined to deal with the cold weather in New York. A hood, edged in faux fur, framed her face.

For some reason, he couldn't look her in the eyes…not yet. "Make yourself comfortable," he said over his shoulder. After shaking the worst of the water from the umbrella, he closed it and stored it in a small closet. Then he retracted the jet's folding steps and turned the locking mechanisms on the cabin door.

"We'll be taking off in about five minutes."

At last, he turned around. Libby stood in the center of the cabin, her purse and coat on a seat beside her.

His heart punched once in his chest. Hard. His lungs forgot how to function. "Libby?" Incredulous, he stared at her. She was wearing a long-sleeve, scoop-necked black dress with a chunky silver necklace and matching earrings. The dress was completely plain. But the slubbed-knit fabric fit her body perfectly, emphasizing every sexy curve.

Even so, the dress wasn't what made the greatest impact. Nor was it the extremely fashionable but wildly impractical high heels that made her legs seem a million miles long. The dramatic jolt wasn't even a result of her darkly lashed green eyes or her soft crimson lips. It was her hair. God, her hair…

His mouth was probably hanging open, but he couldn't help it. He cleared his throat, shoving his hands in the pocket of his suit jacket to keep from grabbing her. "Whoever talked you into changing your color back to normal is a genius. It suits you perfectly." The deep red curls with gold highlights made her skin glow. The new cut framed her face and drew attention to high cheekbones and a slightly pointed chin.

Libby shrugged, seeming both pleased by and uncomfortable with his reaction. She and her mother had been harassed by reporters for months. Looking the way she did right now, it would have been impossible for her to fade into a crowd. Hence the metamorphosis from gorgeous socialite to little brown mouse.

She nodded, her eyes shadowed. "I've been hiding for a long time. But that's over, Patrick. I'm ready to move on."

He couldn't help himself. He closed the distance between them. "You're more than the sum of your looks, Libby."

"Thank you."

He winnowed his fingers through her hair. "It's so light…and fluffy…and *red*." He lowered his voice to a rough whisper. "I want to take you right here, right now. In that big overstuffed captain's chair. You make me crazy."

She looked at him, her soft green eyes roving his face, perhaps seeking assurance of his sincerity. "I want you, too, Patrick. Perhaps I shouldn't. My life is complicated enough already. But when I'm with you, I forget about all the bad stuff."

He frowned. "I'm not sure I want to be used as an amnesiac device."

"Don't think of it that way. You're like a drug. But the good kind. One that makes me feel alive in the best possible way. When I'm with you, I'm happy. It's as simple as that."

Her explanation mollified him somewhat, but he still wasn't entirely satisfied. He wanted to kiss her, but the pilot used the intercom to notify them of imminent take-off. "This discussion isn't over," he said.

They strapped into adjacent seats and prepared to be airborne. Libby turned to look out the window. Her profile was as familiar to him now as was his own. He struggled with a hodgepodge of emotions that left him feeling out of sorts.

He liked being Libby Parkhurst's savior. In the beginning he had resented his mother's interference. But once Libby was installed at Silver Reflections, it made him feel good to know he was helping make her life easier. Now that she had acquitted herself reasonably well in the woods, there was really no reason not to let her finish out Charlise's maternity leave.

But did he honestly want Libby under his nose 24/7? The situation would be perfect fodder for his mother's wedding-obsessed machinations behind the scenes. Patrick, however, was more worried about becoming a slobbering sex-starved idiot.

He had a business to run. Silver Reflections was doing very well, but any relatively new business had to keep on its toes. He couldn't afford to let his focus be drawn away by a woman, no matter how appealing.

The flight to New York was uneventful. Patrick worked on his presentation. Libby read a novel. They spoke occasionally, but it was stilted conversation. Was he the only one feeling shaken by what might happen during the night to come?

Libby felt like a girl in a fairy tale. Except this was backward. She had already been the princess with the world at her feet. Now she was an ordinary woman trying to embrace her new life.

It didn't hurt that Maeve had spoiled her with a suitcase full of new clothes. When Libby was growing up, her mother had bought Libby an entire new wardrobe every spring and fall. The castoffs were given to charity. They were always good clothes, some of them barely worn. Libby had never thought twice about it…other than the few times she had begged to keep a favorite sweater or pair of jeans.

Such excess seemed dreadful now. The clothes she'd brought with her this weekend would have to last several years. They were quality items, well made and classic in style. Perhaps Maeve was more perceptive than Libby realized, because during their wild shopping spree, Maeve had never once suggested anything that was faddish, nothing that would be dated by the next season.

On the other hand, Libby knew it wasn't the clothing that defined her new maturity. The past year had been a trial by fire. She had struggled with the emotional loss of her father, grieved the physical loss of her mother and juggled all of that alongside the almost inexplicable loss of her own identity.

And now there was Patrick. What to do about Patrick?

He disturbed her introspection. "Do you have any current plans to see your father?"

"Will you think I'm a terrible person if I say *no*?"

His smile was gentle and encompassed an understanding that threatened her composure. "Of course not. No one can make that decision for you."

She picked at the armrest. "I've sent him the occasional note. And of course, I called him after Mother, well…you know."

"Was he able to attend the funeral?"

"No. The request to the prison would have had to come from me, and I didn't think I could handle it. I was pretty much a mess. Fortunately, my parents had actually bought plots where my father grew up in Connecticut. They even prepaid for funerals. So at least I didn't have to worry about that."

"Has he written to you?"

"Only twice. I think he's ashamed. And embarrassed. But mostly angry he got caught. My father apparently subscribed to the theory that tax fraud isn't actually a crime unless someone finds out what you've done."

"He's not alone in that view."

"Doesn't make it right."

"How long does he have to serve?"

"Seven to ten. It was a lot of money. And apparently he was not exactly repentant in front of the judge."

"Time in prison can change people. Maybe it will show him what matters."

"I suppose…" But she was dubious. Her father was accustomed to throwing his weight around. His money had made it possible for him to demand *what* he wanted *when* he wanted. She had tried to find it in her heart to have sympathy for him. But she was still too shattered about the whole experience.

Patrick leaned forward and pointed out her window. "There's the skyline."

Libby took in the familiar sight and felt a stab of grief so raw and deep it caught her off guard. Patrick didn't say a word. But he used his finger to catch a tear that rolled down her cheek, and he finally offered her a pristine handkerchief to blow her nose.

"It's not my home anymore," she said, her throat so tight she could barely speak.

Patrick slid an arm around her shoulders. "It will always be your *first* home. And at some point, the trauma of what happened will become part of your past. Not so devastating that you think of it every day."

"I hope so."

"Silver Glen is a pretty good place for a fresh start. I know you came to the mountains to heal and to get back on your feet financially. My mother would be over the moon if you decided to stay forever."

"What about you, Patrick?"

The impulsive query came from her own lips, but shocked her nevertheless. It was the kind of needy leading question an insecure woman asks. "Don't answer that," she said quickly. "I don't know why I said it."

His expression was impassive, his thoughts impossible to decipher. "I have nothing to hide. I've already told you how I feel about marriage. I get the impression you're the kind of woman who will want a permanent relationship eventually. Maybe you can find that in Silver Glen. I don't know. But in the meantime, we've come very close to a line you may not want to cross when you're no longer in fear for your life."

"Don't patronize me," she said slowly. "I mentioned the one-hotel-room thing when I was safely out of the mine and standing in your office. Did you forget about that?"

"A relationship forged under duress doesn't usually stand the test of time."

She scowled, even as the plane bumped down on the runway at LaGuardia. "For a guy who's barely thirty, you pontificate like someone's grandmother."

He sighed, his jaw tight. "Are we having our first fight?"

"No," she snapped. "That happened when you called me a *misfit*."

"So many things are clear now," he muttered, his hot gaze skating from her lips to her breasts. "It's the red hair. I could have saved myself a lot of heartache if I'd known that the woman I interviewed in the beginning was not a mouse, but instead an exotic, hotheaded spitfire."

"Patronizing *and* chauvinistic."

A deep voice interrupted their quarrel. "Um, excuse me…Mr. Kavanagh? We have to deplane now."

Libby groaned inwardly, embarrassed beyond belief. How much had the pilot overheard? Grabbing her coat and shoving her arms into the sleeves, she scooped up her purse and climbed over Patrick's legs to head for the exit. He let her go, presumably lingering to deal with their luggage.

A private limo awaited them, a uniformed driver at the ready. When Patrick climbed in to the backseat with her, she ignored him pointedly, her face still hot with mortification.

How was a woman supposed to deal with a man who was both brutally honest and ridiculously appealing? Was she seriously going to settle for a temporary fling? And what was the time limit? When Charlise came back in six months, did the affair and the job end on the same day?

Patrick took her hand. "Quit sulking."

Her temper shot up several notches. She gave him a look that should have melted the door frame. "I've changed my mind. I want my own hotel room. I need a job more than I need you."

He stroked the inside of her wrist with his thumb. "Don't be mad, my beautiful girl. We're in New York. Alone. Away from my meddling family. We can do anything we want…anything at all."

His voice threatened to mesmerize her. Deep and husky with arousal, his words had the smooth cadence of a snake charmer. She shivered inwardly. "How easy do you think I am?" Her indignation dwindled rapidly in inverse proportion to the increase in her shaky breathing and the acceleration of her rushing pulse.

Patrick lifted her wrist and kissed the back of her hand. "You're not easy at all, Libby. You're damned difficult. Every time I think I have you figured out, you surprise me all over again."

She caught the chauffeur's gaze in the rearview mirror. The man lifted an eyebrow. Libby blushed again and stared out the window. "Not now, Patrick. We're almost there."

Patrick settled back in his seat, but the enigmatic smile on his face made Libby want to kiss the smirk off his face. Fortunately for her self-control, the car pulled up in front of their destination. While Patrick swiped his credit card, Libby slid out of the vehicle, shivering when a blast of cold air flipped up the tail of her coat.

"Where's our luggage?" she asked, suddenly anxious about Maeve's nice suitcases and Libby's new clothes.

"The driver is taking them on to the Carlyle. They'll hold them for us until check-in time."

He took her arm. "C'mon. We're early, but I want to make sure they're ready for us." Ushering her through sleek revolving doors, he hurried her into the building and onto the elevator. Fortunately for Libby, the small space was crowded, meaning she didn't have to talk to Patrick at all.

On the twenty-seventh floor, they exited. An eerily perfect receptionist greeted them. Behind her in platinum letters were the words *Peabody Rushford*. Libby took off her coat, using the opportunity to look around with curiosity. It was difficult to imagine anyone from this upscale environment insisting that executives participate in one of Patrick's field experiences.

Moments later, after a hushed communication via a high-tech intercom system, they were escorted to the boardroom where Patrick would do his presentation. Every chair at the glossy conference table was situated at an exact ninety-degree angle. Crystal tumblers filled with ice water sat on folded linen napkins.

Not a single item in the room was out of place. Except Libby. She felt ill at ease. Why had she agreed to accompany Patrick? Oh, wait. Tagging along had been her idea.

She was still holding out hope that she could convince him to give her the job.

The executives trickled into the room, first one or two, and then three or four, until finally, the entire team was assembled. Eight men, four women. Plus the graying boss. She guessed his *underlings* ranged in age from early thirties to late forties. Libby was easily the youngest person in the room.

Patrick greeted each participant warmly, introducing himself with the self-deprecatory charm she had come to expect from him. He was confident and humorous, and he interacted with both men and women equally well. When everyone was seated, there were three chairs remaining at one end of the table. Libby took the middle one, leaving a buffer on either side.

She was here as an interested observer. No need to get chummy. Not now at least. The future remained to be seen. If she continued to work for Patrick—and it was possible he might decide to let her stay on—then no doubt, she would be meeting these people in April.

Honestly, it was hard to imagine any of this crew getting dirty in the woods. The women wore similar quasi uniforms. Dark formfitting blazers with matching pencil skirts and white silk blouses. Their hairstyles fell into two camps…either sophisticated chignons or sharply modern pixie cuts.

The men were equally polished. Their dark suits resembled Patrick's. Though he wore a red power tie, the executives' neckwear was more conservative. Finally, the room settled, and Patrick began his spiel.

Libby knew Patrick was smart. But seeing him operate in this environment was eye-opening. He spoke to the group as an equal…a man with experience in their world as well as the master of his own domain, Silver Reflections.

As the orientation proceeded, Libby watched the faces

around the table. One of the women and several of the men were actively engaged, frequently asking questions… demonstrating enthusiasm and anticipation. Others exhibited veiled anxiety, and some were almost hostile.

Patrick had shared with Libby that the CEO was an ex-marine…a man both hard in business and in his physical demands on himself. For him to insist that his top management people participate in Patrick's program was asking a lot. Libby wondered if anyone would bail out, even if it might mean losing their jobs.

During the official Q and A time at the end, one of the quieter women who hadn't said a word so far raised her hand. When Patrick acknowledged her, she pointed at Libby. "Does she work for you? I'd like to hear what she has to say."

Patrick gave Libby a wry glance and shrugged. "Libby?"

All eyes in the room focused on her. She cleared her throat, scrambling for the right words. She would never forgive herself if she botched this for Patrick. "Well, um…"

The woman stared at her with naked apprehension. Clearly she wanted some kind of reassurance and saw Libby as a kindred spirit.

Libby smiled. "I certainly understand if anyone in this room, male or female, has reservations about spending a night or two in the woods, particularly if your personal history doesn't include campouts and bonfires. To be honest, I was the same way. But when I came to work for Patrick, it was important for me to try this *immersion* experience. I had to prove to myself that I could step outside my comfort zone."

The woman blanched. "And how did that go?"

Libby laughed softly. "I'll be honest. There were good parts and bad." No reason to go into the mine-shaft fiasco. "On the plus side, the setting is pristine and beautiful and serene. If you haven't been much of a nature lover in the past, I think you'll be one when the weekend is over."

"And the less wonderful parts?"

Though only one woman was doing the interrogation, Libby had a strong suspicion that others around the table were hanging on Libby's comments, looking for reassurance.

"Spending the night on the ground was a challenge, even with a comfy sleeping bag and a small pad. I'm a light sleeper to start with, so I found it difficult to relax enough to sleep deeply, even though I was tired."

"Anything else?"

Libby hesitated. Patrick grinned and nodded, as if not perturbed at all by anything she might have to say. "Well," she said, "there's the issue of using the bathroom in the woods. Women are always at a disadvantage there."

A titter of laughter circled the table.

Libby continued. "But all of this is minor stuff compared to the big picture. You'll learn to rely on teamwork to get simple tasks done like meals and setting up camp and taking it down. I think you'll see your coworkers in a new light. And I promise you that you'll find skills and talents you never knew you had. Patrick is not a drill sergeant. He's a facilitator. His knowledge is formidable. You can feel entirely safe with him in charge."

For a split second, the room was silent. Patrick was no longer smiling. If anything, he looked as if someone had punched him in the stomach. What was he thinking?

The woman asking the questions breathed an audible sigh of relief. "Thank you, Libby. I feel much better about this now."

The boss nodded. "I encourage my people to ask questions. It's the only way to learn."

Now some of the men seemed chagrined. Suddenly the woman in the group who had seemed like the weakest link had earned the boss's respect. Libby was pleased that her own small contribution had helped.

After the session adjourned, most of the staff returned to their offices. The boss lingered to speak with Patrick, expressing his opinion that the orientation had gone extremely well.

Then it was time to go. Patrick and Libby retraced their steps to the lobby, both of them quiet. Libby stood on the sidewalk, huddled into her coat. "Do we split up now? And meet at the hotel later?"

Patrick pulled up her hood and tucked a stray strand of hair inside. "Is it important for you to be alone when you revisit your old building?"

She searched his face. "No. Not really. But I assumed you had other things to do."

He kissed the tip of her nose. "My business is done. I'd like to take you to lunch, and then we'll face your past together."

"I might cry."

Patrick chuckled. "I think I can handle it. C'mon, I'm starving."

Eleven

Patrick hailed a cab and helped Libby in, then ran around to the other side and joined her. Heavy clouds had rolled in. The sky overhead was gray and menacing. He gave the driver an address and sat back. "If you don't mind, Libby, I thought we would try a new place Aidan recommended. It's tucked away in the theater district, off the beaten path for tourists. He says they have the best homemade soups this side of North Carolina."

Libby smoothed the hem of her coat over her knees, unwittingly drawing attention to her legs. He had plans for those legs.

She nodded. "Sounds good, but I'm surprised. I thought men needed more than soup to consider it a meal."

"I might have forgotten to mention the gyros and turkey legs." His stomach growled on cue.

Libby laughed. "Now I get it."

"You were amazing back there," he said. "I never realized how much better these weekend trips would be if all the participants have the opportunity to calm their fears beforehand. Everything you said was perfect."

"But you've always done orientations…right?" She frowned.

"I have. Yes. But the dynamics of these high-powered firms are interesting. No one wants to appear weak in front of the boss."

"Then how was today different?"

"I think your presence at the table connected with that woman. She saw you as an ally. And perceived you to be truthful and sincere. So that gave her the courage to speak out. Truthfully, I think there were others in the room who shared some of the same anxieties. So even though they didn't *ask*, they also wanted to know what you had to say."

"I'm glad I could help."

Patrick glanced at his watch. "Now, we're officially off the clock…business concluded."

"There's a lot of the day still ahead."

He leaned over, took her chin in his hand and kissed her full on the lips. "I'm sure we can find some way to fill the time."

"I'll leave the planning up to you." Her demure answer was accompanied by a teasing smile that made him wish he could ditch the rest of the day's agenda and take her back to their room right now. Unfortunately, waiting wasn't his strong suit.

The change in her appearance still threw him off his stride. The Libby with whom he had communed out in the woods and down in the mine was spunky and cute and fun. He'd been aroused by her and interested in bedding her.

This newly revamped Libby was something else again. She made him feel like an overeager adolescent caught up in a surge of hormones that were probably killing off his brain cells in droves. His libido was louder than ever. *Take Libby. Take Libby. Man want woman.*

To disguise his increasing agitation, he pulled out his phone. With a muttered "excuse me," he pretended to check important emails. Libby was neither insulted nor overly perturbed by his distraction. She stared out the window of the cab, perhaps both pleased and yet anxious about revisiting her old stomping grounds.

That was one thing he loved about her. She wasn't jaded, even though a woman from her background certainly could be. Perhaps she had always been so fresh and open to life's surprises. Or maybe the places she and her mother had lived after being kicked out of their lavish home had taught Libby to appreciate her past.

The café where they had lunch was noisy and crowded. Patrick was glad. He wasn't in the mood for intimate conversation. His need to make love to Libby drowned out every other thought in his head.

Libby, on the other hand, chatted happily, her mood upbeat despite the fact that she was facing an emotional hurdle this afternoon.

He drank his coffee slowly, absently listening as his luncheon date conversed with the waitress about what it was like to be an understudy for an off-Broadway play. At last, the server walked away and Libby smiled at Patrick. "Sorry. I love hearing people's stories."

He raised an eyebrow. "Yet I haven't heard all of yours. What did you study in college? Who did you want to be when you grew up? How many boyfriends did you have along the way?"

A shadow flitted across her face. "I was an English major."

"Did you want to teach?"

"No. Not really. My parents wouldn't have approved."

"Too plebeian?" he asked, tongue in cheek.

Libby rolled her eyes at him. "Something like that."

"Then why the English major?"

She shrugged, her expression slightly defensive. "I loved books. It was the one area of study where I could indulge my obsession with the printed word and no one would criticize the hours I spent in the library."

"Is that what your parents did?"

Her smile was bleak this time. "They told me no man would want to marry a woman who was boring. That I should learn to entertain and decorate a house and choose fine wines and converse about politics and current events."

"Sounds like a Stepford wife."

"I suppose. It became a moot point when my father decided to defraud the government. My standing in society evaporated, not that I minded. At least not on my own account. I did feel very sorry for what it did to my mother. She never signed on for coupon clipping and shopping at discount clothing stores. My father spoiled her and pampered her, right up until the day he was carted away in handcuffs."

"That's all behind you now. Nothing but good times ahead."

He heard his own words and winced inwardly. What did *he* know about the struggles Libby faced? Even several years ago when he decided to give up his career in Chicago, it wasn't a huge risk. The Kavanagh family had deep pockets. He had started Silver Reflections with his own money, but if he had run into financial difficulties, there would have been plenty of help available to him. Never in his life had he faced the challenges that had been thrust upon Libby.

She wiped her mouth with a napkin and reapplied her lipstick. Watching her smooth on the sultry red color was an exercise in sexual frustration.

When she looked up, she caught him staring. He must have put on a good show, because she didn't appear to notice how close to the edge he was. Instead, she grimaced. "Let's go see my building before I get cold feet."

The sentence would have made sense, even if the words had been literal. The temperature outside had to have dropped at least ten degrees since they had arrived in the city.

He hailed another cab and looked at Libby. "You'll have to give the address this time."

"Of course." She nodded, her expression hard to decipher. But as they whizzed through the streets of the city, he saw her anxiety level rise.

When he took one of her hands in his, it was ice-cold. "Where are your gloves?"

"I didn't have any that matched this coat, and I wanted to look nice for your business associates."

"Oh, for God's sake, Libby. Here. Take mine." The ones in the pocket of his overcoat were old and well-worn, but they were leather, lined with cashmere. At least they would keep her warm in transit.

She barely seemed to notice his offering, but she didn't protest when he slid the gloves onto her hands. Finally, the cab stopped. "We're here," she said. For a moment, she didn't move.

"Libby? Are we going to get out?"

She looked at him blankly.

"Libby?" He kissed her nose. "C'mon, darlin'. There's no bogeyman waiting for you. Nothing but bricks and mortar."

"I know that."

Even so, when they stood on the sidewalk, she huddled against him, pretending to shelter herself from the wind. But they were shielded by the building, and the biting breeze had all but disappeared.

He put his arm around her shoulder, at a loss for how to

help her. "Which floor was yours?" he asked…anything to get her to talk.

"The penthouse. Daddy liked looking down on Central Park."

Patrick stood quietly, holding her close. "I'm here, Libby. You're not alone."

At last, she moved. He thought she meant only to walk past the impressive building, but she stopped in front of the double glass doors and, after a moment's hesitation, stepped forward to open them.

Before she could do so, a barrel-chested, white-haired man in a gray uniform with burgundy piping flung them wide. "Ms. Libby. Good God Almighty. I've been worried sick about you. I'm so sorry about your mother, baby girl. Come let me hug you."

Libby launched herself into the man's embrace and wrapped her arms around his ample waist. "Oh, Clarence. I've missed you so much."

Patrick watched in bemusement as the two old friends reconnected. He entered the lobby in deference to the cold, but hung back, unwilling to interfere with Libby's moment of closure.

At last, the old man acknowledged his presence. "Come on, Libby. Tell me about this handsome young fellow."

Libby blushed, her face alight with happiness. "That's my boss, Patrick Kavanagh. Patrick, this is Clarence Turner. He's known me since I was in diapers."

Clarence beamed. "Sweetest little gal you ever saw. And she grew up as beautiful on the inside as she was on the outside. For my sixtieth birthday, she made me a banana cream cake from scratch. Nicest thing anyone had ever done for me since my wife died."

Patrick stuck out his hand. "An honor to meet you, sir."

Clarence looked at Libby, his face troubled. "I'd take you upstairs if I could, but I think it would upset you. The new owners redid the whole place. You wouldn't recognize it."

"It doesn't matter," Libby said. "Seeing you is enough. I always thought my parents and I would give you a big, awesome gift when you retired…maybe a trip to Hawaii… or a new car. Turns out you'll be lucky to get a card and a pack of gum from me now."

She smiled and laughed when she said it, but Patrick knew it troubled her not to be able to help her old friend in any substantial way. Patrick made a mental note to follow up on the situation and see what he could do in Libby's name.

Clarence shot Patrick an assessing glance. "I thought maybe the two of you were an item," he said, not so subtly. "A man could do a lot worse than to marry Libby Parkhurst."

Before Patrick could reply, Libby jumped in. "Patrick and I are just friends. Actually, I'm working for his company temporarily. Patrick's mother and mine were good friends. Maeve Kavanagh has been helping me get back on my feet." She hugged Clarence one more time. "We have to go. But I promise to write more often. You're still at the same address?"

"Yes, indeed. They'll have to take me out of there feet-first." He looked at Patrick one more time and then back at Libby. "You're going to be okay, Libby. I never saw a girl with more grit or more light in her soul."

"Thank you for that, old friend."

When Patrick saw Libby's soft green eyes fill with tears, he decided it was time to go. "Nice to meet you, sir. I hope our paths will cross again."

Though Libby glanced over her shoulder and waved one last time as they braved the cold again, she didn't protest. Patrick had a feeling that the emotional reunion had taken more out of her than she realized.

On the sidewalk, he tipped up her chin and kissed her forehead. "How 'bout we go on the hotel and check in? I think we both could use a nap. If we're going to have a night on the town, you need your beauty sleep. And now that I think about it, I probably should get some play tickets."

They climbed into a cab and Libby took his hand. "What if we skip a play and just go out to dinner? That way we'd be back to the hotel early."

He swallowed, aware that the cabbie was perhaps listening, despite the fact that he had his radio on. "I'd like that very much." He clenched his other fist. "I want to be alone with you," he muttered.

"We could skip the nap, also."

In her eyes he saw everything he wanted and more. "I booked two rooms," he said hoarsely. "I didn't want to take advantage of you."

"I'm not weak, Patrick. I can take care of myself. And I was mad when I asked for that second room. We don't need it. I don't expect anything from you except pleasure."

"Pleasure?" His mouth was dry, his sex hard as stone. His brain had for all intents and purposes turned to mush.

She leaned into him. "Pleasure," she whispered. "You're a smart man. You'll figure it out."

Fortunately for Patrick's sanity, it was a brief cab ride. He paid the fare, aware all the while that Libby watched him.

He couldn't bear to look at her. He was too close to the edge.

At the front desk, the polite employee didn't blink an eye when Patrick canceled one of the rooms. The clerk dealt with the credit card and handed over the keys. "We've been holding your luggage, Mr. Kavanagh. I'll have it sent up immediately, along with a bottle of champagne and some canapés. Is there anything else we can do for you?"

Patrick swallowed, his hand shaking as he signed the charge slip. "No. Thank you."

He turned to Libby. "You ready to go upstairs?"

Twelve

Libby linked her hand in his. "I'm ready." She was under no illusions. If she hadn't pushed the issue, Patrick might well have ignored the spark of attraction between them. He was wary of hurting Libby, and he had a healthy respect for his mother's good opinion.

Libby rested her head on his shoulder. They were alone in the elegant elevator. "No one will know about this but you and me, Patrick. You're not interested in a relationship, and I'm not, either. But that doesn't mean we can't enjoy each other's company."

His grip tightened on her hand when the elevator dinged. The bellman had come up on the service elevator, so there was a busy moment as Patrick opened the door and the luggage was situated. A second bellman came on the heels of the first, this one pushing a cart covered in white linen. The silver ice bucket chilled a bottle of bubbly. An offering of fancy cheese spreads and toast fingers resided on china dishes, along with strawberries and cream.

Once the efficient Carlyle employees disappeared, tips in hand, Patrick leaned against the door. "May I offer you a strawberry…or a glass of champagne?"

Libby nodded, her heart in her throat. "The latter please." She was accustomed to drinking fine champagne, but it had been a very long time. When Patrick handed her a crystal flute, she tipped it back and drank recklessly. The bubbly liquid was crisp and flavorful.

Patrick followed suit, although he sipped his drink slowly, eyeing her over the rim. "Have I told you how sexy you look in that dress?"

She was crestfallen. "I thought it was suitably professional."

"It *is* suitable," he said. "And professional. But the woman inside makes it something else entirely."

"Like what?" She held out her glass for a refill. Her knees were shaky. Was she going to chicken out now? She couldn't remember the last time she had experienced such genuine, shivery, sexual desire.

Patrick filled her flute a second time. But before he handed it to her, he took a sip…exactly where her lipstick had left a faint stain. "Tastes amazing," he said.

She kicked off her heels and curled her toes against the exquisite Oriental rug. Ordinarily, she hated panty hose with a passion, but the weather today had been a bit much for bare legs. There was no good way for a man to remove them…romantically speaking.

"Will you excuse me for a moment?" she asked, setting down her half-empty glass.

"Of course."

In the opulent bathroom, she covered her hot red cheeks with cold hands. She was going to have sex with Patrick Kavanagh. Casually. Temporarily.

Good girls didn't do such things. But then again, she'd

been a good girl for much of her life, and look where it had gotten her.

Rapidly, she stripped off her panty hose and stuffed them in a drawer of the vanity. She fluffed her hair and then held a damp cloth to her cheeks, trying to tame the wild color that was a dead giveaway as to her state of mind.

When she could linger no longer, she returned to the sitting room. It was lovely, with pale green and ecru walls. Antique French furnishings lent an air of romance. Patrick had even lit a candle, though it was the middle of the day.

He came to her and slid his hands beneath her hair, his smile holding the tiniest hint of male satisfaction. "Are you shy, Libby love?"

"Maybe. A little bit. I'm suddenly feeling rather unsophisticated."

"I don't want sophistication. I don't need it." His eyes had gone all dark and serious, the blue-gray irises like stormy lakes.

She curled her fingers around his wrists, not to push him away, but to hold on to something steady as her emotions cartwheeled. "What *do* you want and need, Patrick?"

He scooped her into his arms. "You, Libby. Only you."

On the way to the bedroom, he stopped to pick up the heavy pillar candle. But he couldn't manage it and Libby, too. Not without tumbling them all to the floor in a pile of hot wax. The image made her smile.

Patrick scowled. "Are you laughing at me?"

She looped an arm around his neck. "I wouldn't dare. I was merely contemplating all the ways I could use hot wax to drive you wild."

He stumbled and nearly lost his balance. His jaw dropped. Not much. But enough to let Libby know her little comment had left him gobsmacked. It felt good to have the upper hand, even if for only a moment.

The bedroom was something out of a fantasy…soft lavender sheets, fresh violets in a crystal vase…a Louis XIV chaise longue upholstered in sunshine-yellow and aubergine brocade. The ivory damask duvet had already been folded back. All Patrick had to do was gently drop Libby on the bed.

"Don't move," he said. "I'm going back for the ambience."

She barely had time to blink before he returned. He put the candle on the ornate dresser, a safe distance away. Then he closed the drapes, shutting out the gray afternoon light.

Libby propped her elbows behind her. "I thought you wanted a nap," she teased.

"Later," he said.

His jaw was tight, his cheekbones flushed. As he walked slowly toward the bed, he stripped off his tie and shirt and jacket with an economy of motion that was both intense and arousing…as if he couldn't bear to waste a single second. Libby's breath caught the first time she saw his bare chest.

"Nice show," she croaked. Her throat was dry, but the champagne was in the other room.

When he stood beside the bed, he unbuckled his belt and slid it free. Next went the shoes and socks. When he was down to his pants and nothing else, he crooked a finger. "Come here and turn around."

Trembling all over, she got up on her knees and presented her back to him. His fingertips found the top of her zipper and lowered it slowly. He cursed.

She looked over her shoulder, alarmed. "What's wrong?"

His expression was equal parts torment and lust. "You're too young. Too vulnerable. Too beautifully innocent."

"I'm not *entirely* innocent."

"I'm not talking about that kind of innocence," he said gruffly, stroking the length of her spine. He unfastened her bra, sliding his arms around her and palming her achy breasts. "It's *you*. All these things have tried to defeat you and yet you're still like a rosy-eyed child. As if nothing bad could ever happen."

She took one of his hands and raised it to her lips. "I'm only young in calendar years, Patrick. Life gave me an old soul, whether I wanted it or not. Now, quit agonizing over this and come to bed."

Patrick knew he was a lucky man. At this point in his life, he possessed most everything he'd ever wanted. But he had never wanted anything or anyone the way he wanted Libby Parkhurst. He wanted to be her knight, her protector, her one and only lover. The intensity of the desire overwhelmed him and left a hollow feeling in his chest. Because to have Libby in his life on a permanent basis would mean changes he wasn't prepared to make.

He wasn't in love with her. This was about sex. Nothing more.

He helped her out of the black dress. Underneath it, her bra and panties were pink lace. He'd never particularly been a fan of pink. But on her, it was perfect.

When she was completely naked, he sucked in a breath. "Get under the covers," he said gruffly. "Before you freeze."

He wondered if she saw through his equivocation. The room was plenty warm. But he needed a moment to collect himself. Turning away from the bed, he stripped off his pants and briefs. His erection could have hammered nails. He ached, almost bent over with the need to thrust inside her and find peace. When Libby flicked off the only remaining lamp, he turned around.

In the light from the single candle, her hair glowed like a nimbus around a naughty angel.

She curled on her side, the covers tucked to her chin. "I'm feeling nervous," she said quietly.

Did the woman have no filters? No emotional armor? "I'm feeling a bit shaky myself," he admitted.

Her eyes widened when she spotted the physical evidence of his excitement for the first time. "Really? 'Cause from over here it seems like you're good to go."

Her droll humor made him laugh. He flipped back the covers and joined her, his legs tangling with ones that were softer and more slender. "You have no concept of how much I want to make love to you."

"Why, Patrick? Why me?"

"Why not you?" He teased the nearest nipple, watching in fascination as it budded tightly.

"That's not an answer." She cried out when he bent to suckle her breast. But she must have meant for him to continue, because she clutched his head to her chest, her fingers twined in his hair.

She smelled like wildflowers and summer love affairs. In the midst of winter, she brought warmth and sunshine into this room, this bed.

He kissed her roughly. "Not everything in life can be explained, Libby."

Her arms wrapped around his neck, threatening to choke him. "Try."

"You give me something no one else ever has," he admitted quietly. "When I'm with you, everything seems right."

He saw in her eyes the recognition of his honesty. It wasn't something he planned. In fact, he felt damned naked in more ways than one. But if he couldn't give her forever, at least he could give her this.

"Make love to me, Patrick."

It was all he needed to hear and more. Later there would

be time for drawn-out foreplay and fancy moves. But at the moment, all he could think about was being inside her.

Reaching for the condoms he had dropped on the nightstand, he sheathed himself matter-of-factly, trying not to notice the way Libby's gaze followed his every motion. "Now, my Libby. Now."

He eased on top of her, careful to shield her from his entire weight. For a moment, he couldn't move. He was hard against her thigh, shuddering with the need to take and take and take.

Libby reached up and cradled his face in her hands. "I want you, too, Patrick."

"You wouldn't lie about not being a virgin…would you?"

Her eyes darkened with an emotion he didn't understand. "I don't lie about *anything*."

That was the problem. Few people in life were as transparent as Libby. If he hurt her, either physically or emotionally, he would know it. Immediately. Was he prepared for that responsibility? The first one, yes…no question. But the second?

Slowly, he eased inside her, pressing all the way until he could go no farther. Her sex was warm and tight. Yellow spots danced behind his eyelids. Every muscle in his body was tense.

Libby curled her legs around his waist, unwittingly driving him deeper still. "This is nice," she said, catching her breath.

"Nice?" He clenched his teeth. He was damned if he would come like a teenage boy—all flash and no substance.

Libby squeezed him inwardly, her mouth tipped up in a tiny smile that told him she enjoyed flexing her newfound power. "I give you high marks for the opening sequence. Very impressive delivery. Appealing package."

He choked out a laugh. "Haven't you ever heard of calling a spade a spade? You can refer to it as a co—"

She clapped a hand over his mouth with a move that was beginning to seem familiar. "No I can't."

"Where did you say you went to school?"

"Catholic everything. My parents were Protestant, but they liked the idea of surrounding their baby girl with nuns."

"Can we please not talk about nuns right now? It's throwing me off my game."

She nipped his chin with sharp teeth. "Proceed. You're doing very well so far."

When he flexed his hips, he managed to erase the smile from her face. "How about now?"

Libby tipped back her head and sighed, arching into his thrust. "Don't ever stop. What time is checkout tomorrow?"

The random conversation confounded him. As a rule, his bed partners were not so chatty. "Eleven. Twelve. Hell, I don't know. Why?"

Green eyes, hazy and unfocused, gazed up at him. "I want to calculate how many more times we can do this before we have to go home."

Libby was in deep trouble. She'd been lying to herself so well, she didn't even see the cliff ahead. And now she was about to tumble into disaster. Again.

At sixteen there had been some excuse. Not so much in her current situation.

Patrick was big and warm and solid, and that wasn't even taking into consideration the body part currently stroking her so intimately. He surrounded her, filled her, possessed her. The smell of his skin, the silky touch of his hair against her breasts. She could barely breathe from wanting him.

"Hush now, darlin'," he groaned, his Southern accent more pronounced as he ground his hips against hers. When he zeroed in on a certain spot, she cried out, her orgasm taking her by surprise.

The flash of climax was intense and prolonged, wave after wave of pleasure that left her lax and helpless in his embrace. But Patrick was lost, as well. His muffled shout against her neck was accompanied by fierce, frantic thrusts that culminated in his wild release.

When the storm passed, the room was silent but for their harsh breathing.

Coming back to New York had triggered an avalanche of feelings. And not only about her father's fall from grace. There was that other business, as well. The thing that still shamed her and made her question her judgment about men. She had never wanted to be so vulnerable again. But Patrick wouldn't hurt her, would he? At least not the way she'd been hurt before.

Thirteen

Libby was having the most wonderful dream. She was floating in the ocean, the sun beaming down in gentle benediction. The temperature was exactly right. A warm blanket cocooned her as the breeze ruffled her hair.

Some sound far in the distance brought her awake with a jerk. Every cell in her body froze in stunned disbelief. Patrick Kavanagh lay half on top of her, his regular breathing steady and deep.

Holy Hannah. What had she done? Other than make it perfectly clear to Patrick that she was ready for dalliance with no expectation of anything more lasting than a weekend fling…

She eased out from under her lover, wincing when he muttered and frowned in his sleep. Fortunately, he settled back into slumber. He wasn't kidding about the nap. On the other hand, he probably needed it. The preceding week hadn't been a walk in the park. Maybe Patrick had experienced the same disturbing nightmares she had.

Caves with endless tunnels. Suffocating darkness. Musty air. Crypts and death. That's what came from having a too-vivid imagination.

Tiptoeing around the bed, she made her way into the other room and found her carry-on with her toiletry bag. Since she was naked as a baby at the moment, it also seemed prudent to locate her gown and robe. Patrick didn't stir when she quietly opened the bathroom door.

Once she was safely on the other side, she exhaled shakily. Nothing in the course of her admittedly limited sexual experience—much of it negative—had prepared her for Patrick's lovemaking. He was thorough. And intense. And enthusiastic. And generous. Did she mention generous? She'd lost track of her own orgasms. The man was a freaking genius in the bedroom. Who knew?

She wrapped a towel around her hair to keep it dry, and took an abbreviated shower. The thought of getting caught in the act was too terrifying to contemplate. The man had seen her naked. But that didn't mean a woman didn't like her privacy.

When she was clean and dry, she put on her silky nightwear. The soft ivory gown and robe were old, but still stylish and comfy. The fact that they were very thin gave her pause, but it was better than being nude.

Her hair did well with nothing more than a good brushing. Now all she had to do was pretend to be blasé, make her way through a fancy dinner and convince Patrick to sleep on the sofa.

She needed to put some distance between them. A barricade against doing something stupid. He'd already told her that marriage wasn't in the cards for him. Which meant this relationship was going nowhere.

If she let herself share his bed again, all bets were off. She might end up begging, and that would be the final indignity. He'd already called her a misfit once. She was sure as heck not going to let him pity her for crushing on him like a teenage girl.

She sat on the edge of the bathtub for ten minutes, trying to decide how to stage her return to the bedroom. In the end, Patrick took the matter out of her hands. He jerked open the door without ceremony and sighed—apparently in relief—when he saw her.

"I didn't know where you were," he complained.

The man was stark naked, his body a work of art. His *penis*—she could whisper that word in the privacy of her own head—hovered at half-mast, but was rapidly rising to attention. And apparently, the man had no modesty at all, because he stood there in the doorway, hands on hips, and glared at her. Not seeming at all concerned with his nudity. His spectacular, mouthwatering nudity.

"Where would I go?" she asked, trying not to look below his waist.

He ignored the question and strode toward her, dwarfing the generous dimensions of the bathroom. "I fail to see why you're wearing clothes. Aren't you the one who was doing mathematical calculations about potential episodes of sexual activity per hour?"

"That wasn't me," she lied, leaning back as his *stuff* practically whacked her in the nose.

His good humor returned. Without warning, he scooped her into his arms. "For future reference, no pj's unless I say so. And now that I think about it, no pj's at all."

Her cheek rested over the reassuring *thump-thump* of his heart. "These aren't pajamas. It's a peignoir set."

"I don't care if it's Queen Elizabeth's royal dressing gown. Ditch it, my love. Now."

He set her on her feet and, without further ado, lifted the two filmy layers over her head, ignoring her sputtering protests. "Patrick!"

He tossed the offending garments aside and ran his

hands from her neck to her shoulders, to her breasts, and all the way down to her bottom. "God, you're beautiful," he muttered.

"Oh, Patrick."

"Oh, Patrick." He mocked her gently. "Is that 'Oh, Patrick, I want to have sex with you again' or 'Oh, Patrick, you're the best lover I've ever had'?"

She caught her bottom lip with her teeth, torn between honesty and the need to keep his ego in check. "Well, both. But to be fair, you're only number two, so there's still room for comparison down the road."

His gaze sharpened. "Only number two?"

"I'm barely twenty-three."

"Yes, but a lot of girls are sexually active at sixteen."

"Not in my family. You do remember the nuns, right?"

"There you go again. Mentioning nuns at inappropriate moments. For the record, I knew one or two good little Catholic girls who taught me a lot about life. And sex."

Her eyes rounded. "Well, not me."

He thumbed her nipples, sending heat streaking all the way down to the damp juncture between her thighs. "You were amazing, Libby. Who taught you that thing you did there at the end?"

She shrugged demurely. "I read books."

"I see."

"You don't believe me?"

"You're awfully talented for a relative beginner."

The compliment was unexpected. "That's sweet of you to say."

"You want to tell me about number one?" Patrick seemed troubled, though she couldn't understand why.

She didn't. Not at all. The memory made her wince. "Maybe another time."

"Fair enough." He tipped his head and nibbled the side of her neck. "This will be slower, I promise."

She shuddered, her hands fisting at her sides. "I had no complaints."

Again, he scooped her into his arms, though this time he sat on the edge of the bed and turned her across his knees. "Do you have any spanking fantasies?"

She looked at him over her shoulder. "I can't say that I do, but feel free to test the hypothesis."

The sharp smack on her butt shocked her, even as the heat from his hand radiated throughout her pelvis. "That hurt, Patrick."

He chuckled. "Isn't that the point?"

The truth was, there was more to the sharp-edged play than hurt, but she didn't want to give him any ideas. She wriggled off his lap and knelt on the floor, resting her elbows on his bare knees and linking her hands underneath her chin. "I'll bet you know all sorts of kinky stuff, don't you?"

He grabbed handfuls of her hair and tugged gently. "Like the scenario where the desert sheikh takes the powerless English woman captive."

"I'm not English," she pointed out.

Patrick smiled tightly, sending a frisson of feminine apprehension down her spine. "We'll improvise. For the moment, let's see how you do on the oral exam. If you don't object, how about getting a washcloth and cleaning me up?"

"You mean so I can...?" Her voice trailed off. His erection bobbed in front of her. "Um, sure." She scuttled to the bathroom, painfully aware of his gaze following her progress. When she returned, he had leaned back on both hands. He didn't say a word.

But his challenging gaze tested her mettle. The balance of power was already unequal. He saw her as naive. Susceptible to being charmed by a man of experience. Though any and all of that might be true, she was determined to knock him off his feet.

Feigning confidence she did not possess, she sat at his hip and ran the washcloth over his intimate flesh, squeezing lightly. She smiled inwardly when he gasped, even though he tried to pretend it was a cough. "Too hard?" she asked, her expression guileless.

"No." Sweat beaded his forehead.

She continued to do her job, around and around, up and down. When she was finished, his flesh had turned to stone, and his chest rose and fell with every rapid breath.

Dropping the wet cloth on the floor, she bent, placed a hand on each of his thighs and took him in her mouth.

Patrick was pretty sure he had died and gone to heaven. He'd had blow jobs before. But none like this. His skin tightened all over his body. Libby's mouth was in turns delicate and firm. He couldn't predict her next move, and the uncertainty ratcheted up his arousal exponentially. He had promised her slow this time around, but already, he was at the breaking point. "Enough," he said, the word hoarse.

She looked up at him, her wide-eyed innocence no doubt damning him eternally for the lustful thoughts that turned him inside out. Putting his hands under her arms, he dragged her up onto the bed and kissed her recklessly. "Tell me what you want, Libby."

"I've never been on top."

Sweet holy hell. He swallowed hard. "Is that a request?"

She shrugged. "If you don't mind."

He took care of protection and moved onto his back. "You're in charge," he said, wondering if it were really true. He would hold out as long as he could, but the odds were iffy.

Libby seemed pleased by his gruff words. "I don't feel

very graceful," she complained as she attempted to mount the apparatus.

"The view from this side isn't bad."

When she slid down onto him without warning, he said a word that made her frown. "That's what we're doing, but you don't have to call it that."

She leaned forward, curling her fingertips into the depressions above his collarbone. "Don't you like this position?"

No one could be that naive. He gripped her firm ass and pulled her against him more firmly. "I've got your number now, Libby. You think you can drive me insane. But that's a two-edged sword. Wait until later when I tie your wrists to the bedposts and tickle you with a feather. You won't be so smug then, now will you?"

Her mouth formed a small perfect O. Her eyes widened. "Isn't that kind of advanced? We haven't known each other all that long. I think we should take things slowly…you know, get comfortable with each other before we branch out."

"I'm pretty damn comfortable right now." He put his hands under her breasts and bounced them experimentally. "These are nice."

She flushed. "Why are men so obsessed with boobs?"

"Maybe because we don't have any. I don't know. But you have to admit, they're beautiful."

"Now you've made me all weepy." Suppressing a smile, she leaned down and rested her forehead against his. "I didn't know it would be like this with you."

"Like what?"

"So easy. But so scary."

"I scare you?" He lifted her and eased her back down, making both of them gasp.

Without warning, she went for the dismount, nearly unmanning him in the process. She bounced off the bed and stood there, arms flung wide, her expression agitated. "You're ruining me for other men. I won't be able to find a husband after this."

He frowned. "I thought you were concentrating on rebuilding your life. That you didn't want a husband."

"Not today. Or tomorrow. But someday." She shook her head. "Now every guy I go to bed with is going to have to measure up to *that*." She pointed at his erection, seeming aggrieved by its very existence.

"You're overreacting. My co—" He stopped short. "My male *appendage* is perfectly normal," he said. "And people have casual sex all the time. Once we leave this hotel, it won't seem like such a big deal."

She folded her arms around her waist, apparently forgetting that she was bare-ass naked. "You know this from experience?"

"I have more than you, apparently. So, yes. And PS—it's bad form to walk out in the middle of the performance."

"I'm sorry." But she stood there so long he began to be afraid that she was actually going to call a halt to their madness.

He sat up and held out a hand. "Come back to bed, Libby. Please."

Her small smile loosened the knot in his stomach. "Well, if you ask that nicely…"

When he could reach her hand, he tugged, toppling her off balance and happily onto his lap. Libby sputtered and squirmed and protested until he flipped her and reversed their positions. Staring down at her, he felt something break apart and reform…a distinct seismic shift in his consciousness. Fortunately, he was good at ignoring extraneous details in the middle of serious business.

"Tell me you want me," he demanded.

"I want you."

"That wasn't convincing."

She linked her hands at the small of his back. "Patrick Kavanagh...I'll go mad with lust if you don't take me... right now."

"That's better." He shifted his weight and slid inside her, relishing the tight fit, the warm, wet friction. This was rapidly becoming an addiction, but he couldn't find it in his heart to care. His brain wasn't in the driver's seat. "I want you, too," he said, though she hadn't asked.

Libby's expressive eyes were closed, leaving him awash in doubt. What was she thinking? In the end, it didn't matter. His gut instincts took over, hammering home the message that she was the woman he needed. At least for now.

He felt the inner flutters that signaled her release. At last, he gave himself permission to finish recklessly, self-ishly. Again and again, he thrust. Scrambling for a pinnacle just out of reach. When the end came, it was bittersweet. Because he realized one mind-numbing fact.

Libby Parkhurst had burrowed her way beneath his guard. And maybe into his heart.

Fourteen

"Hurry up, woman. We have dinner reservations in forty-five minutes."

Libby laughed, feeling happier than she had in a very long time. "I'll be ready in five." She leaned toward the mirror and touched up her eyeliner, then added a dash of smoky shadow.

After asking her preferences earlier in the day, Patrick had made reservations at an exclusive French restaurant high atop a Manhattan skyscraper. The evening promised to be magical.

She resisted the urge to pirouette in front of the mirror. The dress Maeve had bought for her was sexy and sophisticated and exceedingly feminine. The fabric was black lace over a gold satin underlay. The skirt ended modestly just at the knee, but the back dipped to the base of her spine.

Patrick rested his hands on her shoulders and kissed the nape of her neck, his hot gaze meeting hers in the mirror. "We could skip dinner," he said.

He was dressed in an expensive, conservative dark suit. The look in his eyes, however, was anything but ordinary.

She put her hand over one of his. "We need to keep up our strength. And besides, it would be a shame to waste all this sartorial splendor on room service."

"I could live with the disappointment," he muttered. He lifted the hem of her dress and stroked her thigh. "You can't go bare legged. It's cold outside."

"I thought you would be a fan of easy access."

"Maybe in July. But not tonight. I care about you too much to see you turn into a Popsicle."

Despite her distaste for the hosiery, she knew he was right. With that one adjustment to her wardrobe, she was ready. At least her black coat was fairly dressy. At one time she had owned an entire collection of high-end faux furs. But those were long gone.

Their cab was waiting when they got down to the lobby. It was dark now, and the wind that funneled between the buildings took her breath away as they stepped outside. Patrick didn't have to say, "I told you so." At least her legs had a layer of protection from the elements.

On the way, he played with the inside of her knee. "We could stay another night," he said.

The words were casual, but they stopped her heart. Because she wanted so very badly to say yes, she did the opposite. Too risky. She was letting him too close. "I don't think so," she said. "Your sister-in-law Zoe offered to help me move to Dylan's apartment Sunday afternoon, maybe find a few pillows and pictures to spruce it up. You probably remember she did a stint as a vagabond for a couple of years, so she has a good eye for a bargain."

"I see. We'll go back, then."

Had she wanted him to talk her into staying? Was she hurt that he dropped the idea so easily?

She didn't want to answer those questions, not even to herself.

They made it to the restaurant with ten minutes to spare. An obsequious maître d' seated them near the floor-to-ceiling windows at a table overlooking the city. Patrick tipped the man unobtrusively and pulled out Libby's chair.

"Does this suit your fancy?"

"Perfect," she sighed. The restaurant was new. And crowded. Discreet music filtered from hidden speakers overhead. Their fellow diners—men and women alike—dazzled in stunning couture clothing. Expensive accessories. Flashy jewelry. At one time, this had been Libby's life.

Patrick touched her hand across the table. "You okay?"

She shook off the moment of melancholy. "Yes. More than okay."

Another puffed-up employee, this one their waiter, appeared at the table. "Would Monsieur like to order for the lady?"

Patrick shook his head, smiling. "I don't think so."

Libby picked up her menu, and in flawless French ordered her favorite dish of scallops and prawns in cream sauce. The man had the decency to look chagrined before he turned to Patrick. "And you, sir?"

"I won't embarrass myself in front of the lady. Please bring me a filet, medium, and the asparagus in lemon butter."

"My pleasure."

When they were alone again, Libby grinned. "You set him straight, but so very nicely."

"The owners probably taught him that spiel. It's not his fault."

Libby gazed out the window, soaking in the vista of the city she considered home. "I don't think I'll stay in Silver Glen after this summer," she said impulsively. It would be impossibly difficult to be around the man who didn't want marriage and forever.

Patrick, caught in the act of sipping his wine, went still, his glass hovering in midair. "Oh? Why not?"

The reality was too painful, so she fed him a lesser truth. "I need to be independent. If I lean on your mom or even the Kavanaghs in general, I won't know if I really have the guts to rebuild my life. Here in New York, at least everything is familiar. I know the turf…and I have contacts…maybe even friends if I can figure out which ones still care about me now that my bank account is empty."

"So you don't see yourself becoming part of a place like Silver Glen?" His expression was curiously blank.

"I think we've established that I'm not much of a country girl. The concrete jungle is more my speed. I know which deli has the best pastrami, and I can tell you the operating hours of the Met and Natural History. I memorized the subway system by the time I was fourteen. I've seen the Rockettes dance every December since I was three years old…well, except for this past one. New York is home to me."

"I see."

His gaze was odd, turbulent. Did he think she was somehow insulting his beloved hometown?

"Don't get me wrong," she said hurriedly. "North Carolina is incredibly beautiful. And I'm happy to be living there for the moment. But when I think about the future, I can't see myself in Silver Glen."

In the heavy silence that followed her pronouncement the waiter returned, bearing their meals. The food was amazing, the presentation exceptional. But the evening had fallen flat.

She was honestly mystified. Patrick should be glad she wasn't going to hang around. He was the one with the matchmaking mother. And he'd made no secret of the fact that he was not ever going to get married.

For Libby's part, it made sense to decide from the beginning that she and Patrick were nothing more than a blip on the radar. She had suffered enough trauma in her life during the past year, without adding a broken heart to the mix.

Falling in love with Patrick Kavanagh would be the easiest thing in the world. Maybe she was partway there already. But she wasn't a fool. People didn't change. Her father hadn't. Her mother hadn't. And in the end, their inability to be the people they could have been desperately hurt their only daughter more than they could have imagined.

Still, Libby was tormented by one simple question. She knew she wouldn't be satisfied until she knew the answer.

Over dessert, she took a chance. "Patrick…"

"Hmm?" Distracted, he was dealing with the credit card and the check for their meal.

"May I ask you a personal question?"

He lifted an eyebrow, his sexy smile lethal. "I think we've reached that point, don't you?"

Maybe they had, and maybe they hadn't. But she risked it even so. "I know what happened to you when you were in high school. And I get that it was deeply painful and upsetting. But why have you decided that marriage is not for you?"

For a moment, he froze. She was certain he was going to tell her to go to hell. But then his shoulders relaxed and he sat back in his chair. "It's pretty simple really."

"Okay. Tell me."

"I've already done it. And messed it up. I choose not to take it so lightly again."

"I'm confused."

He fidgeted with his bow tie, his tanned fingers dark against the pristine white of his shirt. "Five of my brothers have gotten married so far. They've each stood in front of

God and family and made a solemn vow to one particular woman. To love and to cherish…till death do us part… all that stuff…"

"And you don't want to do that?"

"I'm telling you," he said, his voice rising slightly. "I already did it. But I cheapened the meaning of marriage. I bound myself to a woman, a girl really, whom I didn't love. And I knew I didn't love her even while I was repeating the vows."

"But you weren't an adult…and you were doing what was expected of you."

"Doesn't matter. The point is, I had my chance, and I made light of a moment that's supposed to be sacred. So I'm not going to take another woman in front of the altar knowing that I've already betrayed her before we ever start."

It made a weird sort of sense.

Poor Patrick…chained by the strength of his own regrets to life as a bachelor. And poor Libby…on the brink of falling for a man who didn't want anything she had to offer in the relationship department. It might have been funny if it hadn't been so wistfully sad.

Over one last cup of coffee, they sat in silence. Her question and his answer had driven an invisible wedge between them. She played with the silver demitasse spoon, watching the blinking lights far below…the traffic that never ceased. The Empire State Building off to her left was lit up, but the colors puzzled her. "I wonder why they went for pink and white this weekend," she murmured.

Patrick leaned forward. "Seriously? Tomorrow is Valentine's Day, Libby."

"Oh. Well, this is awkward."

"Why? Because you don't know what day it is?"

She lifted her chin. "No. Because you and I are the last two people who should be having a romantic dinner."

"Humans are good at pretense." The tinge of bitterness was unlike him.

But since her Cinderella experience was winding down, she chose to ignore his mood. She reached for his hand. "I don't want to fight with you, Patrick." She rubbed her thumb across the back of his hand. "Let's go back to the hotel. Please."

Patrick was not accustomed to self-doubt. He made decisions and followed through. He was mentally, physically and emotionally strong. People respected him…admired his integrity.

Then why did he feel as if he were failing Libby on every level?

He was so rattled by his jumbled thoughts that he forgot to call a cab before they got down to the street. "Stay inside a minute," he said.

But Libby had already gone on ahead, calling out to him with excitement in her voice. "Come look, Patrick. It's snowing…"

He followed her and pulled up short when the scene slammed into him with all the force of a freight train. Libby stood in the glow of a streetlight, arms upraised, her face tipped toward the sky. She was laughing, her features radiant. The sheltered heiress who had lost everything and been forced by harsh circumstances to grow up in a hurry, still had more joie de vivre in her little finger than Patrick could muster at the moment.

She had made love to him…openly, generously. Never once holding back or trying to protect herself from his *rules* for relationships. Even knowing that he was an emotionally locked-up bastard, she gave him everything. Her sweetness…her enthusiasm…her amazing body.

He should be kneeling at her feet and begging her forgiveness. Instead, he was going to commit the unforgivable sin. He was going to let her go.

As the snowfall grew heavier and the wind stilled, the whole world became hushed. Although he was miles from home, this particular gift of winter was the same everywhere. People stopped. Time stopped. Quiet descended. The swirl of white was an experience linked to childhood. Simple joy. Breathtaking wonder.

When he finally managed to hail a cab, he and Libby were coated in white. Strands of damp hair clung to her forehead, and her cheeks were pink. She laughed at him when he tried to brush the melting flakes from her shoulders. "Leave it," she said. "We'll be home soon."

He knew it was a slip of the tongue. A hotel, however lovely, was not home. But he was almost certain that Libby possessed a talent he lacked…the ability to make a real home with nothing more than her presence and her giving heart.

The trip from the cab to their suite seemed inordinately long. He shook, not from the cold, but from an amalgam of fear and desperation. This was it, most likely. His last chance to be with her intimately. His last opportunity to memorize the curve of her breasts, the softness of her bottom pressed to his pelvis as they curled together in sleep.

Libby's mood had segued from delight to quiet introspection. Perhaps she had picked up on the chaos inside him. But no matter the reason, she gave him space. Made no requests. He almost wanted her to demand something from him. To beg him to change. To plead with him to make an exception for her.

Libby, however, treated him like a grown man. She respected his choices, even as she made plans to go her own way. It was the most painful "letting go" he could have imagined.

As he fumbled with the key to their door, Libby slipped

her arm through his and leaned her head on his shoulder. "I think that last glass of wine was one too many," she murmured.

The door opened, and he scooted her through, backing her against it when it closed. His hands clenched her shoulders. His forehead rested against hers. "I need you." He meant to say more than that, but she understood.

She smiled at him as she unbuttoned her coat. "I know, Patrick. And it's okay, I promise. I won't ask for more than you're willing to give." She tossed the coat aside. "But we have tonight."

Fifteen

He undressed her reverently, as if she were a long-awaited Christmas gift. Either Libby was very tired, or she understood his need to be gentle in this moment, because there was no mad stripping of clothes, no sex-crazed fumbling to get naked. With her head bowed, she submitted to his hands, even when those hands trembled and even when he cursed a stuck zipper.

At last, she was nude. He lifted her in his arms and carried her a few steps to the settee. Depositing her carefully, he stepped back and removed his own clothing. She watched him drowsily, her green eyes glowing with pleasure.

Her gaze was almost tactile on his bare skin. At last, it was done. He held out a hand. "Come with me."

That she obeyed instantly messed with his head. Was she trying to win him over? Or was she humoring a slightly deranged man who temporarily held her captive?

Did it matter?

As soon as she stood up, he recognized the possibilities in the elegant piece of furniture. "How do you feel about playacting the emperor and the concubine?"

"On someone else's furniture?" She was scandalized. "Not without something to protect it."

"Don't move." He raced to the bedroom and grabbed the blanket off the foot of the bed, along with a strip of condoms. When he returned, Libby had taken him at his word.

She stood, arms at her sides, and stared from him to the settee and back again. "I never took gymnastics classes. So don't get any kinky ideas."

"Kinky ideas are the best," he said. Teasing her was almost as much fun as making love to her. She sputtered and blushed and scowled adorably. Giving her a moment to get used to the idea, he flipped the thick duvet out and over the settee and sat down, palms flat on his thighs. "I'm ready."

Libby tilted her head to one side and pursed her lips. "Clearly."

"Well, come on."

"And do what?"

"Sit on my lap."

He watched as she assessed every possible permutation of that suggestion.

"Umm…"

"Don't be a chicken. You're a fearless woman who survived a night in the mine. Surely you're not afraid of a little role-playing."

"I'm not afraid of anything," she said firmly.

"I know it. And now you know it, too."

The look on her face was priceless. Libby had changed. She had grown. She was no longer the same woman who had professed timidity during her job interview.

"I don't know what to say. Thank you, Patrick."

He tucked his hands behind his head. "Don't thank me. You're the woman who has been slaying dragons."

She inhaled, making her breasts rise and fall in a way that would turn any man's brain to mush. "Okay, then…"

"Wait. Stop." He'd forgotten the protection. But, within seconds, he was sheathed and ready to go. "Come and get me."

"Isn't that supposed to be my line?"

He tickled the insides of her thighs as she gingerly straddled his lap. "I think an emperor would expect more bodily contact." He grabbed her butt and kneaded her warm, resilient flesh. "We should have a mirror," he complained, wishing he had been more prepared.

Libby cupped his neck with her hands and leaned in to kiss him. "Focus, Kavanagh. You have a naked woman on your lap."

"That's my problem," he complained, thoroughly aggrieved. "I forget my name when I touch you. It makes decision-making dicey at best."

"I'll help," she promised. "Give me something to decide."

"Well," he drawled. "It would be nice if you could get a little closer."

Fortunately, Libby was a smart woman. "Like this, you mean?" She lifted up and lowered, joining their bodies perfectly.

He buried his face in her scented breasts. "Exactly like that."

This particular position might have been a miscalculation. The visual stimulation combined with a somewhat passive role on his part made his body burn. He had barely entered her, and already he wanted to come.

Damn it.

But as much as he wanted to move, the urge was strong to simply hold her there. And pretend she was his to keep.

She tapped him on the head. "Hello in there. The last emperor who wanted me was a bit more…um…*active.*"

"You want active, little concubine?" he muttered. "How about this?" He surged upward, burying himself so deeply inside her, he wasn't sure he could find his way out.

"Patrick!" Libby cried out, stopping his heart.

"Did I hurt you?" he asked, pulling back to examine her face.

"You didn't hurt me." She bit her lip. "But it was definitely…"

"What? Definitely what?"

One shoulder lifted and fell. "Wicked. Memorable. Deep."

He swallowed hard. "I see. Would you consider those positive adjectives?"

She wiggled her butt, making him squeeze his eyes shut as he counted to ten and tried to hold on.

"Oh, yes, my emperor," she whispered. "Very positive indeed."

Libby might have lied a little bit. That last move on Patrick's part left her hovering on a line between pleasure and pain. She had never felt more desired, nor more completely possessed.

He trembled against her…or maybe that was her own body shaking. Was good sex always this momentous? Her basis for comparison was woefully inadequate. She'd had one terrible experience and now this one.

She raked her teeth along the shell of his ear. "Make love to me, Patrick. I want it all. Don't hold back."

Her request tore through his last thread of restraint. He lunged into her once…twice…then a third time, before he tumbled them both onto the floor and lifted one of her legs over his shoulder.

Suddenly, she felt exposed…vulnerable. Their bodies were no longer joined. Patrick was talented, but even he couldn't manage that trick while airborne. He stroked a fingertip in her damp sex, making her squirm as he stared at her intimately.

"Do you trust me, Libby?"

"Of course, I do."

"Close your eyes."

"But I…"

"Close them."

She obeyed the command, quivering in his grasp. "What are you going to do?"

"Hush, Libby."

She sensed him moving, and then she arched her back in instinctive protest when she felt his hands spread her legs apart. Moments later, his warm breath gave her the first warning of what he was about to do seconds before she felt the rough pass of his tongue on her sex.

A groan ripped from her gut, shocked pleasure swamping her inhibitions. She tried to escape, even so. But he locked her legs to the rug and continued his lazy torture.

She came more than once…loudly. And in the end, she barely had the breath to whisper his name when he moved inside her and drove them both insane…

It was still dark when Libby awoke. She was sore and satiated but oddly uncertain. Some sound had dragged her from a deep sleep. Patrick breathed quietly at her back, his arms wrapped around her waist, his face buried in her hair.

"Patrick," she said, turning to face him. "I think your phone is vibrating." It had to be bad. No good news ever came at…what was it? Four in the morning?

Her companion grumbled, but reached for his phone on the bedside table. "What?"

Patrick sat straight up in bed. "How bad is it?"

The tone in his voice alarmed her. "What's wrong?"

He ignored her until he finished the call. "It's Mia…

Dylan's wife. She's in the hospital with a ruptured appendix. And there are complications."

"Oh, no…"

"There's nothing we can do to help."

"Are you trying to convince me or you? Come on, Patrick. You know we need to go back. At least we can be there to lend moral support. People die from a ruptured appendix sometimes. Dylan must be out of his mind."

"Thank you for understanding," he said quietly.

They barely spoke as they gathered up their things and dressed. Patrick hardly acknowledged Libby's presence. She forgave him his silence, though, because she knew what it was like to be sick with fear.

A car waited for them when they exited the hotel. Apparently nothing ruffled the overnight desk clerk, even guests rushing out with their hair askew and wearing rumpled clothing from the night before.

At the airport, the pilot was ready. The flight back to Silver Glen seemed endless. Patrick stared out the window. Libby dozed. By eight in the morning, they were touching down on the new airstrip.

James was waiting for them, the car warm and toasty, despite the frigid early-morning air. As James stowed their bags into the trunk, Patrick helped Libby into the backseat and then joined James up front.

"How is she?" Patrick asked. "And tell me what happened. I didn't wait for details earlier when Liam contacted us."

James grimaced. "Apparently, she started having severe pain sometime after midnight, but she didn't wake up Dylan, because she didn't want to have to get Cora out of bed. By three thirty, it was so bad she had no choice. Dylan didn't take her. She went by ambulance. She's in surgery right now."

"Damn it, women are stubborn."

"Yeah."

Libby stayed silent in the backseat, hearing the concern in the siblings' voices...and the faintest hint of panic. These were big strong men. But they loved their sisters-in-law and treated them as blood relations, integral parts of this large, tight-knit family.

At the hospital, Libby staked out a seat in the waiting room and tried to become invisible. Through the glass walls adjacent to the corridor she had seen Maeve, the brothers and most of their wives from time to time, pacing the halls. Still wearing her coat to cover her inappropriate clothing, Libby closed her eyes and leaned her head against the wall. This setting brought back too many painful memories of her mother's early suicide attempts.

When Patrick finally sought her out, almost two hours had elapsed. He plopped down in a chair across from her and rested his elbows on his knees, head in his hands. Wearing his tux pants and wrinkled white shirt, he looked exhausted.

"Patrick?" Alarm coursed through her veins. "Did something go wrong? Is Mia okay?"

He sat up slowly, his expression taut with stress. "She's going to be. At least I hope so. The surgery went well, but infection is a concern. She was in recovery for forty-five minutes. They've brought her up to a room now. We've been taking turns going in to see her."

"How is she?"

"Cranky at the moment. She hates being out of control."

"I'm sure it's scary for her."

"Yeah." He pushed his hair from his forehead, his eyes weary, but laden with something else, as well. "Dylan is an absolute wreck."

At that moment, Maeve walked into the waiting room. Normally, Patrick's mother was the epitome of vigor and

elegance, never a hair out of place. This morning, however, she looked every bit her age.

Patrick jumped up. "Here. Take my seat, Mom. I'm
going to find some coffee."

Maeve managed a smile, but her hands trembled as she
sat down and looked at Libby. "It's a hard thing to watch
your children suffer. My poor Dylan is stoic, but I was
afraid he was going to have a heart attack. He loves Mia
deeply. And I do, too, of course. A man's love for his wife,
though, is a sacred thing."

"I'm so glad it looks like Mia is going to be okay."

"Would you mind driving me home, dear? I told Patrick I was going to ask you. He's already had your things
sent up to the lodge."

"Are you okay, Maeve?" The older woman was definitely pale.

Maeve nodded. "I'm fine. Just a little shaky, because I
never ate breakfast. My car is in the parking lot."

They made their way downstairs, pausing to speak
to various members of the family. But Patrick had not
returned. As they exited the hospital, Libby's stomach
growled. "Would you like to stop at the diner for a meal?"

"Actually, that sounds wonderful. Thank you, dear."

The little restaurant wasn't crowded. Maybe because it
wasn't a weekday. Libby and Maeve grabbed a booth and
ordered bacon and eggs with a side of heart-shaped pan-
cakes in honor of the holiday. Coffee and orange juice came
out ahead of the food. Libby drained her cup in short order,
hoping the jolt of caffeine would kick in soon. Maeve did
the same, but she eyed Libby over the rim.

"I'm glad you suggested breakfast, Libby. I wanted to
ask how the New York weekend went. I see you're still
wearing that lovely dress."

Libby drew the collar of her coat closer together, thank-
ful that the temperatures justified her attire. "We left in

such a hurry this morning, we both just grabbed our clothes from last night."

Maeve's smile was knowing. "I wasn't making a judgment call...merely commenting. So tell me...did things go well?"

"The orientation at Peabody Rushford was fascinating. Although it wasn't for *my* benefit, I learned a lot."

Maeve shook her head, her dark eyes sharp with interest. "I'm not really asking about Patrick's business dealings. My son is an astute entrepreneur. I would expect no less. Mine was a more personal question."

Most people wouldn't have the guts to pry. But Maeve was not most people. Libby could do nothing about the flood of heat that washed from her throat to her hairline. "I'm not sure what you mean."

The server delivered the food. Libby scooped a forkful of eggs, hoping the distraction would derail Maeve's interrogation.

But Patrick's mother was like a dog with a bone... a very tasty bone. "I don't expect a blow-by-blow description, but I would like to know if the two of you connected on an intimate level." She locked her steady gaze with Libby's flustered one.

Blow-by-blow? Good grief. Libby managed to swallow the eggs that had solidified into a lump in her throat. "Um...yes, ma'am. We did."

"But?"

"But what?"

"You hardly seem the picture of a young woman who has been swept off her feet by romance."

"I haven't had much sleep, Maeve. It's a long way from New York."

"Give Patrick a chance," Maeve begged. "I know he doesn't go in for big gestures and declarations of undying passion, but he's a deep man. You can unpeel the layers if only you'll be patient."

Libby reached across the table and took Maeve's hand, squeezing it for a moment. Then she sat back in the booth and sighed. The delicious breakfast had lost its appeal. "Patrick is an *amazing* man. But he's been very honest with me from the beginning, and I have to honor that. For you to interfere or for me to weave daydreams based on nothing at all, would be wrong."

Maeve's face fell. "But you care about him?"

"Of course I do. He's a lovely man. But that doesn't make us soul mates, Maeve."

"I don't want my son to spend his life alone."

Tears glistened in Maeve's eyes. Given Patrick's mother's talents for benign manipulation, Libby had to wonder if the tears were genuine. But then again, Maeve was capable of deep feeling. Everything she did came from a place of abundant love.

"Some people like being alone, Maeve. I know tons of single people who are very happy and content with their lives. Patrick has a rewarding career and a circle of intimate friends. You can't box him into a *relationship* corner he doesn't want or need."

"You sound awfully wise for a young woman of your age."

"Life is a tough teacher."

"So what you're telling me is that you won't even consider letting yourself fall in love with my son because he's told you he doesn't want to get married."

"That's about the sum of it. I may stay for the duration of Charlise's leave…as long as things don't get awkward. But I've already told Patrick that I'm thinking of going back to New York permanently. This weekend's trip told me I can handle it. I wasn't sure, to be honest. I didn't want to think about my mother's death and my father's crime every second of every day. But I think it's going to be okay."

"Well…" Maeve scowled at a strip of bacon. "It sounds like you know your own mind."

"Yes, ma'am. And don't worry about Patrick. He knows what he wants and what he doesn't want."

Maeve leaned forward. "So what *does* he want?"

"He wants to build his life here…among family. He wants to be close to you and his brothers, and their wives and children, both physically and emotionally. He wants to grow Silver Reflections and know that he's making a difference in people's lives. He wants to spend time in the mountains and to draw strength from this place you all call home."

"For a woman who hasn't found her soul mate, you surely sound as if you know a great deal about my son."

"Stop it, Maeve. I'm serious. This last year has taught me that I can't always bend the world to my will. I have to accept reality and deal with it as best I can. And even under those circumstances—sometimes difficult, sometimes tragic—I can be happy. Or at least content."

Maeve held up her hands. "You've convinced me. I'm officially done with playing Cupid…though it's awfully hard to say that on his special day."

Libby laughed, finishing her meal with a lighter heart. "Maybe *we* should be worrying about *you*, Maeve. You're still very youthful and attractive. I'm sure there are tons of eligible men out there who would like to find a woman like you."

Maeve blanched. "If that's blackmail, I stand forewarned. I like my life the way it is. I had one husband. That was enough."

"If you say so. Now please pass the syrup, let's finish breakfast so I can go back to the lodge and get out of these clothes."

Sixteen

Patrick kicked a log, not even flinching when pain shot from his toe up his leg. He liked the pain. It helped distract him from the turmoil in the rest of his body. It had been over twenty-four hours since he had seen Libby. Longer than that since they'd had sex. He was like a junkie jonesing for the next hit.

But therein lay his problem. He had to stay away from her.

The conviction had been born in an intimate New York hotel room and solidified in the antiseptic corridors of a hospital. He couldn't afford to fall in love with Libby Parkhurst. It was too dangerous.

Little memories of Friday slipped into his thoughts when his guard was down. The smell of her hair on his pillow. The humorous, self-deprecating way she spoke to his clients about sleeping in the great outdoors. Her delighted laughter as she tipped her face toward the sky while snowflakes fell on her soft cheeks.

Even the way she hugged an old man in a uniform and let him know that he was important in her life.

Libby made everything brighter, more special. If he'd been inclined to find a lover and hang on to her, that woman might be Libby. But he couldn't. He wouldn't.

Without realizing it, he'd been on his way to changing his life plan. Having Libby in his bed, turning him inside out, had begun to convince him that he might be smarter about marriage a second time. After all, he wasn't a kid anymore.

But then yesterday happened. Mia's emergency surgery. Patrick knew his brother Dylan as a laid-back, comfortable-with-the-world, confident man. But in Dylan's eyes yesterday, Patrick had seen raw terror. With the woman Dylan loved in danger, Patrick's older brother had been helpless... scared sick that he was going to lose his whole world.

Patrick didn't want that kind of responsibility or that kind of grief. He remembered well the bitter taste of failure and loss when his youthful marriage ended, and that was for a girl he hadn't even loved.

How much worse would it be if he let himself get addicted to Libby and then he lost her? Death. Divorce. Infidelity. There were any number of forces waiting to tear couples apart.

Why would he subject himself to such vulnerability?

The hours he'd spent with Libby in the Carlyle hotel had literally changed him. Her sweet, sultry beauty. Her gentleness. Her shy, eager passion. He could have wallowed in their lovemaking for days on end and never had enough.

But when he broached the subject of extending their stay, Libby hadn't jumped at the idea. Worse still, she'd spoken of returning to New York permanently. Of leaving Silver Glen. Of leaving him.

It wasn't too late to correct his mistakes. He hadn't

gone all the way into obsession. He could end this thing and walk away unscathed.

But to do so meant suffering through one very unpleasant conversation. Today was Sunday. Thank God, Valentine's Day had come and gone. There was no reason not to intercept Libby's plans before she returned to Silver Reflections Monday morning.

When he contemplated what he was about to do, the bottom fell out of his stomach. Much like the first time he'd stood atop the high dive as a ten-year-old and wondered if he had the guts to make the jump.

He took out his cell phone and started to punch in a number. Libby carried a cheap pay-as-you-go phone. But at the last minute he remembered that Zoe was helping Libby get set up in the apartment over Dylan's bar.

The two of them had vowed to hit up thrift stores and outfit Libby's new digs. Should he stop Libby before she spent any of her hard-earned cash on things she might not need?

Damn it. He'd never had to deal with any of this with Charlise at his side.

At last, he decided he had to make the call.

Libby answered on the first ring. "Hello?"

Her voice reached inside his chest and squeezed his heart. "Are you and Zoe still occupied with your move?"

"She had to cancel. But I may go over to the Silver Dollar later to get the lay of the land. What's up, Patrick?"

"We need to talk," he said gruffly. "What if I pick up some sandwiches, and you and I go for a drive?"

"It's not really picnic weather," she said, laughter in her voice.

The day was infinitely dreary, sheets of rain drenching the mountains, temperatures hovering at a raw 38 degrees.

"I know that," he said. "But I've eaten in my car before. It won't kill me."

"If you say so."

"Can you be ready in an hour?"

"Of course."

"See you shortly." Now that he had made up his mind, he wanted to get this thing done...

Libby had a good idea what was coming. Patrick was going to tell her that an intimate relationship was not a good idea since she was going to be working for him. The thing was, she sort of agreed.

At this point in her life, she needed a good job more than she needed a love interest. Maybe in time this physical attraction between the two of them might blossom into something stronger...something lasting. She was a patient person. And if that were never going to happen, then she would be a big girl and face the truth.

Despite her brave talk, the prospect of seeing Patrick again made her insides go wobbly. They had gone from sleeping in each other's arms, to panic, to rushed travel to the hospital, to nothing. Patrick had left to get coffee, and that was the last she had seen of him.

This afternoon, with one guarded phone call, he was evidently prepared to set her straight. A fling in New York was one thing. Now it would be back to business as usual.

Since they weren't going anywhere fancy, she dressed warmly in jeans, boots and a thick, forest green sweater. The pleasant weather when Patrick had taken her out in the woods was nothing but a memory. Winter had returned... with no sign of relenting.

She was waiting on the front steps of the hotel when Patrick pulled up in his sporty sedan. It didn't seem like a good idea to meet him inside where his mother might happen to see them and get the wrong idea.

Ever the gentleman, he got out and opened her door, despite the fact that a uniformed parking attendant stood nearby, ready to lend a hand. She wanted to smile at Patrick and say something light and innocuous, but the words dried up in her throat.

This man had seen her naked. He had done wonderfully wicked things to her and with her. They had slept like exhausted children, wrapped in each other's arms.

Looking at Patrick's stoic face right now, no one would ever guess any of that.

Once they were seated practically hip to hip in the interior of the car, things got worse. The windows fogged up and the tension increased exponentially. She literally said nothing.

Patrick followed her lead.

She wanted to ask where they were going. But Patrick's grim profile in the waning afternoon light didn't invite questions. Chastened, she huddled in her seat and watched as the world flew by her window.

He drove like a man possessed, spiraling down the mountain road at least ten miles above the speed limit, and then racing on past town and out into the countryside. If he had a destination, she couldn't guess what it was. Her gut said he was driving at random.

When thirty minutes had passed from the moment he fetched her at the lodge, he finally slowed the car and rolled to a stop. The scene spread out in front of them was the definition of *middle of nowhere*. If she hadn't known better, she might have been worried he was going to dump her out and drive away, leaving her to find her way back home.

Their meal was in the backseat, but she wasn't hungry. And since she'd never been one to put off unpleasant tasks, she decided to cut to the chase. "I've been expecting this conversation," she said quietly. "You're going to say that we can either be lovers or coworkers, but not both."

Patrick's hands were white-knuckled on the steering

wheel. "The rain has stopped. I need to get out of this car. Do you mind?"

His question was clearly rhetorical, because before she could respond, he had already climbed out. She joined him on the side of the road, her arms wrapped around her waist. Even with a coat over her sweater, she was cold. The graveled edges of the pavement were waterlogged and muddy. The tops of the surrounding mountains were invisible, shrouded in low clouds, though the sun was trying to peek through.

Patrick stood a few feet away, physically and emotionally aloof, with aviator sunglasses obscuring part of his face. His khakis were crisply creased. He wore a white shirt underneath a brown bomber jacket. The leather was soft and scarred, clearly the real deal. Who had given it to him? Maybe it had been a gift when he first earned his pilot's license.

A light breeze ruffled his hair. Though she couldn't see his eyes, she guessed they were more gray than blue in this light. "Are you asking *me* to decide? New York was incredible, Patrick. I want to pick sex with you and say to hell with everything else. But we don't know each other all that well, and I was serious about learning to stand on my own two feet."

"You've misunderstood me," he said, hands shoved in his pocket.

"Does that mean *you* get to choose? I have no say in the matter?"

His expression was grim, his jaw so tight he would surely have a headache soon if he didn't already. It wasn't the face of a man who was going to choose physical pleasure over their work relationship.

He held up a hand. "Stop, Libby." His voice was hoarse. "You're making this harder."

Disappointment set up residence in her stomach.

Clearly the sex that had seemed so incredibly intimate and warm and fun to her had meant nothing to him. Well, she wouldn't be an object of pity. If he thought she was going to pine away for him, he was wrong. As far as she was concerned, they could work together and pretend the past weekend never happened.

She mimed zipping her lip. "Say what you have to say."

He took off his sunglasses and tucked them in his pocket. In the battle between the clouds and the sun, the clouds had won. "I'm not asking you to choose, Libby. I think you were right. You should go back to New York."

Trembling began deep in her core and worked its way to her extremities. "I don't understand."

In his face, she saw no remnant of the tender, funny man who had made love to her so passionately and so well. He stared at her impassively. "You gave it your best shot, Libby. I admired your resolve in the woods and in the mine, but you're not who I need while Charlise is gone."

You're not who I need. The blunt statement took her breath away.

"And our physical relationship?" Now her entire body shook. She tightened her arms around herself, trying not to splinter into a million tiny pieces of disbelief and wounded embarrassment.

"One night does not make a relationship. We were great in bed, but I've already told you how I feel about marriage. If you stay in Silver Glen, and you and I *continue* to end up in bed, things will get messy.

"Messy..." She parroted the word, her thought processes in shambles.

"You have to go home, Libby. Your instincts were good about that. Silver Glen is not the place for you, and I'm not the man you want. It's better to put an end to this now with no harm done."

Somewhere, she found the strength to smile evenly,

even as jagged, breathless pain raced through her veins and threatened to cripple her. It was a hell of a time to realize she was in love with him. She inhaled and exhaled, calling upon all of her acting skills. "I can't say I'm surprised by your decision. I never really thought you were going to give me the job anyway."

He must have seen through her layer of calm. For the first time, something in him cracked...visibly. For a split second, she could swear she saw agony in his eyes. "Libby..." He took an impulsive step in her direction and reached for her arm.

She jerked away, backing up so quickly she nearly lost her footing in the loose gravel. "No. Just no. Please take me back to the hotel. I have plans to make."

The return drive seemed endless. In front of the Silver Beeches Lodge, Patrick rolled to a halt and locked all the car doors with one click. His chest heaved. "Libby..." he said her name again.

But his time she had no escape route. He leaned across the console and tangled his hands in her hair, pulling her to him for a hard, desperate kiss. It took guts and fortitude, but she didn't respond. At all.

When he finally released her and sat back, she slapped him hard across the face. In seconds, his cheek bore the dark red mark of her fingers. "You're a selfish, heartless jackass, Patrick Kavanagh...and an emotionally stunted shell of a man. I don't ever want to see you again...not even if your face is on a Wanted poster. Go to hell."

Seventeen

Patrick had known it was going to be bad…but not that it would hurt so damned much. He unlocked the doors and watched Libby exit his car and his life in one fell swoop. His throat tight, he lowered the window and called her name urgently. "Libby!"

She never hesitated…never turned around.

Patrick struggled through the next several days as if the hours were quicksand threatening to pull him under. Though he found a replacement for Charlise—a male grad student in desperate need of extra cash who was willing to work for five months and then go back to chipping away at the course work for his degree—Patrick felt no sense of relief.

He went through the motions of preparing for his first outdoor adventure group, but the tasks that normally energized and excited him felt burdensome.

Even worse, he was forced to hide out from his family.

He knew his mother well. She had surely put two and two together by now. As Libby's champion, she would have his hide for hurting her.

Even a scheduled trip to LA, a city he normally enjoyed, was torture. All he could see in his mind's eye was Libby sitting at the conference table in her stylish black dress, handing out advice to skittish executives.

Far worse were the two nights he spent in a California hotel, flipping channels when he couldn't sleep. Libby was everywhere. In the big king-size bed, the marble tiled shower, the love seat that was a close twin to a certain settee in New York.

As much as he wanted to avoid facing the music in Silver Glen, he quickly wrapped up his assignment and headed home. His mother's birthday was in two days. Zoe and Cassidy were coordinating a huge bash in the ballroom of Silver Beeches. Though Liam and Maeve had run the lodge together for years, Maeve had finally decided to step down and devote herself to her rapidly expanding crop of grandchildren.

There was no possible way for Patrick to miss such an event. Nor did he want to. But it went without saying that Libby would be in attendance, as well. Even thinking about the possibility of seeing her again made him hard. He hadn't slept worth a damn since she ran from his car.

He relived that moment time after time. In every way he spun the conversation, the truth was, Libby was probably right. But even if he had it all to do over again, he didn't think he could change. The prospect of loving her was too scary.

What if he let himself love her and something happened to her? He had watched Dylan come apart at the seams. Fortunately, Mia was on her way to a complete recovery, but even so, Dylan was probably hovering over her, making sure she obeyed doctor's orders.

Patrick was following the only possible path. He had to keep his distance. He wouldn't let love destroy him.

At last, he came up with what he decided was a rational, well-thought-out plan. He would go to the Silver Dollar—surely Libby had finished moving in by now. And she wouldn't have left town yet—not without taking a few weeks to make some plans about her future and to look for a place to live in New York. He would track Libby down in her upstairs apartment over the saloon and discuss how they would comport themselves during Maeve's celebration.

His heart beat faster at the thought of seeing her again. She wouldn't be able to call him out on the validity of his visit. Neither one of them wanted to hurt or embarrass Maeve.

To mitigate his nervousness and postpone the inevitable, he stopped downstairs in the bar first. It was midafternoon on a Friday. Only a handful of customers lingered after what would have been a predictable lunch-hour rush.

Dylan was behind the bar doing something with the cash drawer. He looked up when Patrick approached. "Howdy, stranger. I thought you'd left town. Nobody's seen or heard from you all week."

"Been busy." He sat down on a leather-topped stool.

Dylan poured him a beer. "You want to go in with Mia and me for Mom's birthday gift? We were thinking about getting her a three-day visit to that new spa over in Asheville…with the works. It's not something she would buy for herself."

"Sounds good. Just tell me how much I owe you." He drained half of his beer and felt his chest tighten. "Do you happen to know if Libby is upstairs at the moment?"

Dylan frowned. "What do you mean?"

"Well, she lives here now, doesn't she? I thought you might keep track of her comings and goings."

Dylan wiped his hands on a clean bar towel, his expression troubled. "She's not living upstairs, man."

"But she was planning to move her stuff here from the hotel. She told me."

"Libby stayed for one night. Then she went back to New York."

Patrick made some excuse to his brother and departed, scraped raw by the look of sympathy on Dylan's face. Patrick felt hollow inside. Life had kicked the heart out of him, and it was his own fault. He hadn't really thought Libby would leave. Granted, he'd told her to go back to New York, but he'd assumed Maeve had helped her get a more suitable job here in Silver Glen while Libby decided if a return to the big city was the right thing to do.

Why would she go back to New York and the friends who had shunned her after her father's arrest?

His stomach curled as he imagined innocent, open-hearted Libby living in some roach-infested apartment in a bad part of town. Possibly in actual physical danger.

God, what had he done?

He raced home and packed a bag. Then he lay awake almost all night to make absolutely sure he knew what he had to do. This was his mess. He was going to make it right. Fortunately, the jet was not in use the next day.

In a moment of absolute clarity, he saw the arrogant blunder he'd made. He'd been so entrenched in the notion that he had no business marrying anyone, he hadn't seen how much he was hurting the one woman who meant the world to him. He loved her. Right or wrong. And he couldn't let her go.

He filed his flight plan and was airborne before 8:00 a.m.

LaGuardia was busy. He had to execute a holding pattern until he was given permission to land. By the time he made it into the city, it was almost noon. He took care of several errands, then checked into the Carlyle and left on foot to walk to Libby's old building.

His idea was far-fetched, but it was the only hope he had of finding her. Fortunately, the doorman was the same old guy Libby had hugged with such fierce affection.

The man recognized Patrick right away. Patrick's plan called for bold-faced confidence.

Patrick smiled. "Hello, there. I'm hoping you can help me. I've come to see Libby and surprise her at her new place, but somehow I lost the address she gave me. Do you perhaps remember what it is? I know the two of you are close."

The elderly gentleman stared at Patrick for the longest time, leaving no doubt that he saw through Patrick's lie. But at last, he relented. He reached in his pocket and took out a scrap of paper. "Don't make me regret this."

Patrick jotted down the information in the note app on his phone and sighed in relief. At least he knew where to start. "Thank you," he said. "I appreciate your help." He pulled a folder from his pocket and handed it to Clarence. "This is an open-ended reservation at my family's hotel. For a two-week stay. You've meant a lot to Libby, and she wanted you to have this."

Hopefully, the tiny white lie would buy him goodwill in both directions.

Clarence smiled broadly. "Tell Miss Libby thank you. And I'll talk to her soon. This is mighty nice. Mighty nice."

Unfortunately, the new apartment was not in walking distance. Patrick was forced to grab a cab and slowly make his way downtown in rush-hour traffic. Contrary to his worst fears, the address pointed him toward TriBeCa... and a trendy collection of redesigned lofts.

This was far beyond anything Libby could afford right now. Had she found a man...an old friend willing to take her in? His gut cramped at the possibility. He took the elevator and rang the bell for 2B. Moments later, he heard footsteps. But nothing happened. There was a security peephole in the door.

Taking a chance, he stared straight at it. "Open up, Libby. I know you're in there, and I'm prepared to stand out here all night."

Libby leaned her forehead against the door and fought back tears. To peek outside and see Patrick in the flesh decimated her hard-won composure. She'd thought she had herself under control.

Turned out, she was wrong.

She cracked the door open, but left the chain on. "Why are you here?" she asked, her tone carefully dispassionate. Obviously it wasn't to declare his undying love for her.

"Maeve's birthday party is tomorrow night. Are you planning to be there?"

The hand behind the door, the one he couldn't see, clenched in a fist. "No. It's too expensive to fly and I don't have a car."

"You're willing to disappoint your mother's good friend…the woman who has done so much for you?"

She was getting tired of trying to read his mood through the crack. But she knew him well enough not to let him in. "Maeve will understand. She knows my financial situation."

"I brought the jet to pick you up, so money is not really an issue."

"I said I'm not going. Goodbye, Patrick."

He stuck his large leather shoe in the opening, foiling her attempt to shut him out. "Now who's being selfish and emotionally stunted?"

Had her words actually wounded him? Why else would he remember them almost verbatim? What would it take to make him leave her alone? And more importantly, what would it take to convince herself she hadn't fallen in love with him?

"What do you want?" she asked. Her heart was in shreds, and she didn't have the will to fight. The past few days had almost done her in. She wanted the man on the other side of the door with every fiber of her being. But she wasn't going to beg. Her dignity was all she had left.

"Please let me in, Libby."

She glanced behind her at the clock on the wall. Spencer would be home soon. This awkward confrontation couldn't last too long. "Fine," she said. "But only for a moment. I have things to do."

After disengaging the chain, she stepped back and let him come in. The dimensions of the loft were generous, but Patrick's size and personality made an impact, even so.

"Have you eaten?" he asked.

"Yes, sorry." But she wasn't sorry at all. And she wasn't going to offer to cook for him.

"This is quite some place."

"Yes. It's very nice."

"I thought all your friends dropped you when your dad went to prison."

"Spencer was doing an eighteen-month stint with the Peace Corps in Bangladesh. Manhattan society news travels slowly over there."

"And now Spencer is back and took you in?"

"Yes."

"And your future employment?"

"Zoe loaned me some money. I interviewed today for a position as a personal shopper at Bergdorf Goodman. Turns out I have skills in that area. As soon as I'm able, I'll be paying her back…"

"And Spencer, too?"

"Of course."

Patrick's expression was moody, as if he resented the fact that she had landed on her feet. What was it to him? He hadn't been willing to give her a job or a place to live… or even a tiny piece of his heart.

"Shall I tell Maeve that I flew up here to get you, but you were too busy to come to her birthday party?" He leaned against the wall in the foyer, his hands shoved in his pockets.

"Why would you do that?"

"To get my way."

Wow. There it was. Not even dressed up.

At that moment, the door opened without ceremony and a large, handsome blond man entered. He stopped short when he saw Patrick. Then he lifted an eyebrow. "Libby?"

"Patrick was just leaving," she said hurriedly. She took the newcomer by the arm and dragged him toward the kitchen, but he refused to go very far. Instead, she had to whisper in his ear.

He straightened after a moment and eyed Patrick with distrust. "I see."

She squeezed his arm. "I'm going back to Silver Glen for a couple of nights. But don't worry about me. I'll be fine."

"You'd better be."

Ten feet away, Patrick practically vibrated with incensed testosterone overload. She had to get him out of the apartment. "You win, Patrick," she said. "But I need some time. I'll meet you at the airport in two hours. Take it or leave it."

He nodded once, scowled at her and walked out.

The blond man chuckled. "Poor bastard. He's madly in love with you and you let him think you're living with me."

"Well, I am living with you," Libby said, giving him a big hug.

"Yeah, but with me *and* Spencer, who happens to be my beautiful, sexy wife."

Libby winced. "I might possibly have led him to believe that Spencer is male…and that *you* are Spencer."

"That's stone-cold, love. But he probably deserved it."

Libby threw some things in a bag, her heart racing with adrenaline. She didn't have a gift for Maeve, but Maeve would understand. Coat, keys, phone, small suitcase. In forty-five minutes, she was running downstairs and out to the street.

Then she stopped dead, because leaning against a lamp-post was Patrick Kavanagh. "I said I would meet you at the airport," she protested.

He shrugged. "I didn't trust you not to run."

There was accusation in his voice…and something else. Fatigue? Sadness? What did he want from her?

"Well, I'm here."

They faced each other silently. Being this close to him ripped apart the web of lies she had told herself to keep going every day. The truth punched her with a ferocity that took her breath. She was madly, deeply, unfortunately in love with Patrick Kavanagh.

He raked a hand through his hair, for the first time revealing a trace of vulnerability. "The airport is shut down for fog. We can't leave until tomorrow morning."

She swallowed. "Okay. Call me and let me know what time." She turned to go back inside the building.

Patrick caught her in two steps, his hands warm on her shoulders. "We need to talk, Libby. Come back to the hotel with me. We'll have dinner there. Casual. Nothing fancy. I'll get you a room if you want it. Or—" He stopped short as if he hadn't meant to say that.

"Or what?"

"Nothing," he muttered. "Never mind. Come have dinner with me. Please."

He was the last person on earth she wanted to have dinner with. And the only person. He didn't deserve to be given the time of day. But she let herself be persuaded. And not because she was weak, and he smelled wonderful. She would hear him out, for Maeve.

After that, Patrick was a complete gentleman. He kept his distance in the cab. At the hotel, he handed her bag to a bellman and steered Libby toward the dining room. The restaurant was conservatively old-school, reminding her of birthday dinners with her parents.

She ordered the lobster bisque. Her appetite lately had been almost nonexistent, but the rich, warm soup was perfect. Patrick chose the duck. Because the captain and servers were attentive, it was easy to let conversation touch on innocuous topics.

But at last, over cappuccino and crème brûlée, Patrick made an overture she hadn't expected. "We need some privacy, Libby. Will you come upstairs with me?"

What did he mean, *privacy*?

Well, hell. She wasn't going to be a coward about this. "For talking? Or something else?"

His throat flushed dark red and his eyes flashed with some strong emotion. "I'll let you make that call."

When he stared at her with storms in his blue-gray irises, she was helpless to resist. Or maybe that was the lie she told herself, because she didn't *want* to resist.

She folded her napkin and set it on the table. "Fine. We'll go upstairs."

The tension in the elevator would have been unbearable except for the older couple who joined them during the brief ride to an upper floor.

At Patrick's door, Libby waited nervously for him to fish the key from his pocket. It was a different room, of course. But the furnishings were similar enough to remind her of every last thing she and Patrick had shared just days earlier in this same city…this same hotel.

Libby took a seat. Patrick stood and paced.

"If you're feeling guilty, I absolve you," she said, the words flat. "You were right. The job at Silver Reflections wasn't suited for me. But you needn't worry. I've landed on my feet, and things are going very well. I should thank you for firing me."

"I didn't exactly *fire* you," he protested, the muscles in his neck corded and tight.

"What would *you* call it?"

He exhaled. "A mistake. A bad mistake. I acted like a complete ass, and I hope you will find it in your heart to forgive me."

"I make no promises. What about the sex?" she asked recklessly, fighting for her happiness, unwilling to let a blindly stubborn man ruin what they had.

"I can't deny it was incredible. But my life was rocking along pretty damn well until you came along." His voice faltered.

"Well, mine wasn't. A thousand apologies, emperor." She made her tone as snide and nasty as she could manage. And she leaped to her feet, no longer content to sit and let him scowl at her.

He grabbed her wrist to reel her in, his chest heaving. "I will not fail at marriage again, Libby."

Eighteen

Her heart dropped to her feet until she looked deeply into his eyes and saw the secret he was trying so hard to keep. Her jaw dropped. "You love me..."

"No I don't." His denial was automatic but totally unconvincing.

She cupped his face in her hands. "I love you, too, Patrick. But we don't have to get married," she said softly, "if that's what scares you. We can live in sin. You'll be the black sheep of the family."

At last the line between his eyebrows disappeared. "It's the twenty-first century. You'll have to do more than that to get me ostracized."

"I'll try my best. But it will have to be something really awful, won't it? Like maybe you and I making a baby without a ring on my finger? Your mom would hate that."

She saw the muscles in his throat work. "I'd hate it, too," he muttered. "This isn't how things should be, Libby. I've already stood before a priest and repeated marriage vows.

You deserve a man who can come to you with a clean past, a blank slate."

Going against all her instincts, she released him and put the width of the room between them. Still, she couldn't sit down. Too much adrenaline pumped through her veins. She busied herself at the minibar. "Would you like something to drink?"

"No. Look at me, Libby. You know I'm right. You're young and sweet and you deserve all the traditional trappings of an extraordinary wedding. You deserve to be the perfect bride."

She set down the small unopened bottle of liquor. "Here's the truth, Patrick…the last year has taught me that life is seldom perfect. I won't have my father to walk me down the aisle, because he's in prison. My mother won't be at my side helping me pick out a dress, because she took a bottle of pills."

"I'm sorry about all those things."

There was one more secret she knew she should disclose. Something that might make him understand. "Patrick?" She forced herself to perch on the sofa. The gas logs in the fireplace burned cheerfully. "Please sit with me. I want to tell you a story."

His expression guarded, and with reluctance in every line of his body, he nodded. But instead of joining her, he took a chair opposite, putting a low antique table between them as a barrier. "I'm listening."

This was harder than she had thought it would be. But if she didn't tell Patrick, perhaps she would never be free. "You keep calling me innocent, but you had to realize that I wasn't a virgin when you and I made love."

"I knew that. But neither was I. I've never approved of the double standard for women. I don't care about the men in your past, Libby. It's not important."

She leaned forward, her hot face in her hands. Shame flooded her stomach. "Well, it sort of is," she muttered.

Patrick made some kind of motion. "I don't want to hear your confession."

She sat up and stared at him before looking away and shaking her head. "I'm not giving you a choice. I was a very rebellious teenager, Patrick. I'd been spoiled and pampered, and I thought the world was my oyster. I'd barely dated at all, because my parents were so strict."

Patrick inhaled sharply. "Libby..."

"Don't interrupt. Please. The thing is, my father's best friend was newly divorced that year. He began flirting with me every time he came over to the apartment. I didn't really think of it as flirting. But I was smug about the fact that an older, sophisticated man was interested in my thoughts and opinions. It made me feel very grown-up."

Beneath his breath, Patrick said a word that was succinct and vehement. She had to ignore him to get through this.

"I turned sixteen in February. That fall was the beginning of my senior year. Most of my classmates had boyfriends, but I didn't. So I started telling everyone about *Mitch*."

"Was that his real name?"

She shrugged. "His middle name. I wasn't entirely stupid. I didn't want to get him or me in trouble. But as time passed and no one ever saw my 'boyfriend' at parties or other social occasions, they began to accuse me of making him up. The more teasing I took at school, the closer I grew to my father's friend. The attention of this handsome, very masculine man soothed my adolescent feelings of inadequacy."

"A man old enough to be your father."

"It didn't seem that way. To me, he was close to perfect."

"So what happened?"

Apparently, in spite of himself, Patrick wanted to know.

"In October, my father had to go to a financial seminar in Chicago. He wanted my mother and me to accompany him. But the trip sounded beyond boring to a teenage girl, even though my mom promised me shopping. I insisted that I was almost an adult and that they could certainly trust me. I begged them to let me stay home for the two nights they would be away."

"Oh, Libby…"

"It wasn't really a big deal. I planned to watch *inappropriate* movies on cable and paint my toenails and text with my friends. Maybe even sneak into my parents' liquor cabinet and have a single glass of sherry. I felt very daring and independent."

"And then Mitch came over."

"How did you know that?"

"It's not that hard to figure out. He knew you were going to be alone."

Libby grimaced. "I was an easy mark. He pretended he dropped by to see Daddy, and then feigned surprise that my father wasn't home. Later on, of course, I understood that Mitch knew exactly where my parents were and that I hadn't gone with them to Chicago. But at the time, it seemed like a happy accident. I asked him to come in."

Patrick had gone white beneath his tan. "He raped you."

Even now, the memory of that night made her shudder. "I wish it were that simple. I didn't understand all that much about men. I certainly didn't know that when they started drinking they were more dangerous. But I was having so much fun and he was complimenting me on my looks and my intelligence…anyway, when he kissed me the first time, I thought it was okay. For a minute."

"And afterward?"

"Something inside me said I should go to my bedroom

and lock my door. But I didn't want him to think of me as a child. So I ignored that little voice. And I paid the price."

"God, Libby…"

Tears stung her eyes, though she didn't let them fall. "It was a long time ago. And I'm fine…really I am. I just wanted you to know that I wouldn't come to marriage unscathed, either. Not that you've asked me, but you know…"

Patrick staggered to his feet, his heart and his composure shattering into pieces like brittle glass. He went to the sofa and sat down, scooping her into his lap. For a long time, they just sat there…not speaking, her head tucked against his shoulder.

He stroked her fiery hair, wanting desperately to find the son of a bitch with the middle name Mitch and avenge Libby's honor.

At last, he drew a deep breath and let go of the past that had held him with invisible chains. "I adore you, Libby Parkhurst. How could I not? You're beautiful and brave and you have the most extraordinary outlook on life." He tipped her backward over his arm and kissed her, shuddering with relief as she kissed him in return.

When they separated and sat side by side, her green eyes were damp, but then his were, too, so they were even. "Don't move," he said.

Her face expressed first puzzlement and then astonishment when he slid off the sofa and onto one knee, pushing the table aside. Reaching into his pocket, he pulled out a turquoise leather box and flipped it open. "Marry me, Libby," he pleaded, the words hoarse, his throat raw.

She stared at the multicarat single stone as if it were a snake. "You have a ring?"

Her bewilderment made him feel lower than low. "Of course, I do," he said. "I'll change this for a diamond if you want, but I've always thought redheads should wear emeralds." Libby didn't protest when he slid the simple platinum band with the exotic jewel onto her finger.

She held her hand up, her eyes wide. "It's extraordinary."

"I have no doubts about us, Libby, not anymore. And it's not because of your confession. You've opened my eyes to how stupid I've been to deliberately throw away something so amazingly good. I'm sorry I insulted you and fired you and tried to break your heart. I was an idiot. I bought the ring this afternoon, but then I got cold feet." He rested his forehead against her knee. He'd said his piece. The outcome was up to her now.

Her silence lasted too damn long. When he felt her fingers in his hair, he braced for a refusal.

But Libby took him by surprise. She slid down beside him, her legs curled to one side. "This is a very beautiful rug," she said. "I suppose we shouldn't do anything to ruin it."

He scowled at her. "Damn it, Libby. Don't toy with me. I've had a hell of a day."

"And whose fault is that?"

"I know I said I didn't care about other men in your life, and I really don't, but tell me one thing. Is Spencer expecting to share your bed? He's a big guy, and I want to know if I'm going to have to fight for your hand."

Libby's eyes widened, and she laughed, staring down at her fingers as if mesmerized by the brilliant green stone Patrick had spent several hours choosing. "Spencer is my dear friend. She and I were best buddies in school. The man you met at the loft is her husband, Derek."

Patrick exhaled, torn between frustration at Libby's deliberate deception and relief that no one else had a claim on his fiancée. "You're going to lead me in a merry dance, aren't you? I'll never be able to turn my back. And when you gang up with my sisters-in-law, Lord help us all."

He stretched out his legs and banged his shin on the table leg. "Wait a minute," he said, aggrieved. "You haven't said you'll marry me."

"I didn't?" Guileless green eyes looked up at him.

He started to sweat. "Say it, Libby. Right now."

She sighed, leaning forward to unbutton his shirt. "Yes, Patrick Kavanagh. I will marry you. Now, are you satisfied?"

He kissed her hard, moving over her and pressing her into the sofa. But it was a damned uncomfortable position. "I'm not satisfied at all," he stuttered. "Bedroom. Now." He dragged her to her feet, trying to undress her and walk at the same time. They made it as far as the still-closed door, but his patience frayed.

He lifted her hands over her head, trapping her against the polished wood with the weight of his body. Her breasts, mostly exposed in a sexy bra, heaved.

Libby's gaze was dreamy. "Let's come here for our honeymoon," she said.

"But during the summer. When you don't have to wear so many clothes." He gave up on the wrist-holding thing and unzipped her pants. "Help me, woman."

Finally, aeons later, they were both nude. He held her tightly, his face buried in her hair. "This is forever. I hope you know that."

Libby sighed deeply. "I'm counting on it, my love."

Twenty-four hours later, Libby stood in one of the private salons at the Silver Beeches Lodge and hid a yawn behind her hand. The emerald ring hung on a chain tucked inside her dress. All around her, the Kavanagh family, along with an intimate circle of friends, laughed and danced and partied. Maeve, the guest of honor, beamed continuously, delighted to have all her loved ones under one roof.

By prior agreement, Patrick and Libby had arrived at the festivities separately. For the past two hours they had stayed on opposite sides of the room. Either Dylan or Zoe must have warned everyone not to make a big deal about Libby's presence after a weeklong absence, because no one said a word out of place. All the attention was centered on Maeve—as it should be.

Still, it was a good bet that all the Kavanaghs knew Libby was no longer working for Patrick, and that things had ended badly.

After a sumptuous dinner, Maeve opened gifts. Her family and friends showered her with offerings of love and affection. For a brief moment, Libby allowed herself to grieve the fact that her own children would have only one grandmother. But then the moment passed.

She was luckier than most.

At last, when the babies were asleep and even the grown-ups were starting to fade, it was clear the party was over. Patrick stepped to the center of the room and gave his mother a hug. "I have one last gift for you, Mom."

Maeve seemed confused. "But I thought the spa thing had your name on it, too."

Little by little, the room fell silent. All eyes were on Patrick. "This is something more personal," he said.

Unobtrusively, Libby removed the emerald from its resting place and slipped it onto her left finger. It had pained her not to wear it, even for this one brief evening.

Patrick stood—tall and strong—with an almost palpable air of contentment and joy surrounding him.

Maeve stared at her boy, her brow creased. "Well, don't keep me in suspense. Where is it?"

Patrick grinned broadly, crooking a finger. "It's not an *it*. It's a *who*."

Libby threaded her way through the crowd, smiling as

the swell of exclamations followed her progress. When she joined Patrick, he put an arm around her.

"Mom," he said. "I'd like to present my fiancée, Libby Parkhurst, soon to be the daughter of your heart."

Maeve burst into tears, and the entire room fairly exploded with excitement. Libby lost track of the hugs and kisses and well wishes.

When some of the furor finally died down, Maeve held her close and whispered in her ear. "Thank you, Libby. Look at him. He's beaming."

And indeed he was. Libby's heart turned over. If she had harbored any last doubts, seeing Patrick like this in the bosom of his family and so obviously exultant and happy made her own heart swell with emotion.

Patrick finally reclaimed his fiancée and dragged her out to the car. He leaned her against the hood and kissed her long and slow. "Come home with me, my love."

Libby wrapped her arms around his neck, feeling the beat of his heart against hers. "I thought you'd never ask…"

* * * * *

MILLS & BOON®

Desire™

PASSIONATE AND DRAMATIC LOVE STORIES

MILLS & BOON®

The Billionaires Collection!

This fabulous 6 book collection features stories from some of our talented writers. Feel the temperature rise with our ultra-sexy and powerful billionaires. Don't miss this great offer – buy the collection today to get two books free!

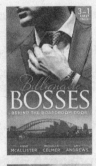

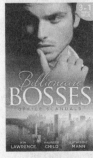
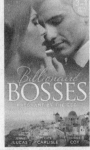

Order yours at
**www.millsandboon.co.uk
/billionaires**

MILLS & BOON®

Let us take you back in time with our Medieval Brides...

The Novice Bride – Carol Townend

The Dumont Bride – Terri Brisbin

The Lord's Forced Bride – Anne Herries

The Warrior's Princess Bride – Meriel Fuller

The Overlord's Bride – Margaret Moore

Templar Knight, Forbidden Bride – Lynna Banning

Order yours at
www.millsandboon.co.uk/medievalbrides

0116_MB519

MILLS & BOON®

Why shop at millsandboon.co.uk?

Each year, thousands of romance readers find their perfect read at millsandboon.co.uk. That's because we're passionate about bringing you the very best romantic fiction. Here are some of the advantages of shopping at www.millsandboon.co.uk:

* **Get new books first**—you'll be able to buy your favourite books one month before they hit the shops

* **Get exclusive discounts**—you'll also be able to buy our specially created monthly collections, with up to 50% off the RRP

* **Find your favourite authors**—latest news, interviews and new releases for all your favourite authors and series on our website, plus ideas for what to try next

* **Join in**—once you've bought your favourite books, don't forget to register with us to rate, review and join in the discussions

Visit **www.millsandboon.co.uk**
for all this and more today!